T. L. Johnson

THE ROSE AND THE SHADOWS

www.tljohnsonauthor.com

Published by Midnight Haven Books

www.MidnightHavenBooks.com

First Print Edition, 2026

Library of Congress Control Number: 2025906652

ISBNs:

Hardcover: 979-8-9923666-3-1

Ebook (Kindle): 979-8-9923666-4-8

Paperback: 979-8-9923666-5-5

Cover design by Jacie Neher

For those who have made peace with the fire.
For those who learned that
gentleness is not surrender.
Your strength hums quieter now, but deeper.
It is calm. It is steady. It is yours.

"Perhaps strength is nothing but gentleness that has learned to breathe in fire."

—Alphonse de Lamartine

Contents

Preface

Every story is a mirror, even the dark ones.

I didn't write this story to create a fairy tale.

I wrote it to trace the scars we carry, the ghosts we outgrow, and the beauty that manages to bloom anyway.

If you've ever felt unseen, unheard, or unlovable, these pages are proof that your story still matters.

This world isn't built for softness.

But in these chapters, softness becomes a weapon.

Love becomes a rebellion.

And survival becomes its own kind of poetry.

Welcome to *The Rose and the Shadows*.

Welcome to the places where light meets ruin.

~ T. L. Johnson

Content Advisory

Like many storms, this story carries moments of darkness: emotional trauma, fear, obsession, and the long shadows left by past harm.

It includes depictions of stalking, references to emotional and psychological abuse, and brief scenes of physical confrontation.

This book also contains a scene involving poisoning and a subsequent life-saving CPR attempt.

Open-door intimacy is present but not central; these moments are written with intention, rooted in connection, not shock.

The Rose and the Shadows is a story of survival, trust, and the fragile strength it takes to begin again.

If you're carrying your own scars, please read with compassion for yourself, and know that what lies ahead is not just the storm, but the bloom that follows it.

Take breaks if you need them.

Stories can be powerful, but your peace comes first.

If you find yourself overwhelmed, it's okay to pause.

To rest.

To breathe.

You matter more than any page.

CHAPTER 1

The Storm Repeats

"Don't scream," a voice hissed, close and low, hot against her ear. "Don't make this harder than it has to be."

The words slithered under her skin before her body caught up.

Arden fought.

She twisted, kicked—instinct, not strategy—but his arm clamped around her ribs, tight and unsteady. The grip wasn't practiced; it shook. His breath hitched against her ear, cologne soured by sweat.

He wasn't in control.

I can use that.

She let her weight collapse like a stringless puppet, head dropping, breath catching hard in her throat.

It worked. His stance shifted for one precious second.

Arden took it.

Her heel slammed into his shin. A grunt broke against her ear as he staggered, and she spun, driving her elbow back into bone. Cartilage gave beneath the strike; blood spilled across his face like ink flooding a page.

"Fucking bitch." He spat the words, one hand clutching his nose.

It was the only warning she got.

His other hand darted to his pocket.

The blade flashed.

Adrenaline lit her nerves, sharp and merciless. Arden scanned the alley in a single sweep: trash can, lid, steel edge. She lunged.

Metal met metal. The clang shuddered through her arms, into her teeth, but she held fast.

"You don't want to do this," she said, voice low, even despite the riot beneath it. "You're bleeding. Broken nose. Shallow breath. You're dizzy."

He faltered. The knife wavered.

"Shut up."

But his hand shook harder.

"Stop fighting me!" he snapped.

She didn't.

She swung.

The lid struck steel again, glancing, but enough. The knife flew. Arden shoved him into the brick, hard enough that his shoulder cracked against the wall.

He hit, grunted, staggered.

Then he ran—gone in seconds.

And the alley held its breath.

Arden stood frozen in the aftermath, breath jagged, arms aching from impact. The lid clattered to the concrete beside the discarded knife. Blood dripped down her sleeve, seeping from scrapes she hadn't noticed until her body remembered it could hurt.

She bent and picked up the knife with shaking fingers.

No witnesses. No evidence left.

The alley seemed to pulse as she turned toward the bar. Light spilled from the doorway—warm, golden, safe—but her feet wouldn't move. Her hand pressed against her ribs where his arm had crushed the air from her lungs; her skin still burned there, memory sharp as heat.

Her gaze dropped.

A rose.

Red. Blood-smeared. Bent at the stem.

Still fresh.

What the fuck?

This wasn't JT. The build was wrong—leaner, twitchier. The grip hadn't known her. Erratic. Untrained. And the voice carried no reverence, no sick devotion dressed as tenderness. Only control. Cold and blunt and ugly.

She was a target.

So what did he want?

She'd never let it get that far.

Fuck.

No theatrics. No chance for his script. She had fought, survived, stayed upright when some older version of herself might have disappeared inside the fear.

Still—a rose.

If it was random... why?

Unless it wasn't supposed to make sense. Unless sense wasn't the point. Maybe it was only meant to keep her guessing, keep her afraid, keep her looking over her shoulder until the fear became another hand around her throat.

She stared at the bloom, its edges blurring as blood slid warm down her sleeve. Her pulse roared in her ears.

Nothing made sense.

Not now. Not again. Not here.

She stepped over the rose and walked.

One foot.

Then the other.

The world felt borrowed, as if she had slipped into a life that should have ended twenty minutes ago.

Inside, the bar buzzed with laughter, music, and clinking glasses. Penny's voice rang near the jukebox, clear and easy, and Arden flinched.

Too bright. Too loud. Too fast.

Still, she kept moving.

Penny spotted her first. The smile faltered.

"Wait—Arden?"

Her voice carried, but her body was faster. She pushed past a booth, face dropping, hand reaching before the question finished.

"Is that blood?"

Arden tried to smile. It cracked. "I'm fine."

"You're not—"

"Not here." The words cut sharper than she meant. "Not... here."

She slid into the booth, muscles trembling from the comedown. Her hands fumbled for her phone—not because she needed it, but because she needed something solid. The screen was cool and slick, wrong against her shaking grip.

It lit.

Unknown number.

Her stomach lurched.

> I saw them all watching you tonight but I only had eyes for you.

Her breath caught.

She blinked and read it again.

No name. No thread history.

Her thumb hovered. *Delete? Pretend?*

But her hand was already moving.

The bar dulled around her, sound warping as if she'd gone underwater. Her hands shook. She told herself it was adrenaline, not fear. Not him.

She stared at the screen, thumb trembling over the reply bubble.

Then she backed out in one decisive motion. New message. Typed fast.

Something happened. I'm safe. I'll explain later.

Sent.

Gideon's reply came instantly.

Where are you? I'm coming.

INSIDE, the bar buzzed with laughter, music, and clinking glasses. Penny's voice rang near the jukebox, clear and easy.

Arden flinched.

Too bright. Too loud.

Too fast.

Still, she kept moving.

Penny spotted her first. The smile faltered.

"Wait—Arden?"

Her voice carried, but her body was faster. She pushed past a booth, face dropping, hand reaching before the question finished.

"Is that blood?"

Arden tried to smile. It cracked. "I'm fine."

"You're not—"

"Not here." The words cut sharper than she meant. "Not... here."

She slid into the booth, muscles trembling from the comedown. Her hands fumbled for her phone—not because she needed it, but because she needed *something* solid. The screen was cool and slick, wrong against her shaking grip.

It lit.

Unknown number.

Her stomach lurched.

I saw them all watching you tonight but I only had eyes for you.

Her breath caught.

She blinked. Read it again.

No name. No thread history.

Her thumb hovered. Delete? Pretend?

But her hand was already moving.

The bar dulled, sound warping, like she was underwater. Her hands shook. She told herself... adrenaline, not fear. Not him.

She stared at the screen, thumb trembling over the reply bubble.

Then in a decisive move, she backed out. New message. Typed fast:

Something happened. I'm safe. I'll explain later.

Sent.

Gideon's reply came instantly.

Where are you? I'm coming.

SHE HAD SLIPPED out of the bar alone.

Good girl.

Her breath still carried the last note of the song—low, aching, grief wrapped in silk. Rain dampened her hair. Her eyes searched the night, sharp and restless, as if some animal part of her already knew she was being watched.

But she didn't see him.

Sebastian stayed at the edge of light, brick at his back, shadows gathered at his side. Every muscle held still. He wasn't here to frighten her.

He was here to watch. To study. To remember why this mattered.

Arden.

Little Fire.

She'd grown sharper edges. He liked that. The flame burned hotter now, contained but dangerous.

Alive.

Then someone else stepped in.

Not stumbling. Not lost.

There.

A man. Certain. Too near to be accidental. Not a stranger, either—closer than that. He moved like he belonged near her. Like he knew her.

Sebastian's breath stilled.

Arden twisted with purpose.

He couldn't hear the words. He didn't need to. Her body spoke louder.

Collapse.

Feint.

Snap.

Boot. Elbow. Blood.

Then steel. Trash can lid. Redirect. Disarm. Strike.

She burned.

The man bolted.

Arden stood in the aftermath, blood on her sleeve, knife at her feet. Unbroken.

Sebastian stayed in shadow, gaze fixed on the place where the stranger had touched her.

Not me.

He hadn't touched her.

Hadn't planned for anyone to.

The moment had been his gift—a song, a memory, a whisper meant to remind her she wasn't alone. The message had been left earlier, precisely timed.

Ritual. Not panic.

But now—

Now someone else had marked her skin.

His jaw clenched. Molars ground together. If he stepped into the light now, he wouldn't stop until someone broke.

Arden turned toward the doorway, shoulders stiff, steps measured. Her hand brushed her ribs, then paused.

She saw the rose.

Stepped over it.

Didn't flinch.

Didn't look back.

Good.

Let her think she was in control. Let her walk away proud.

But she had felt him. Somewhere deep, she knew.

She'd find the message waiting.

I saw them all watching you tonight but I only had eyes for you.

She'd read it. He didn't need to see it happen to know.

Because that moment—the second her fingers touched the screen, her lips parted, her pulse stuttered—would belong to him.

CHAPTER 2
Through the Cracks

The apartment door shut with a soft click, sealing the city behind them. Manhattan's murmur faded, but the night clung to Arden: damp rain in the fibers of her jacket, the low hum of traffic still vibrating through her bones.

Penny hovered close as Arden shrugged off her jacket. It slipped from her shoulders and landed in a heap on the chair, the movement pulling a wince from her before she could stop it.

"You need ice," Penny said, nodding toward the bruise blooming across her forearm.

"I'm fine," Arden murmured.

"You're not," Penny snapped, already digging through the freezer. "And I'm not letting you pretend otherwise."

Arden didn't argue. She barely had the strength.

Her phone buzzed.

She glanced at the screen, pulse stuttering.

Gideon: I have Dan with me. We're downstairs.

Her thumb hesitated before she typed.

Door's open.

I'm not someone who needs rescuing.
But God, I want him to anyway.

Even the thought of him pressed in close—perceptive, impossible to fool. Comfort braided with danger. Relief threaded with heat.

Penny returned with ice wrapped in a dishtowel like a battlefield bandage.

"Who was that?" she asked, though the edge in her voice said she already knew.

"Gideon," Arden said. "And Dan."

Before Penny could reply, a knock thudded against the door.

Her eyes cut to Arden, sharp and searching, before she went to answer it.

Gideon stepped in first; the room adjusted around him, as if gravity had shifted. Dan followed, alert eyes already tracking the shadows.

Gideon's gaze found Arden. It lingered on the bruise, on the way she held herself as if her bones no longer fit.

He said nothing at first.

Then, low, "Are you all right?"

"I'm fine," Arden said too quickly.

"She's not," Penny cut in, arms folded. "And she needs to talk."

"She's right," Gideon said.

Arden sighed and gestured toward the couch. "Sit. This'll take a minute."

Dan claimed the armchair, posture still military. Gideon hesitated before lowering himself beside her, and the tension in him vibrated through the cushion.

Silence thickened.

Arden tightened her grip on the ice pack. "It wasn't random."

Gideon's jaw shifted. "What wasn't?"

"Tonight. The rose at the café. The messages." She steadied her voice. "None of it was random. This has happened before."

Penny dropped into the chair, her face draining of color. "What do you mean, before?"

"In Morgantown." Arden's fingers brushed the faint scar on her palm. "I had a stalker."

Dan's jaw locked.

"He left notes. Flowers. Just enough to scare me, but not enough for the police to act." She swallowed. "I moved. Changed everything. I thought I outran it."

Her voice faltered.

"But now...now I don't know."

Gideon leaned forward, elbows on his knees. "Tell me what happened tonight."

Arden drew a breath. "I needed air. I stepped out of the bar. It was misting rain. I thought I was alone."

Her hands trembled. Her voice didn't.

"I didn't hear him. One second I was standing there, and the next his arm was around me, dragging me back."

Penny gasped.

"His grip was tight. His voice was too calm." Arden swallowed. "He said, Don't scream. Don't make this harder than it has to be. Like he'd rehearsed it."

Gideon's fists curled, knuckles whitening.

"I didn't fight. Not at first. I stayed still. Listened." She met Gideon's gaze. "He was shaking. Breathing fast. Not in control."

Dan nodded. "Adrenaline. Still dangerous."

"That's what I counted on." Her tone sharpened. "I went limp, threw him off balance. When he adjusted, I hit him. Heel to shin, elbow to his face. Broke his nose."

Dan let out a whistle.

"He pulled a knife."

Penny's hand flew to her chest. "Jesus, Arden."

"I didn't stop. I grabbed a trash can lid, blocked his swings. Lied and told him he was bleeding too much, that he'd pass out..." Arden's grip tightened around the ice pack. "It worked. He hesitated."

"And you struck," Gideon said, voice steel-flat.

"I did. Knocked the knife away. Pushed him into the wall. He ran."

Gideon's eyes hardened. "Where's the knife?"

Arden reached into her coat and drew it out.

The blade caught the light.

Dan broke the silence. "We need to call it in."

Arden hesitated. "I don't—"

"Arden." Gideon's voice gentled. "We can't let you carry this alone."

Her defenses sagged. "Okay. Call."

Dan dialed without another word.

The tension lingered long after.

"They'll be here soon," he said quietly.

"I'm making tea," Penny announced, already moving. "We all need something warm."

"You don't have to—" Arden began.

"I do," Penny said. "Tea fixes everything."

Dan followed her into the kitchen. A kettle hissed to life. Steam curled through the apartment, and the ordinary sounds only made Arden's nerves buzz harder.

Gideon hadn't moved. He seemed held there by the sight of her, as if the careful architecture of him had found the one fracture it couldn't ignore.

Then he shifted closer, slowly, hands visible. He reached for her hand, thumb brushing her knuckles, his touch cautious enough to give her room to pull away.

"You're here," he said softly. "You're standing. You're safe."

Her throat closed.

"I'm fine," she said again, thinner now. Less defense than threadbare lie.

Gideon didn't argue. He sat beside her, close enough to feel her shaking.

"You're not," he said, his grip tightening. "And I'm not fine seeing you like this."

"I'm still standing." Her chin lifted. "He didn't win."

"No." Quiet fire edged his voice. "But he tried."

Gently, he lifted her hand and pressed his lips to her knuckles, fierce and intimate in its restraint.

"You scared the hell out of me," he murmured. "And I know how strong you are. But for tonight..."

He paused.

"Let me carry this for you."

Something cracked. She didn't deflect. Didn't retreat.

"Okay," she whispered.

The kettle whistled.

Dan's voice drifted out from the kitchen. "Do you even have sugar?"

"Next to the microwave!" Penny called back.

When she returned with the tray, Arden straightened. Gideon let go of her, though the warmth lingered like a phantom.

"Tea time," Penny said briskly, setting the mugs down. "I added honey."

"Thanks, Pen," Arden murmured.

They sat. Sipped. Let the quiet hold.

Then a sudden, hard knock struck the door.

Arden and Penny both flinched.

Gideon was already on his feet, calm and focused. "I've got it."

He crossed to the door with intention.

When it opened, a tall woman filled the frame. Uniformed. Sharp-eyed.

"Officer Harris," she said, clipped, not cold. Her gaze swept the room, quickly assessing. "I'm here to take your statement."

CHAPTER 3
Close Enough to Break

"Thanks for coming," Arden said, motioning toward the couch.

She sat carefully, wincing as the ice pressed against her bruised arm. Penny slid in beside her, one hand resting lightly on her shoulder. Gideon stayed near the door, eyes fixed on Arden, unmoving and unreadable, while Dan leaned against the wall with his arms crossed, expression grave.

Harris didn't sit. She clicked her pen. "Let's start at the beginning. Walk me through what happened tonight."

Arden inhaled slowly. "I stepped out of the bar after karaoke. There's an alley nearby. I didn't hear anyone. I thought I was alone."

The pen scratched. "Go on."

"I didn't hear him." Her voice stayed steady, though her chest tightened beneath every word. She shifted, fingers twisting together. "One second I was alone. The next, someone grabbed me from behind. His arm locked hard around my ribs."

Penny flinched.

"His voice was so...calm," Arden said. "He told me not to scream. Said not to make it harder than it had to be. Like he'd practiced saying it."

Gideon's jaw flexed.

"I didn't panic. I froze on purpose. His grip was trembling. His breathing was shallow. He didn't seem in control."

Harris nodded once, making notes. "What did you do next?"

"I went limp to make him adjust his hold. When he did, I moved." Arden glanced at Penny, then down at the ice. "I learned it in nursing school. Dead weight throws people off balance. Gives you a chance to break free."

Dan gave a small nod.

"I drove my heel into his shin. Twisted out. Elbowed him hard." Arden swallowed. "I heard his nose break."

Penny's hand tightened on Arden's shoulder.

"He pulled a knife."

The words landed heavy. Harris didn't flinch. Gideon didn't either, but the air around him went colder.

"I grabbed a trash can lid. Blocked him. Lied and told him he was bleeding too much, that he'd pass out. It made him hesitate."

Harris's voice stayed even. "And then?"

"I knocked the knife away. Shoved him into the wall. He ran."

Arden reached into her pocket. The blade glinted as she set it on the table.

Harris slipped on gloves and bagged it with practiced ease. "Did you see his face?"

Arden hesitated, fingers brushing the scar on her palm. "Not clearly. He came from behind. When I broke free, I saw blood. One hand over his nose. White male. Average height. Dark hoodie. That's all."

"It helps." Harris jotted it down. "Change your locks. Install a camera. This wasn't random."

"She will," Gideon said flatly, before Arden could speak.

Arden shot him a look but said nothing.

When Harris left, the door clicked shut.

Quiet rushed back in.

GIDEON STEPPED CLOSER and crouched until they were eye-level.

"You didn't freeze," he said. "You're strong. You fought and survived. That matters."

"I don't feel strong," Arden whispered.

"You are." His voice softened. "And you're not alone."

The door had barely shut before Gideon's phone was out, his voice shifting into something clipped and tactical.

"Christian. I need a security upgrade. Tonight. Full setup. Locks, cameras, everything."

Arden opened her mouth, but he lifted a hand, eyes on hers.

"No debate," he said, not sharp but firm.

She swallowed the protest.

"Leo," he said, already on the next call. "I need you on a stalker case. Old files from Morgantown. Flowers, notes, female target. Arden Rose Rivers. Cross-reference Silverbranch. Full report by morning."

Penny let out a low whistle, leaning in. "Wait—he knows your middle name?"

Arden flushed. "Oh, Pen. It...never came up."

Penny's mouth curved, small and knowing. She said nothing, but reached for Arden's hand and gave it a brief, firm squeeze.

Gideon ended the call and turned back. His stance was rigid, but his gaze softened.

"We're not guessing anymore."

"We?" Arden echoed.

"We," he said. "You're not doing this alone."

Arden crossed her arms, spine straight. "This is too much. I don't need bodyguards. I need space to think."

"This isn't too much," Gideon said evenly. "You were attacked. That's reality."

"I'm not running," she snapped. "Not again."

His expression didn't change. "I'm not asking you to run. I'm asking you to let me help."

Before she could fire back, Penny cut in. "He's right. You've carried too much alone already. It's okay not to want to be strong right now."

Arden's voice dropped. "I'm not leaving my apartment."

"You won't have to," Gideon said. "But I'm staying close."

"You can't just—"

"I can," he said. "And I will...if you'll let me."

Dan cleared his throat. "We can help too. Take shifts. Make it less intense."

Arden looked at each of them—Penny, Dan, Gideon. A fortress forming around her without her asking, but not one of them blocking the door.

She exhaled. "Fine. But I'm not a prisoner. If I say I need air, I mean it."

Penny smiled. "Deal. But you're not walking through this alone."

Gideon's phone buzzed. "Christian's team is en route. Full security before morning."

Arden's fingers brushed the scar on her palm. "I don't know how to do this," she admitted. "Letting people in."

Gideon rested a hand lightly on her shoulder. "You don't have to do it all at once. Just don't shut us out."

Dan nodded. “We’ve got you.”

“Always,” Penny said.

For the first time in years, Arden believed them.

The shadows were still there.

But she wasn’t facing them alone anymore.

CHAPTER 4
Quiet Knives

Morning came gray and heavy, the sky pressing down on the city as if it knew what kind of night had passed. Sunlight filtered weakly through the clouds, dulling everything it touched.

Arden stirred beneath the blankets. Her body ached in all the wrong places; bruises bloomed along her ribs, and her palm tingled with the memory of what it had held.

For one fragile second, she let herself pretend everything was fine.

Her phone's vibration shattered the illusion.

> Penny: Coffee's ready. Come out whenever.

She sat up slowly, joints stiff, bruises pulsing. But the weight in her chest wasn't pain.

It was memory.

Last night hadn't faded. It had fossilized.

She pulled on an oversized hoodie and padded barefoot into the living room, drawn by the smell of coffee. Penny stood at the counter in chartreuse sweatpants and a paint-splattered T-shirt, hair in a messy bun, mug clutched tightly between both hands.

"Morning," she said gently, sliding a cup toward Arden. "Figured you'd need this."

"Thanks."

Arden took a sip. Warmth bloomed down her throat, settling deep in her bones.

The quiet wasn't uncomfortable, but it was dense, like fog gathering before the storm breaks.

Then came the knock.

They froze.

Penny moved first, stepping toward the door, knuckles white around her phone. "Probably Dan," she said, peeking through the peephole.

Her brows drew tight. "There's no one."

Arden set her mug down and crossed the room in three quick strides.

When Penny opened the door, cold air spilled in.

At their feet sat a small package, neat and unassuming. Brown paper. Twine knotted with care. No label. No return address.

Penny started to bend.

"Wait—" Arden's voice cut clean as a blade.

Penny straightened. "Um, okay, but what the hell is that?"

Arden grabbed a pen from the counter and nudged the package. The knot loosened too easily. The paper unfolded with the soft reluctance of something private.

Inside was a worn hardcover.

Her breath hitched.

Anne of Green Gables.

She didn't move. Didn't speak.

Penny leaned closer. "Is it—?"

Arden nodded, eyes locked on the book as if it might vanish. "It's mine. From when I was a kid. I haven't mentioned it to anyone."

Not to Penny.

Not to Gideon.

Not even to herself in years.

She reached for it like it might break and opened the cover.

A folded slip of paper slid free.

The scent hit first.

Roses—faint, sweet, unmistakable. Familiar in the worst way.

Her stomach revolted.

She managed to open the note.

I know you better than anyone else does. You'll see.

Her vision tunneled. The room pulled away.

Her knees buckled.

Penny's hand clamped around Arden's arm. "What is it?"

Arden held the note out with shaking fingers. "He knows. He knows things he shouldn't."

Penny read it, the color draining from her face. "Oh my God." She grabbed her phone. "I'm calling Gideon—"

"No." Arden's voice was taut. "I will."

She pulled out her phone and dialed with shaking hands.

Gideon answered on the second ring. "Arden?"

"There was a package," she said, throat raw. "Or...a gift. Outside my door."

"What kind?" His voice dropped, controlled and lethal.

"A book." She swallowed. "Anne of Green Gables. My favorite. But no one knew. Not even Penny."

Silence.

Then, "I'm on my way. Don't touch anything else. Is Penny with you?"

"She's here."

"Good. Christian and Leo are coming. Dan too. We'll figure this out."

She hesitated. "Gideon...the note. It said, 'I know you. Better than anyone else does. You'll see.'"

His breath left him hard. "Stay put."

The line went dead.

She lowered the phone. Penny's grip stayed firm around her arm.

"What did he say?"

"He's coming," Arden said. "And not alone."

Minutes stretched thin.

Penny paced. Arden sat rigid on the couch, staring at the book as if it might breathe.

When the knock finally came, her body jolted.

Penny checked the peephole. "It's them."

Gideon stepped in first, coat damp with mist. His gaze swept the room, found Arden, then cut straight to the package.

Dan followed, coiled and quiet, already mapping the space.

"This it?" Gideon asked.

Arden nodded.

He picked up the book like it might burn, turned it once, then set it down carefully.

"Anyone in or out since it showed up?"

"Just us," Penny said.

"I used a pen to open it," Arden added. "No contact."

"Good." His jaw tightened. "Christian and Leo will take care of it, run an analysis."

"You think he slipped?" Arden asked.

"We'll see." Calm words. Fury underneath. "But this isn't just surveillance. This is communication."

Penny crossed her arms. "We shouldn't stay here."

"I'm not leaving," Arden said flatly.

"You should," Gideon countered. "At least for now."

She bristled. "So I let this guy win?"

"It's not running," Penny said gently. "It's reloading."

Gideon stepped closer. "My place is secure. Cameras. Alarms. People I trust. You'll be safer there."

"And if I say no?" Arden crossed her arms.

"I won't force you," he said. "But I'm asking you."

His voice shifted, steel threaded with a plea.

She looked at Penny. Then at Dan.

"Fine," she said. "A few days. Nothing more."

Relief flickered across Gideon's face. "Deal."

Penny grinned. "Good. Because I wasn't leaving you alone anyway."

Dan muttered, "Guess I'll shift some meetings."

Penny blinked. "Wait—you live nearby?"

"Yep. Couple doors down."

She stared. "This explains so much."

Gideon arched a brow. "Does it?"

"I don't have the bandwidth for this," Penny muttered, sipping her coffee like whiskey.

The tension shifted—not gone, but redistributed.

"I don't know how to do this," Arden said softly. "Letting people in."

"You don't have to know," Gideon said. "But don't shut us out."

She didn't answer.

But she didn't pull away.

A lighter knock came at the door.

Gideon opened it, and Christian and Leo stepped inside. Christian went straight to the book, gloves snapping on.

"Team's outside," Christian said. "We'll handle it."

Leo offered Arden a small smile as he bagged the note. "No one's invisible forever."

As they worked, Arden sank back into the couch. Gideon sat beside her and gently took her hand.

SEBASTIAN HAD CHOSEN the book on purpose.

Not because it was old. Not because it was hers.

Because it was his favorite version of her—the girl who stayed up late escaping into words. The one who believed in kindred spirits.

She still wanted to believe.

That was the best part.

He watched the feed. Watched her fingers hover over the note, her eyes widen, the faint tremor at her lips.

She didn't scream.

He knew she wouldn't.

She never screamed.

He allowed himself a smile.

Let them play at safety.

Let Gideon Blackwell throw money at ghosts.

They would always be too late.

CHAPTER 5
Safe Haven

Arden stood in her bedroom, staring at the packed bag as if it might unpack itself if she waited long enough.

Penny zipped her own bag with more force than necessary.

"This isn't forever," she said gently, not pushing. "Just until things settle."

Arden nodded, her voice buried beneath the tightness in her chest. She couldn't tell if this was surrender or survival.

Penny squeezed her shoulder, brief and steady, then carried both bags to the door.

The ride to Gideon's felt empty at first. Penny tried to fill it with soft chatter about packing light and strange beds, but the words passed through Arden like a ghost. She leaned her head against the window, eyes half-lidded, tracking the blur of streetlights as they slid past.

Last night pulsed behind her ribs: the alley, the knife, the book.

The note.

She didn't speak. She counted her breaths.

In for four.

Hold for four.

Out for eight.

Again.

Gideon's brownstone came into view, waiting for them with its clean lines and tall windows. Solid. Real. Something she could lean on, if she let herself.

At the steps, Penny spoke softly. "This is all...temporary."

"I know." Arden adjusted the strap on her bag, but everything still felt too heavy.

The front door opened before they could knock.

Gideon stood framed there, dressed down but alert, his eyes scanning them both before settling on Arden.

He lifted their bags without a word and stepped aside.

Inside, warmth wrapped around her like an embrace she didn't want, but leaned into anyway. Hardwood floors. Dim light. The air smelled faintly of coffee and cedar and him.

"This way," he said, already leading them upstairs.

He opened the first door on the right. "Penny—this is yours. Bathroom's down the hall."

"Thanks." Penny offered him a small, grateful smile, then glanced back at Arden. "You good?"

Arden nodded.

Not a lie exactly.

Gideon met her gaze, and the gentleness she found there took her breath away.

"Come on," he said more quietly. "I'll show you to your room."

He opened the next door and stepped back.

Warm light. Deep wood. A room that felt as if it had been waiting, not for a guest, but for her.

He placed her bag at the foot of the bed.

"This is you," Gideon said. "...I'm right down the hall."

Her throat tightened. "Thank you."

His gaze didn't waver. "You don't have to do it all yourself."

Before she could answer, his hands settled gently on her shoulders.

Arden exhaled and leaned in, her forehead resting against his chest. His heartbeat was unhurried.

Real.

"It's okay to let someone else carry the weight for a while," he murmured.

One hand brushed the back of her neck. His lips pressed a light kiss to her temple.

When she stepped back, her fingers lingered at the fabric of his shirt.

"I wish I were here under different circumstances," she said, managing a smile. "But I think I'm going to lie down."

He nodded. "If you need anything," he said, voice rougher now, "I'm here."

"Goodnight, Gideon."

She slipped inside and closed the door.

Only then did she allow herself to smile.

GIDEON LAY IN HIS BED, staring at the ceiling for answers it didn't hold. The house was still.

Too still.

Arden's voice echoed back to him—thin, worn, still trying.

Thank you.

He closed his eyes. Tried to let go. Tried to let her be.

Then came the sound.

Soft. Strained. Familiar in the worst way.

He sat up, listening.

A choked breath.

A muffled whimper.

Arden.

Gideon moved before thought could catch him.

He paused outside her door, hand hovering at the knob, every instinct in him already over the threshold. For one second, he listened again, giving restraint its chance.

Then decision took over, and he turned it.

The bedside lamp glowed.

She lay tangled in the covers, breathing fast, caught in the grip of a dream. Her body trembled, fists clenched tight.

He was beside her in an instant.

"Arden," he said softly, kneeling at the bed. "Hey. You're okay."

She didn't wake.

He touched her arm, light as a question. She flinched, then softened. Her breath hitched, but her eyes stayed shut.

Only then did he slide beneath the covers and draw her close.

She settled almost immediately. Her head tucked beneath his chin, her breath evening out. One hand found his arm and clung like memory.

He exhaled, pressing a kiss into her hair.

"I've got you," he whispered. "You're safe."

She murmured his name, maybe, and curled deeper against him.

He stayed still. One arm firm around her waist, the other tracing slow, soothing circles down her arm. Her weight against him kept him present, held him inside the room instead of inside every violent thing his mind wanted to do.

His eyes drifted shut.

For now, she was safe.

And for now, that was enough.

CHAPTER 6
Light Between Shadows

The soft murmur of morning filtered through the brownstone—floorboards creaking, the faint clink of a mug on tile. Sunlight slipped through the curtains in golden strips, thinning the night's shadows.

Arden stirred. The scent of warm sheets and cedar cologne clung to the pillows, grounding her before memory caught up.

The attack.

The note.

The arms that had held her while she slept.

She didn't move for a while. She let the memory of Gideon's presence settle around her like another blanket.

Then Penny's voice shattered the morning with zero regard for timing or volume.

"Rise and shine, Sleeping Beauty!"

She swept into the room with a tray in one hand and her phone in the other. Toast. Coffee. And—was that a mimosa?

Arden blinked, groaned, and yanked the blanket over her head. "You are absolutely relentless."

"And yet, you love me for it," Penny said, setting the tray down with a flourish before plopping onto the bed. "Now up. We're having a morning. Snacks, trash TV, and a full debrief on why the whole Gideon thing has you looking both dreamy and personally attacked."

Arden peeked out, hair wild, expression unimpressed. "There is no Gideon thing."

Penny's eyes gleamed. "Oh, there is absolutely a Gideon thing. This is classic forced proximity, slow-burn escalation." She sniffed the air. "Also, why does this room smell like his jawline and emotional repression?"

Arden laughed despite herself. "It's too early for questions."

"Nope. You're deflecting," Penny sang, lifting her mimosa. "You're practically living in his presence. His scent has moved in. That's not a vibe—it's aromatherapy with benefits."

Arden rolled her eyes, but warmth crept into her cheeks. "You're ridiculous."

"Ridiculously correct." Penny toasted the air. "So. What's the plan? Denial or full surrender?"

"I'm not planning anything," Arden said, quieter now. "It's complicated."

Penny's smile softened. "All the best love stories are."

DOWNSTAIRS, Gideon paused mid-step as Penny's laughter rang through the house like sunlight cracking open a storm.

His shoulders eased a fraction as he stepped into the living room.

Arden was curled on the couch, a blanket draped around her shoulders, hair loose and unbothered. Penny sat beside her, gesturing wildly at the screen, and the coffee table looked like a snack explosion.

He let himself watch for a moment, not because he didn't belong, but because this version of Arden was rare.

Open.

Unwound.

"Trash-TV day?" he asked, leaning against the doorway.

Penny beamed. "Don't knock it, Blackwell. This is healing."

Arden looked over, eyes bright. "It's...oddly cathartic."

Gideon gave a low chuckle. "I'll pass." His gaze lingered. Her posture was different—still alert, still guarded, but lighter. Softer at the edges.

"I'm heading into the office," he said, voice pitched to her now. "You'll be all right?"

"We'll be fine," Arden said, straightening slightly. The blanket slipped to her lap, her hair falling over one shoulder.

The way she already looked like she belonged here twisted something in his chest.

She followed him to the front door. Penny said nothing, but turned the volume up on the reality show.

At the threshold, Gideon pulled on his overcoat.

"Thank you," Arden said quietly.

He glanced down. "For what?"

"For letting me stay. For last night. For..." She trailed off, looking away. "All of it."

His fingertips brushed hers. "You don't have to thank me. I'm glad you're here."

The honesty in his voice caught her off guard.

She stepped closer and pressed a kiss to his cheek—light, cautious, intentional.

Her breath hitched as their eyes met, and for a second, the world tilted toward inevitability.

His hand settled at her waist, thumb tracing a slow arc. Neither of them moved closer. Neither of them moved away. The tension drew tight...then held.

"Be careful today," she whispered.

His smile was faint, but his voice carried weight. "I always am."

Light as breath, intimate as a promise, he brushed his thumb across her cheek. Then he stepped back, and the contact broke like a string pulled too tight.

"Try not to let Penny talk you into anything outrageous."

"No promises," Arden said, smiling despite the ache blooming low in her chest.

He hesitated, fingers curling around the doorknob.

Then he was gone, coat billowing behind him as the cool morning swallowed him whole.

Arden stayed where she was, forehead resting against the doorframe.

Under different circumstances, this might have felt like one of those Avonlea mornings: soft light, borrowed peace, the promise of good things just out of sight.

But life hadn't given her Gilbert Blythe and rose gardens.

It had given her surveillance bugs and borrowed safety.

And still, she stayed.

She exhaled, steadying herself.

This wasn't the chapter she would have written.

But it was hers.

And that was enough.

It had to be.

The elevator doors opened into the glass-and-marble hush of Hawthorne Holdings.

Inside Gideon's office, Leo stood by the desk, Christian by the window. Both alert. Focused. Waiting.

"Let's hear it," Gideon said, shrugging out of his coat before taking his seat.

Leo opened a file. "If it's the same guy, he's escalating. If it's someone new —" He glanced up. "They've done their homework."

Christian added, "We identified surveillance gaps. At her apartment and at your brownstone. This wasn't random. Whoever it is knows how to move."

Gideon's jaw tightened. "This isn't amateur work."

"No," Christian said. "It's surgical."

Leo nodded. "I've got people combing old Silverbranch cases. If this ties back to her past, we'll find it."

"Cross-reference everything," Gideon said. "And don't let up on Sebastian or Alex. If they know something—"

"They won't for long," Christian cut in. "There's more."

The room seemed to still around those words.

Christian paused. "Her apartment was bugged. Audio and visual."

Gideon went still.

"Streaming devices," Christian continued. "Miniature cameras. Concealed. Hardwired and wireless. Whoever placed them wasn't just listening. They were watching."

A muscle jumped in Gideon's jaw. "And no one caught it."

"They were professionally embedded," Christian said. "Designed not to be."

Gideon exhaled slowly, the kind of controlled breath that kept violence behind his teeth. "Remove everything. Sweep it again. Then sweep it twice more. No gaps."

Leo's voice dropped. "We'll find him."

Gideon didn't look up. "You always do."

LATER, in the glass-walled conference room, Dan ran point on quarterly projections while Gideon stared a little too hard at a column of numbers.

Dan texted under the table.

You're a million miles away. You good?

Gideon glanced at the screen.

Fine. Keep going.

Dan didn't press. He didn't have to.

When the meeting ended, the room cleared quickly. Dan lingered.

"You're distracted," he said. "Want to talk about it?"

"It's Arden."

"Leo filled me in. How's she holding up?"

"She says she's fine." Gideon's voice stayed even. "I don't buy it."

"And you?"

"She's all I can think about." A pause. "Whoever's behind this knows too much. And I can't stop it. Not yet."

Dan leaned back, arms crossed. "You care."

Gideon didn't blink. "She's important."

Dan's smile was slow, knowing. "That's one way to put it."

A buzz cut through the room.

Gideon checked his phone.

Arden: Trash-TV marathon update: awful show, worse outfits. Penny's thriving.

Something in his jaw eased a fraction.

His thumbs hovered over the screen.

He didn't reply.

Dan arched a brow. "Arden?"

"She's...okay."

"For now," Dan said quietly. "But you'll handle it. You always do."

When Gideon returned to the brownstone, the house was still.

No laughter. No movement.

But the faint scent of lavender and honey lingered in the kitchen—proof she'd been there. That she still was.

Safe.

For now.

CHAPTER 7
Swaying in the Shadows

Gideon's place felt different without Penny.

Like the pause between heartbeats. Like breath caught in the chest, waiting for release.

Arden stood in the living room as golden evening light spilled through the tall windows, catching on polished wood and the shadowed corners of Gideon's carefully curated world. The brownstone didn't feel like hers, but it didn't feel foreign either.

Penny had invited her to spend the evening with her family. Had tried to insist. Arden had declined.

She wasn't ready to pretend things were fine. The calm here, and the pull of Gideon's presence, were the only things that made sense.

She leaned against the kitchen island, cradling a mug of coffee, when Gideon appeared.

Gone were the sharp lines of his suit. In their place, soft denim and a black sweater that clung in all the right ways.

He opened the fridge, scanned its contents, and frowned in a way she was already learning to recognize.

"Empty," she asked, "or nothing you actually want?"

He glanced over his shoulder, mouth twitching. "Trying to decide if there's anything worth throwing together. But I'm guessing your standards for dinner are higher than this."

Arden smirked over her mug. "Last meal was Penny's chips. You're safe."

"Then takeout it is." He pulled out his phone. "Thai okay?"

"Thai is always okay."

Her lips curved. "Do you feed all your houseguests, or is this a special perk for the emotionally unstable?"

He didn't miss a beat. "Manners," he said, gaze sharp but warmer now. "And maybe a little bit of a you thing."

Heat crept up her neck. She dropped her gaze, watching the coffee swirl in her mug. He made her feel...disarmed. Like there was room for her here.

"You're annoyingly good at this normal thing," she muttered.

"Annoyingly?" His smirk deepened. "I'll take that as a compliment."

The moment lingered, easy and unforced, as the city darkened beyond the glass, gold fading to indigo, lights blinking awake.

Later, they sat in the sitting room, lamplight soft against the walls. Empty takeout containers crowded the coffee table, Pad Thai from the place Gideon swore was the best in the city.

He was right. Of course he was.

"You weren't kidding," she said, setting her container aside. "If I didn't know better, I'd think you were bribing me into staying."

"Bribe you with food?" He poured bourbon into two glasses and handed her one. "Could be worse plans."

She arched a brow, accepting it. "Do those plans usually involve bourbon?"

"Only the good ones." His tone was dry, gentled at the edges. "Consider it a remedy for a long day."

She sipped. The burn bloomed warm in her chest, lingering heat that mirrored her pulse.

They sat across from each other, the space between them small but charged. The fire popped low. Outside, the city breathed.

Arden felt the shift, the tether between them drawing taut.

A held note. A thread pulled tight and waiting.

Gideon stood slowly, then extended his hand.

"Dance with me."

His voice carried conviction. Not a demand—an invitation.

She didn't blink this time.

She knew this version of him now. The one who didn't try to fix her, only made space. The one who reminded her she didn't always have to hold her survival like a blade.

Arden set her glass aside and met his gaze. "You really don't like to ask, do you?"

"Not when I already know the answer."

Her fingers slid into his. No urgency. No pressure.

"All right," she said softly. "Lead the way."

He guided her to the center of the room, his hand settling at her waist—light, sure, without claim.

There was no music at first, only the soft crackle of firewood and the hush of breath between them. Then somewhere, a low melody drifted in. She didn't know if it came from hidden speakers or her imagination.

She didn't care.

They swayed, unhurried and measured, until her head rested briefly against his shoulder and the tension eased from her chest in slow release, like something long held finally letting go.

No words.

None needed.

Her body found his rhythm instinctively. It wasn't a complicated dance. That was the point. To be held. To lean in. To let the walls soften enough to breathe.

And for a few minutes, in the hush between firelight and shadow, she did just that.

"Do you always take the lead?" she murmured, lips curving against his sweater, a challenge softened by the smile she couldn't quite hide.

Gideon tipped his head, firelight catching in his eyes. "Only when you let me."

Her brow arched. She leaned in, breath brushing his neck. "And if I don't?"

His hand pressed firmer at her waist. Not to control, but to answer. Attuned. "Then I'll follow."

Her defiance flickered, gentling into something else. A pulse of trust.

Their steps slowed as the melody thinned to the edges. The moment stretched, suspended.

She looked up, pulse stuttering. Everything lived in his gray eyes: restraint and hunger held in balance, the weight of wanting without demand.

Neither moved.

Then the sway returned, smaller now, closer. A conversation in breath and motion.

She took him in by fragments: the clean line of his jaw, the crease between his brows that smoothed only when he looked at her, the warmth of his palm at her back.

No promise of forever. Only presence. Steadiness. The kind of safety she hadn't known she craved until he offered it.

Her forehead came to rest against his shoulder. Her eyes closed.

And for the first time in days, she let go.

A dance.

A choice.

She was trusting him.

Arden had no idea what time it was when they finally started up the stairs.

At the landing, she turned to him. "Thank you. For everything. You've made the last couple of days...easier than I thought they could be."

"You never have to thank me, Arden."

Her name softened in his mouth, still carrying weight. A vow woven into the syllables.

He stepped closer, unhurried.

When he leaned in, she didn't flinch.

She met him halfway.

The kiss struck like lightning—swift, consuming, irresistible.

His hand rose to cup her jaw, thumb brushing her cheekbone with a tenderness that made her chest ache. The other settled firm at her waist.

She melted into him.

Her hands slid into his hair, threading through the soft strands as she tilted her head, deepening the kiss. His strength and presence wrapped around her like heat, stoking something deeper than desire.

Every shift of his hand.

Every press of his mouth.

Wild beneath her skin.

Gideon groaned low, his grip tightening at her waist. The kiss deepened, controlled but unraveling. His restraint was palpable; so was the edge of it. Want, barely leashed, matched her heartbeat for heartbeat.

Her back met the guest-room doorframe, the cool wood a shock against the fire climbing through her. His fingers skimmed her lower back, his other hand tangling in her hair as he claimed her mouth again.

This kiss was a reckoning.

A release.

A promise.

When he finally pulled back, their eyes locked.

Neither moved.

Neither blinked.

His thumb stroked her waist in a slow rhythm, soothing and dangerous in the way it unraveled her.

She slid her hands down, palms flattening against his chest, as if she needed the contact to keep from collapsing. The erratic hammer of her heart matched the thrum beneath her touch.

"Gideon," she whispered, trembling with everything she couldn't shape into words.

He answered with another kiss, softer this time. Gentle. A promise pressed to her lips.

His hand lingered at her waist, tightening briefly, as if he couldn't quite let go.

"Goodnight," he murmured, voice intimate enough to wrap around her like warmth itself.

Her eyes fluttered open. Their gazes held.

In his expression she saw everything unsaid, longing and care threaded with an understanding that stole her breath.

"Goodnight," she whispered back, a faint, almost shy smile tugging at her lips despite the fire still burning beneath her skin.

Neither moved.

The moment stretched, thick with want and gentled by restraint.

Finally, Gideon stepped back, his eyes never leaving hers as she slipped into the room.

She closed the door softly behind her, fingertips brushing her lips as if she could keep the memory there.

Even in the stillness, she felt him: the echo of his heat, the weight of his presence, the pull of everything left unsaid.

She lay awake in the dark. The sheets were soft, the bed comfortable, but sleep wouldn't come.

Her mind circled the kiss—the heat, the care, the way it had reached past her body and settled somewhere deeper. Her center. Her core.

Her lips still tingled, haunted by the memory of his mouth. No tossing, no turning could silence the ache blooming low in her chest.

She didn't want to admit it.

But she did.

She wanted him.

Not only the way his hand found her waist like it belonged there, or the way his mouth claimed and cherished in the same breath. She wanted the stillness he gave her. The steadiness. The space to exist without performing survival.

Her hand curled in the sheets, frustration sparking against the thrum of longing.

And then—she moved.

She didn't let herself think. She slid from the bed, the night air cool against her skin as she padded into the hallway.

At his door, she hesitated.

Her hand hovered over the knob. The sensible part of her whispered: mistake. Go back. Lock the door. Lie still. Wait.

But the pull was louder.

She turned the knob slowly. The door creaked open.

Gideon lay on his back, covers low at his waist. His chest rose and fell in an even rhythm, but his eyes were open.

They met hers across the dim room.

He didn't ask why she was there.

He didn't move to stop her.

He only watched.

Arden stepped inside.

Uncertain.

Certain.

Each step was soft against the hardwood until she reached the bed. Her hand brushed the mattress.

Gideon shifted, making space.

And without a word, she slid in beside him.

The sheets were cool. The room hushed. Shadows pooled at the edges, the city's distant breath pressing faintly through the glass.

Then his arm came around her waist, drawing her gently in.

Warmth spread through her chest as she settled against him, her head tucked beneath his collarbone. Her hand found his heartbeat, the steady thump holding her in a way nothing else had all night.

He exhaled, and her hair stirred with the quiet rise and fall of him.

His arm tightened, just enough to say—

I've got you.

She closed her eyes, absorbing it: the feel of him, the promise in his breath, the stillness inside her that hadn't existed in days.

She didn't know what tomorrow would bring.

She didn't know what this meant.

But here, in this narrow sliver of night, wrapped in his arms, she felt more herself than any mirror had ever shown.

Arden finally let herself rest.

And for the first time since everything shattered—she slept.

CHAPTER 8
The Edge of Home

Morning sunlight filtered softly through the curtains, laying gentle bands of gold across the room. The light was warm and forgiving, the kind that softened the edges of everything it touched.

Gideon stirred first.

His body, tuned to early hours, moved before his mind fully caught up. When he glanced down, Arden was still curled against him, one hand resting lightly on his chest. Her breath was slow. Even. The tension she wore so faithfully had smoothed away in sleep.

Carefully, he eased himself out of bed. The mattress dipped, and Arden stirred, her hand brushing the empty space he left behind.

She didn't wake.

He dressed quietly in dark slacks and a button-down, each motion smooth: the hush of fabric, the soft click of his belt.

He was almost to the door when her voice broke the stillness.

"Sneaking out on me already?"

He turned.

She was barely awake, lashes heavy, a lazy smile tugging at her mouth. Her hair haloed her face, her voice raspy with sleep, mischief threaded through it.

"I have to run into the office." He crossed back, bracing one hand on the mattress as he leaned in. "I'll be back as soon as I can."

Her smile deepened. "Guess I'll rifle through all your things while you're gone. Find your secrets."

A laugh slipped out, low and warm. "You won't find anything. I don't keep secrets from you."

She cracked one eye, skeptical. "None at all?"

"None," he said again, softer now. Steadier. His gaze didn't waver.

For a moment, he simply looked at her.

Unguarded.

Tender.

His fingers brushed her cheek, his thumb tracing a gentle line along her skin.

"I love you."

The words hung in the stillness. Unplanned. Unguarded. True.

Arden's breath caught. The teasing slipped from her smile.

"Gideon..."

"You don't have to say anything," he murmured, his hand still at her cheek. "I just needed you to know."

She covered his hand with hers. "Thank you," she whispered. "You didn't need to say it. But...thank you for saying it anyway."

They held the moment for a heartbeat, eyes locked, the world receding around them.

He pressed a kiss to her forehead, lingering as if he were memorizing the shape of her breath.

"Go back to sleep," he said gently. "I'll be back soon."

She hummed, already sinking into warmth. Her hand curled into the hollow he'd left in the sheets, holding the imprint of him.

Gideon straightened, chest tight and full all at once.

At the doorway, he looked back once more. She hadn't moved, but the early light threaded copper through her chestnut hair.

It felt like home.

He carried that with him as he stepped into the day.

Arden was mid-stretch, one hand wrapped around a coffee mug, when the sound of the front door opening reached her.

She tiptoed barefoot across the living room, dressed in one of Gideon's crisp white button-downs. It hung loose, brushing her thighs, bare skin beneath. When she saw him step inside, she froze mid-step.

"You're home early," she said, a slow smile curving at her mouth. Casual tone. Less casual gaze.

Gideon's eyes darkened.

He let the door fall shut, his attention lingering on the shirt, open enough to suggest everything. A smirk tugged at his mouth.

"I thought you might need a nap."

She leaned against the back of the couch, brow arching. "A nap, huh?"

"That's what I said."

Her eyes sparked. "Is that...code for something?"

He crossed to her, unhurried. "Like what?"

"Oh, I don't know." Her voice dipped, warm and teasing. "A reason for you to press your body against mine?"

His gaze swept her slowly, hunger edged with amusement. "If that's your definition of a nap," he murmured, "then yes. Exactly that."

Her laugh was low, knowing. She stepped closer. "Well, in that case—"

She didn't finish.

His hands found her waist, drawing her flush. Her arms slid around his neck, fingers threading into his hair as his mouth met hers.

The kiss was slow and deep, memory and promise stitched together. Not hurried. Not wild. Tension hummed beneath it, restraint sharpening every brush of his lips.

She matched him, teasing fingers tugging him closer. His coiled strength answered hers, measured and sure.

When he pulled back, his breath grazed her cheek. "Let's take that nap."

She smirked, lips brushing his. "I thought I was the one who needed rest."

"Maybe I do." His hand slid down her spine, slow and certain. "But only if it involves you."

She let him lead her to the couch, steps easy and unhurried.

They sank into the cushions, laughter lingering as her head settled against his chest. His familiar warmth wrapped around her.

The kiss stayed with them, not forgotten, only softened.

The world outside slipped away.

There was only the hush of the brownstone, their breathing in rhythm, and the comfort of closeness that didn't need proving.

They didn't speak.

The hushed sounds of the house wrapped around them like a blanket.

Gideon leaned back into the couch, one arm slung loosely around Arden. She rested against his chest, lulled again by the beat of his heart. Afternoon sunlight streamed through the windows, golden and soft, chasing the sharp edges from a frayed week.

For the first time in days, the weight on her chest eased.

Then Gideon's phone buzzed against the table, low and insistent.

He exhaled through his nose, brushed a kiss into her temple, and reached for it. "It's Christian."

Arden sat up slightly, fingers tracing the folds of the oversized shirt she wore. His, but it felt like hers now. She watched as he paced, phone to his ear.

"Yeah, Christian. What's the update?"

The light caught the darker threads in his brown hair and sharpened the line of his profile. Even mid-crisis, he moved with composed ease. Unshaken. Like she could lean on him without him breaking.

His voice shifted. "And the bugs?" A pause. "Good. And her apartment—everything's in place?"

He nodded once, listening.

"I trust you. Keep me updated."

The call ended. When he turned back, the edge in his posture softened as he crossed to her again.

"We've made progress."

Relief and dread tangled in her chest. "What does that mean?"

"Your apartment's clean," he said. "Christian swept it—no more bugs. We upgraded the locks. Cameras in the hall and on the balcony. You'll have access to the feed on your phone."

She went still.

Her hand tightened in the fabric at her waist. "And the bugs—did you figure out who planted them?"

His jaw ticked. "They're gone. No trail. Whoever placed them knew what they were doing. Leo's working the leads."

"And the stalker?"

"We're narrowing it down," he said. "This wasn't impulse. It was calculated. That helps us focus."

She looked away, fingers brushing the faint scar on her palm. "You've done so much. All of this...it's a lot."

A faint smile touched his mouth. "I'd do it again. Every bit of it." His gaze held hers. "You're not in this alone, Arden."

Her chest tightened. His voice carried more than reassurance; it held intention. Commitment. Something feral at the edges, but controlled.

"Thank you," she whispered.

"There's more." His tone shifted. "Christian and I think it's safe for you to move back...if you're ready."

Her head snapped up. "Already?"

He nodded. "You don't have to decide now. But it's secure. And Christian's team will stay close."

She didn't answer right away. Her gaze drifted to the sunlight striping the hardwood.

The brownstone had become a shelter, safe in a way that felt borrowed. It wasn't home. And staying too long might make her want things she wasn't ready to name.

"I'll think about it," she said finally.

"Take your time." His voice softened. "It's your call."

Before she could reply, Penny's voice floated in from the kitchen. "Hey! Are we getting pizza or what? I want a vote on toppings."

The tension fractured.

Arden's mouth curved as she glanced toward the kitchen. "You've been warned," she murmured.

Gideon's smirk returned, easier now. "Noted."

He stood, stretching as he headed toward the kitchen. "Penny, you get one topping. Don't make it pineapple."

"Pineapple is elite, Blackwell!" Penny shot back, scandalized. "You clearly have no taste—or joy."

His low chuckle carried down the hall.

Arden leaned back into the couch, a faint smile tugging at her lips.

It didn't quite reach her eyes.

Because when the laughter faded, the shadows crept back in.

The stalker.

The surveillance.

The threat waiting beyond the door.

But for now, for a little longer, she let herself stay in the light.

The decision hung between them like fog.

Arden leaned forward, elbows on her knees, hands clasped tight. Across the room, Gideon stood at the counter, arms folded. His expression was relaxed, but the tension in his jaw betrayed him.

"I can't stay here," she said at last.

His gaze sharpened.

"Arden," he said carefully, weight threaded through her name. Half warning. Half prayer. "You don't have to decide now. There's no pressure."

She shook her head, eyes fixed on her hands. "It's not about pressure. It's about not hiding."

When she looked up, her gaze didn't waver.

"If I don't go back, I let them win. And I can't live like that. I won't."

The words landed harder than he expected. He stepped forward without thinking.

"You know it's still dangerous," he said, voice lower now. "Going back doesn't make you braver. You don't owe anyone anything."

"It's not about proving anything." Her voice softened, but it didn't bend. "It's about claiming what's mine. I won't let fear take that from me."

His jaw flexed. He dragged a hand through his already tousled hair, tension rolling off him in waves. "And nothing I say will stop you."

Her smile curved, rueful and warm. "You know me too well."

In two strides, he was in front of her. His hand lifted, knuckles brushing her cheek. The tenderness of it stole her breath.

"I want you safe," he said, voice rough.

"I know." She leaned into his touch. "And I will be. Because of you."

The silence between them stretched.

His hand fell slowly. He exhaled through clenched teeth.

"If this is what you need," he said at last, "I'll make it happen. No gaps. No slip-ups. Full detail."

Her throat tightened. "Thank you."

He gave a single nod.

Not dismissal.

A vow.

They didn't move.

In the silence, they felt it: something deeper than safety, stronger than fear.

Not retreat.

Not distance.

Return.

CHAPTER 9

More than Survival

Morning light filtered through the windows of Gideon's brownstone in long, honey-warm streaks, catching on book spines and brushed brass.

Arden curled into the corner of the couch, one knee drawn beneath her, a book open in her lap.

She wasn't reading.

The words blurred, slipping past her focus like mist. Her body was still, but her thoughts paced, restless and uncontained. Too much tension for sleep. Too much exhaustion for action.

She felt him before she saw him.

His presence was deliberate. He didn't speak at first, only stood there, waiting. The way he always did. Giving her the choice to look up.

She didn't stop him.

He crossed the room and sank beside her, close enough that she felt his warmth, not so close that he pressed against the edges of her defenses. His forearms rested on his knees, fingers loosely laced. His gaze moved over her, unsettling and stable all at once.

"I want to do something for you," he said softly.

Arden turned her head. "Gideon—"

"I know." His jaw flexed as he met her gaze. "You don't want to be managed. Or protected. You don't want to feel boxed in."

He held her eyes like it mattered to say it out loud.

Maybe it did.

"This isn't that," he said, softer now. "You haven't had a second to breathe since it happened. I can't undo any of it." A pause. "But I can give you a distraction. For a little while."

No agenda.

No pity.

An offering.

Her fingers traced the frayed corner of the book in her lap. Her chest tightened and loosened at the same time.

"What are you suggesting?" she asked.

"A spa day," he said, lips twitching. "You and Penny. My treat."

She blinked. "A spa day?"

"I booked it already," he admitted. "Facials, massages, the works. Just...space. Time. Somewhere you can stop bracing."

Before she could respond, Penny's voice rang down the hall. "Did someone say spa day?"

Arden groaned, dragging a hand down her face. "Of course you heard that."

Penny breezed in, phone in hand, grin wide. "Gideon Blackwell, I retract everything terrible I've ever said about you."

His brow lifted. "You'll say worse by dinner."

"Fair." Penny spun to Arden, practically glowing. "Okay. I know you hate pampering. But this is medically necessary. A licensed stranger is going to rub your shoulders while we sip cucumber water and pretend we have no trauma. It'll be great."

Arden arched a brow. "You're not selling it."

"Massages," Penny intoned. "Also, I'm picking your nail color. Judge me if you dare."

Gideon's gaze stayed on Arden. His voice softened, meant for her alone. "I'm not trying to fix anything. I want to treat you. No strings. No expectations."

Her throat tightened. The part of her still armored wanted to joke, to deflect.

But maybe...she did need it.

She looked between Penny, who could drag her through hell and still make her laugh, and Gideon, who never pushed and always left the door open.

"Fine," she yielded.

Penny threw her arms up. "Yes! Victory!"

"You're unbearable," Arden said, but her lips twitched.

"And you," Penny said, pointing at Gideon, "are now my favorite billionaire. Temporarily. Don't blow it."

"I'll try to survive the pressure," he deadpanned.

As Penny launched into an enthusiastic breakdown of spa packages, Arden leaned back, her gaze drifting to Gideon.

He didn't gloat.

Didn't even smile.

He gave her the smallest nod.

Good, it said. You deserve this.

And for the first time in days, she let herself believe it.

The air smelled of acetone and florals, softened by the hum of dryers and low chatter.

Arden leaned back in her chair, legs stretched into the bubbling foot bath. Across from her, Penny crouched like a general, scrutinizing a rack of polish swatches with absurd intensity.

"I swear, Arden," Penny said, "if you pick black again, I'm going to riot."

Arden smirked. "Relax. I'm branching out."

Penny's eyes narrowed. "Define branching out."

With playful flourish, Arden lifted a bottle. "It's called Good Girls Gone Plaid."

Penny gasped. "Is that purple?"

Arden nodded solemnly. "Deep purple. Very bold of me."

Penny beamed, practically vibrating. "This is historic. Actual color. You're healing."

"Don't get greedy," Arden warned, warmth threading her tone.

The nail tech brushed on the first coat while Penny hovered like a judge at a bake-off.

A rich violet bloomed across Arden's nail.

Penny clapped once. "Yessss. Now this is growth."

By the third coat, her expression faltered.

"Wait."

Under the UV lamp, the polish cured to a glossy, almost-black sheen. The purple only whispered when the light hit it at the right angle.

Penny squinted. "Arden..."

The topcoat sealed it.

Penny's jaw dropped. "That's basically black."

Arden tilted her hand, admiring it. "No. It's Good Girls Gone Plaid."

"You played me."

"You played yourself." Arden's smirk deepened. "Rookie mistake."

Penny flopped back in her chair with a groan. "You're a villain in an origin story."

Arden wiggled her fingers. The faint plum undertone caught like a secret. "Perfect."

"Of course you think so," Penny muttered, scandalized. "I believed in your growth arc, and you dragged me straight back to noir."

"I warned you."

Penny peeked through her fingers, torn between outrage and admiration. "That is the most you thing I've ever seen."

"Exactly."

They fell silent for a beat, the salon's hum filling the space. Arden let herself sink into the warmth, the ridiculousness, the ordinary comfort of sitting beside someone who knew the difference between a color choice and a small act of mercy.

She hadn't realized how tightly she'd been holding herself until she felt it begin to loosen.

Penny broke the silence. "Next time...glitter. Gloss. Full commitment."

Arden raised a brow. "You'll have to sedate me."

"Noted."

The drive back felt strangely weightless, buoyed by Penny's relentless commentary. She cycled through possible ways to celebrate Arden's return: trash-TV marathons, ordering enough Chinese food to spark a diplomatic incident, or rearranging furniture for feng shui and spiritual dominance.

Arden didn't say much, but her lips curved often. Penny's familiar rhythm—insistent, ridiculous, impossible not to love—knocked loose tension Arden hadn't realized she was still carrying. For once, she didn't shove it back down.

But when they pulled up to the curb, the shift was immediate.

The building loomed larger than memory, exterior unchanged, interior remade. Security cameras blinked above the door. Locks gleamed like surgical steel. Stark reminders of what had driven her out.

Still, Arden stepped forward.

Inside, the scent of her space hit first: citrus cleaner and the faint herbal note of a candle left uncapped weeks ago. She ran her fingers along the edge of the counter, and the texture centered her more than she expected.

Penny hovered. "You okay?"

Arden exhaled, nodding once. "Yeah." Her voice was low, anchored. "It's good to be home."

Penny studied her. "And you're really going back to work tomorrow?"

"I need to." Arden turned. "It's rhythm. Proof I'm still me."

"Rest is allowed," Penny said gently. "Brave doesn't mean burned out."

"I'm not trying to be brave." Arden's voice softened. "I'm trying not to disappear."

That stilled Penny. Then she nodded. "Okay. But I'll be lurking like a feral little barfly anyway."

Arden laughed, warm and surprised. "You're terrible at lurking. You'd flirt with the bouncer before I clocked in."

"Multitasking queen," Penny said, grinning.

The weight on Arden's shoulders eased further.

As Penny flopped onto the couch to build a nest of blankets and snacks, Arden slipped into her bedroom to unpack.

She moved slowly. Folded clothes. Brushed her fingers over the spines of books on her nightstand. Everything where she'd left it.

And yet—not.

Still, she moved with intention, pressing her claim. This was her space. Her sanctuary.

Not retreat.

Return.

The apartment wasn't only shelter now; it was choice.

She paused in the doorway, watching familiar shadows stretch across the hardwood.

I'm still here.

And for tonight, she let herself appreciate it.

THE LIGHTS FLICKERED ON, spilling warmth into the apartment as Arden stepped through the doorway—chin lifted, shoulders squared.

A queen reclaiming stolen territory.

On the grainy feed, Sebastian watched.

The camera caught her silhouette, gold against dark. They thought they'd erased him.

Fools.

They hadn't even looked here, at the margins. The forgotten angles of her sanctuary.

The door shut. The image jittered. It didn't matter. Watching her cross the threshold was enough: the hesitation in her step, the inhale before she entered.

A symphony composed for him alone.

She had no idea.

And her ignorance was perfect.

He leaned closer to the monitor, cold light carving his features into sharp planes. Her lips moved, teasing Penny no doubt.

He couldn't hear.

He didn't need to.

He knew her rhythms. The tilt of her brow. The way her smile curved when she was pretending nothing hurt. Every gesture etched into him like scripture.

She thought she was safe.

How naïve.

The locks. The cameras. Gideon Blackwell's gleaming arsenal—knight's armor polished bright.

As if walls could keep him out.

He knew this apartment better than she did: the way morning light spilled across tile, the faint protest of a cabinet hinge, the refrigerator's hum when the room went still.

Her home wasn't hers anymore.

It was his world now.

Her laughter pulled his gaze back to the screen. Soundless—but he knew its rise and fall. The way her head tipped when Penny joked. Maddening, how natural she looked.

How easily she believed she had reclaimed it.

As if she could erase him.

As if he hadn't been there first.

His fingers moved, pulling an older feed.

The hallway. Weeks ago. Arden lingering outside her door, auburn waves damp, exhaustion softening her posture. A flicker of hesitation. Guard lowered.

Exquisite.

She thought no one had seen.

But he had.

And it had been beautiful.

The present feed snapped back. Penny stepped fully inside. Arden shut the door. The lock clicked.

He smiled.

Meaningless.

He didn't need to be inside to own the space. He was already there—in the air, in the walls, in every shadow that brushed her skin.

Let her believe she was secure. Let Gideon play protector.

It changed nothing.

The cracks were forming. He saw them in the set of her jaw, the pause before each movement, the way her hand lingered on the counter as if she were convincing herself she still belonged.

She wasn't untouchable.

She was breaking.

Slowly.

Beautifully.

And when she fell, he would be there.

Penny's voice rose faintly in the background. Meddling. Temporary. She would leave. They always did.

Arden would be alone again.

Like before.

His fingers hovered over the keyboard. The itch to leave a mark burned beneath his skin. A reminder. Subtle. Unmistakable.

Not yet.

Timing was everything.

For now, it was enough to watch. To know she was his, even if she hadn't realized it yet.

Her gaze flicked toward the window.

His breath stilled.

For a moment, he thought she felt him. The weight of him, beyond the glass.

But she turned away.

Oblivious.

Always oblivious.

Let her believe in her fortress. In her knight.

It wouldn't undo what he had already taken.

When the moment came, when the mask slipped and the walls finally failed, she would understand.

There would be no more pretending.

No more hiding.

And no one left to save her.

CHAPTER 10

In the Shadow of Flames

Morning light filtered through the blinds, casting bands of gold across Arden's bed. She blinked and reached by instinct for the other side of the mattress before memory caught up.

Empty.

The absence hit harder than she wanted to admit. Gideon's warmth, so constant these past days, was gone, and though part of her relished the solitude, the ache beneath her ribs told a less convenient truth.

She exhaled slowly and took in the contours of her room.

Her room. Her space. Home.

It wasn't perfect. It wasn't safe—not entirely—but it was hers.

Arden slid out of bed and stretched, muscles stiff from too many nights spent half-sleeping with adrenaline wired beneath her skin. Today felt lighter. Traffic hummed outside. A horn blared. Footsteps tapped from the floor above. The city, loud and indifferent and alive, steadied something in her.

She wasn't only surviving anymore.

She moved through the apartment with purpose, fingers brushing the windowsill as she straightened a frame and opened the blinds slat by slat. Beyond the glass, the city stared back, unapologetic.

In the mirror, her reflection met her evenly. The wariness in her eyes hadn't vanished, but steel had settled behind it.

She pulled on a fitted black tank beneath a slate button-down, then slim jeans and boots that made her stand taller. Not practical, exactly.

Intentional.

I'm still me.

Still, Gideon lingered—in the scent clinging faintly to her pillow, in the warmth tucked beneath her ribs. She let the memory stay for one breath...then set it aside.

One step at a time.

The low hush of conversation met her first, then the clink of glasses, the gleam of polished wood, the familiar shape of the room settling around her like breath returning to the body. Cedar and citrus traced the air from the candles Gideon insisted on, warm and clean beneath the sharper scents of liquor, ice, and old wood.

Arden brushed her fingers along the bar's edge as she slipped behind it, her spine straightening.

Home.

"Look who's back," Marco called, grinning. "Place hasn't been the same without you, Mama."

Arden smirked. "It's your bar when I'm not here, Marco. I'm just the bartender."

"You're more than that, and you know it. Don't make me emotional. It's too early."

At the far end, Fatima waved, curls bouncing. "Arden! Finally. Marco's been insufferable. I've had to endure a five-day rant about glass-stacking."

"Glass-stacking is an art form," Marco declared.

Arden laughed easily this time, and something loosened deep in her chest.

She moved through the bar like she had never left. Bottles aligned. Garnishes checked. Regulars greeted by name. Drinks poured with muscle memory. Banter traded mid-shake. The familiar rhythm reclaimed her by inches, not as performance, but as proof.

Out of the corner of her eye, always him.

Gideon.

Not hovering. Not intruding. Passing his office door. Pausing at the edge of shadow. Present in that restrained, impossible way of his, as if he had made himself part of the architecture without once asking her to lean.

A tether she didn't yet have language for.

The hours passed in suspended ease, shakers flashing silver beneath the lights, laughter warming the corners, the cadence of work returning her to herself. For the first time in weeks, she didn't flinch at every movement behind her.

She was back.

Not free of shadows.

But no longer shrinking from them.

As the night slowed, Arden slipped into the rear hallway. The sounds of the bar dulled behind her, softened by distance and walls. She untied her apron, draped it over her shoulder, and leaned back against the cool plaster.

The hush here wasn't empty.

It was earned.

Moments later, she felt him before she saw him.

Gideon emerged from the dim light, posture relaxed, eyes sharp. "How's it going?"

His voice was low, threaded with attention.

"Surprisingly normal," she said. "And good. I needed that."

"That's the goal." His gaze held hers. "If anything feels off, you tell me."

She nodded.

Then she stepped into him.

Her arms slid around his waist, her cheek coming to rest against his chest. Gideon exhaled, one hand firm at her back, the other settling at her neck with a care that made something in her ache. She felt breakable there, held between his hands and the quiet.

But not broken.

He didn't speak. He didn't have to.

In the stillness, her breath found his. She softened into him, into the steadiness of his body and the restraint in his touch.

Not rescue. Not surrender.

Chosen.

When she pulled back, her fingers lingered at his elbow. Her eyes felt gentler now, the edges eased.

"Thanks," she said. Simple. Weighty.

His thumb brushed her wrist. "Always."

She slipped back into the bar's glow, into clinking glasses and conversation. Behind the counter again, her body remembered its rhythm: the reach, the pour, the polish. Citrus and cedar drifted through the air like memory.

Gideon lingered a moment at the edge, then retreated to his office.

Not hovering.

Not needing to.
His presence was already woven into the night.

"Arden," Marco called down the bar, "our guy in the corner wants your take on a whiskey flight."

She glanced over. Early sixties. Silver hair. Navy suit. Fingers resting lightly on the rim of his glass.

"Hmm...feeling adventurous," she asked, "or looking for comfort?"

"Surprise me," he said, cultured voice, sharp eyes. "You look like someone who knows how to choose."

She selected three bottles with care, letting instinct lead where muscle memory followed.

"Start here." She poured the first. "Smooth. Vanilla on the front, clean finish. A classic."

She slid the second glass forward. "Layered. Cinnamon, stone fruit. A little wild."

Then the last. "Smoky. Bold. Like dusk—if dusk had a taste."

The man chuckled, swirling the glass. "That's quite the description."

"It's been that kind of night," she said.

He sampled each one, then nodded once. "You chose well."

As she moved away, Fatima caught her eye.

A subtle nod passed between them.

Two women standing still, reclaiming what had nearly broken them.

The bar settled into its final rhythm. Velvet chairs emptied. Chandeliers dimmed. Marco and Fatima moved in sync around her, closing drawers, stacking glasses, wiping down the night until only its sheen remained.

Arden wiped the bar, her reflection flickering in the polished wood. For a moment, her hand stilled around the towel. Jazz hummed low through the room, soft as a secret, and the woman staring back at her looked tired, wary, whole.

For the first time in what felt like forever, she didn't feel like a shadow passing through her own life.

She was here.
Fully present.
Herself.

THE FIRST TIME Sebastian saw her step through those doors again, it was like dry kindling catching flame.

Arden Rivers.

Untamed. Unyielding.

Back where she belonged.

For days stretched thin into weeks, she had been hidden inside Blackwell's curated prison. A flame behind glass. No shadow at the window, no trace of her fire in the world. Sebastian had paced through the hours, counting absence like a penance.

And now here she was.

She moved behind the bar like it was a throne, as if the crown had never slipped. Every motion was fluid, precise, confidence crackling through the air around her, sharp and electric.

He had missed this.

Missed her.

The way she lit a room without trying. The rare curve of her smile, striking like a match in the dark.

She hadn't merely returned. She was alive again—lit from within, exquisite in the way only fire could be exquisite.

Except for the reason she'd been gone.

Gideon.

The arrogant bastard who had caged her, wrapped her brilliance in high-thread-count sheets, and called it sanctuary. Who fancied himself a savior. A protector.

Gideon didn't understand her fire.

Didn't deserve it.

Sebastian let the fury settle, thinning into smoke. It didn't matter. Arden's fire couldn't be contained. It would burn through Gideon the way it burned through everything else.

It already had.

He saw it in the sharper lift of her chin. In the return of her laughter, a language reclaimed.

He stayed in the shadows, watching.

Her laugh stole his breath.

She never laughed like that in Blackwell's world. There, she'd been muted. Silence behind her eyes. Tension etched into her spine.

But here? Here she was free.

Marco. Fatima. The others. They orbited her with chatter, blind to the depth beneath her surface. They thought she was a bartender. A survivor.

They were wrong.

She was more.

She was his muse.

His Little Fire.

His future.

Then she stepped into the hallway.

Alone.

His pulse surged.

She leaned against the wall, apron draped over her shoulder, exhaling as if she could shed the night in one long breath. Stripped of performance, she was sharper. Realer.

Perfect.

And then—

Gideon.

Goddammit.

His silhouette cut in like a blade. Pretentious steadiness. Counterfeit calm. Sebastian's stomach turned as he watched Arden soften, watched her step into Gideon's arms, her body yielding as if it belonged there.

It didn't.

She didn't need Gideon's rules. His watchful control. She needed someone who saw her. Who understood her chaos, her brilliance, her fire.

Not someone who tried to smother it.

Sebastian's fists clenched as Gideon's hand settled at her waist—gentle, possessive. A performance. Lies in tailored wool.

But Arden—

She would remember.

Sooner or later, she would recall what it felt like to be seen. To be loved not in spite of her edges, but because of them.

For now, he watched.

He etched the moment into himself: the angle of her body, the tilt of her head, the flicker of hesitation in her smile. Every detail became another piece in the structure he was methodically building.

She thought she was in control again.

She thought this was her life.

She had no idea how deep his reach ran. How long he had been there, watching, listening, wanting.

Waiting for her fire to burn bright enough to see him.

Soon, she would understand.

And when the truth came crashing down, it wouldn't be Gideon she turned to.

It would be him.

CHAPTER 11
The Appeal

The club buzzed with low conversation and the rhythmic clink of crystal. Arden barely noticed.

She was in her element.

Hands moving with practiced ease, sliding a cocktail across polished wood. Ears tuned to the room's cadence: the scuff of heels on marble, the shifting tempo of laughter, the low hum of old jazz from hidden speakers.

Polished. Controlled.

Until she heard them.

Laughter. Too loud. Too sharp. Not joy, but performance.

Tori Langston.

Arden didn't need to look. That voice carried—honeyed and barbed, lacquered in judgment. A voice made for cliques and courtroom gossip, for slipping knives between shoulder blades while smiling through lip gloss.

"I don't get it."

Arden wiped down the bar, constantly moving.

"Get what?" someone asked.

"Arden Rivers." A sip. The casual flick of a manicured wrist. "Sure, she's... confident. But Gideon Blackwell? He could have any woman in this city."

Arden's grip tightened on the towel.

She didn't flinch. Didn't fumble. She folded it once, pressed her thumb into the seam, and contained the heat.

"Maybe it's a phase," another voice chimed in, amusement oil-slick beneath the words. "Some men like the wounded-bird thing. Makes them feel heroic."

That did it.

Not embarrassment.

Insult.

She let the voices drip behind her like condensation on crystal. Let them underestimate her. Let them frame the narrative the way they always did: softness mistaken for damage, survival rewritten as spectacle.

She kept moving, because she knew something they didn't.

This wasn't appeal born of injury. It was gravity.

And gravity didn't need to announce itself to be felt.

"Doesn't it make you wonder?" Tori pressed. "What is the appeal?"

Then—

"Let's ask her."

Arden looked up.

Tori's eyes were already on her, smile slow and curling like smoke at the edge of a burn.

"Arden. Darling." A raised glass, saccharine sweet. "Be a gem and come over?"

Arden could have ignored it. Could have stayed where she was and let them rot behind polished veneers.

Instead, she smoothed her shirt and walked over.

Not because they had summoned her.

Because they had forgotten who she was.

Not the bartender.

The storm they thought they could name.

She stopped at the table, cool, composed, utterly unimpressed.

Tori's smile widened. "We were just talking about you. Specifically how you managed to capture Gideon Blackwell's attention." A sip. The bait gleaming. "No offense, but some of us are dying to know what the appeal is."

Arden blinked.

Once.

Slowly.

Then she laughed.

Not polite. Not nervous. A low, indulgent laugh that dropped the pressure in the room like a sudden storm front.

Tori stiffened.

"You've been sitting here all night discussing me?" Arden asked, voice velveted and sharp.

Silence.

"We were curious—" someone tried.

"No, I get it." Arden tilted her head. "I'd be curious too. If I'd spent years trying to catch Gideon's eye and all I had to show for it was—"

Her hand gestured vaguely.

Mercilessly.

Across the table.

Tori's jaw ticked.

"Excuse me?"

"Oh, don't be embarrassed." Arden smiled, soft and precise. "When someone like Gideon chooses someone else, of course people start asking questions."

"It's...surprising," Tori said tightly. "That's all."

"Mmm." Arden's smile deepened. "And yet—here I am, and he's with me."

She let the silence do the rest.

"Not you."

Check.

Mate.

Tori's fingers whitened around her glass.

"Really, girls?"

The voice wasn't loud, but it sliced clean.

Cate Blackwell.

Reclined in her chair like a woman born immune to scrutiny, shoulders relaxed, champagne coupe balanced like an afterthought. Her tone wasn't cruel. Just bored.

"This is embarrassing. For you."

Tori went pale. The others shrank.

Arden didn't move. She only watched, one brow arched, faint amusement lighting her stillness.

Cate never glanced over.

Apathy landed heavier than insult.

"We should go," another friend whispered.

"I'm finishing my drink," Tori hissed.

Arden smiled, knowing and silk-smooth. "Take your time."

Poised and unhurried, she turned away.

Because she had already won.

They all knew it.

SEBASTIAN LEANED back in his seat, savoring the aftermath.

Not a conversation.

Not a power play.

A slaughter.

Tori Langston sat rigid, nails biting into crystal as if it were the only thing keeping her upright. Her friends whispered frantically around her, pretty masks cracked at the edges.

Pathetic.

Sebastian swirled the amber in his glass, the motion slow and indulgent.

Arden hadn't just won.

She hadn't even had to try.

His mouth curved.

Little Fire.

My girl.

Not yet.

But soon.

Because this was the truth: Tori played at power.

Arden was power.

Sharp-edged. Unapologetic. Untouchable.

And still—

She stood at Gideon's side.

The thought lodged in his chest, heavy and insulting.

Gideon Blackwell hadn't earned her. He hadn't fought for her. He had simply arrived first.

The room shifted. A low hum moved through it, as if the space itself had inhaled.

Gideon had entered.

Not loud. Not dramatic.

He didn't acknowledge the tightening air. He never did. He moved like a man who owned the room without needing permission.

Tori flinched as he passed, chin lifting in brittle defense.

Futile.

He didn't even look at her.

His focus was singular.

Arden.

And worse—

She felt it.

Sebastian saw it in the subtle shift of her posture, the lift of her head, the way she didn't turn because she didn't have to.

She knew Gideon was there.

The ice in Sebastian's glass clinked, sharp against his teeth.
Gideon's claim wasn't performance.
It was presence.
Real.
And Arden didn't seem to mind.
Sebastian forced a slow sip, burying the flare of rage beneath practiced ease.
He could wait.
He always had.
Because Gideon might think he had her. Might think he understood her fire.
But he didn't.
Not the way Sebastian did.
And that—
That was a mistake.
One Sebastian would correct.

CHAPTER 12
To Resilience

Arden woke with sunlight warming her face.

Mornings like this made breathing feel possible. Light on skin. The world still turning. Golden streaks filtered through the thin curtains, striping the hardwood in fractured gold as she stretched beneath the sheets, her muscles tight from too many restless nights.

But the ache felt different now.

Less like weight.

More like memory.

The rhythm of recent days had begun to settle inside her: her return to the club, the easy cadence of her team, and most of all, Gideon's presence, steady in ways she hadn't expected and careful in ways she didn't know she needed. She hadn't gone looking for that kind of constancy.

It had found her anyway.

Unshakable.

A tether in the dark.

Safety hadn't erased survival. It had simply given the storm somewhere to rest.

In the kitchen, a whisper of unease curled low in her gut. Not panic, exactly. More like a breath held too long.

She exhaled and let it pass.

The scent of coffee cut through the stillness, familiar enough to settle her. This was her space. Her routine. The shadows didn't get to take that from her.

By late afternoon, she stepped through the doors of The Blackwell Room, and the familiar scent wrapped around her like a hug from an old friend.

The bar pulsed with motion: staff weaving in practiced rhythm, voices low, hands sure. The sight filled her chest with something close to pride.

"Ah, the prodigal bartender returns. Again."

Marco's voice rang from behind the counter, mischief curled at the edges. His black hair was styled to flawless perfection as always. "I was starting to think we'd scared you off for good."

Arden rolled her eyes as she slid behind the bar. "I've been back for days, Marco. You're losing your touch."

"Touch?" He gestured toward Fatima at the far end. "She's been picking up your slack."

Fatima laughed, curls bouncing. Her blouse, a riot of Moroccan reds and golds, glowed against her skin. "Marco's mad because I stack glasses better than he does."

"Heathens," Marco sighed, setting a glass down with exaggerated care. "You wouldn't understand craftsmanship."

Arden leaned her hip into the counter, smirking. "Still talking about glassware? Or have we graduated to garnish debates and your deeply held beliefs about hair gel?"

Marco clutched his chest in mock betrayal. "You wound me, boss. This hair doesn't just happen. It's a lifestyle."

Their laughter spilled across the bar, blending into the warm hum of conversation and clinking glass.

For hours, everything felt light. Arden teased Marco mercilessly, swapped stories with Fatima, and smiled more than she had in days.

It felt like reclaiming something.

Not a moment. Not a place.

A part of herself she had thought the dark had swallowed.

Later, as the night deepened, the air inside the bar shifted.

Not suddenly, but enough to lift the hairs at the nape of her neck.

Gideon stood near the back entrance, arms crossed, posture easy, gaze unyielding.

"Checking on me again?" she asked.

Her voice was soft, affection tucked beneath the edge as she leaned against the wall beside him.

"Always."

He drew her in, slow and sure. His arms wrapped around her, and she sank into him, fingers curling into the worn fabric of his shirt. His heartbeat steadied beneath her palm, solid as the floor under her feet.

He smelled like oud and clean cotton. Warmth through familiar cloth. The kind of presence that didn't ask; only held.

His lips brushed her hairline.

Barely there.

Still, it rippled through her.

"I'm here," he murmured, low and certain.

When she stepped back onto the floor, the bar surged alive again. Fatima's laughter cracked like sunlight at one end; Marco's sharp wit sparked grins at the other.

The club breathed.

And Arden felt it in her bones.

This was hers.

Vibrant.

Alive.

Until the night began to come apart.

One moment, Marco stood poised, his trademark charm lighting the room.

The next, his body crumpled to the floor with a sickening thud.

The glass slipped from his hand and shattered across polished wood.

Splinters of chaos, frozen in the light.

A collective gasp tore through the room. Conversations severed mid-sentence. The air thickened, constricted, fractured by whispers.

"Marco!"

Arden's voice cut through the rising panic, sharp and commanding.

Before she registered the movement, she was on the floor, knees slamming into hardwood. The cold shock grounded her just enough to dam the adrenaline roaring through her veins.

Her fingers found his neck.

Searching.

Nothing.

Her chest cinched tight.

Instinct overrode fear, razor-sharp and relentless.

"Fatima, call 911!" she barked.

Her voice didn't waver, even as dread scraped claws along her ribs.

She tilted Marco's head back and checked his airway, then laced her fingers and pressed down, hard and fast, into the center of his chest.

"Gideon, clear the area!"

"Out. Now!"

Gideon's voice boomed through the room, baritone thunder. Chairs scraped back. Murmurs died. His presence surged behind her like a wall.

Unmoving.

Unyielding.

Order imposed on chaos.

But Arden's world had already narrowed.

Only Marco.

His slack face.

Her palms driving rhythm into his chest, each compression a prayer made mechanical.

"One, two, three..."

She counted under her breath, arms already burning. Sweat slicked her temple. Her knees screamed against the floor. The cycle became her tether, her only anchor in the storm.

Twenty-eight.

Twenty-nine.

Thirty.

She tilted his head back, pinched his nose, and sealed her mouth over his.

Two breaths.

The taste hit—bitter, acrid.

Wrong.

She recoiled.

"Poison," she said, low.

Then she dove back in.

Hands pressing harder. Faster.

"Come on, Marco. Come on."

Her arms trembled. Sweat made her grip slick. The relentless pound of muscle and will roared in her ears.

What did he take? How much? How long do we have?

"Arden."

Gideon's voice cut through the blur, urgent but anchored.

"Paramedics are on their way."

She didn't look up, but she nodded once, sharp.

Her hands never stopped.

Sirens wailed outside, swelling toward them.

When the medics burst through the doors, Arden was still compressing. Her voice turned clipped, clinical, the tremor buried beneath precision.

"Suspected poisoning. Bitter taste on rescue breaths. No pulse on initial check. Compressions ongoing."

A medic nodded, already placing pads on Marco's chest. Fast. Focused.

Arden rocked back at last.

Arms limp.

Chest hollow.

Adrenaline bled out of her in cold waves.

She watched them lift Marco onto the stretcher, watched his face disappear into the rush of motion, and let the room come roaring back in.

When she tried to stand, her legs buckled.

The room tilted.

Her vision narrowed.

A large hand caught her elbow.

Gideon.

His grip held her upright. His gaze locked onto hers, fierce enough to anchor her.

"You saved him," he said, low and resolute.

She shook her head, breath hitching. "I don't know if it's enough."

The words frayed as they left her.

His hand slid to her shoulder, firm and grounding. "He's alive because of you. You did everything right."

It mattered.

The weight of his assurance hit her like a line thrown into deep water.

She exhaled, shaky, leaning into him even as the knot in her chest refused to loosen.

The paramedics disappeared into the night.

The bar hung hollow.

Broken glass glittered at her feet, jagged and unforgiving; a mirror of the fracture lines spreading inside her.

"I can't—"

Her voice cracked. Her fingers brushed his, then stilled. She shook her head, breath shuddering free.

"I can't do this alone."

"You're not alone," Gideon said.

Steel in his tone.

No room for argument.

"Not now. Not ever."

Something inside her finally gave.

She tipped forward, her forehead coming to rest against his chest.

His arms closed around her, holding her together where she felt herself coming apart.

"I'm here," he murmured.

The words weren't comfort; they were structure.

A shield raised in real time.

And she let herself believe him.

The low rumble of the car engine carried them through the city, the silence between them taut as a string stretched to its limit. Passing streetlights cast fleeting patterns across Gideon's profile—hard lines, set jaw, shadows revealing something unspoken before taking it back.

His focus shifted between the road and the rearview mirror, vigilance constant beneath the charged quiet. The night clung to them, unshaken, its weight settling in the cabin like fog.

Arden sat still, fingers picking at the edge of her jacket while her thoughts churned. Every flash of headlights, every movement at the periphery, twisted low in her gut.

Marco.

Falling.

Unmoving.

The scene looped mercilessly.

She glanced at Gideon: the clenched jaw, the steady grip on the wheel, the fury he had folded down into something useful.

"I'm not leaving you tonight," he said suddenly, voice threaded with steel.

She managed a faint, weary smile. "I figured."

The gratitude in her voice outweighed the humor.

He turned onto her block, and her building came into view. The car eased into a space near the entrance. The engine cut.

Silence followed, thick with things unsaid.

Gideon rounded the car and opened her door. The faint scent of his cologne hung in the cold air, familiar enough to steady her, and she took his hand without hesitation.

The walk to her building felt longer than it should. Each step measured. Every shadow cataloged by his eyes.

His presence didn't only soothe her.

It warned the night to behave.

Inside, the warmth of her apartment wrapped around her.

Not heat—familiarity.

Some of the tension slipped from her shoulders as she dropped her bag and turned.

Gideon was there, closing the door carefully, filling the space without effort. The edges of him had softened a little, though not the part that watched over her.

"I'll grab some water," she said, barely audible.

The task steadied her.

Glass. Faucet. Motion.

A rhythm she could control.

The sound threaded through everything else, a thin, constant hiss she could hang onto. She braced one hand on the counter, fingers splayed against the cool laminate, and let the other hover beneath the stream until the chill bit hard enough to matter.

Too cold.

Too alive.

She pulled back with a sharp inhale.

Behind her, Gideon didn't move.

That was what she noticed next—not footsteps, not a question, not even the shift of fabric. Just the fact of him. Solid. Occupying space without claiming it. Like a wall she leaned against before realizing she had been swaying.

"Arden," he said quietly; not a prompt, not a correction.

She shut off the faucet.

The silence rang louder for a second, her ears protesting the absence before they settled. The refrigerator hummed. Somewhere outside, a car passed, tires whispering over pavement.

Normal sounds.

Civilian sounds.

Her reflection stared back from the darkened microwave door; eyes too bright, pupils blown wide. A smear of water darkened the cuff of her jacket. She peeled it off with careful fingers, folding it once, then again, as though order itself might slow the tremor in her hands.

"He tasted bitter," she said.

The words surprised her. She hadn't meant to say them. They slipped out anyway, raw and unadorned.

Gideon didn't pretend not to hear.

"You noticed," he said.

Not what does that mean? Not are you sure? Just acknowledgment; a fact placed gently between them.

She nodded once.

"I didn't have time to think about it until after," she went on, steady in a way that felt fraudulent. "During—there wasn't room. Just compressions. Timing. Breath. But afterward it wouldn't leave me alone. Like metal. Like...something wrong."

Her fingers curled into her palm. She pressed her thumbnail into the pad of her thumb until the sensation sharpened.

Gideon stepped closer then; not into her space, but near enough that she could feel the warmth of him at her back. He rested his hands on the counter on either side of her, a careful bracket.

Not trapping her.

Just there.

"You did exactly what you were supposed to do," he said. "You saved his life."

The word saved skidded through her chest and struck something tender.

"For now," she said.

Silence followed. Not empty. Not awkward. He let the truth of it breathe.

"For now," he agreed.

She turned then, needing to see his face.

The light from the stove hood caught the planes of him: cheekbone, jaw, the faint line between his brows that appeared only when he was holding too many things at once. His eyes stayed on hers, searching.

She handed him a glass, and their fingers brushed.

"Thanks," he murmured.

His gaze didn't leave her.

"How are you holding up?"

She sank onto the couch beside him, the cushion giving beneath her weight. Her fingers traced the rim of her glass.

"I'm not sure," she said quietly. "Tonight...it was a lot."

"It was," he agreed.

No minimizing. No bright side.

"But you handled it."

A breath slipped out of her, half laugh, half surrender.

"Barely."

"Better than most."

His voice didn't waver.

He rested a hand lightly on her knee.

Warmth moved through her, a counterbalance to the cold still clinging beneath her skin. Her eyes dropped to his hand. Her pulse quickened—not from fear, but from the ease of it.

The safety of that touch.

She leaned into him.

Let herself.

"I'm glad you're here," she whispered.

The words barely formed; they still carried weight.

Her gaze searched his, though she already knew.

"Me too," he said softly.

She folded into him then, and his arms came around her—strong, sure, without urgency. They sat like that for a long while, the echo of the night loosening its grip.

But beneath the moment, something remained awake.

A thread pulled taut.

Held—for now.

THE APARTMENT WAS STEEPED in stillness—not peace exactly, but something more fragile. A quiet so breakable one wrong breath might shatter it.

Streetlight spilled through the curtains, casting fractured patterns across the walls. Light and shadow layered over everything, ghosts of movement barely there.

Arden stirred.

Her dreams had been restless and jagged, and her breath hitched as fading images clawed at the edge of consciousness—familiar, but ungraspable. Fear had a way of slipping in sideways. Her chest rose and fell in uneven rhythm, tension still coiled tight beneath her skin.

Then an arm curled around her waist.

The weight of it pulled her back from the edge.

She wasn't alone.

"Arden."

Gideon's voice was low, thick with sleep, and instinctively gentle.

"It's okay," he murmured. "I've got you."

She turned her head, finding him in the dim light, the sharp edges of his face softened by the glow from the street. The usual watchfulness had eased into something quieter.

Protective.

Present.

His hand moved across her back in slow, even strokes, each one smoothing the static beneath her skin.

He didn't ask.

Didn't press.

"I'm here," he said again, low and certain.

The words wrapped around her, not for fighting, but for rest.

She exhaled slowly, and the tightness in her chest loosened. Turning into him, she let her forehead brush his collarbone, her fingers curling against his chest as if drawn there by instinct. His heartbeat pulsed steadily beneath her touch, a rhythm she could follow.

Soothing.

The silence stretched, not empty but full. Everything they didn't need to say lived there.

His hand slid to the nape of her neck, fingers threading gently through her waves. Unhurried. As if even time had softened its grip to let them have this.

"You don't even know," he murmured, lips brushing her temple, "how much you matter to me."

No flourish.

Just truth, laid bare between breaths.

Her eyes drifted shut. Whatever fragments the nightmare had left behind dissolved under the weight of his voice, and a small, reluctant smile touched her mouth as she tucked closer into him—not to hide, but to rest.

The words lingered in the quiet.

Gideon's arms tightened slightly. His exhale brushed against her temple. The last of the tension slipped free.

She softened into him.

Her breath evened.

Her pulse slowed.

And she slept.

THE NIGHT UNFOLDED LIKE A BLADE.

Sebastian watched from the shadows, each moment a clean incision in the fragile veneer of their world.

Marco's collapse had been the first cut, a beautiful fracture in The Blackwell Room's polished facade. The toxin had been chosen with care: subtle, temporary, enough to bring the bartender to his knees without leaving a trace.

Marco had never been the target.

He was a prop.

A disruption.

The stage had always belonged to her.

Arden.

Watching her bend was poetry.

Her hands, usually so precise, trembled as they moved with frantic determination. The spine that never broke bowed just enough to reveal its fault lines. The fight to save Marco unfolded in real time: instinct over fear, discipline over panic.

It thrilled him.

Strength and vulnerability, colliding.

She was magnificent.

Every fractured second resolved into a composition meant for him alone.

Marco's removal had been necessary. Too many smiles. Too much ease. The way she laughed with him—unguarded, soft. The way comfort crept in when it had no right to exist.

It wasn't jealousy.

It was principle.

A reminder, clean and unmistakable:

Her fire wasn't theirs to share.

She didn't crumble.

She didn't wither.

She burned.

And it was the burn that made her worthy.

Fire demanded patience. Care. Precision.

From the dark, Sebastian conducted his symphony of fear, each note placed with intention, each beat exact.

Not chaos.

Never chaos.

A message carved neatly into the night:

No one was untouchable.

Not golden boy Gideon.

Not even his Little Fire.

As the sirens drew closer, he took one last look.

Arden, still on her knees beside Marco.

Gideon barking orders.

Panic tearing through the room like shrapnel.

Perfect.

With quiet efficiency, Sebastian slipped into the shifting crowd—another startled face, another concerned witness.

No one noticed him leave.

They never did.

CHAPTER 13

A Quiet Promise

Marco's collapse replayed in her mind, but Arden refused to let it paralyze her.

Hiding in her apartment wasn't an option. She needed rhythm. Routine. The pull of a life she was still piecing back together.

This was her world.

And she intended to claim it fully.

The evening wound down, the last patrons filtering out of the club with soft laughter and unhurried goodbyes. Citrus and clean wood lingered in the air, familiar enough to comfort, sharp enough to keep her awake.

Behind the bar, Arden moved with intention, wiping down the counter. Her motions were slow and focused, each pass of the rag an assertion of control. She welcomed the hush of closing time, the way it held everything still without demanding anything from her.

At the far end of the bar, Fatima and Iris worked through their final tasks. Fatima's dark curls bounced as she stacked glasses, cobalt and gold flashing from the embroidery of her blouse. Iris moved beside her with her usual grace, methodical and calm. Their laughter drifted across the space.

It didn't fracture the silence.

It filled it.

A reminder that even in the aftermath of chaos, normalcy could still exist—fragile, yes, but real.

From the hallway, Gideon stepped into view.

His silhouette cut clean against the warm bar lights, edges sharpened by exhaustion and softened only when his gaze found her. He paused there for a moment, as if measuring the room before stepping fully into it.

"Heading out soon?"

His voice was low, laced with the same steady cadence he'd offered her all week.

"Yeah." She set the rag aside. "Just finishing up."

Her tone stayed even, but fatigue threaded through it, unmistakable.

He watched her then. Really watched. His brow furrowed slightly, the tell she had learned to recognize. Gideon had a way of seeing her that made pretense feel pointless.

"You don't have to prove anything tonight," he said quietly.

She met his gaze.

"I know."

And she did.

"But I want to be here," she added. "I need to be."

Something in his expression shifted—not concern, not resistance. Understanding. Respect.

"That's different," he said.

A small smile tugged at her mouth. "It is."

Fatima glanced over, catching the exchange with a knowing look. "We're good here, Arden. Go on."

Arden nodded, gratitude warming her chest more than she expected. She slipped her jacket on, movements unhurried.

When she turned back, Gideon was already waiting near the door.

Not hovering.

Just ready.

As they stepped out into the cool night air, Arden felt it settle over her: confidence beneath the exhaustion.

She wasn't retreating.

She was choosing.

Gideon walked beside her, close enough to feel, far enough to let her breathe. His hand brushed hers once, a question without words.

She answered by threading her fingers through his.

Not because she needed him to hold her up.

Because she wanted him there.

And in that small, unspoken exchange, a promise took shape—unshowy, unbreakable in its own way.

Whatever came next, she wouldn't face it alone.

"You sure you're okay?"

She let out a soft breath. Half a smile tugged at her mouth. "I'm here, aren't I?"

"I guess that's enough for now." Gideon rested a hand on the bar. "Let me drive you home."

Her instinct was to wave him off, to say she was fine and watch the lie land between them like every other reflex she'd outgrown too slowly.

But the look in his eyes stopped her.

No pretending.

Not with him.

The night met them with teeth. Cold air pressed in as they stepped onto the sidewalk, the city quieted now, shadows stretching long across the concrete. Street lamps spilled fractured patterns over the pavement, light breaking itself apart.

Arden tucked her hands into her pockets, breath ghosting in the air.

Gideon walked beside her, unhurried, his gaze tracking the street. Every corner cleared. Every shadow accounted for.

She glanced at him and felt safer than she had in days.

"Gideon."

He turned immediately, focused and present. "What is it?"

She hesitated, fingers worrying the edge of her sleeve as the knot in her chest pulled tighter.

"I still don't know how to do this," she said. Her voice was muted, but it didn't waver. "Letting someone in. Letting you in."

His expression shifted—something easing, not softening into weakness, but opening where it mattered. The sharp edges tempered. Still strong. Still him.

"You don't have to figure it all out," he said. "You just have to let me be here."

Simple.

But it reached her.

It always did.

A gust of wind tugged at her coat. She shivered, folding her arms closer.

Without a word, Gideon stepped nearer. His hand brushed hers before settling lightly at her arm, warmth bleeding through the layers.

"You don't have to do this alone anymore," he said, low and certain. "I'm here."

He didn't add always.

Her breath caught anyway.

The words sank deep—not as a promise meant to bind her, but as one meant to hold. His thumb skimmed her cheek, tender and sure, and it undid something in her.

"Gideon..." she began, but the rest slipped away.

"You have no idea how much you mean to me," he said, voice rough. "What you do to the shape of things."

Then he kissed her.

Not hurried. Not desperate.

His hand slid to the small of her back; the other cradled her cheek as though she were something worth holding carefully.

Arden's fingers curled into his shirt. She leaned into him, not because she needed saving, but because, for once, she didn't have to carry everything alone.

She tilted her head, deepening the kiss.

A slow surrender.

A claiming.

When they parted, their foreheads lingered close, breath mingling in the cold.

"You make me want things I thought I'd already outgrown," he murmured.

Her lips curved. Her voice trembled, but it didn't falter.

"You're not the only one."

He kissed her again, softer this time. A brush of lips. A promise that didn't ask for anything in return.

When they parted, he reached for her hand. His thumb traced her knuckles, familiar, before their fingers threaded together.

"You know," he said quietly, "having you at my place...it felt right."

Her heart stuttered.

"It did," she said. "It really did."

A pause.

"Thank you," she added. "For everything. I don't always know how to say it."

"You don't have to."

Then, gentler still—

"But come home with me tonight."

She looked at him. Really looked.

Then squeezed his hand.

"Okay," she whispered.

A HUSH HAD FALLEN over the city. Streetlights flared and faded across the windshield in uneven rhythm, and Gideon kept his focus ahead.

Arden didn't speak. She sat still, head resting against the window, as if movement might fracture what little calm remained.

Her lashes fluttered shut.

Not sleep yet.

Just a yielding.

The kind that came only after too much had been held for too long.

Outside, the streets slipped past in a blur, familiar and unregistered. Arden didn't look. Her gaze stayed on the dark beyond the glass, but her mind wasn't there.

She was still inside the night.

Inside the things she hadn't said.

Inside the weight of what she had finally let herself feel.

When Gideon turned into the drive, she didn't ask where they were. Didn't hesitate.

She got out and followed him inside.

Not because she was expected to.

Because she didn't want distance.

Not from him.

He didn't say anything.

She crossed the threshold like she had done it before, without mask or performance. Fully there.

Gideon moved through the house with intention, turning on only what light the moment required. No more than that, but enough to keep the shadows from winning.

She stayed silent.

Not withdrawal.

Choice.

And when she exhaled, finally and completely, it was into his space.

For once, she wasn't bracing for what came next; she was letting herself arrive.

HOURS LATER, he stirred.

The room was still.

Moonlight spilled through half-open curtains, silver pooling across the bed. Gideon reached for her, expecting the familiar weight of her body curled into his.

But she wasn't there.

She lay at the edge of the mattress, back to him, tense and folded inward.

Not sleep.

Defense.

The light caught the curve of her bare shoulder. Still. Too still. Her breath stuttered.

She wasn't dreaming.

She was remembering.

Gideon reached for her, his fingers brushing the length of her arm, light enough not to startle, firm enough to say I'm here.

"Arden."

His voice was low, rough with sleep.

She stirred. A small sound escaped her, but the tension in her spine didn't ease.

Not yet.

He slid closer, wrapped an arm around her waist, and drew her back into him, chest to back, full contact. No space left for fear to gather.

"I've got you," he murmured into her hair. "You're safe."

She didn't melt.

Not right away.

Her body stayed taut, the echo of terror still wired into her frame. Then, slowly, she gave. She let herself lean.

Her fingers found his arm and curled tight, as if she were afraid he might vanish if she didn't hold on.

"I hate feeling like this," she whispered.

Not fragile.

Raw.

His hand moved along her arm in slow, even circles.

"You don't have to fight it alone," he said.

Each word was careful. Weighted. Spoken like fact, not reassurance.

Her heart beat hard against him, a tremor beneath the surface. But she didn't pull away.

And that, he knew, was everything.

She pressed back into him and let herself believe him.

If only for tonight.

Her breath slowed. The rigid line of her body softened.

His lips brushed the crown of her head, nothing ceremonial, nothing claimed.

"I'm not going anywhere," he said.

A promise, spoken once and without ornament, because that was all it needed.

She didn't answer.

But her grip tightened a little.

And that was enough.

As sleep claimed her, Gideon didn't move.

He stayed.

Her breath warmed the length of his forearm where it curved around her, and his matched it without thought. Her head fit beneath his chin. His heartbeat kept even against her back.

He didn't try to fix the fear.

He just stayed.

And for now, that held.

Sebastian watched her.

Unnoticed.

As always.

She moved through the club with sheer determination, each step purposeful, as if defying the weight pressing in on her from every side.

She had come back to work.

After Marco's collapse.

After the chaos.

After fear had reached for the edges of the life she had fought to rebuild.

And still, she was here.

Not cowering. Not hiding.

Fire forged in pressure, a blaze that refused to be extinguished.

The others didn't see it. They saw competence. Sharp wit. The effortless grace she carried into every shift.

But Sebastian saw what lived beneath.

The cracks.

The scars.

The exquisite defiance.

That was what made her extraordinary.

She didn't retreat.

She didn't crumble.

Arden Rivers burned brighter when the world tried to snuff her out.

From his vantage point, he studied every detail: the precision of her hands, even under strain; the tilt of her head when she listened; the warmth that flickered in her eyes, carefully rationed and never wasted.

She laughed.

Soft.

Brief.

A sound so fragile it barely existed.

It was real.

And it made something tighten in his chest.

She was strength wrapped in vulnerability, radiant and dangerous in her resilience.

But even flames required tending.

Required control.

And he was the only one who understood how to keep hers alive without letting it consume itself.

This place was her element: the polished bar, the low hum of voices, the amber light spilling across her skin.

Not Gideon's clean, clinical world.

Here, she belonged to herself.

Here, her fire was her own.

She didn't see how close she lived to the edge. Didn't see the shadows waiting just beyond her light.

He did.

And he wouldn't let them take her.

Little Fire.

She was stronger than they knew, stronger than even she knew.

But even the brightest fires could be smothered by careless hands.

And he would not allow it.

Not now.

Not ever.

CHAPTER 14

The Shape of Trust

Morning light filtered through the curtains, casting muted gold across the room.

Arden blinked against the warmth and let the hush of the city hum beneath it: soft traffic, a distant horn, the rhythm of a world still moving.

Gideon's bed was spacious and familiar now in a way it hadn't been before. The first night she'd stayed here, restful sleep had been impossible. Every sound had been too loud. Every shadow, too sharp.

Now, the faint scent of him lingered in the sheets—cedar, spice, clean.

It tugged a smile from her before she could stop it.

She exhaled and let herself feel it.

Not safety, exactly.

But something adjacent.

Earned.

Her phone buzzed.

Penny.

> So... does Mr. Broody make a habit of keeping women hostage with his charm and excessive square footage, or are you a special case? Asking for science.

A laugh slipped out as Arden typed back.

> Pretty sure I'm the only one. I'll let you know if I spot any other captives.

You should. I could stage a rescue. Bring snacks. Make it a whole thing.

And you think I'd leave?

Nah. You're in deep, babe.

So what's the morning-after vibe? Coffee and soft kisses, or business as usual?

Memory surfaced. Gideon leaning close, voice low and sleep-warmed.

I'll be back soon.

A kiss brushed against her temple. The weight of the blankets drawn up around her afterward. Steady. Always steady.

Business. He's handling things.

Of course he is.

The man probably handles financial forecasts with the same intensity he handles you.

Must be exhausting. And also hot.

Arden groaned, smiling despite herself.

Stop.

Never.

Anyway, checking in. You good?

Her fingers hovered, not because she didn't know the answer. Because she meant it.

I'm fine.

Or I will be.

Thanks for asking.

Good because if I don't see you soon, I'm crashing this little cohabitation situation. Just saying.

Arden chuckled as she set the phone aside.

The quiet settled again. Not empty, but full. Even in his absence, Gideon's presence lingered, a tether she hadn't realized she had accepted.

She pushed back the covers and swung her legs over the side of the bed. The cool floorboards creaked faintly beneath her feet, grounding and real.

She wandered into the kitchen still wearing the shirt she had borrowed days ago. The brownstone's stillness calmed her and gave her too much room to think.

The unease from the night before hadn't vanished. It lingered low and watchful, but it didn't own her.

And that felt new.

She poured a glass of water, the sound anchoring her, and leaned against the counter as her phone buzzed again.

On my way back. Hope Penny isn't blowing up your phone.

Always. She's her own force of nature.

Remind me to thank her for keeping you grounded.

Also we're going out today. To talk. And eat. You need a break.

Food and updates? You know how to spoil a girl.

Get used to it.

She stared at the words.

Let them settle.

Let herself believe them.

The phone went silent.

She stayed where she was, palms braced on the counter. The ache in her chest hadn't disappeared, but it had softened. The sharp edge had dulled, replaced by something warmer.

Motion.

Toward something that looked suspiciously like hope.

Later that morning, the crisp air carried the mingled scents of fresh pastries and the faint burn of exhaust.

Arden and Gideon walked side by side, the city's pulse steady around them. Motion. Breath. Noise. A cocoon of anonymity.

But beneath it, tension hummed.

Unrelenting.

Gideon's hand rested lightly at the small of her back. Not possessive. Just there. A silent promise: whatever came next, they would face it together.

"Third compound in Marco's system," he said, voice low and precise. "Obscure. Traceable only to a handful of research labs. Whoever did this knew exactly what they were doing."

Arden slowed, her brows knitting as the implication pressed in behind her ribs.

"Is it something your family would've had access to?"

The question lingered.

He didn't answer right away.

A muscle ticked along his jaw, barely there but unmistakable. Something moved behind his eyes. Anger, yes—but also something older. Something etched in.

When he spoke, his words were measured.

"It matches a string of poisonings," he said. "Back when my grandfather was still running things. The compound was part of a classified program, engineered to vanish in the bloodstream. Undetectable within hours."

He paused.

"A perfect crime," he added, and didn't soften it. "Designed to fail forensics."

Her stomach tightened.

So it wasn't coincidence. It wasn't opportunity.

It was legacy.

"It's tied to Blackwell," she said, certain now. "One way or another."

"Or someone using what's left of it." The edges of his words ground tight. "Leo traced it to a shell corporation. A holding my grandfather offloaded years ago. But the labs—some of them still exist. Off the books. Buried deep."

His gaze stayed on the street ahead.

"Someone's unearthing ghosts," he said. "And weaponizing them."

The truth settled over her like frost. Not loud. Not immediate. Worse than that.

Arden drew a breath and tried to deepen it.

Failed.

Not random.

Not reckless.

"They're not just sending a message," she said.

She straightened, not for show but necessity. The knots were still there. The unease hadn't vanished.

But neither had her certainty.

"They're building something bigger."

"They are," Gideon agreed, voice cutting clean. "And they're counting on us being reactive. Scattered. Alone."

A pause.

"But we're not giving them the satisfaction."

He brushed her hand, brief and almost imperceptible.

Their eyes met with shared conviction.

Around them, the city surged forward, indifferent to the storm forming in its quietest corners.

This was only the beginning.

And neither of them could afford to falter.

Gideon's phone buzzed.

The sound cut through the space between them like glass.

He glanced at the screen. His expression shifted, sharpened.

"We need to regroup," he said, already recalibrating. "Leo's closing in, but there are still gaps."

Arden nodded. Her steps fell into rhythm with his as they turned the corner, her thoughts tightening, threads drawing together as urgency coiled low in her chest.

The path ahead was fragile.

But not impossible.

Then—

The scent reached her first.

Garlic. Warm bread. Something faintly sweet.

A break in the tension.

Uninvited.

Not unwelcome.

Gideon angled his attention toward the café without turning his head. The change in him was slight. Barely there. But she felt it anyway, a softening she might have missed once.

Now, she felt every shift like barometric pressure—subtle, undeniable, signaling change before it arrived.

And this one, this pause, she recognized.

Restraint.

"Let's get lunch," he said, voice dipped low. His gaze met hers, firm and sure, threaded with something unspoken. "We need to keep our strength up."

She hesitated.

Stillness felt exposed. Counterintuitive.

But there was calm in his voice and certainty in the way he stood beside her.

So she nodded.

It wasn't surrender.

It was trust.

And trust, she realized, wasn't something their enemies could seize.

It was something they had to break.

LUNCH IN A TUCKED-AWAY Italian bistro offered the illusion of normalcy—thin as rice paper, but strong enough to hold.

They sat in a corner booth, wrapped in the restaurant's warm golden glow. The air was heavy with garlic, fresh bread, and slow-roasted tomatoes. Around them, voices murmured; forks tapped softly against porcelain.

A fragile barrier between them and everything waiting outside.

For a while, they let themselves slip into the ordinary.

Gideon's voice softened as he spoke about architecture, the subject drawing warmth into his otherwise even tone.

"It's the symmetry of it," he said, fingers moving faintly, as if sketching invisible lines in the air. "The way every element has a purpose, but still comes together to create something larger than itself. A story told in steel and stone."

Arden leaned in, her elbow brushing the edge of the table.

"And The Blackwell Room?" Her tone stayed light, but the question carried weight. "Does it tell your story?"

He hesitated.

His thumb traced the rim of his glass. The question settled between them, neither sharp nor soft.

"Maybe," he said after a beat, voice lowering. "But it wasn't meant to tell mine. It was meant to build something outside of theirs."

She held his gaze. Something unreadable passed through her.

"Sometimes," she said quietly, "that is the story."

Stillness followed.

Not silence.

Something fuller.

Like the air after a bell stops ringing.

When they spoke again, the rhythm had changed. Slower. More careful. As if something had shifted and neither of them needed to name it.

Arden offered pieces of her path the same way: measured, intentional. Years in trauma nursing. The constant balance between heartbreak and healing. The way proximity to pain had taught her the difference between endurance and presence.

"The bar," she said at last, voice softer now, "was never about hiding. It was about breathing. Remembering what it felt like to stand still."

Gideon didn't interrupt.

He didn't rush to answer.

He watched her, listening the way someone does when they know the moment matters too much to fracture.

The rest of the world thinned for a moment. Their edges softened.

And then—

"Sebastian's been asking questions about you."

No preamble.

Whatever ease had settled between them shattered, surface tension breaking.

Arden's grip on her fork stilled. Her fingers tightened, then she made herself set it down. When she looked up, her gaze was clear. Unblinking.

"What kind of questions?"

"Your nursing background. Your connections. Who you trust."

His tone stayed even, but the weight beneath it was iron. Beneath the table, his hand brushed hers, grounding.

"He's either looking for vulnerabilities," Gideon said, "or making sure we know he's looking."

Her mind moved fast. Jagged pieces slid into place.

The precision.

The opacity of the messages.

The shadows that never quite left her periphery.

"Or he's laying a trail," she said. Her voice was surgical. Measured. Built to cut. "Keeping our focus pinned in one direction while the real play unfolds somewhere else."

Gideon's jaw ticked once.

"If he thinks he's running this board," he said quietly, "he's wrong."

Their eyes met and held with the shared recognition that something had shifted. Not theory. Not threat.

An active front.

The low hum of the bistro returned, distant and indistinct, as if the room itself had slipped out of focus around them. But the tension didn't separate them.

It welded them closer.

Whatever Sebastian thought he was orchestrating, he hadn't accounted for this.

When they stepped back onto the street, the city carried on, oblivious. Clouds had thickened overhead, and a fine drizzle whispered across Arden's skin.

Gideon's hand settled at her waist. Not for shelter, but alignment.

"We'll find out what he's planning," he said, voice low and resolute. "And we'll stop it."

She turned to him.

"Together."

One word.

But it carried the weight of every vow they hadn't spoken.

He nodded once, gaze fixed ahead. Unflinching.

"Brick by brick," he murmured. "We dismantle it. Every hidden corridor. Every load-bearing lie. Until there's nothing left to stand on."

Her breath caught—not at the words, but at the precision behind them. This wasn't bluster; it was blueprint.

The architect in him didn't believe in chaos. He believed in method. In pressure applied exactly where a structure failed.

And what they were shaping now wasn't resistance.

It was intent—with design.

Beneath it, an unvoiced, unmistakable warning:

They weren't the prey anymore.

The drizzle thickened as they crossed into Washington Square, forcing them beneath the awning of a boutique with gold-lettered windows. Rain spilled from its edges in silken veils, softening the city's harder lines.

Mist clung to their skin.

Arden exhaled. The air was sharp with rain and the warm, earthy scent of wet brick, rosemary focaccia drifting from somewhere nearby. A lock of hair clung to her cheek; she brushed it back absently, gaze lifting toward the storm-lit sky.

Streetlights fractured across the wet pavement. Each raindrop caught the glow like glass.

The world shimmered.

Suspended.

Between the hush before a reckoning and whatever came after.

Soft acoustic chords filtered through the boutique speakers. Then a piano line rose, gentle and aching.

Arden stilled mid-motion.

"The song," she murmured. "Somewhere Only We Know."

Her voice barely cleared the rain. The tune wasn't merely familiar; it was embedded, a memory folded into her chest years ago and left untouched.

Gideon glanced toward the speaker, then back to her. He stepped closer, his presence cutting the damp chill. Not shielding her, exactly. Steadying.

"It suits you," he said.

She turned, one brow lifting. "What does that even mean?"

He didn't hesitate.

"It means you notice what most people miss," he said. "And you don't let the world grind it down."

Her breath caught. Not from surprise, but recognition.

It wasn't the first time he had seen her clearly.

It was the first time she didn't feel the instinct to retreat.

The melody circled them, melancholic and searching.

"You always know what to say," she said softly.

Not praise.

Admission.

She studied his face, not looking for reassurance, but for proof that this wasn't something she was carrying alone. That he felt the shift, too.

"Maybe," he said, "because I don't say anything I don't mean."

His hand spread gently at her back, anchoring her to the moment. To him.

She didn't step away.

Didn't want to.

Rain clung to her lashes.

He reached out, thumb brushing a drop from her cheek before tucking a curl behind her ear, as if he had done it before. As if the tenderness had already learned the shape of her.

Earned.

Not assumed.

The song swelled, tender and unmistakable.

"We don't get sunsets," he said, voice barely above the rain. "We get storms."

The truth of it struck deep.

Because this wasn't easy.

Wasn't ideal.

It was real.

A connection forged through fracture and heat. Not something that burned out, but something that burned through.

He leaned in slowly.

And the world stilled.

Just two people choosing the same direction.

When his lips found hers, it wasn't tentative. The kiss said what neither of them could quite risk saying aloud: I see you. I'm here.

His hand drew her closer. Her fingers curled into his lapel. She rose onto her toes, deepening the kiss, not from urgency, but inevitability.

He kissed the way he built. Measured. Every touch intentional. Every shift an invitation, never an assumption.

And every part of her answered.

The space between them charged.

He wasn't closing in.

He was making room.

And she stepped into it.

Outside, the storm softened to a hush.

Inside, the air held, dense with warmth and unspent tension. Rain on wool. Skin beneath fabric. The nearness of breath.

Still, neither rushed.

When they finally eased apart, it wasn't retreat.

It was recognition.

A pause to register what had shifted, to memorize the shape of it bone-deep.

Their foreheads rested together in the quiet that followed.

Not surrender.

Not stillness.

Something steadier.

Something chosen.

"I don't think I'll ever hear that song again without thinking of you," he said, voice threaded with everything he hadn't spoken yet.

She didn't look away. Didn't smile. She reached up, fingers skimming the line of his collar, anchoring herself there.

"Good," she said softly. "Because I don't want to forget any of this."

The rain kept falling.

The city kept moving.

But beneath the gold-lettered awning, in the hush between piano chords and passing strangers, they stood.

Close enough to fall.

And still choosing to stay.

SEBASTIAN WATCHED.

Rain traced slow trails down the shop window, smearing the city into softened light and motion. It should have obscured them.

Instead, it framed them.

A portrait rendered in silver and steam.

Her head tipped back slightly. Gideon leaned in, familiar and assured, his hand at her waist like a claim.

The storm didn't hide them.

It revealed.

Shaped them in reflection and shine. Made them look like something lifted from a love story.

But Sebastian knew better.

It wasn't love.

It was performance.

She wasn't his.

She wasn't anyone's.

And yet she had allowed it. Let him that close.

That was the transgression.

Not the kiss.

The permission.

She softened when she should have burned. Bent when she should have risen.

Because Gideon only ever saw the edges of her. The curated surface. Poised. Palatable. Praiseworthy.

But Sebastian saw the rest.

The rage carried in her shoulders. The fracture lines stitched with stubborn grace. The ache beneath her brilliance.

She was a storm pretending to be still water.

And that was what made her extraordinary.

She didn't need protection.

She needed remembering.

He watched as the moment held, rain soaking through his collar, cold biting into his skin. Still, he didn't move.

Didn't blink.

He memorized.

Because this wasn't jealousy.

It was recognition.

The roses.

The tea.

The book.

The subtle shift in the rhythm of her life, one thread at a time.

He had guided it carefully.

Not to harm.

To reveal.

Let her believe she was safe. Let her lean into Gideon's steadiness, his restraint, his armor.

It would make the unraveling cleaner.

Sharper.

They thought this storm meant something. That it marked a turning point. That it changed her.

But Sebastian knew.

It changed nothing essential.

She was still fire.

And she was the only thing that mattered.

Let them hold the moment. Let them believe in it.

Because when it finally broke, when she saw past the structure and remembered what burned beneath, then she would be ready.

And this?

This was only the beginning.

CHAPTER 15
Magnetic Proximity

The rhythmic patter of rain against the windows filled the space as Gideon stepped inside, the door clicking shut behind him.

He didn't scan the room.

His attention went straight to her.

Arden stood a few feet away, damp curls clinging to her cheeks, her posture balanced between resistance and release. Vulnerability flickered across her expression, quick as breath, but it didn't weaken her.

It refined her.

Tempered steel.

The air between them thrummed, familiar and magnetic, no longer content to wait at the edges.

Gideon moved toward her, unhurried, every step deliberate.

When he spoke, his voice was low and warm, threaded with something more dangerous.

"Are you planning to stand there all night," he murmured, "or are you going to let me in?"

A soft laugh slipped free, easing the knot in her chest.

"Let you in?" she said, brushing a curl from her cheek. "I think you're already here."

His smile deepened. Not sharp. Not cruel.

But not empty, either.

"Not all the way."

The words came rougher now. Not a demand. A challenge offered with patience instead of force.

"But I'm not in a hurry. I can be patient."

The pressure of it settled against old armor, not to crack it, but to remind her she didn't need it.

When he reached for her, his touch was steady, as if she were something meant to be met, not taken.

And she stepped forward.

Into the space.

Into him.

Her pulse leapt high in her throat.

"Patience," she said, her breath brushing his collar. A curve touched her mouth, half truth, half dare. "That's a dangerous thing to offer."

His thumb grazed her cheek, slow and certain.

"Not with you," he said.

His voice carried weight.

The storm outside blurred into white noise as she leaned into his palm. In the hush that followed, rain tracing lines down the windows, his gaze steady and close, Arden felt something deeper than want. Deeper than fear.

She felt safe.

And for her, that meant everything.

By the time they reached her bedroom, the energy between them had shifted, molten at the edges. Lamplight spilled warmth across the room, but there was nothing gentle about the tension now.

His hand lingered at the small of her back as he eased the door shut behind them. His fingers brushed hers, then slipped away.

"Close the door," he said.

Not a command.

Not quite a request.

An offering.

A threshold she could choose to cross.

She turned, her hand hovering at the knob.

Not from doubt.

From knowing that once it clicked shut, they would be somewhere entirely new.

She closed it anyway.

The latch settled with a final click.

Then he was behind her.

Heat rolled off him, his nearness blooming across her skin before touch.

When his palms settled at her hips and drew her back against him, the world fractured.

The movement was confident.

Seamless.

And it unmade her.

His mouth hovered near her ear, breath warm along her neck.

"You keep letting me in," he murmured, each word placed with care. "And I don't think you realize how far I want to go."

Her knees softened beneath her. Her palms met the door, fingers bracing against the wood, seeking balance as the truth of it lodged deep.

A fact.

And it shifted everything.

His lips traced the curve of her neck, every touch a vow. One hand steadied her at the waist. The other slid forward, palm settling flat against her stomach.

Not possession.

Presence.

Asking nothing.

Promising everything.

"Tell me to stop," he whispered, voice roughened by restraint, a fracture in his calm.

Not control lost.

Control offered.

She didn't.

"Don't," she breathed.

It wasn't only permission.

It was intention. Truth she hadn't dared give voice to until now.

He turned her slowly, hands careful, like turning a page meant to be read all the way through.

When her eyes met his, there was no uncertainty.

Only fire.

Only yes.

He kissed her then, slow and deliberate. Not rewriting what they had held back, but honoring it.

She answered with equal weight, her hands sliding beneath his coat to the warmth of his chest. Not to pull him closer—he was already there.

But to feel him.

To know this was real.

The storm outside kept its rhythm.

The one between them didn't rage; it burned.

This wasn't collapse or free fall.
It was a choice—clear-eyed, unflinching.

Gideon's hands stayed at her waist, anchoring her even as the current between them surged—heat, hunger, the ache that had lived between them since the moment their lives collided.

His gaze held hers.

No question in it.

Only want, unfiltered and undeniable.

"You make me forget every rule I've ever set for myself," he said. His voice was low, the confession steady enough to cut clean and irreversible.

Arden's hands rose to his chest, fingers trembling with certainty. She traced the sharp line of his jaw before sliding into his hair.

"Rules were made to be broken," she murmured, her lips brushing his. "Especially yours."

He didn't hesitate.

His mouth found hers, deep and all-consuming.

The kiss hit like collision, pressure released in a single, breathless crash. He drew her closer, lifting her with ease, and her breath vanished as his strength wrapped around her like gravity.

It thrilled her.

Terrified her.

Undid her.

When they came down together, tangled in sheets and storm light, it wasn't frenzy that followed.

The kiss slowed.

Softened.

Every movement turned precise, as if they were writing each other into skin and memory.

His hand cradled the back of her neck, thumb tracing slow arcs that kept her centered. Her breath left her in a broken exhale as she pressed her palm flat to his chest, fingers splayed over the pulse beneath.

His heartbeat felt more intimate than any touch, more real than anything she had let herself believe was possible.

And then, as if the words had been waiting too long to be held back, she whispered, "I do love you, y'know."

The truth hit like flame on dry air.

Gideon went still.

His breath caught.

Not from surprise.

From the weight of it.

Of her.

His eyes searched hers, not for doubt, but for confirmation of something he had already surrendered to.

"I know," he said quietly.

Then his hand tightened at her waist, not to pull her closer, but to keep her there, as if he had felt the truth land and wasn't about to let her step back from it.

She laughed, breathless and unguarded, burying her face against his shoulder as if the weight of it all might finally crush her in the best possible way.

"You're so sure of yourself," she murmured.

"When it comes to you?" His brow lifted slightly. "Absolutely."

She rolled her eyes, but didn't pull away.

Didn't want to.

Her body settled into his, muscles loosening, breath finally deep. No vigilance. Just heat and closeness and the violence of being chosen without reservation.

"You're shameless," she muttered.

Yes. This version keeps the explicit physical payoff. I'm not blurring the acts; I'm refining the language so it stays erotic, embodied, and very Arden/Gideon rather than sliding into stock-spice mechanics. Based on the pasted section.

His hand slid from her waist and down her spine, knuckles grazing bare skin before his palm flattened low. He didn't answer. He leaned in, and his mouth found hers again—slow at first, then deeper, rougher, as if her mouth had said something his hands needed to finish.

The kiss pulled her under.

His fingers caught the hem of her shirt and dragged it up inch by inch. The fabric peeled away as she raised her arms and let him take it. Her skin prickled when the air touched her—cool and dry, a sharp contrast to the heat rising between them.

He tossed the shirt aside, his gaze moving over her like he had earned the right to look and still knew better than to take it for granted.

Arden didn't flinch. Didn't hide. Her hands went to his shirt, fumbling buttons one by one, and she pressed her palms flat against his chest as each section came free—heat, muscle, the weight of him real beneath her fingers. She wanted to memorize him. Every line. Every response. Every place restraint lived in him and trembled anyway.

Then they were skin to skin.

And he moved.

His mouth dropped to her chest, lips dragging along her sternum. She arched under him, not sudden, but open, her hands sliding to his shoulders and holding him there as his mouth traced the curve of her breast.

He kissed her slowly. Thoroughly. No urgency. No part of her treated as incidental. When his tongue circled her nipple, she gasped; when he sucked, deep and controlled, she moaned. He shifted, bracing himself on one elbow while his free hand cupped her other breast, thumb dragging over the peak until her hips lifted off the bed.

Her name left his mouth, low and quiet.

Warning and prayer.

Then he moved lower.

She felt every inch of him go with it—his mouth on her stomach, his breath skimming her skin, his hand sliding down to her thigh. He parted her legs with a devastating kind of care, settled between them, and looked up once.

Not to ask.

To make sure she saw him.

To make sure she knew what came next wasn't performance.

It was promise.

He kissed her inner thigh first. Left, then right. Slow. Close. His hands settled at her hips, firm enough to hold, careful enough to let her leave.

She didn't.

Then his mouth found her.

No teasing.

No soft edge of build-up.

Tongue. Lips. Heat.

Full contact, and Arden's head snapped back, a sound tearing from her throat that made him groan against her. She reached for him blindly—his hair, his shoulder, anything solid while his mouth worked her in an unrelenting rhythm.

He knew her now. Knew how to read the twitch in her thigh, the shiver in her breath, the press of her heels into the mattress. His tongue circled her clit, slow at first, then firmer, matching the rise of her pulse. She gasped, hips lifting, and his grip tightened.

Not to restrain.

To hold.

He didn't stop. Not when her voice broke. Not when her hands fisted in the sheets. Not when her body started to tremble beneath him, pleasure gathering too fast and too bright for her to contain. He kept going until she shattered, loud and helpless, all muscle and heat and aftershock.

Only then did he ease off.

He kissed her through the comedown, soft licks and lips brushing skin, his breath warm against nerves still sparking. When she whimpered, he shifted again, slow and controlled, crawling back up her body until he was flush against her.

His cock pressed heavy against her thigh, hard and waiting.

Arden turned her head and kissed him. Deep. Needy. She tasted herself on his mouth and didn't care. Her hand slid between them, fingers wrapping tight around the length of him, her thumb stroking the underside with no hesitation.

He growled, hips twitching into her grip.

The sound lit through her.

He kissed her again, hard and messy, as she pulled him closer and wrapped her legs around his hips. His cock pressed hot against her skin, but he didn't push in yet. He kissed her instead—deep, slow—while his fingers slipped between her legs.

She gasped as he found her clit, rubbing in tight, steady circles until her breath broke.

"Fuck," he murmured, voice rough against her mouth. "You're so wet for me."

Her throat went tight. She nodded anyway.

His fingers slowed. His gaze held hers.

"Say it, Arden."

The command should have made her retreat.

It didn't.

"I want you," she breathed.

His control fractured.

He pushed in with one long, slow stroke, inch by inch, until he was buried deep. Arden arched beneath him, a moan breaking loose as her body stretched around him.

Gideon didn't move right away. He stayed there, forehead pressed to hers, breath ragged.

"Fuck, you feel—"

She shifted her hips, clenching around him.

The rest of the sentence died in his throat.

Then he started to move.

Deep, controlled thrusts that hit hard and true, dragging a broken sound from her every time he sank back in. Her legs wrapped around his waist. Her nails found his back.

"Don't stop."

He didn't.

He moved slowly at first, drawing nearly all the way out before sliding back in, letting her feel every inch of him. The rhythm built fast, each thrust heavier, deeper, until the sound of their bodies filled the room beneath the steady hush of rain.

Her nails dug into his back, dragging lines down his spine as he fucked her harder.

He shifted, one hand bracing at the small of her back, angling deeper until she cried out. Her hips rose to meet every thrust, their pace roughening, sharpening, until it felt like free fall.

No finesse now.

No distance.

His name slipped free, raw and unguarded.

She felt the shift in him, the exact moment restraint bent.

Control didn't vanish.

It transformed.

He growled low in his throat. One hand caught behind her knee, pushing her leg higher, opening her wider. His other arm locked beneath her back, pulling her tight against him as he fucked into her harder.

Their bodies slammed together, rhythm breaking loose, every careful thing between them burning down to breath and skin and the brutal sweetness of being wanted without reservation.

Her body snapped tight.

Legs locked.

Nails dragging down his back.

She came hard, gasping his name like it was the only word the world had left her.

Time unraveled.

The storm outside softened to a hush, its pulse falling into sync with theirs. Breath to breath. Skin to skin. A slow crescendo of want and will.

He followed her over, control finally giving way in a shudder that moved through him hard. Even then, he held her. Through the last thrust. Through the heat. Through the aftershock.

And when they finally stilled, when the world narrowed to the space between heartbeats, there was only the unmistakable sense that something had changed shape.

Gideon's hand came up to her face, fingers curling gently at her jaw. His forehead rested against hers.

"You're mine," he whispered, filled with everything he felt.

Not possession.

Recognition.

Not a claim.

A vow.

Arden didn't waver. Her hands framed his face, her gaze locked to his. There was fire in it, steady and unshaken.

"I'm yours."

The peaceful hush of rain broke beneath the sharp jangle of keys and the unmistakable click of the door unlocking.

Penny burst in like a kaleidoscope: rainbow umbrella dripping onto the hardwood, cheeks flushed pink from the cold, a tie-dyed hoodie peeking out beneath her patchwork coat. She kicked off her mismatched boots with theatrical flair and zeroed in on Arden with surgical precision.

There was no escape.

Perched on the arm of the couch, Arden had been drifting in the afterimage of Gideon's touch. The cadence of his voice. The deferential way he had looked at her, as if nothing existed beyond that moment.

Penny's arrival detonated the reverie with all the grace of a glitter bomb.

"Okay, spill it," she demanded, flinging the umbrella toward the corner without looking. "That look? Not subtle, babe. You're glowing."

Arden rolled her eyes, but the smile betrayed her. "Penny—"

"Oh no. Absolutely not." Penny flopped onto the couch, one arm draped over the back like she was auditioning for a telenovela. "This room reeks of post-swoon energy, and I demand details. And please don't tell me you let Mr. Tall, Dark, and Sexually Responsible walk out into this weather without at least one gratuitous rain-soaked make-out. If you did, romance novel heroes everywhere are weeping."

Arden laughed, soft and helpless, grabbing a towel to mop up the umbrella puddles. "It wasn't like that."

"Oh God, it was better," Penny groaned, throwing an arm over her eyes. "Tell me you gazed into each other's souls. Whispered things meant only for the dead and the devoted. Held hands like it mattered."

"Penny," Arden warned, already smiling.

"I mean it," Penny pressed, sitting up abruptly. "This is slow-burn, fate-fueled, emotionally ruinous romance. You two are that couple. The ones people claim to hate because you're insufferably perfect, but they stay up until two in the morning rooting for you anyway."

Arden tossed the towel onto her lap. "You're ridiculous."

"And you're glowing," Penny said again, this time with a softer smile. "You know what this is? Magnetic-proximity romance. You've been orbiting each other forever. And now?" She snapped her fingers. "Collision."

"Magnetic-proximity romance?" Arden raised a brow. "Do you make these terms up as you go?"

"Only when I'm inspired," Penny said, faux-humble. "And babe, you're inspiring. That glimmer in your eyes? That's 'I can't believe he exists' energy. You're a modern heroine—sassy, trauma-laced, gorgeous. And now your brooding love interest has finally realized he can't breathe without you and absolutely intends to make that everyone's problem."

"I'm not waiting for anyone to sweep me away," Arden said flatly.

"No," Penny agreed, and her tone dropped into something steadier. "Because he's already there."

Arden stilled.

"Gideon would burn the world down for you, Ard," Penny said, the grin giving way to something deeper. "Like strike-the-match, watch-it-burn levels of gone. You see that, right?"

Heat crept up Arden's throat. She looked away, but didn't deny it.

Penny wasn't done.

"And here's the kicker." She pointed with mock gravity. "You'd let him. You'd hand him the match. Hell, I think you'd light the first flame if it meant protecting him."

The truth didn't weigh the room down.

It grounded it.

"I mean it," Penny said. "You deserve this. Let yourself have it."

Arden exhaled. "Goodnight, Penny."

"Goodnight, Queen of I'd-Burn-It-All-for-Love," Penny called as Arden disappeared down the hall.

Once alone, Arden sat on the edge of her bed, phone resting in her palm.

The screen was dark.

Still, she stared at it.

Then her thumbs hovered, and the words came as naturally as breath.

Couldn't sleep if I tried. You?

Her pulse ticked up as she sent it.

The silence stretched. Rain tapped softly at the window, the city blurring beyond it.

Her phone vibrated almost immediately.

Wide awake. What's on your mind?

A faint smile curved her lips as she leaned back against the pillows. Somehow, he felt close, as if the warmth of him had crossed the distance.

She typed quickly.

Maybe I wanted to see if you were thinking about me.

His reply came instantly.

Always. What do you need, Arden?

She paused.

That one hit differently.

The thrill of it curled through her, a spark catching low.

Something to keep me warm.

A beat.

You already have me.

Her heart skipped.

Not because of the words.

Because of the way they felt.

Unshakable.

A promise without ornament.

Her fingers hovered again, the burn of him still under her skin.

Careful, Gideon. I'm starting to think you mean it.

This time, the vibration felt immediate.

I mean every damn word.

Heat rushed through her, slow and insistent, lighting her limbs, threading into her breath.

She set the phone aside, the glow fading as warmth lingered beneath her skin.

She didn't sleep.

She watched the ceiling while rain traced its rhythm outside.

The storm was still here.

So was she.

And when her thoughts circled back to him—to every unguarded word, every unspoken vow—her mouth curved.

Not merely a smile.

A shift.

A knowing.

And it reached all the way to her eyes.

CHAPTER 16
Shadows of Roses

Sunlight shoved through the curtains in blunt streaks, dragging her into consciousness whether she was ready or not.

Outside, the Lower East Side was already barking. Someone yelled into a phone. A gate rolled up with a metal screech. Delivery bikes threaded between traffic, and a cab laid on its horn like it had a score to settle.

The city didn't wake so much as lurch.

Arden stretched, letting the warmth of her comforter cling a moment longer before kicking it off. Her feet met cold hardwood with a familiar creak, the kind of sound that wasn't charming, exactly, but proof the floor hadn't given out yet.

She yanked back the curtain.

From her third-floor window, the neighborhood unfolded in bruised color. Fire escapes rattled in the wind. Trash bags sagged at the curb, slick with last night's rain. Graffiti bled into chipped murals, names scrawled over faces no one had the money or interest to repaint. Storefronts leaned against each other like they were all waiting for rent to come due.

The scent of coffee drifted up from the deli downstairs, burnt but still comforting. Someone shouted for a cab. A pigeon landed on the fire escape and stared at her like it had notes.

This was the LES. Loud. Layered. Unruly.

Penny lived for it. Arden had learned to hold its rhythm like a pulse, one you listened to with your jaw set. It wasn't gentle, but it was honest. And that, more than anything, made it feel like hers.

She dressed on autopilot. Faded jeans. A black sweater soft from wear.

Canvas tote slung over her shoulder. The market would be open. She didn't expect it to fix anything, but maybe the color and cadence could dull the edges.

Fleetwood Mac drifted from the other room.

Arden smiled to herself, already picturing Penny tangled in yarn or glue or some aggressively whimsical side project. She'd been talking all week about her annual sister trip upstate.

Right on cue, Penny appeared, curls pulled into a half-wrestled bun, a denim jacket covered in enamel pins—some ironic, some vaguely occult—and socks that absolutely did not match.

"I thought you were leaving early," Arden said, nodding at the duffel bag by the door. "Upstate woods and sisterly trauma bonding?"

Penny grinned. "You know how it is. One last fashion emergency before departure." She grabbed her bag, then paused. "You gonna be okay holding down the fort?"

"I'll manage," Arden said, reaching for her keys. "Heading to the market."

"Ooh, buy something indulgent. Like cheese. Or revenge."

"I'll see what's on sale."

Penny's grin softened. "Seriously. Don't spend the whole weekend brooding like a noir detective."

"I make no promises," Arden said, slinging the tote over her shoulder.

"Fair. But if you have any hot make-out flashbacks near the oranges, text me. I live for that content."

Arden didn't look back, but her smirk was an answer.

The hallway was cold, the building's walls wearing their usual layers of peeling paint and fading graffiti. When she stepped outside, the city wrapped around her fast and full: steam vents hissing, bread baking somewhere close, the wind carrying something bright and sharp through the morning.

She walked.

Orchard Street was already humming. Vendors shouted prices. Someone blasted old Sinatra. A pair of teenagers argued in overlapping Spanish and sarcasm. Arden let it rush past her.

It didn't erase the fear.

But it reminded her she was still here.

At the market, she moved between stalls like she belonged to the morning. A loaf of sourdough. A wedge of cheese. Apples she didn't need but liked the look of.

She reached for a bunch of carrots, dirt still clinging to the roots, proof they'd been somewhere real.

Then her hand hovered over a pile of lemons.

Bright.

Defiant.

Citrus in winter always felt like a promise.

Not that everything was fine.

But that it could be.

She added them to her bag.

"Arden, shopping for groceries? I didn't expect to see you here."

The voice cut through the market's hum. Paper bags rustled. Vendors laughed. Citrus and fresh bread hung thick in the air.

She stopped cold.

Her grip tightened on the tote. Her pulse jumped, sharp and immediate, the sound of him lifting the fine hairs at the back of her neck before thought could catch up.

She turned.

Sebastian Hawthorne leaned against a crate of oranges, untouched by the damp that clung to everyone else. His coat, deep charcoal and razor-lined, sat immaculate over his frame. Every dark blond hair in place. No smudges. No creases. No human mess.

Calculated control.

His smile came easily. Disarming, if you didn't know better.

His eyes told the truth.

Gray-blue, sharp and watchful, already weighing her like a problem that required solving.

"Sebastian," she said evenly. Crisp syllables. Clean lines. "Could say the same to you. Didn't think this was your scene."

He chuckled, low and smooth.

"What can I say? I'm a man of many tastes."

His gaze traced over her, leisurely and invasive, meant to land like hands. Like entitlement.

Her stomach flipped.

She didn't move.

"What brings you here?" he asked lightly. "Out of all places. Why now?"

She straightened and refused to shrink. "Maybe I'm just living my life. Not everything is a grand mystery, Sebastian."

"Oh, I disagree." His voice dipped, silk stretched thin over something serrated. "You're all mystery, Arden. And I do love a puzzle."

"Funny," she said. "I'm not looking to be solved."

His grin sharpened. "Not by everyone, certainly."

He reached for an apple from the nearest stall, rolling it between his fingers. Too gentle. The kind of softness that implied pressure would come later.

"You know," he mused, eyes never leaving hers, "some puzzles aren't meant to be solved. They're fascinating to watch..."

He tilted his head slightly.

"...unravel."

Heat climbed her throat. Arden slowed her breath and grounded herself where she stood.

"If I didn't know better," she said, "I'd think you were watching a little too closely."

His smile didn't falter.

"Now why would you think that?" he asked, voice honeyed and poisonous. "Surely you're not accusing me of—"

"Should I be?"

The words dropped between them.

A blade.

Clean. Precise.

Sebastian laughed as if he had anticipated this moment and approved of it.

"Paranoia doesn't suit you," he said, his tone velveted—sweet and steeped in rot. "But I understand. Big city. Strange faces. Anyone would be on edge."

He straightened, smoothing an invisible wrinkle from his sleeve.

A performance down to the last detail.

"But remember, Arden," he said, holding her gaze, unblinking, "not everything is about you."

Then he turned.

And he was gone.

Swallowed by the crowd. His silhouette dissolved into motion, the hem of his coat the last flick of shadow.

But the scent of him lingered.

Earthy. Refined. A sharp, acrid undertone beneath it—wrong. Like expensive cologne poured over fire.

Arden exhaled through clenched teeth.

The strap of her bag bit into her palm, fingers numb from a grip she hadn't realized she had taken.

Around her, the market carried on untouched. The vendor behind the apple cart smiled at a child. Laughter spilled down the row, easy and unbothered.

As if nothing had shifted.

But it had.

Her thoughts splintered, chasing the shape of the moment: the timing, the stillness, the way his gaze had held her like a pin through paper.

Could it be him?

The notes.

The roses.

The shadows that kept time with her steps after midnight.

Was it memory turning feral, or something that had finally decided to show its face?

She didn't know.

But her body moved before fear could take hold.

One step.

Then another.

The air burned her lungs, but she didn't let it show.

She didn't run.

She didn't fracture.

She walked, head high, spine locked, into the crowd that had already swallowed him whole.

She wasn't prey.

She was the storm.

The market overflowed with life.

Children's laughter cut through the air. Vendors called out prices in practiced rhythms. A street musician threaded blues notes through the noise.

None of it mattered.

The only rhythm Sebastian registered was hers.

Arden.

She moved like someone who knew she was being watched.

Because she was.

Composed.

Her gaze skimmed the crowd with that careful vigilance he recognized immediately. But beneath the straight spine, the white-knuckled grip on her tote, the slight acceleration in her stride, Sebastian saw the truth.

She felt him.

That, too, had been intentional.

Awareness was delicate. A whisper against the skin. The tightening at the base of the neck. Breath turning shallow. The understanding that anonymity had been breached.

She was always braced. Always scanning.

But she responded.

And he—

He composed.

Every beat of this moment belonged to him, a symphony assembled with patience rather than force. He had learned long ago that inevitability didn't announce itself.

It accumulated.

He had unraveled her life slowly. Methodically. Thread by thread.

Her past.

Her friends.

Her family.

Every tether she believed she had—cataloged, cross-referenced, understood.

The roses.

The notes.

The gifts.

Not warnings.

Not threats.

Markers.

Chapters.

Their story, written in scent and shadow and precision.

Even the messages she ignored carried weight. She hadn't blocked the number.

That mattered.

That meant the door was still open.

She paused at a stall, and for a fraction of a second, her mask slipped.

Barely.

Fingers clenched too tight.

Shoulders locked.

Jaw set.

She was pretending not to see him.

But she saw.

She always did.

And it never stopped thrilling him.

The involuntary flicker when their eyes met was enough. A fault line. A moment she couldn't smooth over.

Like all the others.

Her fire was predictable.

He knew the real tells: the glance over her shoulder, the half-step quicker, the way her voice lifted, then dropped too low.

She believed she was choosing her direction. Believed she could leave the roses behind. The notes. The shadows that kept pace with her nights.

Believed she could outrun him.

She was wrong.

He had carefully built a world around her, one where every path curved back to the same place.

To him.

And no matter how far she went, she would arrive there again.

And again.

And again.

Because this wasn't her story.

It was his.

And she was the necessary center of it.

As he slipped back into the crowd, he didn't look to see whether her eyes followed.

He knew he had left residue.

The space behind him still held her shape: the heat, the static, the awareness.

The world dulled without her at its center. Sound flattened. Color thinned.

But that emptiness never lasted.

He knew how the story ended.

He had written it slowly. Line by line.

And she was already moving toward the final scene.

Right on time.

Little Fire.

Soon, she would see him clearly.

Not as a stranger in the crowd, but as the architect she had always been orbiting.

And when that recognition came, there would be no distance.

No denial.

No escape.

THE WALK back to her apartment stretched.

Each step heavier.

Slower.

The grocery bag weighed almost nothing in her hand. Her chest was another matter, tight and sinking, every shadow humming with threat.

Something was coming.

Every alley mouth bristled with static. Every turn felt like a coin toss between safe and not.

When her building finally rose into view, it didn't feel like refuge. The warmth she used to associate with chipped brick and groaning floors had been scraped away, replaced by something colder.

The dread was worse now.

Quieter.

The kind that lived beneath the skin.

She climbed the stairs.

One.

Two.

Each step groaned beneath her like a warning.

Then she saw it.

Her apartment door stood slightly ajar.

The grocery bag slipped from her hand and hit the floor with a soft thud.

A single crimson rose rested against the doorframe, too perfect beneath the flickering hallway light. Its petals glowed there, beautiful in the way nightmares borrow from dreams. Beside it lay a folded white card, crisp and pristine.

Intentional.

Her breath hitched. Her heart kicked hard against her ribs as she crouched, fingers trembling as they closed around the stem.

Velvet petals.

Thorned stem.

The prick came sharp and sudden, a sting of red at her thumb. The pain did nothing to slow the panic rising in her chest.

Beside the rose sat a box.

Wrapped in dark paper, smooth and cold beneath her touch. Her initials were embossed in gold across the lid—subtle, expensive, personal.

She froze.

The card hovered between her fingers. She hadn't opened it, and already it felt louder than any scream.

Her gaze flicked down the hallway. The emergency exit door stood cracked open at the far end.

A soft creak broke the stillness.

"Eli," she snapped, sharper than she meant to.

Her neighbor stepped out of his apartment, wiping his hands on a paint-smeared rag. A streak of blue marked his cheek. His eyes landed on the rose, the box, the scene she hadn't chosen.

"That's...dramatic," he said lightly. But his gaze lingered. "Did someone—?"

Arden forced a thin smile, fingers curling tighter around the stem. "Someone's feeling poetic."

Eli stepped closer, expression tightening. "Do you know who it's from?"

"No," she said too fast. Then, quieter, "Not really."

He nodded slowly. "Well...whoever it is doesn't understand boundaries."

"No kidding," she muttered.

Her thumb still throbbed, the sting oddly distant, as if it belonged to someone else.

Eli held her gaze. "If you need anything...you know where to find me."

She nodded once, unsure whether the offer steadied her or unsettled her.

His door clicked shut moments later.

Arden was alone again.

With the box.

She didn't want to open it.

She opened it anyway.

The ribbon slid loose beneath her fingers. The paper gave too easily, surrendering to reveal a velvet box the color of flushed rose petals.

Soft pink.

Pretty in a way that turned her stomach.

She opened the card.

Uniquely beautiful, like you.
-Your Secret Admirer

The words sat heavy in her palm.

Arden exhaled slowly, then glanced toward the emergency exit again. The door had nearly closed, but the narrow seam of space left behind felt charged, alive with threat.

Inside, the apartment was cold in its quietude. The low hum of the refrigerator. The distant rush of traffic. Familiar sounds, rendered strange by the weight of what had been left behind.

She bolted the door, sliding the deadbolt into place with a decisive click.

Then she stood there, back against the wood, breathing through the static rising in her chest. Rain tapped softly against the windows—small, insistent sounds, like whispers trying to get in.

On the counter sat the rose.

The card.

The velvet box.

She stared at them.

They didn't belong here.

But they were here.

And no matter how tightly she locked the door, deep in her bones, Arden knew someone had been inside.

Again.

The hallway held its breath, that particular silence where every creak sounded louder than it should.

From the dark, from a vantage designed to be forgotten, Sebastian watched.

The grainy feed glowed on the screen before him, catching Arden's approach to the door. Her steps were measured, but heavy with hesitation.

Every pause, every adjustment of her pace—notes in a composition he had refined over time.

The perfume.

The book.

The roses.

The cards.

Not gestures.

Design.

Each one chosen to lodge beneath her skin and stay there. The rose wasn't a flower; it was a tether. The card—Uniquely beautiful, like you—a phrase meant to echo long after the paper was gone.

A reminder:

No space was ever fully hers.

Not while he held the threads.

This wasn't a gift.

It was a mirror. A signal. Proof she had never been unseen.

He saw her.

More clearly than anyone else ever had.

And the door, left barely ajar—

That was the quietest incision.

Not forced.

Not broken.

Simply open.

An invitation masquerading as a mistake.

A fracture in the belief she still carried: that safety was something she could choose.

This wasn't fear.

Not yet.

It was doubt.

The kind that crept in slowly. That lingered. That started small—a shadow where none should be, a sound that held too long—and then stayed.

Locks.

Walls.

Routines.

None of it mattered.

Not when he moved beneath it all.

Sebastian leaned closer to the screen, gaze fixed.

Devotion sharpened to a point.

She paused at the threshold. Her body betrayed her before her thoughts could catch up: the shift of her weight, the glance toward the emergency exit, the tightening of her grip.

She could feel him.

Not with reason.

Not with proof.

With instinct.

She was close to sensing him.

So close.

But not quite.

She stepped inside.

The soft click of the lock turning made him smile. As if it mattered. As if a bolt could bar him from a space he had already entered.

She had believed Gideon Blackwell's presence—his reach, his resources—could protect her. Believed a fortress built of affection and influence might hold.

But safety was the illusion.

He was the constant.

Sebastian watched the apartment lights bloom across the feed. Her silhouette moved through the space—the pacing, the restless hands, the break in her composure.

She wasn't controlled anymore.

She was coming undone.

And it was exquisite.

His work.

His patience.

Gideon believed he understood her.

But Gideon had mistaken stillness for fragility.

Sebastian knew better.

Fire didn't need shelter.

It needed direction.

Arden Rivers was fire, wild and bright, already burning at the edges of her life.

She simply hadn't recognized it yet.

That she was the axis.

The fixed point his world turned around.

Not obsession.

Something older.

Deeper.

He had been building this for months, thread by thread, page by page.

She believed she could keep moving. That strength alone would protect her.

But her brilliance, her resistance, her spark—

Those were the very things that would draw her closer.

Soon, she would see what he had been showing her all along.

She would understand.

And when that moment came, there would be no shadows left to hide in.

No distance left to run.

No exit.

Only inevitability.

CHAPTER 17
The Shape of Safety

Arden checked the locks again.

Once wasn't enough.

Twice didn't register.

The third time, her fingers slipped against the cold metal, clumsy and numb, as if they no longer belonged to her.

The deadbolt slid home with a hollow click.

Too loud.

Every sound was too loud.

The echo ricocheted through the apartment and didn't stop. It kept going, bouncing off walls, burrowing into her skull, replaying long after the noise itself was gone.

Safety felt thin.

Tissue-thin.

Something that could tear if she breathed wrong.

She stood there, unmoving, chest already tight, already wrong.

On the counter, the items waited.

The rose.

The card.

The velvet box.

She had placed them there with almost surgical care, as if one wrong movement might detonate the fragile calm she was pretending to have. The faint scent of lavender and vanilla clung to her skin, usually grounding, usually familiar, but now it turned heavy. Cloying. Too much.

It tangled with the sharp, metallic taste creeping up the back of her throat.

Uniquely beautiful, like you.

The words crawled back into her head uninvited, dragging memory with them.

That bar.

Sticky floors.

Chad's voice, loud and careless.

The first rose.

That was when it shifted.

When the air changed.

When the shadows stopped behaving like shadows.

Her thumb found the scar in her palm.

A faint crescent. Easy to miss if you didn't know where to look.

She pressed into it harder than necessary, pushing through pain because pain, at least, made sense. A moment when self-defense hadn't been a choice, but instinct.

The wound had healed.

The weight hadn't.

Her gaze slid back to the box.

She didn't want to open it.

Her hands moved anyway.

The ribbon slipped free too easily. The paper peeled back, revealing velvet that looked soft enough to swallow light.

Her breath stalled.

Inside lay a rose-gold bracelet. Lotus flowers, dozens of them, each diamond petal catching the light.

Her vision tunneled.

"Oh my God," she whispered—and then louder, involuntary, "I'm going to be sick."

The room tilted.

Too bright.

Too sharp.

Too close.

The bracelet wasn't jewelry. It was an assertion. Opulence wielded like a hand at her throat. Beauty sharpened into control.

Her phone lay beside it, screen dark.

Heavy.

Unreachable.

Sebastian's face surged up unbidden: the too-easy smile, the way his gaze had lingered, not leering, but measuring, as if he were taking inventory.

That couldn't have been coincidence.

But the rose had been at her door while he was standing in front of her.

Her stomach lurched.

He couldn't have been in two places at once.

Could he?

The thought sparked static down her spine. Illogical. Impossible.

Her heart didn't care.

Am I losing my mind?

The question looped.

Louder each time.

This wasn't before.

This wasn't clumsy or impulsive.

This was precise.

Smart.

Resourced.

Strategic.

Her arms wrapped around herself, reflexive, but the pressure didn't help. Her skin felt too tight. Her chest felt compressed from the inside out, lungs refusing to pull a deep inhale no matter how hard she tried.

Breathe.

Just breathe.

She tried.

Her body ignored her.

Air came shallow and fast, scraping instead of filling. Her pulse slammed against her ribs, erratic, wrong. Her hands shook harder, fingers tingling, then going numb.

The apartment felt smaller.

The fridge hummed—too loud.

A siren wailed outside—too close.

Her own heartbeat roared in her ears until it drowned out everything else.

No.

No, no, no—

She had always handled this. Alone. She had to. That was the rule.

But the rule shattered.

Her thumbs moved before she could stop them.

I need you.

The response came instantly.

I'm on my way.

Relief didn't come.
The panic didn't stop.
Relief didn't come.
The panic didn't stop.

Minutes stretched into something viscous and unreal. Time lost shape. Her knees locked to keep her upright. The bracelet sat open like a threat, velvet gaping, diamonds flashing every time her vision swam.

Then—

Three knocks.

Firm. Controlled.

Her body reacted before her mind caught up. She moved toward the door, each step a negotiation, her legs trembling and threatening collapse with every shift of weight.

She reached the lock.

Her fingers slipped.

She turned it anyway.

The moment the door opened, her body gave up.

The floor rushed toward her.

Strong arms caught her mid-fall.

Gideon.

The solidity of him registered before his face did—hands anchoring her, chest solid beneath her cheek. She clutched at his coat like it was the only thing keeping her tethered to the world.

"Arden."

His voice cut through the noise.

Not loud.

Not urgent.

Certain.

He guided her down with controlled care, lowering her to the couch as if he had done this a hundred times. As if she weighed nothing at all.

"Look at me," he said, hands firm on her shoulders. "You're safe. You're here. With me."

She shook her head, breath stuttering. "I—I can't—" Her voice fractured. "I can't breathe."

"You are breathing," he said, unwavering. "It just feels wrong right now. I'm here. Stay with me."

Her chest seized again. Tears blurred her vision. Her fingers clawed at her sweater, desperate for air that wouldn't come fast enough.

"I feel like—" she gasped. "I'm drowning."

"I know," he said softly. "I've got you."

He didn't rush her. Didn't overwhelm her with words.

He breathed.

Slow.

Measured.

"In through your nose," he murmured. "Just a little. That's it. Hold it. Now out."

He counted.

With her.

For her.

Inhale.

Exhale.

The first breath barely worked.

The second shook.

The third came with a sob torn loose from somewhere deep and ugly.

But it came.

The spinning eased by increments so small she barely noticed until the room stopped collapsing inward. Her pulse slowed from a gallop to something uneven but survivable.

Her hand pressed to her chest, rising and falling with breaths that finally felt like air.

"That's it," Gideon said quietly. "You're doing it."

When he sat beside her and pulled her into his arms, she didn't resist. She folded into him, exhaustion crashing in hard and heavy now that the adrenaline had begun to drain.

His heart beat beneath her ear.

Real.

"I hate this," she whispered hoarsely. "I feel so small."

"You are not," he said immediately, voice steel-sure. "This is your body trying to protect you. It doesn't mean you're weak."

"It feels like I'm trapped," she said. "Like I can't outrun it."

"And yet you reached out." He cupped her face gently, grounding her with the steadiness of his touch. "You didn't disappear. You didn't shut down. That's strength, Arden, even when it feels like hell."

The words didn't fix it.

But they held.

Her breathing evened. The shaking slowed. The panic retreated—not gone, not cured, but pushed back far enough to let her rest.

Gideon leaned back, holding her against him, one arm firm around her, the other tracing slow, grounding circles along her arm. He didn't move when her body finally went slack with exhaustion.

Outside, the city pressed on.

Shadows lingered.

But they stopped at the edges of the room.

Not tonight.

Not while he held her.

THE FAINT GLOW of city light bled through the curtains, casting restless shadows along the walls.

Outside, the rain didn't let up.

Soft.

Constant.

Gideon stayed still, his arms around her, her breath slowing against his chest. The weight of her—warm, real, settling into him—grounded him.

And beneath that comfort, something else.

Not fear.

Not quite pain.

The kind of ache that comes from holding something you know you could lose.

She had unraveled in his arms, not because she was fragile, but because someone had made her feel unsafe in a place that was supposed to be hers.

His jaw locked.

The rose.

The note.

That fucking bracelet.

None of it was random.

Every piece had been chosen.

A message.

A warning.

A line drawn where it didn't belong.

A calculated attempt to strip her of power, to remind her that no lock, no address, no ritual of safety could fully protect her.

The air still carried the imprint of her fear—sharp and visceral beneath the faint scent of lavender, jasmine, and vanilla. The contrast twisted something deep in his gut.

She shifted slightly in her sleep, fingers curling into the fabric of his shirt like muscle memory. Even unconscious, she reached for his steadiness.

And he gave it without hesitation.

His arms tightened around her.

A silent vow.

What haunted him wasn't the panic attack. It was the look in her eyes before it overtook her: a split-second flicker of helplessness, foreign and unbidden.

He had seen her stand unflinching in the face of betrayal, pain, and loss.

But this—

This was different.

This was her past trying to reclaim its hold.

And still, she had fought it.

Still, she had reached for him.

The knowledge settled low and fierce in his chest.

She let me in.

He shifted carefully, mindful not to wake her, the leather of his watch brushing her shoulder as he adjusted. His thoughts returned to the details she had shared. Sebastian at the market. Casual. All charm and sharp edges.

The man was a snake.

Too polished.

Too intentional.

Gideon didn't trust him.

But instinct told him Sebastian wasn't behind this.

Not directly.

No. This was colder. Smarter.

Whoever was orchestrating it wanted to scare her, yes, but more than that, they wanted to own her fear. To curate it.

Not a stalker.

Not a spurned ex.

A strategist.

Someone who understood the power of implication. Someone who knew how to leave space between threat and proof. Someone who planted doubt and let it grow.

Someone dangerous.

Gideon's eyes flicked toward the counter, where the velvet box still sat, blush pink and precise, obscene in its audacity. His fingers flexed once against Arden's spine.

He didn't know who was behind this yet.

But he would.

And when he found them—

They would learn the difference between watching someone from the shadows and touching someone he loved.

Because Arden Rivers wasn't alone.

And whoever had made her feel like she was?

They would regret it.

Hours later, Arden stirred, lashes fluttering as sleep loosened its grip.

The first thing she noticed was the rhythm beneath her ear.

Gideon's heartbeat.

Her fingers flexed slightly against the soft fabric of his shirt as she exhaled, the last of the storm settling somewhere deeper than breath.

"You're awake," Gideon murmured.

His voice vibrated low in his chest, more felt than heard. His hand continued its slow, absent tracing along her back, as if letting go might fracture whatever serenity had formed between them.

"I am," she whispered, sleep still clinging to her voice. "You didn't have to stay."

"Yes, I did," he said simply.

A faint half-smile touched the corner of his mouth, one felt more than seen.

She shifted, tilting her head to meet his eyes. They were still heavy, rimmed with exhaustion, but clear.

"I hate that you saw me like that," she said quietly. Stripped bare. "Helpless. Struggling. Weak."

"I don't see it that way," he said without hesitation. "I saw you fight. That's all I ever see when I look at you, Arden—strength."

Her chest tightened. The emotion came fast, sharp and uninvited.

She dropped her gaze, fingers tracing a wrinkle in his shirt like it might anchor her.

"It didn't feel like strength," she admitted. "It felt like I was breaking. Like I was barely holding on."

"And yet you held on," Gideon said. "You didn't run. You didn't disappear into the fear. You stayed. That's resilience, even when it doesn't feel like it."

Silence settled between them.

Not heavy.

Not hollow.

Full.

She let his words sink in, not as reassurance, but as something sturdier. A reframing she hadn't known how to give herself.

Her breathing evened. Her shoulders softened. The residual tremor beneath her skin faded to a dull echo.

"I don't want to feel like this again," she said, barely above a breath.

His arm tightened around her, not restrictive.

Just there.

"You won't face it alone," he said. "Not ever."

That did it.

Her eyes drifted closed again, the weight of the day finally pulling her under. She shifted closer, breath deepening, her body settling into his as if it had been searching for this exact shape all along.

Gideon stayed still, watching the slow rise and fall of her chest, the crease between her brows finally easing.

When he was certain she was fully asleep, Gideon moved carefully, adjusting his hold before rising with her in his arms.

She stirred faintly, fingers curling into his shirt, but she didn't wake.

There was only the sound of rain against the windows.

A second heartbeat.

He carried her through the dark, nudging open her bedroom door with his foot. The room waited, undisturbed, as if it had been holding its breath.

He laid her down gently and brushed a loose strand of hair from her cheek.

As he straightened, her hand reached for him again in sleep.

Searching.

He hesitated only a moment.

Then he kicked off his shoes and climbed in beside her.

The covers whispered as he pulled them up, his arm sliding around her waist as if it had already learned the shape of her. She melted into him, breath evening, her body soft and unguarded.

And for the first time all night, so did his.

Holding her like this didn't fix the storm. It didn't erase the threat waiting beyond the door.

But it did something else.

It reminded him what mattered.

She was still here.

And as long as she was, he would hold the line.

MORNING CAME QUIETLY.

Arden stirred to the faint light of dawn filtering through the curtains, soft gold casting warmth across the room. Her lashes fluttered open, the stillness almost disorienting after the chaos of the night.

The weight in her chest hadn't vanished.

But it was lighter now.

No longer crushing.

As if the storm had pulled back enough to let her breathe.

The sight of Gideon brought her fully into the present, memory rushing back in.

He lay on his side, one arm draped over the edge of the bed like a barrier. Still guarding her, even in sleep. His sharp features, so often carved with intensity, had softened in the morning light, revealing something rare.

Almost boyish.

Arden pushed herself upright, brushing her chestnut waves back with a slow exhale. Outside, the world felt distant, the faint patter of rain muffling everything beyond the walls. Her fingers tugged absently at the hem of her shirt as she glanced at him again, a faint, unbidden smile touching her mouth.

"I need coffee," she muttered, low and husky with sleep, edged in dry humor.

Gideon's eyes opened.

Steel-gray sharpened, then softened as they focused on her. A low chuckle rumbled from his chest, warm and unguarded—a sound that felt like hers alone.

"I'll make it," he said, sitting up with an ease that belied the tension still coiled beneath the surface. The sheets slipped to his waist, and for a beat she watched him.

Wholly present.

A man who looked like he belonged exactly where he was.

Then he paused.

Turned back to her.

Something shifted in his expression. Intent. Serious.

"But first," he said, voice low, "promise me something."

She arched a brow. "That depends."

A flicker of a smile crossed his mouth, then disappeared almost immediately.

"Don't shut me out," he said.

The words were simple.

They landed like an oath.

"Whatever this is," he continued, holding her gaze, "whatever comes next, we face it together."

The room went very still.

Arden's chest tightened, not with panic this time, but with the weight of being seen. Of being asked, not commanded. Chosen, not claimed.

She nodded once.

"I don't know how to do this perfectly," she said quietly. "But I won't disappear. I won't pretend I'm fine when I'm not."

"That's all I'm asking."

She hesitated, then reached out, fingers brushing his wrist and creating space for them both.

"And you don't get to carry this alone either," she added. "Not everything is mine to survive by myself."

That earned a real smile.

One that stayed.

"Deal," he said.

He leaned in and pressed a brief kiss to her temple. Not a promise of safety.

A promise of presence.

Then he stood, reaching for his shirt.

"Coffee," he said. "Strong. Non-negotiable."

She watched him move toward the kitchen, the confidence of him filling the space he left behind.

Alone in the soft glow of morning, Arden leaned back against the headboard and closed her eyes for a moment.

The chaos hadn't disappeared. The fear, the questions, the threat—all still there. But her thoughts weren't spiraling anymore. They weren't clawing at her from the inside.

They were steady.

Grounded in one word.

Together.

As THE SCENT of coffee drifted through the apartment, Arden allowed herself a brief, stolen moment of peace. A faint smile curved her lips, and this time, she didn't bother to suppress it.

Whatever came next, she wouldn't face it alone.

She stepped into the kitchen, drawn by the rich smell of coffee and the quiet rhythm of domesticity she hadn't realized she craved.

Gideon stood at the stove, barefoot, sleeves pushed up, his silhouette framed by soft morning light filtering through rain-slicked windows. The sight of him—solid, focused, moving with purpose—hit her low and deep, a thrum curling behind her ribs.

God.

Could this man be any sexier?

His dark hair was mussed in a way that made her fingers twitch with the urge to smooth it. A dark line of stubble traced his jaw, new since last night, and somehow he looked even more composed now. Like a man who had slept with one eye open and still risen ready.

Two plates sat on the counter. Eggs. Toast. Nothing fancy, but plated with intention. The kind of simple care that felt intimate enough to undo her a little.

The coffee he'd poured for her steamed beside it, warmth fogging the edge of the mug where the light caught.

But the card and the box still sat near the sink.

Landmines.

Untouched.

Impossible to ignore.

A reminder that even here, inside the warmth of this kitchen, the outside world still had teeth.

Gideon turned, his gaze sweeping her face, attentive. "Do you want to talk about it?"

Her eyes dropped to the bracelet nestled in velvet, cruelly exquisite, and the words caught in her throat.

"Not yet," she said, barely above a whisper.

He didn't push. Didn't step closer. He nodded once, understanding filling the space between them.

"Okay," he said quietly. "But soon."

Then his voice shifted, lower now. Razor-edged.

"I've already pulled Christian in," he said. "We need answers. How it got through. Why it wasn't flagged. There are too many cracks in the system, and someone's moving through them like they know the layout."

Her pulse ticked faster at the name, the implication sharpening her awareness.

Gideon wasn't only offering comfort anymore.

He was preparing for battle.

She moved to the counter and picked up the coffee he'd made for her, wrapping both hands around the mug. For a few breaths, she didn't speak. She only stared at the rain trailing down the glass, the city beyond softened into blurred grayscale.

Then, softly, more to herself than to him, she said, "He knew. Somehow, he knew I would be alone."

Gideon set his plate down and leaned against the counter beside her. His voice was calm, but his eyes were blazing. "Then that was his mistake."

She looked at him.

Really looked.

And Arden realized she wasn't bracing for impact.

She felt someone standing beside her, ready to push back.

The bracelet sat on the counter like it belonged.

It didn't.

Rose gold. Diamond-encrusted.

Too beautiful to be innocent.

Arden stared, not at the sparkle, but at the intention. The message buried in every polished edge.

Her hand moved before her thoughts could catch up.

Her fingers brushed the metal.

Cold.

The chill ran up her arm, tangible proof this wasn't a nightmare she could wake from.

When she spoke, her voice didn't waver; it cut clean.

"You know I got the lotus tattoo after I finished nursing school. I didn't choose it because it was pretty. It was symbolic. About surviving. Growing. Even when everything felt impossible."

Gideon's expression shifted, the hard edge of his fury easing into something quieter.

He leaned forward, elbows braced on the counter, gaze steady on hers. "Why then?" he asked softly, giving her space to gather her thoughts.

She hesitated, fingers curling around the edge of the counter.

"I was burned out," she said finally. "Nursing wasn't what I thought it would be. Or maybe I wasn't who I thought I was in it. I was carrying too much. Other people's pain. My own doubt. And..."

She swallowed.

"...a stalker I didn't realize I'd picked up until it was too late."

The words landed between them like a bruise.

"When I left Morgantown for Silverbranch, I needed a clean slate. The lotus became a promise to myself. I'd bloom, no matter how much mud I came from."

Her gaze dropped to the bracelet.

A gift that was no gift at all.

"Whoever left this," she said, voice faltering before it steadied, "knew what it meant. They didn't choose it because it's pretty."

Gideon's hand closed over hers.

Warm.

Anchoring.

A counterweight to the chill still clinging to her bones.

"They're trying to twist it," he said, his voice steady but coiled tight with fury. "Take something that's yours and poison it. But they can't. You already claimed it. You made it mean survival."

Her throat tightened, emotion cresting too fast to brace for. His words, earnest and razor-sharp, cut through the fog like light.

"It feels personal," she whispered. "Too personal. The lotus wasn't something I shared. Not like this."

Gideon's jaw locked.

"Christian."

The man was already a few feet away, silent and observant, the kind of presence that knew exactly when to step forward.

"I want every lead," Gideon said. "Every point of access. Every name. This isn't random, and it isn't luck. Someone is moving through the cracks, and it's coming from the inside. I want eyes on everyone."

Christian nodded once, thumbs already flying across his phone. "Understood."

When Gideon turned back to her, his hand found her shoulder—firm, reassuring.

"We're not letting them take anything else from you," he said. "Not your peace. Not your voice. Not one more damn thing."

Arden exhaled. Her fingers brushed the edge of the bracelet one last time.

Then she straightened.

"They think they know me," she said. "They think this makes me small."

She met his gaze, clear and unflinching.

"It doesn't. It makes me dangerous."

Gideon's lips curved faintly. A half-smile that meant good—let them try.

"Then let them see," he said. "Let them see what danger looks like when it's done running."

The bracelet stayed where it was.

No longer a threat.

A line in the sand.

And as Arden stood beside him, she felt it: the promise she had once etched into her own skin, rising again like fire.

This wasn't about surviving anymore.

It was about reclaiming.

CHAPTER 18
Poetry in Motion

She'd gotten off the subway two stops early.

Not for any real reason. Only the need to move.

The walk was longer, her boots aching by the time she reached the block, but it gave her space to breathe.

She missed her car.

The one that got totaled in the winter, the same night everything else shattered. It hadn't been fancy, but it had been hers.

Freedom on four wheels. Tinted windows. The ability to leave when she wanted, how she wanted.

Gideon always offered car service.

Always.

And she appreciated it. But something about the subway, grimy as it was, helped her hold on to a piece of herself. Agency in motion. Even if half the time she was wedged between a mariachi band and someone vaping something deeply illegal-smelling.

And she knew.

You never, ever trusted an empty subway car.

Somewhere, someone had absolutely taken a shit in there.

City law.

The more you know.

Tonight, she needed the noise: the clatter of dishes, the low thrum of bass, the flicker of candlelight on polished glass. She needed people talking around her, not to her. Life in motion. Distraction with a pulse.

She needed to choose to walk into the night, not be chased by what lurked inside it.

The club came into view, the subtle B etched into the entrance, familiar now in a way that unsettled her.

Familiarity bred softness.

Softness bred danger.

But she didn't slow.

INSIDE, candlelight stretched the shadows unnaturally, sharpening their edges until they seemed to reach. Arden moved steadily through the room, though every flicker of motion, every too-long glance, set her nerves buzzing. Conversation blurred into a low, indistinct murmur beneath the tension coiled tight in her chest.

But then she saw him.

Sebastian.

He lounged at the far end of the bar, posture almost insolently casual, one arm draped along the back of the chair, his glass balanced lightly in the other hand.

Candlelight caught his features in fragments. A sharp cheekbone. The curve of his mouth. Eyes too still to be harmless.

The air around him felt charged, rippling outward like a held breath.

An unspoken challenge.

Her spine locked.

Not fear.

Awareness.

But she didn't turn away.

His gaze lifted and found hers across the room.

The moment stretched.

Then his mouth curved, just barely.

Not a smile.

Recognition.

Like he had been waiting for her to arrive.

He raised his glass in a deliberate motion, the faint clink of crystal against his ring slicing through the din.

A toast.

A warning.

His smile sharpened, charm lacquered over something malignant.

"Back again so soon?" Arden said as she approached, her tone clipped, her steps measured. She stopped short of his space, close enough to confront, far enough to keep control.

Sebastian's eyes glinted.

"Can't seem to stay away," he drawled. "Though it appears neither can you. Trouble has a way of finding you."

Her fingers brushed the bar, then curled around the edge tighter than intended. His voice slipped under her skin like a familiar toxin.

"I work here," she said calmly. "You don't."

A beat.

His smile didn't falter. If anything, it sharpened.

"If you've got something to say, Sebastian," she said evenly, "say it."

He leaned forward, unhurried. Intentional. His gaze sharpened, finding its mark.

"Careful, Arden," he murmured, low and intimate, meant only for her. "You're starting to sound like Gideon."

A pause.

Measured.

Enjoyed.

"And we both know how he tends to...overstep."

The word lingered.

Not a jab.

A provocation.

"He's always inserting himself," Sebastian continued lightly. "Into conversations. Into places. Into lives where he doesn't belong." He tilted his glass, watching the liquid swirl. "Men like that don't protect out of loyalty. They protect because they need to be needed."

There it was.

Her jaw set before her voice did. The heat in her chest flared, but she didn't blink.

"Gideon's loyalty isn't up for debate."

"Loyalty," Sebastian echoed, tasting it like wine turned sour. His smile twisted, casual in appearance, hollow underneath. "Such a fragile thing. It bends." A beat. "Sometimes it breaks."

The words landed harder than they should have.

Not because she believed him.

Because he did.

Because there was weight there. Knowledge. Something edged in warning.

Still, she held the line.

"Your stories don't scare me," she said quietly. "And your games won't work. Not on me."

For a split second, his smile wavered. A flash of something unmasked—spiteful, possessive.

Then it was gone.

"We'll see," he said lightly.

And then her gaze caught in the window behind him.

Movement.

Not fast.

Not accidental.

A figure stood across the street, half swallowed by shadow, just beyond the reach of the streetlight. Still. Watching.

Her heart hiccuped.

Not from recognition of the figure, but from the feeling.

This stillness wasn't neutral.

It wasn't curiosity.

It was intent.

Sebastian followed her gaze, slow and unhurried, then tilted his head.

"Something on your mind, Arden?" he asked, concern lacquered over every word. Silk-soft. Blade-edged.

She didn't answer.

Couldn't.

The figure hadn't moved. But its attention was fixed. Through glass, through glare and reflection.

On her.

Her lungs locked.

Air thinned.

Her pulse skidded, uneven and too loud inside her ears.

This wasn't being watched.

This was being held.

"I have to go," she said suddenly, the words snapping out before fear could swallow them.

She brushed past Sebastian without waiting for a response.

His chuckle slid after her, low and velvet-slick.

"Run along," he murmured. "The trouble will wait."

The door loomed.

Heavy.

Too slow.

She shoved through it, and the night hit her like a slap.

Cold air burned her lungs. Sound rushed in all at once: traffic, voices, a siren somewhere too close. Her vision narrowed, edges blurring, lights streaking as her body tried to decide whether to freeze or bolt.

And there.

The figure.

Closer now. Across the street. Half in shadow. No movement.

Only presence.

Watching.

Waiting.

Her skin prickled. Her hands went numb. The city didn't feel real anymore, only noise layered over threat.

Too close.

Far too close.

And for the first time since she had stepped inside the bar, Arden knew with absoluteness this wasn't coincidence.

It was pursuit.

Her pulse spiked.

Sound collapsed, bar chatter dissolving into static until only the shape in the street remained.

A target.

She moved before thought could intervene.

Before fear could negotiate.

THE NIGHT AIR cut through the haze, snapping her into brutal clarity.

Her gaze locked onto a figure weaving between parked cars, a silhouette half swallowed by shadow and moving with purpose.

Not wandering.

Leaving.

"Hey!" she shouted, the word cracking sharp through the night.

Her boots struck pavement hard, each step a drumbeat of rebellion and carelessness. Blood roared in her ears. Breath tore from her in short, uneven bursts.

Logic screamed.

This could be a trap.

You don't know who this is.

You don't know what they want.

Anger screamed louder.

Anger at the way fear had slipped into her body. Anger at whoever thought they could watch her, mark her, and disappear untouched.

She refused to feel powerless again.

"Arden!"

Gideon's voice cut through the night behind her, taut and commanding.

She didn't stop.

The figure turned into a narrow alley, slipping into the dark too easily, as if he knew the streets better than she did.

As if he had counted on this.

The world narrowed to motion and breath. Her lungs burned. Her vision tunneled. Her own footfalls thundered beneath her.

She lunged.

Her fingers snagged fabric. A sleeve. Then the edge of a hood.

She yanked hard, adrenaline surging, and spun the figure around with feral force.

It wasn't him.

The man staggered beneath the dull spill of a streetlamp. Scruffy. Patchy beard. A coat worn thin at the elbows. Dirt beneath his nails.

Not a predator.

A survivor.

"What the hell?" he gasped, stumbling back, hands lifting instinctively. His eyes were wide, animal-bright. "What is your problem?"

"What were you doing?" Arden demanded, breath tearing out of her. The fury holding her upright cracked, confusion seeping in fast. "Why were you watching me?"

"I was smoking," he snapped, wrenching free with surprising strength. "Jesus—"

Then he stopped.

Something drained from his face.

The fear vanished.

Replaced by something empty.

Practiced.

His shoulders settled. His breath evened.

His voice dropped, flat and unfamiliar.

"Tell Gideon—"

His mouth curved.

His eyes stayed dead.

"—the game's just starting."

The words landed wrong.

Too clean.

Too precise.

Cold dread curled low in her stomach.

What?

Before she could move, he spun and bolted, vanishing into the maze of shadow with the same ease as before.

Gone.

"Arden, stop!"

Gideon's voice was close now. Urgent. Real. Her name yanked her back like a rope thrown mid-fall.

She stood frozen.

Legs trembling.

Chest heaving.

The night pressed cold against her skin, but the chill wasn't what made her shiver.

It was the message.

Not a warning.

A declaration.

Whoever this was, they weren't finished.

They were just beginning.

Footsteps thundered behind her—not the man's retreat this time, but Gideon's approach.

Arden barely turned before he was there, eyes locking onto hers as his gaze swept her body in one ruthless assessment.

His hands came to her face with impossible gentleness, the kind that steadied her even when everything inside her wanted to fracture.

"Arden," he said, low and firm, his voice cutting through the cold like a lifeline. "Are you hurt?"

His eyes flicked to her trembling hands, then to the alley beyond. His body was coiled tight with restraint, violence barely leashed beneath the surface.

The question cracked something open.

"I thought—" Her breath hitched. "I thought it could've been him. I thought I could stop this."

Her voice fractured mid-sentence, anger flaring through the break. At the situation. At herself. At the way fear had driven her to chase shadows like she could outrun them.

Behind them, Christian's voice slid into the moment. Measured. Unflinching.

"You clocked him," he said. "That was smart."

A beat.

"But chasing someone alone?" His tone dipped, not sharp, not scolding. "That's a risk we can't afford. Not with you."

She didn't mean to flinch, but the truth landed clean.

Not cruel.

Not judgmental.

Weight.

And it settled.

Her shoulders dropped under it, adrenaline draining away in a slow, hollow bleed. What replaced it wasn't panic.

It was ache.

The kind that didn't scream.

The kind that stayed.

"I know," she said quietly.

No argument.

No edge.

Her hands fell to her sides, empty now, useless with nothing left to grip.

Then she turned.

Didn't explain.

Didn't stall.

She walked.

Boots against pavement.

A rhythm built from failure and fury. From the knowledge that intent wasn't enough.

Every step away from the alley carried the weight of something she hadn't meant to lose.

Behind her, the men stayed.

Christian scanned the darkness like it owed him answers.

Gideon didn't move. His jaw ticked once, rage contained so tightly it was almost worse than violence.

They didn't speak.

They didn't have to.

Christian saw it in Gideon's eyes.

This wasn't escalation.

This was a message.

A miscalculation.

Because whoever had orchestrated that moment hadn't only underestimated Arden Rivers.

They had underestimated who would bleed for her.

ARDEN WALKED, her mind caught on a single sentence that wouldn't stop repeating.

Tell Gideon...the game's just starting.

It sat behind her eyes like smoke. Scraped at the back of her throat. Made the air feel thinner.

Fear moved through her.

Hot.

Familiar.

But beneath it, something older lifted its head.

Grief. The kind of pain that didn't scar skin so much as carve instinct. The kind that taught her how to stand when her knees wanted to fold. A shield no one could see until she needed it.

She wasn't the girl who hid anymore.

She wasn't even the woman who flinched.

Most days.

She wasn't waiting for safety.

Her pulse still ran too fast. Her hands still wanted to shake. But fear didn't get to drive.

She had been marked. Tested. Pushed.

And she was still walking.

So let them play.

She'd meet them where they wanted her.

Yes.

But she would decide what it cost.

Somewhere in the rhythm of her steps, something shifted.

Not peace.

Not relief.

Resolve.

Poetry in motion.

This time, with teeth.

FROM THE SHADOWS, Sebastian watched.

Fascination settled into him first—slow, viscous, unwelcome only in how thoroughly it took hold. Arden Rivers moved through the night like a storm wrapped in restraint.

Every line of her body, every step, dared the world to test her.

My girl.

The thought arrived fully formed, automatic. It always did. And just as quickly, the correction followed.

Not his.

Not yet.

Arden was more than he had anticipated.

That unsettled him.

More precise. More volatile. She didn't flee the dark; she advanced into it, jaw set, eyes sharp, fear repurposed into momentum.

That was the misjudgment most people made about Arden Rivers.

They thought fear weakened her.

It sharpened her.

When she lunged and her fingers caught the edge of the decoy's hood, something inside Sebastian tightened. For a single fractured second, it felt like contact, as if her defiance had brushed against him directly. As if the connection he had been building finally had weight.

Then it snapped.

Gideon Blackwell cut through the night, all blunt force and intervention. He reached her too fast, pulling her back into his gravity.

Sebastian's mouth flattened.

"Always in the way," he muttered, the words thin and brittle.

The decoy disappeared into the alley's throat.

Fine.

This wasn't failure.

It was calibration.

But Gideon.

That name tasted wrong.

Intrusive.

The bond Arden gave him so easily, the trust, felt like a misallocation of something rare. Gideon didn't see what mattered. He didn't recognize the discipline beneath her fury, the edges she kept sheathed.

He mistook containment for fragility.

Sebastian exhaled slowly, irritation smoothing itself into patience.

There would be time.

There was always time.

His focus returned to Arden.

She stood alone in the rain, tension wound tight through her posture. Not collapsing. Not unraveling. Searching. Measuring.

Vulnerable, yes.

But not diminished.

The urge to step forward, to let her see him, to test what she would do with truth instead of absence, flared sharp and insistent.

He restrained it.

She didn't know how close she already was. How much of this had been shaped.

The bracelet had been deliberate.

Every detail chosen. The lotus wasn't decoration; it was leverage. Symbol and incision in one. A way to take something she believed belonged only to her and reframe it.

Gideon would never understand that.

It wasn't a gift.

It was narrative control.

Forty thousand dollars wasn't extravagance.

It was emphasis.

A way to ensure she couldn't dismiss it as coincidence or impulse.

She deserved precision.

And truthfully, he hadn't found the detail alone.

A memory surfaced: Chad Dawson, sloppy and bitter, talking too much, spite thick in his mouth.

"A lotus," Chad had sneered. "Like she thinks crawling out of the mud makes her untouchable."

Sebastian had disliked the tone, but he had noted the information.

Chad saw arrogance.

Sebastian saw armor.

So he inverted it.

Turned survival into vulnerability; strength into access.

When Arden finally turned away, spine straight, pace measured, he didn't follow.

He watched.

Fire was dangerous when chased. It revealed itself when observed.

Gideon Blackwell could stand between them, mistaking vigilance for understanding. But Gideon didn't know how to hold fire without trying to contain it.

Sebastian did.

Little Fire, he thought.

Not fond.
Not gentle.
Possessive in the way collectors were possessive of rare things.
He would wait.
Let her resist.
Let her burn brighter.
Fire always consumed eventually.

Gideon didn't run to catch up.

He ran because she moved like a woman who didn't care what it cost.

And she had already paid enough.

By the time he rounded the corner, the alley had swallowed her whole, and whatever she had found there had already left its mark. Not on her body. On her face. Her eyes. The distant, hollow focus of someone who had seen something she couldn't yet name.

Again.

Every instinct in him screamed to pull her in. Lock doors. Seal exits. Turn the world into something defensible.

But Arden Rivers wasn't built for cages.

Not even the ones disguised as protection.

So he let her walk.

His hands curled at his sides, nails biting into his palms as restraint won out over rage. For now. Shoulders tight. Spine straight. Breath controlled down to the bone.

And he hated it, how completely he understood her silence.

How she didn't need to explain what she was feeling because he felt it too.

She wasn't running from her fury; she was aligning herself with it.

She was preparing for war.

And so was he.

Christian watched her go, boots scuffing asphalt, spine rigid with anger, not fear.

And that was the problem.

Arden didn't flee threats. She confronted them head-on. No flinching. No hesitation. Rage in motion, sharp and dangerous.

And for a few critical seconds, completely alone.

He bit back the instinct to follow. It wasn't his job to trail every emotional aftershock, but as her silhouette dissolved into the night, his jaw locked hard enough to ache.

This should never have happened.

Someone had gotten too close. Close enough to draw her out. Close enough to provoke pursuit. That wasn't chance.

That was leverage.

Christian didn't need intuition to tell him that.

He needed data.

This wasn't a near miss. It was a breach. Clean. Executed like someone had studied the system instead of stumbling into it.

His team had protocols for this. Overlap coverage. Pattern recognition. Behavioral flags that should have tripped the second the situation shifted.

And yet Arden had gotten within arm's reach of a potential threat before anyone had eyes on her.

Unacceptable.

Gideon moved past him, fast and controlled. Christian clocked it instantly: the way Gideon scanned her, hands careful, gaze lethal.

Not possession.

Responsibility.

That was the difference between them.

Gideon would bleed for her.

Christian would make damn sure no one ever got close enough to try.

Still, watching her hands shake with fading adrenaline, watching frustration fracture her voice, something cold and heavy settled in his gut.

Guilt.

Because no matter how tight he had drawn the net, someone had slipped through.

Twice.

His voice had come out level. Professional.

You clocked him. That was smart.

He had paused, then spoken more quietly.

But chasing someone alone? That's a risk we can't afford, Arden. Not for you.

Her shoulders had dropped.

And with them, Christian's tolerance.

The system had failed.

His system.

And if this was a test, if someone was probing for weaknesses, they had found one.

Christian turned back toward the alley, already replaying the escape: gait, stride length, weight distribution, the cadence of retreat.

There would be cameras. Partial angles. Reflections in glass. Traffic flow.

A mistake buried somewhere in the pattern.

He would find it.

And it wouldn't be Gideon who reached the man first.

It would be Christian.

Next time, nothing would slip past.

CHAPTER 19

Between Fire and Shadow

The candlelight stretched the shadows unnaturally, sharpening their edges until they seemed to reach for Arden. The sounds from the lounge couldn't drown out the sentence looping in her head.

Tell Gideon...the game's just starting.

The words tugged like a loose thread, unraveling everything she had worked to stitch back together. But it wasn't fear crawling in.

It was fury.

They wanted her cornered. Shaken. Cowering in the dark.

She wasn't that woman anymore.

Behind her, Gideon's footsteps matched her pace. Heavy. Intentional. The current of him filled the space until he was beside her at the marble bar, his hand brushing hers.

"Arden," he said, low but commanding.

His gaze searched hers, the storm inside him shifting when he caught the fire still burning there.

"I'm fine," she said too fast. Sharp.

A beat later, she shook her head, breath ragged.

"No. I'm not. I'm pissed, Gideon. Pissed he's still out there. Pissed that he's... playing a game."

His hand slid to her back. "Then we stop playing." His voice was unwavering, carrying weight like a drawn blade. "He wants fear. We don't give him that."

Christian appeared, tablet in hand, his presence like a stone dropped into still water.

"We've got a start," he said without preamble. "Alley footage. The angle's tough, but we tagged the man Arden confronted. Facial recognition should work."

Arden's chest tightened. "And if it doesn't?" The edge in her voice scraped against the words. "What if we're chasing ghosts?"

"Then we keep chasing," Christian said evenly. His voice never wavered. "This isn't an end, Arden. It's a beginning."

He didn't show frustration, but she saw it anyway: the rigid set of his jaw, the fraction of tension in his shoulders.

His system had failed.

Twice.

For a man built on precision, that wasn't an inconvenience.

It was war.

Gideon's attention cut back to her. "This is what they want. Doubt. But you saw him. You touched him. That's more than they planned for." His eyes locked onto hers. "And that's enough to make them slip."

Her pulse steadied, the fire sparking higher under his words. Not much, but enough to grab onto. She straightened, fingers releasing their chokehold on the bar.

"Okay," she said, quieter but surer. "What's next?"

Christian tapped the tablet. Maps lit the screen in a pale glow. "Connections. Whoever's pulling strings isn't alone. This is organized. Systematic. They're playing the long game."

"And that means?" Arden pressed.

"It means we don't wait for them to come to us," Christian said bluntly. "We dig. Hard."

Gideon's hand pressed firm against her back, not moving her, but anchoring. "And it means no more chasing shadows alone. If you see anything, you call me. Or Christian."

Her instinct was to argue. To bite back. But the echo of that man's voice stilled her.

"Fine." Her jaw tightened. "But I'm not on the sidelines. If they want a game, they'll get one. On my terms."

Christian's mouth twitched, the faintest ghost of a smile. "Good. Then let's make sure they regret starting it."

The cool night air cut across her skin as she and Gideon stepped outside.

His hand lingered at the small of her back as they crossed to the car, protective as ever.

"I'll have Christian and Leo update us first thing in the morning," Gideon said, voice calm but edged. "This doesn't go unanswered."

Arden nodded, but her steps faltered at the door. "I can't stop thinking about how close they've gotten. None of this is random, Gideon. They know exactly where to hit."

"They do." His jaw flexed, gaze cutting sharp. "But they're underestimating you. You didn't freeze. You fought back."

She exhaled slowly. It helped. A little.

But as her fingers brushed the car door, she stopped.

"I need some time," she murmured. "Not far. A bookstore. Coffee. Something ordinary. I need to remember what that feels like."

His eyes held hers for a long beat. Hard edges softened, but not much.

"Home first," he said. "Then decide."

The brownstone's warmth wrapped around her as they stepped inside. Gideon's presence stayed at her back, steady as a shield.

"You should rest," he said. Not unkind, but final.

Arden set her bag down, chest still tight, thoughts still circling.

"I need air," she murmured. "Not far. Just a walk. Maybe the bookstore." Her faint smile was brittle. "I need something that's mine."

Concern sharpened his features. "Take the car," he said finally, voice low and even. "Christian stays on standby. And you call me the second anything feels off."

"Deal," she said, though her smirk hinted at reluctance.

"Arden."

His hushed voice carried steel.

Not a plea.

A vow disguised as one.

"Promise me."

Her gaze held his. Softer now, but steady.

"I promise."

Arden kept her word.

Mostly.

She stopped at the bookstore on the corner and picked up a few finds: a new notebook, blank pages waiting, the kind she always told herself she would use to pin down the chaos before it swallowed her whole.

Ink as a weapon in her arsenal.

Control in lines and margins.

Later, she stood at the window, fingers tapping absently against the sill. The rain had softened to a drizzle, streetlights smearing into pale halos of gold beyond the glass.

It should have felt safe.

It didn't.

"I don't want to stay here tonight," she said at last, her voice low, carrying the weight of something that wouldn't let her breathe. "Not in the brownstone. Not anywhere that feels borrowed."

Gideon's gaze flicked to her, sharp and assessing. "Where then?"

"My place." She met his eyes, the words heavy in the air. "I need to know I can walk back into it. That I'm not—" She cut herself off, shaking her head. "I just need to be there."

He studied her for a long beat, then crossed the space between them.

"If you're going back," he said, "then so am I."

Her brow arched, the faintest tease tugging at her lips. "Protective much?"

"Call it stubborn." His mouth curved into the kind of smile that didn't erase the storm in his eyes, only made room for something else. "Or call it self-preservation. If you think I'm letting you spend the night there alone, you're out of your mind."

"Sounds like overstepping," she murmured, though the spark in her tone softened it.

"Maybe," he allowed, brushing a stray curl from her cheek. "But you don't scare me off with that word."

The air between them shifted. Still taut. Still threaded with danger. Warmer now, too—alive with the current that had always pulled them closer, no matter how dark the world pressed in.

The drive back was quiet, the silence not hollow but full, as if both of them were gathering air before the next plunge.

When they reached her building, Arden's chest tightened at the sight of the familiar brick, the faint glow from her windows.

Home, and not.

She glanced sideways, catching Gideon's profile in the dim wash of streetlight. Solid. Unflinching.

"You really don't have to stay," she said, softer now, the edge gone.

"Too bad." He cut the engine. "I'm already here."

Her laugh came out surprised.

Small, but real.

It broke through the heaviness of the night.

The door shut behind them with a hollow click. Arden slid the locks into place—bolt, chain, deadbolt—each one snapping home with the same thin promise of safety.

Gideon shrugged out of his coat and draped it over the back of the chair like he had already decided he wasn't going anywhere.

He didn't move past her immediately. His gaze tracked the room first: windows, corners, shadows. Always assessing. Always calculating. Only then did his attention return to her.

"You don't have to patrol," she said, tossing her keys onto the counter, the sound sharper than she intended. She leaned back against it, arms crossing loosely. "It's just my apartment. Not a crime scene."

His brow arched. "Arden, your door was left open with a rose and a five-figure bracelet waiting inside. Forgive me if I don't treat it like casual real estate."

A reluctant smile tugged at her mouth. "Five figures?"

He gave her a look. "Don't test me. I checked."

She exhaled, some of the tension slipping, though not all of it. "So what now? You stand guard while I pretend this is normal?"

"Something like that." His gaze held hers, steady and unyielding. "Unless you've got a better idea."

Her mouth curved, defiance softening into something quieter. "I have a few."

The silence that followed wasn't heavy.

It hummed, alive and charged.

He stepped closer, his presence filling the space between them. "You wanted to come back here," he said, voice lower now. "So here we are. What next?"

Arden leaned against the counter, arms crossed over her chest like armor she didn't really mean to wear. "I don't know. Maybe I make tea. Pretend I'm normal. You stand in the corner and glower at the walls. Seems like your thing."

His mouth curved, slow and deliberate. "Glowering isn't my thing."

"No?" she asked, chin tipping in challenge.

"No." He stepped close enough that the warmth of him pressed against the tension still coiled in her chest. "You are."

Her pulse stuttered. For a moment, the apartment was too still, the air between them low and electric with possibility.

"You're impossible," she rasped, though her voice lacked any real bite.

"And you're exhausted," he countered gently, brushing a strand of hair from her cheek. "Go shower. Change. Breathe."

Her throat tightened. Not with fear this time, but with something heavier. Harder to name.

"And if I say I don't want you to leave?"

"Then I won't," he said simply.

No hesitation.

His eyes softened, though the steel beneath never wavered. "Not tonight. Not ever, if I have my way."

The banter slipped into silence.

She didn't move away.

Neither did he.

For the first time all night, the storm beneath her skin eased enough for her to let him in.

THE SCENT of lavender soap floated in the hall.

Gideon sat on the edge of the couch, elbows braced on his knees, jaw tight, eyes fixed on nothing. He had meant it when he told her he would be here.

But waiting felt like hell.

Every creak in the pipes, every splash against tile, every muffled movement on the other side of the door pressed beneath his skin. He wanted her safe. Wanted her steady.

Wanted her.

When the handle finally turned, his body reacted before his mind caught up.

He was already rising.

The door cracked open, steam spilling into the dim apartment light. Arden stepped through, towel clutched to her chest, damp strands clinging to her neck and collarbone. She froze when she saw him—close, too close, the bathroom glow catching the sharp set of his shoulders.

"I told you I'd be here," he said, voice low.

"You meant outside," she whispered, pulse jumping beneath skin still wet from the shower.

"Did I?" His mouth curved, slow, but his eyes didn't move. Didn't blink.

Her grip tightened on the towel. She should have laughed. Should have sent him back to the couch.

She didn't move.

Couldn't.

The air between them thickened, heavy now with something darker than tension.

Hungrier.

"Gideon..." Her voice cracked on his name.

He crossed the space in one breath, lifting a hand to brush a wet strand from her cheek. His thumb lingered, warm against her skin. His hand didn't shake, but his restraint felt like something strung tight between his teeth.

"I'm not here to guard the door," he murmured. "I'm here for you."

Her chest rose sharply, the towel loosening under her grip.

She didn't fix it.

Steam curled into the hallway as Arden let the towel drop.

It hit the floor in silence.

She stayed still beneath the heat of his gaze, bare and damp and flushed, her skin glowing in the soft spill of light. Her nipples tightened in the cool air—or from the way he looked at her, as if restraint were the only thing standing between them and ruin.

Gideon didn't touch her.

Not yet.

He only stared, every inch of him straining with control. His hands curled at his sides. His jaw clenched. A muscle ticked in his cheek.

He looked one breath away from devouring her.

"You're sure?" he asked, voice pulled from somewhere deep in his chest.

Not a challenge.

A tether.

The last open door.

Her answer was movement.

She stepped close, her bare chest brushing his shirt, her hand sliding up his abdomen to fist lightly against his chest. "I wouldn't be standing here like this if I wasn't."

That broke the line.

He took her face in both hands and kissed her hard, fast, fierce—no lead-up, no caution left to spend. His mouth crashed into hers, his hands dragging down her back, pulling her flush against him as if he needed every inch of her skin against his.

She gasped, and he swallowed the sound, his kiss deepening until thought narrowed to heat and mouth and the brutal relief of wanting without pretending otherwise. One hand found the nape of her neck. The other spanned the curve of her hip. When she fisted his shirt, he tore it off in one clean motion.

Her palms found him—hot skin, solid muscle, strength barely held in check. She dragged her nails across his chest and felt him shudder.

The sound that left him went through her like a struck match.

He grabbed her thighs and lifted her. Her legs wrapped around his waist, the wet heat of her body pressed against the hard line of him through his jeans. She moaned, hips shifting for friction, and he gave it to her, grinding slow and hard enough to tear another gasp from her throat.

His mouth dragged fire down her neck. The scrape of his stubble left her skin raw, sensitized, awake everywhere he touched.

"Gideon—" Her voice broke around his name, need turning sharp.

He didn't answer. He carried her through the apartment as if he had already memorized the dark. The bedroom door struck open beneath his shoulder. Then the mattress caught her, and he was over her—hot, heavy, hovering long enough to meet her eyes.

No words.

Only heat.

The question again, silent but clear.

She pulled him down, mouth to mouth, kiss to kiss, her thighs opening for him, her fingers dragging down his back.

"I want you," she whispered. "All of you."

The rest came fast.

He shed his jeans, fabric dragging over her skin as he pressed close again. Her hands mapped every muscle, every scar, every place his control had begun to fracture. His mouth traced down her ribs, tongue flicking over the curve of one breast, then the other, before dragging back up to kiss her hard enough to make her forget where the room ended and he began.

When he lined himself up and pushed into her, it wasn't careful.

It was deep.

Full.

A single thrust that stole the air from her lungs.

Arden gasped, hips lifting, body arching to take him deeper.

He went still for one fractured second, buried inside her, his forehead dropping to hers as his breath tore loose.

"Fuck, Arden—"

"Don't stop."

He didn't.

His thrusts were deep and rhythmic, brutal in their precision. Her fingers dug into his back, her cries catching against his shoulder as he drove into her like nothing else existed beyond the heat of her body and the sound of his name breaking from her mouth.

The wet sound of skin on skin filled the room. Her legs wrapped tighter. Her nails dragged red down his back. Every shift of his hips pushed her higher, pleasure building hard and bright until there was nowhere left for it to go.

She broke first, body locking, breath fracturing, a cry tearing from her as she came undone around him, tight and pulsing.

He cursed, rough and helpless, hips jerking as he followed her over. He thrust deep, shuddering into her, his mouth buried at her throat, groaning her name like it was the only thing left to hold on to.

For a long moment, he stayed over her.

Inside her.

Breathless.

Sweat slicked their skin. The sheets twisted beneath them. The air smelled like lavender and steam and sex.

Arden wrapped her arms around his back, not ready to let go. His weight settled heavier over her, grounding instead of trapping, and for the first time that night, her pulse slowed.

So did his.

No roses.

No shadows.

No past.

Just this.

Just them.

The air stayed warm around them, thick with heat and steam and the scent of skin.

Neither of them moved right away.

Gideon's chest pressed into hers, solid and slow, his breath still uneven against her neck. Her thighs stayed wrapped around his hips, holding him in place more from instinct than need.

The silence didn't press.

It settled.

His hand slid up her side, fingers dragging through the sweat-slick path along her ribs. Not sexual now. Just touch. As if he had to keep feeling her beneath him to believe she was still there, still breathing, still his.

Arden didn't speak.

She traced lazy lines across his back with her fingertips. Down his spine. Over the ridges of muscle. She felt every subtle tremor he hadn't burned out yet.

He shifted slightly, bracing on his elbow to ease some of his weight from her chest.

Not all of it.

She didn't want all of it gone.

"Okay?" he asked.

She nodded. "Yeah."

Her throat still felt raw from the way she had said his name. From the way she had cried out.

His eyes stayed on hers. "You sure?"

"You're still inside me, Gideon," she said, dry and a little hoarse. "If I wasn't okay, you'd know."

The corner of his mouth twitched.

Not quite a smile.

Close.

Then his gaze dragged over her face again, down to the red blooming under her jaw, the marks he had left. His jaw clenched.

"What?" she asked, fingers brushing his temple.

He didn't look away. "I didn't like tonight."

"Me either." Her voice softened. "But we're here now."

His forehead dropped to hers. He exhaled slowly, breath catching on the way out.

"You scared me," he murmured. "I wanted to hit something. I wanted to—" He cut himself off, jaw flexing. "Then I saw you standing there in that doorway and forgot everything else."

She didn't answer.

She kissed him slowly.

He rolled to the side, pulling her with him. She went easily, settling against his chest, one leg thrown across his thigh, her hand splayed over his center as if she needed to feel his heartbeat to keep her own in rhythm.

The room was dim. The only light came from the cracked bathroom door down the hall. The apartment was still again.

She pressed closer.

His hand moved up her back, fingers tracing her spine with slow, absent care. She felt the tension flow out of him inch by inch, leaving only heat and exhaustion behind.

"Do you think it's over?" she asked quietly, already knowing the answer.

He didn't reply right away.

"I think we just turned a corner," he said finally.

His lips brushed her collarbone before he added, "Whatever happens...don't withdraw from me."

"I won't."

Her hand curled at his chest. His hand cupped the back of her head.

They stayed like that, close and still slick with sweat and sex and too many things left unsaid.

But the air between them was no longer tense.

It was real.

It was steady.

CHAPTER 20
Unseen Strings

The coffee maker hummed in the hush, steady and stubborn, like a pulse refusing to falter.

Arden sat on the edge of the couch, the hem of her robe brushing her thighs, soft cotton grounding her in the now. Outside, dawn bled into the skyline—pale gold, ghost-gray, the city's awakening fragile and borrowed.

On the counter, the rose and the card remained.

Elegant.

Menacing.

Even in stillness, the threat breathed.

In the kitchen, Gideon moved with the kind of steadiness that came from habit, not peace.

When he returned, he set two mugs on the table. The scent rose between them: fresh coffee, sharp and dark, curling like visible heat.

His eyes flicked to the card once. A shadow crossed his face, brief as a blink.

"You okay?"

The way he asked steadied her pulse. Not because she was fine, but because he would stay if she wasn't.

She wrapped her hands around the mug, let the heat bite her palms, and made herself meet his gaze.

"I will be."

It didn't sound like truth.

It sounded like a covenant.

Her thumbs traced the mug's rim. "Last night, it felt like everything was closing in...like it did back then. But this time—"

The words fractured.

Gideon didn't let them scatter.

"This time, you're not alone," he said. "You don't have to carry it anymore."

Her throat tightened. She hated how much she wanted to believe him.

The silence that followed wasn't empty. It breathed. Held room for the truth without demanding she say it out loud.

Her gaze drifted to the counter.

The rose.

The card.

Still there.

Still waiting.

Gideon's eyes followed hers. His jaw ticked, the name landing between them like a verdict.

"Sebastian."

She nodded once, slow.

"The way he looked at me—the things he said. It wasn't random. It was deliberate. He was probing. Testing for weakness."

"He was," Gideon said, his tone turning blade-sharp. "That's what he does. He studies. Watches. Waits until you start doubting your own foundation."

Her shoulders tightened, a reflex she hadn't invited.

She tightened her grip on the mug. "You think it's him? The roses, the notes—all of it?"

His silence was answer enough. His gaze pinned the card like he could dismantle it through sheer focus.

"If it's him, he's not acting alone," he said finally. "This isn't impulsive. It's designed. Someone's orchestrating this, and doing it well."

A chill traced her spine.

Not fear.

Recognition.

The kind that rang like a warning bell.

"Then we find out who," she said. "And we end it. On our terms."

Something fierce flickered in his eyes. "We will. And if it's Sebastian, or anyone else, they'll regret touching you."

He reached for her hand, his grip sure.

She leaned into the contact. It reminded her she was still here.

When he released her, the warmth didn't fade.

They rose together, mugs cleared, coats gathered.

The rose and the card stayed where they were.

Impossible to ignore.

So was the resolve in their eyes.

"We'll start with Leo," Gideon said, pulling on his coat. "If there's a leak in the system, he'll find it."

Arden slid into her jacket.

"Then let's find it."

Her gaze cut to Gideon. "What's the next move?"

He didn't hesitate. "We start with Westchester, then the Queens facility."

Each word was precise.

Surgical.

"If anything's left—records, samples, a shred of intel—we get to it before they do."

"And if it's already gone?"

The question settled heavy in her chest, all gravity and no air.

Gideon's jaw flexed once.

"Then we find where they moved it."

His knuckles brushed hers, the faintest contact, barely there.

"This isn't just about stopping them," he said, voice pitched for her alone. "It's about making sure they never get near you again."

Across the table, Leo leaned back, assessing them both with that cold precision of his. Calculating, but not unfeeling.

"I'll pull security footage from your building. Cross-check entry points. Christian's already scrubbing frame by frame, but if they slipped the cameras..." He exhaled through his nose. "Then we've got a different kind of problem."

Unbidden, the image struck her: the rose on her counter, red as accusation.

"They shouldn't have gotten that close," she said, the words edged with anger that had nowhere to go. "Not with the team outside."

Gideon's expression hardened. "Which means someone knows the blind spots."

A pause.

"Or worse," he said quietly, "someone inside is feeding them."

The air seemed to contract.

Arden's spine chilled, but she didn't fold. She knew the shape of fear; this wasn't it. This was intent—hot and low, catching at the edges.

She straightened, voice clear. "Then we find out who."

Leo rose, chair scraping against tile.

"I'll loop in Christian," he said. "Coordinate surveillance. If there's a weak link, we cut it clean."

Gideon gave a short nod. "Keep me updated. No delays."

At the door, Leo paused. His gaze softened when it found her.

"You're tougher than most people I've worked with," he said, simple truth, no decoration. "Don't let them make you forget it."

The words struck something deep, a place between hurt and belief.

"Thanks, Leo."

Her voice came hushed, but unwavering.

He nodded once, then disappeared down the hall, footsteps fading toward command rooms and monitors humming with static light.

The door clicked shut.

Silence stretched, alive with thought.

Gideon didn't look up. He reopened the file, eyes moving, shoulders tight, as if the paper might confess. In the lamplight, he looked carved from tension and intent.

Arden watched him a brief second, then reached out, fingertips grazing the inside of his wrist.

Not to stop him.

To remind him she was still here.

Still fighting.

The morning met them cold and clean, the kind of air that scraped the lungs awake.

Arden tightened her coat, the manila envelope locked between her hands. The wind caught the edges of her hair, a chill against her skin she barely registered. Leo's voice still echoed through her head, each detail from the meeting ringing like a far-off alarm she couldn't silence.

Gideon moved beside her, a shadow built for daylight. His gaze swept the street with practiced vigilance, the kind born of years spent reading danger in ordinary places. He didn't fidget. Didn't speak. Every measured step dared the dark to show itself.

"You okay?"

His voice cut through, low and steady. His hand hovered near hers, warmth radiating between them.

She met his gaze, her eyes steady though her pulse drummed beneath the surface.

"Not yet," she said. "But I will be."

He didn't press. Only let the smallest shift cross his features, the unspoken promise behind it unmistakable.

"We'll figure this out."

The words carried weight.

"Whatever it takes."

Arden's fingers tightened around the envelope. The paper's corners bit into her palms, anchoring her where fear couldn't.

"They know too much," she said softly. "About me. About Marco. About everything."

The weight of it settled again, heavy and personal.

"That's the point," Gideon replied calmly. "They want you second-guessing. Your instincts, your safety...yourself. But that's where they miscalculate."

He looked over, eyes sharp beneath the surface.

"They think fear will break you."

Arden drew a slow breath. The burn in her chest returned—not panic, but something older, tempered.

"They're wrong."

His mouth curved, voice dropping to a rasp. "Damn right they are."

They reached the car, a sleek black shape meant to disappear, though every line of it promised danger and discipline.

Gideon opened her door, movements precise and practiced. But before she could step inside, he paused, hand braced on the frame, his gaze locking on hers.

"Christian's team is closing the gaps," he said. "The net's tightening. Whatever they're planning..."

He held her eyes.

"They won't get close enough."

There was no reassurance in it.

No performance.

Just certainty.

Her throat tightened. Trust had always been the harder weapon to draw.

But she did trust him.

God help her, she did.

She nodded once and slid into the passenger seat. The leather met her palms, cool and smooth. Gideon closed the door with a soft, final click before circling to the driver's side.

The envelope lay in her lap—thin, unassuming, heavy as confession.

So much of her life had already been reduced to files and surveillance footage.

But not this.

Not her.

Whatever waited inside that facility, they would find it.

And when they did, there would be no more running.

The muffled murmur beyond the conference-room doors barely touched the tension inside.

The club was meant to be a refuge: low light, unspoken opulence, curated calm. But tonight it felt especially cold, and it wasn't the air.

Monitors bathed the walls in spectral blue, looping silent footage of concrete stairwells, narrow halls, and shifting shadows that looked too deliberate to be random.

Christian Sampson stood before the largest screen, his broad frame backlit by the flicker. Pleasantries were never his habit.

"We've combed the feeds," he said, voice deep and unhurried as he gestured toward the display. "No forced entry. No visitor logs. No elevator pings. But—"

He tapped the screen.

A still frame sharpened: an emergency stairwell door, cracked open. Shadows spilled through like smoke.

Arden stepped closer, stomach tightening.

"That door was open when I got home," she said, clipped and contained.

Christian nodded once, jaw hard. "Whoever did this knew exactly how to move. They stayed out of frame. Every camera, every blind spot. Watch."

He toggled another angle. The door eased shut again, silent.

"Calculated," he said. "Not luck. Practice."

Gideon's gaze darkened. His hands flexed once, then went still.

"What about inside?" he asked, tone low and controlled, danger threaded through.

Christian hesitated only long enough to be precise, then pulled up another feed.

The screen jumped to the faint glow of Arden's apartment.

A hooded figure stepped into frame.

No rush.

No panic.

The rose in one hand. A card in the other.

They crossed the room with the familiarity of someone who had already mapped it, knelt, placed the items with care, and left the door ajar as they slipped away.

The feed cut to black.

Silence held.

"They wanted this seen," Christian said finally, his voice stripped of its usual calm. "This wasn't a message. It was a performance."

Arden's breath hitched. She folded her arms, posture held even as the chill settled beneath her skin.

"They were in my apartment."

A whisper.

More fury than fear.

Gideon moved beside her, his hand brushing hers. Not possessive, but present.

Christian folded his arms, the stance of a man bracing for impact. "Perimeter's reinforced. Every door. Every exit. Blind spots patched. Shifts doubled. They won't get that close again."

Gideon didn't look away from the frozen screen. His voice dropped, silk over steel.

"They think they're controlling the board."

A pause.

"But that wasn't surveillance. That was a test."

He turned slightly, the monitor's glow cutting across his profile.

"They're watching how we react—timing, pressure, pattern. It's a larger play."

Arden's hands closed into fists.

"Then we stop waiting," she said, voice clear despite the tremor beneath it. "We make the next move."

Gideon's nod was sharp. Immediate.

"Christian—peel back everything. Employee records. Former security. Vendors. Contractors. Anyone with access. If there's a breadcrumb, I want it."

Christian's fingers were already moving. "On it. But we move quietly. Let them think we're rattled. That gives us cover."

The monitors flickered as data streamed.

Gideon's phone buzzed. He glanced down, eyes narrowing.

"Leo," he said, already in motion. "He's found something."

Adrenaline surged through Arden, clearing the fog and tightening her focus. She met Gideon's gaze.

"Then let's go."

❦

The drive passed in weighted silence, thick with thoughts neither of them dared to voice.

Streetlights streaked the windshield in ribbons of gold, brief flashes painting and erasing the tension on Arden's face. She sat upright, one hand braced against the door, the other locked tight in her lap. With every block, the pressure in her chest wound tighter, a coil refusing to ease.

Outside, the city whispered its usual lullaby: tires hissing on wet pavement, a siren crying somewhere far off, rain beginning to trace the glass.

None of it reached her.

Then Gideon reached over.

His fingers brushed hers. Paused. Closed around her hand.

"It's not just your fight," he said, eyes on the road. "And it's not just mine. We do this together. Every step."

His voice was low, granite-firm, but the promise beneath it vibrated like a pulse.

The touch sent a ripple through her, a stone dropped into dark water, pulling her back from the spiral.

She turned to him. Met his gaze. Her eyes, guarded for so long, softened as they held his. The weight of his words slipped past her defenses and settled somewhere deep, somewhere still unarmored.

"I know," she said at last, voice steadier than she felt. "I'm not used to leaning on anyone. I don't."

Gideon's grip tightened once, then eased.

"You don't have to," he said quietly. "Not anymore."

The air between them shifted, quieter now, charged and full of everything neither of them said.

Arden leaned back against the seat and exhaled through her nose. The tension didn't leave.

It changed shape.

Her fingers brushed the bracelet at her wrist, cold metal against skin. Gold and diamonds, beautiful as a scar. A reminder of how close danger had come and how much closer it could still get.

Rain thickened, sliding down the windshield in slow rivulets. The city blurred, thinning to quieter streets. Each turn drew them closer to Leo's office and whatever waited beyond that door.

Arden straightened, breath even, eyes clear.

She wasn't calm.

She was ready.

❦

The club's murmur dimmed behind the door. Inside, the light was low, and the evidence lay across the table like a confession: folders, printouts, a half-full coffee. Small order in a room wound tight with intent.

Leo met them at the threshold, composed as ever, though the set of his jaw and the flash in his eyes betrayed the work he had done overnight.

"Come in," he said. "We've got a lot to cover."

Monitors cast the walls in sterile gray. Footage scrolled in patient loops: stairwells, corridors, angles that seemed to be waiting for something to move.

Arden stepped forward, fingers trembling as she flipped through the pages. Images stared back at her—derelict facilities half-swallowed by vines, contracts threaded with legal traps, clinical records sterile in phrasing but saturated with consequence.

It wasn't the invasion that chilled her.

It was the intimacy of it.

The way someone had catalogued her life like a file to be opened and weaponized.

"They've been tracking you," Leo said, heat threaded through his even tone. "Not only Gideon. You. Medical files, addresses, coworkers, rotations. This is targeted."

Her grip tightened; the folder's corner bit into her palm.

"Why?" she asked. "What do they want?"

Leo didn't soften the answer.

"Control."

A pause.

"Of you. Of him. Of the Blackwell name."

He set a document on the table. A highlighted address pulled their eyes.

"The Westchester facility. Blackwell sold it years ago. Then it resurfaced under a shell—Obsidian Holdings. Dig deeper, and guess whose name sits in the shadows."

He flipped the page.

Sebastian Hawthorne.

The name crawled along Arden's spine.

"Sebastian," she whispered.

The word scraped.

"He's a spider," Leo said, voice low. "And this web reaches farther than

Blackwell. Scientists. Enablers. People like Lila and Colton. This isn't leverage—he's burning a legacy and trying to make you both go up with it."

Gideon's knuckles whitened on the table. "This stopped being business a long time ago."

A beat.

"It's personal."

Leo pushed a photograph toward them, Sebastian's name scrawled across the dossier like a verdict. Arden stared, chest tight.

"I've faced shadows before," she said, low and hard. "They never liked it when I fought back."

Something shifted in Leo's expression—respect, quick and unguarded.

"That's their mistake," he said. "I think they assumed you wouldn't still be standing."

He tapped another stack.

"But this is bigger. Evelyn's involved."

The name landed like a stone.

Evelyn.

Public smile. Private scalpel.

"She's bankrolling pieces of this," Leo continued. "Colton's her enforcer, delivering ultimatums to anyone who knows too much. But Sebastian isn't her puppet. He's weaponizing her assets. Lawyers. Scientists. Quiet hands planted inside your operations."

"He's dismantling it," Gideon said, low. "Piece by piece."

"Which is why we don't move yet," Leo replied firmly. "If we tip our hand, they vanish. Every trail gone. They'll torch it before we can stop them."

Gideon's jaw ticked.

"You want us to wait while they're in her home?"

"I want you to be smarter than them," Leo said. "Let them think they've rattled us. That gives us the edge."

Arden exhaled, sharp and reluctant. The logic was sound.

It still felt like swallowing glass.

"So we watch."

Gideon's gaze locked with hers, storm and steel.

"And when the time comes—"

"We strike," she finished.

Together.

CHAPTER 21
Shadowed Meetings

The café huddled beneath taller facades, its faded awning sagging under the rain. A muted sign swung above the door, its letters half gone, plain by design and unmarked on purpose; a forgettable face in a city that kept its truths in quieter places.

Inside, conversation moved in careful trades. Information slid across tables like contraband. Anonymity was currency.

Across the street, in a rain-slicked car, Gideon watched the door with slow, relentless focus. The windows fogged around them, streetlight smearing into fractured gold, but his eyes never left the entrance. His jaw was set hard, a faint twitch at his cheek marking the narrow margin where control had begun to fray.

Beside him, Leo sat like a predator at rest—still, alert, cataloguing exits, reflections, the angle of every shoulder inside the room. Everything in him was tuned to possibility.

In the backseat, Arden held herself like a statue, spine straight, hands folded as if guarding a secret. Her pulse thudded in time with the rain on the windshield. The city's murmur pressed at the glass, but her thoughts stayed tight and clear.

Not afraid.

Focused.

"This isn't your usual stakeout," Gideon said, his voice cutting through the hush, soft and taut. "Why drag us along?"

Leo didn't shift. His gaze slid to the rearview, catching Arden's reflection with a cold, quick appraisal.

"Because you'd be here regardless," he said. "Better to have you close than cleaning up the pieces."

He turned the mirror back to the street.

"And because she's not a bystander."

Arden straightened.

"If I'm in this," she said, voice held calmer than she felt, "I'm in it."

No plea. No performance. No explanation.

Leo's mouth twitched in approval, small and dangerous. He tipped his chin toward the café entrance.

"Good. Because this is where it starts getting messy."

The café door opened.

Three pairs of eyes shifted toward the rain-slicked figure stepping inside.

"There he is," Leo muttered, leaning forward.

Sebastian Hawthorne moved through the room with the practiced ease of a man accustomed to being watched. His tailored coat parted, revealing the rigid lines beneath. To most people, he would have read as control incarnate: refined, relaxed, quietly dangerous, always five moves ahead.

Arden watched differently.

She saw the tension threaded through his shoulders. The way his gaze clipped the room. The small, almost imperceptible tick at his jaw.

He wasn't composed.

He was bracing.

Her pulse nudged higher. Her fingertips brushed the fogged glass. "He looks...off," she said.

"Cornered," Gideon replied, low and flat. "And dangerous."

Sebastian slid into a seat by the window, arm slung over the chairback, posture too loose, too casual, as if the shape of ease alone could prove he had nothing to fear.

The door opened again.

A woman entered, and the building seemed to register the change. Her black coat framed a face carved from ice—elegant, remote, precise.

"That's her," Leo said, his tone sharpening. "Dr. Lila Whitaker."

"She's the scientist?" Arden breathed.

"More than that," Gideon said. His gaze narrowed, the word landing like a warning. "She's a player."

Sebastian's hand twitched, brief and involuntary. The first real crack in his performance.

Lila didn't react. Her stillness looked practiced, but Arden leaned forward, attention catching on the smallest betrayal.

"Look at her hands."

They watched.

Her fingers were tense. Edged. She tried to hide it and failed.

"Why now?" Gideon asked. "Why him? What's her tie to my family?"

Leo answered without pause. "She ran the research facilities your grandfather shut down. The ones with no oversight. Records that should've existed—gone. If there's a linchpin in this mess, it's her."

He nodded toward the café. "And Sebastian's either pulling the strings or—"

"Cutting them," Arden finished.

The door opened once more.

The air shifted harder, something metallic sliding through it.

A tall man entered and owned the space. Every measured step spoke of control and consequence: the coat, the shoes, the economy of movement. Someone comfortable with strategy and violence.

"Colton," Gideon said.

Flat.

A breath, nearly swallowed. Gideon's knuckles whitened.

Leo's tone sharpened. "Evelyn's enforcer."

Colton crossed the room in long, arrogant strides, his coat sweeping like a blade. The click of his shoes became a countdown.

"What's he doing here?" Arden whispered.

"Delivering a message," Leo said. "Evelyn doesn't send Colton unless she wants to drive a point home."

At the table, Sebastian straightened subtly. His shoulders stiffened; his jaw tightened. For the first time, he looked unsettled. Power was shifting, and not in his favor.

Colton said nothing. He set a sleek black envelope on the table with precise finality. His eyes held Lila's, daring her to hesitate.

She did.

Her composure cracked. Her fingers betrayed her. She reached, breath hitching, and opened it.

"What is it?" Arden asked, her voice small and sharp.

Leo adjusted the zoom on the feed.

"Leverage," he said. "Evelyn tightened the screws."

Color drained from Lila's face. The envelope's contents folded her composure inward like a snapped wire. Pages creased beneath her trembling grip, and the room seemed to constrict around her.

Sebastian's face darkened. He shot Colton a glance edged with fury, his mask splintering at the seams.

Colton, by contrast, leaned back, untroubled. The faint curve of his mouth was mockery.

"What's his angle?" Arden demanded.

Gideon didn't look away. "Evelyn's. He's here to remind them who's in charge."

"Or force their hand," Leo said. "This is control, not theatre."

Colton rose. One last adjustment of his coat. A final look at Lila. Then he pushed through the door and vanished into the drizzle as if nothing had happened.

Lila stayed frozen, the envelope clutched to her chest. Her eyes flicked to Sebastian—pleading, frightened, tethered to leverage she couldn't outrun.

Sebastian leaned forward, expression venomous.

"Evelyn's tightening her grip," Gideon said. "She wants them to know she's watching."

Leo started the car. "We've seen what we need. Move before they know we were watching."

As they pulled away, Arden peered through the rain at the café window. Sebastian sat straighter now, spine taut, gaze cast outward and scanning.

Hunting.

There was a flinch in his stare, a small, sudden narrowing, as if some animal part of him had felt them slip away.

"He's unraveling," Leo muttered, hands firm on the wheel.

"And that's what we need," Gideon said.

Rain swallowed the café.

Arden leaned back, the storm in her chest sharpening into fierce awareness. This wasn't only Evelyn.

It was all of them.

Gideon's hand found hers briefly. Presence without promises.

"Then we take them down," he said, low and certain.

"One by one."

Arden's pulse quickened. The images from the café still flickered behind her eyes: Lila's composure splintering, Colton's surgical dominance, Sebastian's fury barely held beneath the skin.

Then something outside caught her attention.

A figure stood beneath a flickering lamppost across the street.

Still. Unmoving.

The hood shadowed his face, reducing him to something more silhouette than man, a ghost cut against the city's restless pulse. He didn't belong there.

And he didn't care who noticed.

"Leo." Arden's voice cut through the stillness as she pointed. "We're not the only ones watching."

Leo followed her gaze, posture snapping taut. Across the street, the hooded figure tilted his head, slow and deliberate.

A predator acknowledging another in the dark.

Arden's breath caught. It wasn't the stare that chilled her; it was the calm. The calculated stillness of someone who wanted to be seen.

A warning dressed as witness.

Then, without urgency, the man turned and melted into the passing crowd.

No rush. No trace.

The silence in the car thickened until it buzzed.

"Who the hell was that?" Arden asked, eyes locked on the empty patch of pavement.

Gideon's gaze swept the street, his voice a low rumble. "Someone who doesn't belong."

He turned toward Leo. "Did you get him?"

Leo shook his head, clipped. "Not cleanly. But that wasn't random. He moved like training, not instinct. He wasn't passing through."

Arden leaned forward, the knot in her chest hardening into something colder. "Was he watching us—or them?"

Leo didn't blink. "Both. But that kind of stillness? That's not intimidation. That's data collection."

Surveillance.

The leather creaked beneath Gideon's tightening grip on the wheel. His voice stayed clear, stripped to iron.

"Then let them watch."

A pause. Low. Certain.

"We'll be ready when they think they've seen enough."

Rain trailed the windows as the city blurred past in liquid motion. A dense silence settled inside the car.

Arden watched the world dissolve beyond the glass. Streetlights melted into gold ribbons. Faceless crowds disappeared into mist. Her thoughts refused to slow: Sebastian's performance, Lila's shaking hands, Colton's precise cruelty. Each detail looped back on itself, a tightening thread in a web whose edges she could no longer see.

Beside her, Gideon drove in silence, his face shadowed, his jaw working in a slow rhythm. Practiced calm. The faint tic at his temple betrayed everything beneath it.

She hesitated, then said softly, "You okay?"

His reply came after a pause, measured as a trigger pull.

"I will be," Gideon said, hands tight on the wheel, "if we get ahead of them."

Leo's voice cut clean through the charged quiet. "Colton showing up means Evelyn's paying attention. She's not letting Sebastian steer this, but don't mistake that for loyalty."

Arden's gaze flicked between them, her chest tightening around the question she couldn't shake.

"And the man outside?" Her voice carried more edge than she intended. "Who's he working for?"

Leo leaned forward, eyes sharp as glass. "That's the question. But if he's tracking us, we've rattled someone."

A beat.

"And that's leverage—if we use it before they do."

The tires hissed over wet pavement, the city thinning into rain.

Inside the car, the silence didn't return.

It recalibrated.

Heavier.

More aware.

Sebastian stood at the penthouse window. Rain carved ragged rivers down the glass, fracturing the city into a glittering, jagged mosaic.

In his hand, a photograph: Arden in the rain, hair plastered to her face, chin lifted.

Unbowed.

Defiance clung to her like a second skin.

"She doesn't see it yet," he murmured, voice low, reverent with dark hunger. "But she will."

The café replayed in his mind. Colton's arrival had irritated him—sharp, disruptive—yet useful all the same. Evelyn's paranoia was swelling around her empire like rising water. Let it. He would twist her fear into fuel. Let her tighten the noose until she felt its bite and mistook the pressure for control.

Evelyn was chaos he could manage.

Arden was not.

Arden was weather. Fire. Power without apology. She did not clutch at control the way Evelyn did; she embodied it. She didn't belong to Gideon. She would never belong to anyone.

A slow smile spread across his face, cold and precise. The kind that planned ten moves ahead and never touched the stain.

By tomorrow night, the Blackwell world would begin to splinter.

Arden would see Gideon plain: a man wrapped in loyalty to disguise fear, conviction worn as camouflage, unworthy of her fire.

"And me?" he whispered, setting the photograph down with careful fingers. "I'm the only one who understands her."

His gaze shifted to the single crimson rose beside the sleek black envelope. The weight of what came next settled over him like thunder.

Every turn had been measured. Every thread pulled with intent.

He lifted the envelope. The penthouse seemed to hold its breath.

The rose waited—left or forgotten; it made no difference.

"Soon," he said, the word swallowed by the storm. "She'll see. She'll see everything."

The rain followed them home. It tapped against the loft windows in uneven rhythm, a soft percussion filling the silence Arden had left behind.

Gideon stood at the kitchen counter, the city's glow cutting a thin line across the room. His coat hung over the back of a chair, forgotten. The coffee beside him had long gone cold.

He should have felt relief. They had made it through another night, another strike without loss.

The unease wouldn't settle.

Every detail from the café replayed in fragments: Sebastian's calm, Lila's terror, Colton's smirk, the man beneath the lamppost.

Watching.

Waiting.

Gideon dragged a hand across his face. This wasn't exhaustion from lack of sleep. It was the weight of carrying too much truth and still not having enough to stop what came next.

On the table, the file Leo had given him lay open, pages splayed like wounds. Names. Dates. Coordinates. Every thread looped back to a single point.

Her.

Arden.

He didn't need to look at the photograph tucked inside the folder; he already knew the expression she wore. Determined. Tired. Unbreakable.

"She doesn't deserve this," he said quietly, to no one but the city's hum.

The words tasted like failure.

He closed the folder and pressed his palm to its cover, grounding himself in the decision he had already made.

They were closing in. Sebastian. Evelyn. Whoever that man in the shadows was. And Gideon could no longer afford to keep playing defense.

By morning, he would move first.

Whatever the cost.

Outside, the storm deepened, thunder rolling like distant artillery. Gideon reached for his jacket, movements controlled.

Surgical.

If Sebastian wanted a war, he'd get one.

But not the kind he expected.

CHAPTER 22
Shadowed Sanctuary

The city blurred through rain-dappled glass as Arden stepped from the car, drizzle brushing her skin like a whisper. For a breath, a single borrowed moment, the chaos receded. No messages. No threats. Only the hush of water against pavement and the faint hum of a city exhaling around her.

Washington Square shimmered ahead, hushed and glistening. Wet cobblestones caught the amber glow of streetlamps, light pooling in puddles like spilled gold. At the far end of the square, the arch had begun to glow—pale against the gathering gray, its lights not yet fully awake.

She drew her coat closer at the collar, eyes tracing the edges of the square until they found the small storefront tucked into the far corner.

A single lantern burned in the window, spilling warmth across the slick sidewalk.

The bookstore.

Warm light. A battered door. A flicker of life behind glass.

She crossed the square with purpose, boots tapping a steady rhythm against stone. The bell above the door chimed softly as she entered, and the scent of aged paper, cedarwood, and leather rose to meet her like memory. It was the kind of smell that settled into the bones.

Safe.

Familiar.

She didn't need a plan. Her fingers wandered the shelves on instinct, skimming spines without reading titles. This wasn't escape, exactly. It was rhythm. Texture. Proof the world still held quiet things. Solid things. Stories that waited without asking anything from her first.

A worn paperback caught her eye, its corners softened by use, its cover dulled by time. She lifted it, letting the weight settle in her hands. Another followed, a slim novel bound in red thread, its title echoing the half-forgotten songs her mother used to hum.

At the counter, the shopkeeper greeted her with an unguarded smile. Their exchange was brief. Gentle.

One of those small mercies you don't know you need until it finds you.

When Arden stepped back into the rain, a small paper bag tucked beneath her arm, something inside her had stilled.

Not the fear. Not the fury.

Only the part of her that needed to breathe.

The drizzle kissed her skin as she crossed the square, her breath fogging in the cold. Figures drifted along the paths, umbrellas bobbing, voices softened by rain and distance, until the fountain's faint rhythm swallowed sound and a shape cut through the mist.

A lean, familiar silhouette.

Standing beyond the fountain, where the air shimmered with ghost-thin ribbons of water.

He didn't bother to hide. Didn't step back when someone passed behind him.

Chad Dawson.

The smirk gave him away before the light did: curled, venomous, practiced.

He did not belong here. Not in her space. Not in her city.

Arden stopped mid-stride, pulse spiking against her ribs. The paper bag creaked beneath her tightening grip. He stood still, arms loose, head tilted, watching her with the easy confidence of someone who had mistaken proximity for power.

A threat draped in familiarity.

The instinct to run flared hot and fast.

She smothered it.

She was done running.

Straightening, she let the rain bead on her lashes and soak through her coat. Step by step, she closed the distance—not reckless, not careless, leaving enough space for the crowd to stay between them.

"Arden."

His voice sliced through the drizzle. Too loud. Too cheerful.

Mocking.

She froze, and the fragile quiet inside her shattered.

Chad spread his arms like a performer taking his cue. The smirk widened, brittle and knowing.

"Well, well, if it isn't my favorite nurse-turned-bartender."

Her stomach twisted, but she didn't move.

"Chad." Her voice stayed flat. Clipped. "What are you doing here?"

He shrugged, exaggerated beneath the lamplight. "Living the dream. Big Apple, bright lights. Thought I'd check in on an old friend."

"Cut the bullshit." Her tone cut clean through the rain. "Why are you really here?"

The grin faltered, then re-formed, smaller and sharper. He stepped closer, voice dropping to a low hiss.

"Just here to give you a friendly warning."

Her fingers clenched around the paper bag, the edge biting into her palm. "What kind of warning?"

He leaned in, not touching, but close enough to claim the air between them. Rain streamed down his face; he didn't blink.

"You think Blackwell's your white knight," he whispered, acid-soft. "Think again. He's the next ghost who'll leave you bleeding."

Her pulse kicked, anger flaring bright. "You don't know a damn thing about him."

"Oh, but I do." The smile returned—mean, sardonic. "I know what he's hiding. I know what it'll cost you."

She said nothing.

The silence stretched. Taut. Dangerous.

He moved closer. "You're not untouchable, Arden. And neither is he. The Blackwells are rotten. Money built on the backs of others. One good shove and the whole tree falls."

Her throat tightened. Not fear—precision. Gideon's family. The aim was surgical.

"What are you talking about?" she asked, the words slicing through the rain.

Chad tilted his head, mock-pity gleaming in his eyes. "Well, let's just say... you might want to start packing. That club you love so much? It won't be yours for long. Not once everything comes to light."

Thunder cracked overhead, sudden and close.

Arden didn't flinch.

Chad stepped back with that same knowing smirk, then turned and walked into the dark, unhurried. No look back. A man confident in the damage he'd done.

Arden stood motionless, rain running cold down her face. Her pulse roared in her ears, louder than the storm. The city blurred to color and noise around her.

But his words—

They stayed razor-sharp.

The car eased to a stop outside Gideon's place, rain showering lightly against the windows like the city whispering secrets it didn't want overheard.

Arden stepped into the mist, cool air clinging to her skin. She drew her coat tighter, but the damp that followed her inside wasn't from the weather. It was Chad's voice, still curling like smoke through her thoughts.

Inside, Gideon's hand brushed lightly against her back as he guided her through the doorway. The warmth of the house closed around her, wrapping her in something almost like memory.

She crossed to the kitchen and set the small paper bag from the bookstore carefully on the counter, needing the ordinary weight of it. Something solid. Something real.

"Arden."

His voice cut through the barrage of thoughts torturing her.

She turned. He stood a few steps away, gaze sharp.

"You're distracted," he said. Not accusing. Observant.

Her fingers traced the edge of the counter before she looked up. "Chad...I saw him tonight."

The change in Gideon was subtle. A coil drawn tighter beneath the surface. "Where?"

"Washington Square. He said he was 'checking in on an old friend,' but he knew things—where I work, where I live. It wasn't random."

Gideon's jaw hardened. His fingers flexed once, then curled into tight fists. "Do you think he's working with someone?"

She nodded. "Chad couldn't have orchestrated anything like this alone. But someone's feeding him information. Someone who wants me to remember how easily they can get close."

"Sebastian."

The name landed like a blade.

Arden's breath caught. She nodded once.

"He said something else." Her voice thinned, low and controlled. "About you. Called you my 'knight in shining armor.' Then said you're worse than I realize."

The air between them shifted, pressure rising like static before a strike.

Gideon stepped closer. No anger in his eyes. Only truth, honed to steel.

"Don't let him in your head," he said. "Doubt is how they work. You know me. You've seen me, Arden. All of me."

"I know."

The conviction surprised her.

The chill in her chest did not.

"Still," she said quietly, "they're not going to stop, are they?"

He didn't reach for false comfort. Only her hand, solid and real.

"No," he said. "But neither will we."

The steadiness in his tone felt like a brace.

Arden straightened, her pulse settling into rhythm with his resolve. "We need a plan. First thing tomorrow—Christian, Leo, all of it. We move fast."

Gideon's mouth curved slightly, that shadow of a smile that passed for tenderness.

"Agreed. But tonight..."

He reached for the cabinet and pulled down two glasses.

"Tonight, we regroup. Tomorrow, we fight."

The aromatic pour of bourbon filled the room, rich and low. He slid a glass across the counter.

"To tomorrow," he said, lifting his.

Arden hesitated a breath, then met his glass with her own.

The crystal chime rang through the stillness, clean and sharp.

She took a sip. The bourbon trailed heat down her throat, blooming warm in her chest.

Then, softly—

"We should forget all of it," she said, a ghost of a smile tugging at her lips as she leaned back against the counter. "For tonight. No plans. No threats. No ghosts. Just us. A break."

Gideon's gaze lingered, reading the plea threaded through her words. Not escape from danger, but from vigilance.

Without breaking eye contact, he reached for the bottle and poured again, unhurried and sure. Then he lifted a brow, the edge of a smile softening his otherwise hard features.

"Forget everything?" he echoed, voice low, teasing. "You think that's possible?"

"Why not?" She raised her glass. "We could start by warming up. A hot bath sounds like heaven after being soaked in the rain."

His gaze swept over her, a faint glint of mischief sparking. "That does sound like a good idea."

Before she could reply, his arms slipped beneath her, lifting her off the floor in one smooth motion.

"Gideon!" she gasped, laughter breaking through the last remnants of tension as her arms flew around his neck. "What are you doing?"

"Helping you forget," he said, already carrying her down the hall, that small smirk deepening.

"I can walk, you know."

"I'm aware." His tone softened, threaded with warmth. "But you're already in my arms. Seems inefficient to stop now."

She shook her head, but the weight of the night had already begun to slide from her shoulders.

In the bathroom, he set her down on the edge of the tub and turned to the faucet. Steam unfurled through the room in delicate ribbons as the basin filled. He tested the temperature, then leaned back against the counter, his gaze never leaving hers.

"You don't have to do all this," she said, brushing a damp strand behind her ear.

"I know," he murmured. "But why would I stop now?"

His fingers found the hem of her shirt—gentle, unhurried—and eased the damp fabric away. She shivered, though not from the cold. His gaze moved over her with focused hunger, the kind that studied before it touched.

"Really," she managed, lighter now. "I've got this."

He paused, fingertips brushing her collarbone as the shirt slipped free.

"And I've got you," he said softly. "No harm in being thorough."

She laughed under her breath, the last thread of protest dissolving. "You're incorrigible."

"And you're perfect."

The words landed without charm or pretense. Her breath caught as she searched his face for irony and found none.

He helped her out of her jeans without hurry, every movement patient, every touch chosen. There was heat in it, but not haste; desire held in the careful discipline of his hands.

When she stepped into the bath, warmth gathered around her in slow waves, drawing a sigh from deep in her chest. Water cradled her body, steam blurring the room until every hard edge softened. For the first time all night, she let herself sink.

Gideon crouched beside the tub, one hand resting along the porcelain rim.

"Better?" he asked, hushed.

She nodded, voice loose now. "Much. Thank you."

He lingered a heartbeat longer, gaze moving over her face as if checking the places no bruise could show. Then he stood.

"I'll be right outside," he said quietly. "Call if you need anything."

Before he could move, she dipped her hand into the water and flicked a splash his way.

Droplets struck his shirt, darkening the fabric in scattered bursts.

He blinked once, feigning outrage. "What was that for?"

She tilted her head, a grin ghosting her lips.

"Your clothes are already wet," she said, voice light and threaded with mischief. "Might as well take them off and join me."

His brows lifted. A slow smirk curved his mouth as he leaned in, palms braced on the tub's edge, the space between them humming.

"You're bold tonight, Arden."

"Think I can't handle you?"

The question hung between them, teasing and dangerous.

His gaze sharpened, reverence flickering behind the amusement.

Then, slowly, he straightened, reached for the hem of his shirt, and pulled it over his head. The fabric clung for a heartbeat before sliding free, leaving him bare beneath the soft gold light.

Her breath caught.

The moment bent around it.

"You're serious," he said quietly, undoing his belt.

She leaned back into the water, steam blurring the outline of her body.

"Completely."

He didn't rush. He never did. Every motion was measured, precise—a man built for control, choosing when to surrender it. When he stepped into the tub, the water rose between them, warm and restless.

The space felt smaller now. Denser. Steam curled against their skin like breath.

Her toes brushed his leg beneath the surface. The contact sent a shiver through her, subtle but undeniable.

"See?" she murmured. "Much better."

Gideon's low laugh rippled through the air—rough, indulgent. His fingers found hers beneath the water, their hands tangling in silence.

"You might be right," he said.

The playfulness softened into something slower. Quieter. Not less charged, only deeper; fire settling into coals.

He didn't pull her closer. Didn't push. He simply held her hand, his thumb tracing the faint line of her pulse. The restraint was its own kind of intimacy.

Arden felt the stillness stretch, not hesitant but full. The room steamed around them; her guard melted by degrees.

"Thank you," she whispered. "For giving me space...and not letting me spiral."

His eyes lifted to hers, clear as ever.

"Always."

He didn't add more.

She could feel it in the way he held her hand. In the way he waited. In the way he didn't ask her to come closer—but made her want to anyway.

The water had cooled, its warmth lingering only in the closeness between them. Gideon's fingers brushed hers beneath the surface, a faint smile tugging at the corner of his mouth as he leaned in and pressed a kiss to her forehead.

"We should get out before we both freeze," he murmured, voice low and roughened by amusement.

Arden tilted her head back, her grin softening around something tender. "Fine. But only if you promise I won't immediately regret leaving this cocoon."

He chuckled, rising first. The water rippled as he moved, steam curling from his skin. She watched him reach for a towel, muted light catching the carved lines of his frame. Her breath hitched for a second before he turned and held it open for her.

"Not a chance," he said, warm. Teasing.

She stepped into it, and his hands wrapped the fabric around her with careful, comforting intimacy. That same tenderness followed them into the bedroom, where the chill in the air faded and the weight of the day began, at last, to loosen its grip.

Gideon pulled back the covers. Arden slipped beneath them, sheets cool against her skin, hair spilling across the pillow. He joined her moments later, the mattress dipping gently under his weight.

For a while, they lay in silence, breathing the same hush, wrapped in the same calm.

She turned toward him, studying the shape of his face in the dim light. "This feels...strange," she murmured. "Like nothing else matters."

His hand found hers between them, fingers brushing before they threaded together. "It doesn't," he said. "Not here. Not now."

A small smile ghosted across her lips. "You're dangerous, you know. Making me believe in moments like this."

His thumb traced slow arcs along her hand. "What do you want, Arden?" he asked, tone low and edged with challenge.

The question caught her off guard. Her breath hitched, and the truth rose before she could temper it.

"I don't know," she whispered. "Peace. Stability. Maybe even...a future I can't quite picture yet."

His gaze didn't waver. "Then that's what you'll have," he said simply. "Whatever you want. However you want it."

The weight of his words settled around her, unshakable.

She didn't answer. Instead, she leaned in, resting her forehead against his shoulder. His arm came around her, firm and sure, drawing her close until his warmth sank into her skin.

The silence that followed wasn't empty. It was full of breath and heat and all the things they hadn't yet said; full of something real taking root between them.

"I love you," she murmured, so soft it could have been mistaken for breath.

But he heard it.

Of course he did.

Gideon stilled. Then his hold tightened.

She had only said it once before, but this time it landed differently—truth finding its echo.

When she lifted her head, his eyes were waiting.

"I know," he said quietly, a faint smile catching at his mouth. "I love you too."

The simplicity of it was a revelation.

She breathed in the rawness of him.

The world could wait.

For now, there was only this.

Arden smiled into his skin, her breath warm against his collarbone. The words had already been spoken—the I love yous, the promises, the ache between them threaded with something heavier than lust.

But when Gideon shifted beside her, when his hand slid from hers and skimmed slowly up her thigh beneath the sheets, she knew this wasn't over.

Not yet.

Not when there was still fire under her skin. Not when he was still watching her like that.

She didn't need coaxing. She was already lit.

"Still cold?" he murmured, voice roughened by the weight of her name in his throat.

"No," she breathed. "But I still want you."

Something dark flickered in his eyes. Hunger. Possession tempered by reverence. The raw pull of a man who didn't only love her, but needed her and knew the danger of needing anything that much.

He kissed her like he knew exactly how she liked it: deep, slow, possessive. The kind of kiss that stole her breath and replaced it with his.

Their bodies moved easily together now, with no awkward fumbling, no tentative searching. Only muscle memory and raw need. His hands on her hips. Her mouth at his neck. His voice dropping into a low growl when she dragged her nails over his shoulder blades and shifted beneath him, legs locking around his waist.

This wasn't soft. It wasn't slow. This was desperation barely held in check; familiar and primal, tenderness burning hot enough to bruise.

Her back arched as he pressed into her, his breath ragged at her ear.

"Look at me," he said, voice hoarse.

She did.

Eyes open. Bodies locked. Not only skin to skin, but something deeper, the terrible intimacy of being known and choosing it anyway.

It was a claiming, yes, but never possession. Recognition. Rhythm. Rightness.

The tempo built fast, stuttering with need. Her moan caught around his name. His grip tightened at her hips, hard enough to leave proof.

She shattered first, the wave breaking over her mid-thrust, hands clenched in the sheets, her whole body trembling beneath him.

He followed, a low, guttural sound tearing from him, her name like a benediction on his tongue.

And then...stillness.

Their chests rose and fell in tandem, sweat cooling on their skin. He didn't move to pull away. He stayed wrapped around her, inside her, his face buried against her neck as if the world could end beyond that room and he would still choose this last breath against her pulse.

"I'll never get tired of this," she whispered.

"Of me?" he asked.

She smiled. "Of us."

His lips curved where they brushed her skin.

"Good," he said. "Because I'm just getting started."

Arden didn't have time to answer.

He rolled them in one smooth, practiced motion, her back meeting the mattress with a soft gasp as he settled between her legs again. Not heavy, but undeniable. Absolute.

His mouth was already at her neck, warm and urgent, as though her skin had asked a question and he meant to answer with every breath. His stubble scraped gently across her collarbone, his tongue following the burn. She arched beneath him, and he groaned low, the sound vibrating through her chest.

"I mean it," he murmured, fingers sliding down her side. "I'm not done with you. Not until I relearn every part of you."

"I haven't changed," she whispered, though her voice trembled as his palm cupped the underside of her breast.

"Wrong." His thumb traced a slow circle around her nipple, watching it tighten beneath his touch. "You're softer here." He kissed the place between her ribs. "Tighter here." His hand slipped between her thighs, spreading her gently, reverently. "And wetter than I've ever felt you."

She gasped, and his mouth curved.

He kissed her then, deep and claiming, all tongue and heat and need. She clawed at his back, her legs falling open beneath him, and the moment his fingers curled inside her, she moaned into his mouth.

He was wrecking her.

Already.

Again.

And he wasn't finished.

He withdrew his hand and lifted it to her mouth, two fingers glistening with her arousal. "Look at this," he rasped. "You're dripping for me."

She kissed his fingers, sucked them into her mouth, and watched his control fracture.

"Fuck, Arden." His voice cracked. He reached down, guiding the thick length of himself to her entrance. Just the tip—slow, deliberate, torturing them both.

She rocked her hips up. "Gideon."

"I know." He pressed forward slowly, devastating in his control. The stretch was exquisite. "I've got you."

He filled her inch by inch, groaning as her body took him in. The connection hit hard, sudden as a jolt. They both froze, trembling beneath the gravity of it.

"God, you feel so fucking good," he growled against her throat. "So perfect. So mine."

"Then take me," she whispered, legs wrapping around his hips. "Make me forget everything but this."

And he did.

He moved inside her with punishing grace, each long, rolling thrust stroking deep, dragging pleasure through every nerve until the world narrowed to his body, his breath, the brutal tenderness of his hands. His fingers found her wrists and pinned them above her head. His mouth hovered over hers, breath hot, as he fucked her into the mattress.

"Yes," she gasped, already close again. "Don't hold back."

And he didn't.

He unleashed every ounce of tension still burning in his muscles, every broken whisper she had ever given him, every second they had spent apart. He drove into her until she cried out, raw and glorious, her body arching to meet him.

When she shattered again—hot, clenching, pulsing around him—he kept moving, grinding deeper until his release slammed through him like a wave.

He spilled inside her with a sound that was half curse, half confession. Even then, he didn't stop moving. Not when loving her felt like the only thing still tethering him to the earth.

Even after he came. Even after she shattered.

He stayed buried inside her, hips grinding slow and deep, like he was trying to memorize how it felt to be home. His forehead pressed to hers, breath hot against her lips. Their skin was slick. Her thighs trembled.

"Still with me?" he murmured, voice ruined. Hoarse and low and barely holding on.

She nodded, breath hitching when he rolled his hips again—slow, teasing, deep enough to destroy. "I don't think I ever left."

His laugh broke against her cheek, barely more than breath. He kissed her jaw, her mouth, her neck, until she writhed beneath him again.

"Gideon..." Her voice was raw, rasped open. "I'm not done."

"I know." He dragged his tongue down the curve of her neck, tasting the sweat at her collarbone. "I can feel it."

His fingers slipped between them, finding her again—swollen and sensitive, but still greedy for him.

"You're still begging."

And God help her, she was.

Every inch of her strained toward him. Every gasp turned into a moan. And when he started moving again in earnest—deeper, harder, without pretense—she sobbed his name like a prayer, all vowels and need and unfiltered ache.

"You want more?" he rasped, voice shaking with restraint he no longer had.

"Yes," she gasped, nails scoring his back. "God, yes."

He grabbed her thigh, pushed it higher on his waist, and started driving into her, unforgiving and relentless. The bed jolted with every thrust, the sound of skin and breath and sweat crashing through the room. She met him stroke for stroke, wild and wanton and completely undone.

"You're mine," he growled, fucking her deeper. "Say it."

"I'm yours," she sobbed. "Gideon—I'm yours. I always have been—"

He kissed her then, hard and brutal, all teeth and tongue and adoration.

He didn't only want her to come; he needed it. Needed to feel her break beneath him one more time. Needed the proof of her pleasure, the surrender she chose and the trust it cost her to give.

When his thumb found her clit again—slick, fast, perfect—she exploded.

Her entire body clenched, locking around him as the orgasm ripped through her in wave after violent wave. She shook. She cried out. She shattered, and he followed her straight into the dark.

He came again, deeper this time, with a guttural sound ripped from his chest like it cost him. His whole body convulsed, muscles trembling, head buried in the crook of her neck. Messy. Raw. So fucking real.

And still, neither of them let go.

THEY DIDN'T MOVE for a long time.

Not because they couldn't, but because neither of them wanted to.

Their bodies stayed tangled, sweat-damp and flushed, his chest rising against hers in erratic pulses. She felt every heartbeat, every exhale, every aftershock still flickering low in her core. Her leg remained hooked around his waist. He was still inside her—softening, but not gone.

Not even close.

Gideon's hand skimmed up her side, fingertips tracing the ridges of each rib like a path he could follow blind. His ragged breath brushed her temple.

"You okay?" he murmured, voice so gravel-rough it barely made it out of his throat.

She didn't answer right away. Then she shifted her hips a fraction.

He groaned.

"Was," she said, lips brushing his collarbone. "And now I want more."

He pulled back to look at her, gray eyes blown dark, hair a mess, jaw tense like he was still holding himself together by threads. "Arden..."

"I'm serious." Her fingers skimmed his ribs, slow and dangerous. "I don't want sweet. I don't want careful. I want to come apart again, and I want it from you."

That broke him.

He surged forward, crashing their mouths together in a kiss made of tongue and teeth and desperation. There was no finesse this time. Only need. Filthy, aching, addictive need.

Her fingers tangled in his dark hair, tugging hard enough to make him growl.

"You drive me crazy," he breathed against her mouth, already hardening between them again. "Do you know that?"

She rolled her hips, grinding against him without shame. "Good."

He caught her wrists and pinned them above her head, forearms bracketing her face. "You want to be reckless tonight?" he asked, voice low and guttural, his cock sliding slick and heavy between her thighs.

Her eyes glittered with challenge. "I want to feel something that isn't fear."

That undid him.

He let go of her wrists and pushed her thighs apart again, rougher this time, gripping the backs of them and spreading her open until she cried out. Then he drove into her—fast, hard, deep.

It was collision. Every word they hadn't said. Every threat they couldn't outrun. Every brutal inch of the night turned into heat and motion and her name broken in his mouth.

He pounded into her, hands gripping her thighs hard enough to bruise. She arched beneath him, hands scrambling for purchase on his back, the sheets, her own hair—anything to hold on while he took her exactly the way she had asked him to.

The sound of him filled the room: grunts, curses, breathless growls of her name.

"Harder," she gasped. "Please, Gideon...don't stop—"

"Never," he bit out, snapping his hips against hers. "I'll give you everything."

And he did.

With every brutal thrust. Every filthy whisper. Every graze of his teeth at her throat. He gave her the heat, the pressure, the beautiful violence of wanting without fear, and when she came with a strangled cry, nails raking down his back, her body clamped around him—tight, pulsing, wringing him dry.

Still, he chased it.

Chased her.

Until he was shaking above her, thrusting deep one last time as his release hit him.

They collapsed together, breathless and broken and whole in the same damn breath. But even then, even in the wreckage, his hand slid to her hip. His mouth pressed to her shoulder.

He didn't let her go.

Arden was already moving—bold, unbothered, and starving for him. She shifted, climbing into his lap with a slow grace that made Gideon groan through clenched teeth. Her thighs bracketed his hips as she settled over him again, her hair falling in wild waves around her face, down her shoulders, across her back like a crown undone.

She didn't wait.

Not for permission. Not for breath.

She reached between them, gripping him—hard, hot, thick—and guided him inside her. They both gasped as she sank down, inch by inch, her body taking him with a slow, sinful rhythm that made his head fall back and his hands clench in the sheets.

"Fuck, Arden..." His voice cracked, completely wrecked. "Look at you."

She did. Through heavy lashes, she met his gaze, flushed and fierce, all bright eyes and parted lips. Her breath was already breaking, but her movements were steady, grinding down on him with a slow roll of her hips that left them both trembling.

Gideon's hands found her thighs, then slid up to grip her waist as she rode him—harder, needier, every shift of her body dragging another curse from his throat.

"You're unreal," he rasped, watching her with open hunger, eyes dark and ravenous. He reached up and cupped her breasts, thumbs brushing her nipples before he pinched them gently, rolling the sensitive peaks between his fingers until she cried out and arched into his touch.

Her rhythm stuttered, then surged. She chased it, taking everything he gave and giving it back twice as hard.

His eyes rolled back as her pace quickened, wet heat and clenched muscle dragging him to the edge. "You're going to undo me," he growled, one hand sliding to her ass, gripping, guiding her, encouraging every shameless grind.

She leaned forward, palms braced on his chest, her hair falling over her shoulders like silk. "Then let go," she whispered against his mouth. "Fall with me."

"Greedy girl," he breathed against her throat, teeth grazing her skin. "You don't ride me like that unless you want me to lose it."

"Lose it," she gasped, voice ragged and defiant, eyes flashing with the kind of challenge that begged to be met.

Gideon's breath caught, then snapped.

In one swift, primal motion, he gripped her hips and rolled, flipping her beneath him with a growl that rumbled from deep in his chest. The mattress jolted beneath the shift, and before she could so much as gasp, he drove back into her in a single, ruthless thrust.

She cried out, head thrown back, thighs clamping around him as he filled her again—deeper, sharper, the angle brutal in the best way.

"Don't pretend to be surprised when I fuck you like you asked for," he rasped against her throat, his mouth dragging fire across her skin.

His hands pinned hers above her head, fingers laced tight as his hips snapped harder, demanding and deliciously unrelenting. He claimed her with each thrust, every stroke of his body a declaration she felt in her bones.

And still, she met him there.

She dragged her teeth along his jaw, moaned his name like a curse, a prayer, a promise.

He grunted into her mouth, fingers slipping between them again, circling her clit with tight, devastating precision.

"Come for me, baby," he demanded, voice dark and trembling.

She shattered again.

Harder this time.

Screaming his name as her body clenched around him, pulsing, spasming, dragging him over the edge with her. His rhythm faltered, hips stuttering as he came with a strangled groan, spilling into her with a shudder that rocked them both.

They collapsed, tangled in sweat and breath and limbs that couldn't let go.

Still joined. Still wrecked. Still burning.

And neither of them even thought about stopping.

THEY STAYED TANGLED LONG after the storm inside them quieted—limbs knotted beneath rumpled sheets, slick skin cooling by slow degrees. His chest rose and fell against her back, one arm draped over her waist as if he didn't trust the world to let her go.

Arden's breath was still uneven. Not from the pace, though her body hummed from the way he had pushed her to the edge and held her there, but from everything that had spilled between them. The heat. The ache. The silent, reverent way he had looked at her afterward.

Not like a man who had conquered.

Like a man who had come undone.

She found his hand beneath the covers and laced her fingers through his. "We should sleep," she whispered.

Gideon pressed a kiss to her shoulder. "We should," he said, but didn't move.

They didn't speak again.

Eventually, the night took them both.

CHAPTER 23

Storms Within and Without

The scent of dark roast pulled Arden from sleep before the light did.

She blinked into the late-morning haze, the warmth of the sheets no match for the slow thrum beneath her skin or the delicious ache lingering low in her belly. Every stretch reminded her where his hands had been, how many times he had made her come. Her thighs carried the memory with every shift of linen.

A laugh slipped free, equal parts soreness and satisfaction.

Downstairs, the muted clatter of dishes broke the hush, followed by Gideon's voice from the hallway.

"Leo's here. Dining room in ten."

She groaned and flopped back into the pillows. "Cruel, cruel man."

"I made coffee," he called back, far too smug for someone already dressed.

"That better be code for espresso and an apology."

She dragged herself upright, muscles humming in protest. The sheet pooled around her waist. Her hair was chaos, her body wrecked in the most pleasant ways, and still, she couldn't summon a shred of regret.

"Black. Two sugars," he said, footsteps fading.

Arden smirked and reached for her robe. Whatever spell last night had cast had softened with the morning, but its echo remained—in her bones, between her thighs, in the way the world felt marginally more survivable.

And now—

Time to face the fallout.

Rain streaked down the tall windows of Gideon's dining room, its patter a fragile counterpoint to the pressure mounting inside. The table between them had become a war room, strewn with files, photographs, and documents stamped with the Blackwell name. Each page felt like a ghost from a legacy Gideon had spent years trying to exorcise.

Leo's fingers moved over his laptop keys, the rhythm sharp against the hush. Without looking up, he slid a photograph across the polished wood.

"Chad Dawson and Dylan Tate," he said. "Taken two weeks ago outside a Blackwell-linked facility in Queens."

Arden leaned forward, breath catching. Chad's smug expression was unmistakable, but it was the man beside him that iced her blood.

"Dylan..." Her voice thinned. "What the hell were they doing there?"

"Running messages," Leo said. "Delivering instructions. And Dylan Tate isn't just any errand boy—he's a known associate of Sebastian's."

"Hawthorne doesn't operate alone," Leo continued. "Not anymore. He's been moving through legal channels Harlan oversees."

Across the table, Gideon's jaw flexed, the muscle ticking like a metronome.

"The facility," he said tightly.

Leo opened a folder and spread several pages across the table: scans of ledgers, inspection reports, photographs that looked smuggled out under pressure.

"One of the old Blackwell research sites," he said. "Officially shut down in the eighties by Richard Blackwell II after he realized how deep the damage went—ethically, environmentally. These were the projects he buried. Purged from the portfolio."

His eyes lifted.

"Until now."

Arden's chest tightened as she skimmed the images: rotting labs, rusted tanks, chemical waste permits that should have been incinerated decades ago.

"They're reviving them," she said, anger sharpening her voice. "They're not just dragging skeletons out. They're breathing life back into them."

Leo's tone dropped. "And they're doing it under the Blackwell name. Everything we've found points to forged authorizations tied directly to you, Gideon. Emails. Contracts. Internal memos. It's intricate. Intentional."

"Wait." Arden's fury flashed hot. "They're setting you up. Making it look like this came from the top...from you."

Leo nodded once, grim. "If this breaks, it won't just damage your reputation. It'll raze the company. The board will turn. Investors will walk. But that's not the point."

He met Gideon's gaze, unflinching.

"This isn't corporate sabotage. It's personal. They're isolating you. Discrediting you. Making you a pariah from the inside out."

Leo hesitated, then added, "And there's more. The burner phones coordinating all of this—the digital traces lead back to someone with deep access to the Blackwell archives. Financial. Legal."

A beat.

"We believe Harlan Atwell is involved."

Gideon's hand curled into a fist, knuckles whitening against the table's edge.

"Sebastian's twisting my grandfather's legacy to destroy everything—and now Harlan?" His voice dropped, disbelief tightening every word. "He's been with my family for decades. He drafted my grandfather's will. Why would he turn now?"

Arden's lip curled. "Because he's feeding Sebastian everything he needs to pull this off."

Disbelief hardened in Gideon's eyes, cooling into resolve. "He thinks Sebastian's going to win."

"Exactly," Leo said. "And Harlan knows where the bodies are buried. He understands the structure—what to exploit, what to mimic. He's dangerous because he can move in the dark and leave no trace."

A pause.

"Until we have proof," Leo finished, "we can't act openly."

THE STORM OUTSIDE SWELLED, wind rattling faintly against the windows, an echo of the pressure coiling in the room.

Arden's grip tightened on the edge of the table. "Sebastian thinks he has you cornered," she said. "Because of me."

Gideon reached for her hand.

"No," he said quietly, eyes locked on hers. "He thinks you're my weakness. But he's wrong."

His voice softened, the truth unflinching.

"You're my strength."

The words settled between them, their weight shifting the air itself.

Arden didn't speak. She only tightened her fingers around his, her silence answering more than words ever could.

Leo cleared his throat, the sound slicing clean through the moment. "If Harlan's aligned with Sebastian, they're already anticipating a counter-move.

We keep everything under wraps. Act like nothing's changed. Let them believe they're ahead."

"And while they're celebrating," Gideon said, the edge in his tone honed to precision, "we gut their operation from the inside out."

He turned to Leo. "Find me the proof. Every forged document. Every wire transfer. Every thread Harlan's touched."

Arden's voice came firm, laced with conviction. "And when we have it?"

Gideon met her gaze. "Then we end this."

The room fell silent again, the only sound the soft percussion of rain.

Arden stood slowly, her body protesting in ways that made her bite back a smile. Not only sore, but marked; claimed in ways that had nothing to do with possession and everything to do with belonging. Every ache hummed with memory—his hands, his mouth, the heat they had built between them—but the night was over now, and this wasn't finished.

Not yet.

Her phone buzzed on the counter. Penny's name lit up the screen.

> Okay babe. You better not be dead. Or pregnant. Or kidnapped. BRUNCH. NOW.

Arden exhaled a laugh. Tension still clung to her like smoke, but it was time. Penny deserved the truth. So did the girls.

Another message stacked beneath it.

> 👀 Seriously, lovebird. Spill.

> I've given you space (read: barely survived not stalking you), but if you duck brunch, I will crash date night in sweatpants and spite.

> And do I have to pretend I didn't see Gideon's hands all over you on the news?

Arden smirked, thumb already moving.

> Nolita Café. 12. Bring your chaos. I'll bring the damage report.

> And you're the one who told me to ride the storm. I just took you literally.

The reply came instantly.

OH MY GOD

If you don't tell me everything, I will move into that fancy brownstone, claim the guest room, and turn the thermostat to 82.

Try being hot and bothered and sweaty.

Outside, sunlight began to edge through the kitchen windows, catching in bright little fragments where rain had tried and failed to linger. Arden stood at the sink, a mug of coffee cupped between both hands. Her body still hummed from the night before, lazy-sore in a way she had almost forgotten was possible. Deep in her hips. Behind her knees. Low and warm.

She shifted her weight, the satisfying ache drawing a smile.

Then the air thinned.

Gideon and Leo's voices echoed back—Harlan. Burner phones. A fuse already lit and trailing straight toward the Blackwell name.

Her phone buzzed again.

Penny.

Arden took one more sip before unlocking the screen.

YOU MADE TIKTOK

👀

You and lover boy were spotted outside The Blackwell Room.

Someone did a voiceover like it was a wildlife documentary.

"The Billionaire and the Mystery Brunette"

Another message followed.

I CAN'T

Also Mystery brunette??? Disrespectful.

You trended on Threads for SEVEN hours

SEVEN.

Page Six ran it under Evelyn's gala announcement.

You were THE SIDEBAR.

"Spotted: Blackwell with an unidentified woman in SoHo."

Sidebar, Arden. Like a raccoon they caught sneaking through the garbage.

Arden snorted into her mug. Typical Penny. Zero chill. Half the reason she loved her.

She fired back.

I am NOT the sidebar. I am the whole damn page.

Say that again QUEEN.

Also, we've been a little busy unraveling corporate sabotage and dodging stalkers, so forgive me for missing my tabloid debut.

Wait what

WHAT.

ARDEN

Brunch. Girls. Noon. Non-negotiable.

Jade and Rach are in.

We're ordering every carb on the menu and I am bringing my nosiest questions.

Okay. But I'm wearing sunglasses and ordering first.

Oh babe. You're sitting center table and telling the story like it's church and you're the pastor. I want hands raised and souls saved.

She laughed softly, the sound easing something tight in her chest.

Fine.

Late-morning light filtered through the tall windows, golden and soft, pretending the world wasn't quietly combusting.

Gideon stood near the front door, coat in hand, his gaze fixed on Arden as if he were committing her to memory all over again. She leaned against the frame, barefoot, wearing one of his button-downs half undone and her smirk fully intact.

"You'll call if anything feels off?" His voice dipped lower than necessary, intimate as if they were the only two people left standing.

"I'll call," she said. "But only if you stop texting me mid-conversation like a dad who just discovered emojis."

His smile flickered—there, then gone.

She caught it. The way his guard slipped only when he touched her. So she closed the distance and laid her hands against his chest.

"Hey," she murmured. "You're not alone in this."

His hands found her hips in the next breath, and then he kissed her.

Not sweet.

Not careful.

A claiming.

The impact knocked the breath from her, ignition trailing right behind it. Her knees buckled, barely holding. One of his hands fisted in her hair, tight at the root, pulling her head back to bare her throat. The other slid low across her back, anchoring her hard against him.

Then his mouth found hers—rough, ravenous, taking without apology. He kissed her like he needed to taste her down to the breath. Her moan broke free, raw and unfiltered, and she didn't even try to hold it in.

When he finally pulled back, her lips were kiss-bitten, her pulse thundering beneath his palm.

"Damn," she whispered. "You always say goodbye like you're going to war."

He leaned in, brushing his nose against hers. "Feels like I am, some days."

"Tell Dan to keep you in check."

The faintest smirk curved his mouth. "God help us both."

And with one last look, he was gone.

The two men sat in a back booth at Walker's Diner, a no-frills joint Dan swore by for strong coffee and bacon that didn't taste like regret.

Dan raised a brow as Gideon stirred a sugar packet into his espresso with surgical precision.

"You're doing that thing."

"What thing?"

"The moody brooding thing," Dan said. "Where I have to guess whether you buried a body or got laid so hard you saw your ancestors."

Gideon's mouth curved. "Why not both?"

Dan gave a low chuckle. "No wonder Arden hasn't bothered texting me back in two days."

"She's safe," Gideon said with a wicked grin.

Then the humor drained from his voice.

"For now."

That stripped the smile clean off Dan's face. "So...how bad is it?"

Gideon pulled out his phone and tapped the screen. A grainy image filled the space between them—Chad Dawson and Dylan Tate outside the Queens facility.

"Bad," he said. "Sebastian's accelerating. And Harlan's helping him."

Dan exhaled, long and slow. "That snake. Figures." He leaned back. "So what's the play?"

"We find proof. Leo's digging. I'm keeping Arden close."

A beat.

"They're using her to get to me."

Dan shook his head. "You're not rattled. You're in lockdown mode. I know that look."

"It's not only me they're targeting," Gideon said, setting the phone down. "Arden's break-ins. Threats. Surveillance. They're trying to isolate her. Make her question everything."

Dan's jaw ticked. "They don't know who they're messing with."

"No," Gideon said, draining his espresso in one swallow. "They don't."

Dan leaned forward, voice dropping. "What do you need from me?"

"A distraction. Another set of eyes." Gideon met his gaze. "Someone she trusts who isn't me."

Dan's grin crept back in. "So you want me to hang out with your girlfriend while you go play corporate Batman."

"I'm saying she needs a friend who won't let her out of their sight," Gideon said evenly, "and won't make it feel like surveillance."

"You're lucky I like her."

Gideon clapped him on the shoulder. "We both are."

Dan arched a brow. "You say that like you're not the one deep in his feelings."

Gideon didn't answer.

Dan shook his head, half a laugh, half a warning. "Damn, brother. You've got it bad."

Gideon ran a hand through his hair, not denying it. He couldn't. Not when she was still in his blood—the taste of her kiss, the sound of her voice, the way she looked at him like she saw everything he tried to hide and stayed anyway.

Dan let the silence hang, then smirked.

"Alright, lover boy. Let's move before I start writing vows for you. We've got recon to do."

CHAPTER 24
Brunch Among Girlfriends

The scent of espresso and overpriced pastries curled through the café as Arden stepped inside. Warm clinks of silverware and the low hum of weekend chatter wrapped around her—easy, practiced, pretending the world wasn't actively unraveling.

Penny sat near the back, legs crossed, sunglasses on, hair twisted up like she had places to be but nowhere she wanted to go.

She looked up, slid the shades down her nose, and skipped the greeting entirely.

"Do you have any idea how chaotic it's been not knowing if you're half-dead or dickmatized?"

Arden laughed as she slid into the seat across from her. "Both. But I lived. Barely."

"Good." Penny reached for her oat milk latte, extra cold foam. "Now explain—in order—how we went from 'maybe this is a thing' to 'Gideon Blackwell has left visible proof you belong to him.'"

Arden leaned in, lowering her voice. "You remember those threatening gifts we weren't sure were escalating?"

Penny's expression sharpened. "Oh—yeah?"

"They escalated."

The words settled between them. Arden filled in the edges, enough to sketch the shape of the danger without stepping into the darkest parts.

Penny listened, her face cycling through concern, disbelief, fury, and finally a kind of reluctant awe.

"Jesus," she muttered, dragging her mimosa closer. "That's not brunch gossip. That's witness-protection-level mess. Why didn't you call me?"

Arden's tone softened. "Because I didn't want you involved. You'd throw hands with the wrong person and end up sued."

"I will absolutely still throw hands," Penny said, indignant. "Just...more selectively." She paused. "Also, for the record, I'm crashing with Rachel this week. I love you, but I'm not watching you and Gideon eye-fuck across every available surface like a live-action tension reel."

Arden grinned. "Noted. I'll keep the theatrics to a minimum."

"Please don't," Penny deadpanned. "I'm bored. Give me a show."

Before Arden could reply, the café door opened and Jade and Rachel swept in.

Jade arrived first, draped in a slouchy cashmere cardigan like she had manifested it out of thin air—serene, observant, already clocking the room. Rachel followed close behind, red lipstick sharp, ponytail tighter than most people's boundaries.

Penny perked up. "And now the council convenes."

Penny leaned forward, eyes locked on the slow-motion disaster unfolding at the hostess stand. A woman—painfully overdressed for casual brunch—was berating the hostess as if the girl had personally sabotaged her morning and salted the eggs.

"I just..." Penny gestured with her fork. "Why is she like that? Aggressively unpleasant to a girl who's just trying to do her job?"

Jade didn't bother looking up from her coffee. She stirred once. "Guarantee she brags about how 'honest' she is. Like being rude is a personality trait."

Arden snorted. "Or claims she has 'high standards.' As if basic decency is beneath her."

Rachel, who had zero tolerance for civilian nonsense, tossed her hair and took a slow, teasing sip of her cappuccino.

"If you're gonna be a bitch," she said calmly, "you have to be hot. You can't be mean and ugly. Pick a struggle."

There was a beat of stunned silence, then Penny wheezed into her napkin. "Jesus, Rach."

Rachel didn't blink. "I'm just saying. If you're going to terrorize brunch staff, at least have the cheekbones to justify it."

Jade shook her head, half scandalized, half impressed. "And people think I'm the mean one."

Arden leaned into her chair, stretching until her back finally loosened. "We all have our skills."

Penny lifted her glass. "To balance in the universe."

Rachel clinked hers. "Exactly."

The table dissolved into laughter, the deep, unrestrained kind that made the server hesitate before approaching.

"I swear," Penny said, swiping beneath one eye, "this is why I missed you. Not your cryptic one-liners or your emotionally unavailable boyfriend. This."

Rachel raised her mimosa. "If you're implying I'm emotionally unavailable—rude."

Jade didn't look up. "No, she's implying Arden's man is. And we're not doing that at brunch."

"Agreed." Arden smirked, shifting in her seat. "Gossip is fine. Therapy isn't covered by bottomless mimosas."

Rachel sipped. "Speak for yourself. I'm ordering the emotional-unpacking combo. Comes with pancakes."

A beat passed.

Penny pointed her fork toward the hostess stand again. "Still yelling. That woman has absolutely screamed 'Do you know who I am?' in a Michaels."

Jade arched a brow. "The real question is—does she?"

Arden snorted into her latte. "She definitely calls the cops when her salad comes with croutons."

"And has a favorite cashier she terrorizes," Rachel added. "Name starts with a K. Spells it with a Q."

Penny nodded solemnly. "Kristopher-with-a-Q. Patron saint of restraining orders."

The server returned with a tray of small plates—smashed avocado toast, lemon ricotta pancakes, and a wild mushroom flatbread Penny had sworn was for the table but reached for first.

Conversation paused as plates landed and forks shuffled, but the current between them didn't break. It hummed beneath the surface, warm and familiar.

Like coming up for air.

Arden bit into her toast, the crunch returning her to normalcy by degrees. She needed this: the noise, the jokes, the harmless judgment of strangers. It cut through the heaviness she had been carrying like sunlight through fog.

Jade reached for the syrup with a sigh. "Sometimes I forget what it's like to laugh with people who don't want anything from me."

Arden glanced up. "Right? No games. No questions. Just pancakes and poor life choices."

"Speak for yourself," Penny said through a mouthful. "My only poor choice this week was skipping a background check on that guy from Hinge. Turns out he thinks Trader Joe's is for 'liberal elites.'"

Rachel made a face. "Girl—no."

"He said almond butter was a scam," Penny added. "Like—passionately."

Even Jade laughed at that.

Arden smiled, her gaze drifting around the table. Penny mid-rant. Rachel on her second mimosa, satisfied in the way of a woman who had never once doubted her own taste. Jade beginning to unwind, shoulders lowering, eyes losing their wary edge.

This was hers. Not borrowed. Not fragile.

Real.

A small, necessary line back to herself.

And she didn't take it for granted.

It was proof the world hadn't burned completely.

Not yet.

THE LAST ROUND of lattes came and went, replaced by mimosas and the kind of laughter that left Arden's throat raw in the best way. They lingered longer than they should have, each woman quietly resisting the pull of the world waiting beyond the glass.

But time didn't stop because brunch had been sacred.

Eventually, Penny looped her arm through Arden's as they stepped outside and gave her a soft squeeze. "You okay?"

"I'm getting there," Arden said, and meant it more than she expected to.

Penny nodded, her tone light, her eyes anything but. "Good. Because you're still not allowed to ghost me. And if your man even thinks about monopolizing your recovery time, I will drag you out of there by your gorgeous hair and make you do squats in public."

Arden laughed. "You just miss yelling at me while I'm sweating."

"I do," Penny said easily. "But you miss it too."

Arden didn't answer.

She didn't have to.

❦

The gym smelled like sweat, mats, and memory.

Arden paused in the doorway, her heart thudding—not with fear, but recognition. The kind that settled deep in her muscles. Her temple still carried the faint ghost of a scar. Her body, a constellation of old bruises.

Not broken.

Only paused.

Kasha looked up from her stretch and froze.

"Well, shit," she breathed. "Look who crawled out of witness protection."

Damon stepped out from the back room, stopped mid-stride, and stared. "Arden?"

Her mouth curved. "Told you I wasn't dead."

"You didn't tell us anything," Kasha said, already crossing the mat to pull her into a fierce, unceremonious hug. "We thought you joined a cult. Or moved to Vermont to make cheese."

Damon's gaze swept over her, not judgment but assessment. "You sure you're ready?"

"No," Arden said honestly. "But I'm here anyway."

He nodded once. "Alright then."

She stepped onto the mat. Her movements were tight at first. Careful. But with each stretch, each strike, each measured breath, something familiar began to wake.

Not the woman who hid behind sarcasm and locked doors, but the one who knew how to plant her feet. How to fall. How to get back up.

It wasn't about winning.

It was about not disappearing. About taking her body back.

Arden exhaled, reset her stance, and smiled.

Her palms hit the mat, breath coming fast as she held the plank. Damon circled like a hawk, nodding once in approval, but not easing up.

"Hold it," he said. "You wanted this."

"Thirty seconds ago," she muttered, "I wanted more pancakes."

Kasha coughed a laugh from the corner, still wrapping her hands. "That's what brunch is for. This is for vengeance."

Arden grinned, though her arms trembled—not from weakness, but effort. Refusal. The private discipline of not letting herself coast.

Damon clapped once.

"Up."

She rose, rolled her neck, and reset her stance. Sweat slicked her spine, soaking the band of her sports bra, but it felt good. Earned. Like her body remembered how to be hers again.

"Let's spar," she said.

Kasha lifted a brow. "Thought you'd never ask."

They moved to the center of the mat. No warmups. No light taps.

Kasha came in hot—sharp, fast jabs meant to test reflexes, footing, grit. Arden pressed back, snapped forward with a left hook that drew a laugh from Kasha even as it landed.

"You been holding out on us, princess."

"I've had a lot of rage to organize," Arden said, breath ragged.

A low sound of satisfaction left Damon as he leaned against the wall. "Looks like she's reorganizing just fine."

The next exchange came faster. Kasha clipped her ribs, but Arden twisted, swept low, nearly took her down.

They reset.

Again.

Hit. Block. Duck. Grit teeth. Breathe.

The rhythm wasn't elegant, but it was honest.

And when Arden finally called it, arms limp at her sides, sweat dripping from her temple, she was smiling.

Not because she had won.

Because she hadn't quit.

CHAPTER 25
Back in the Saddle

The brownstone greeted her with the warm scent of coffee and the faint trace of rain. Gideon must have cracked a window to let in the late-afternoon breeze. From the corner, soft jazz played low, threading itself through the room.

Her shoes thudded softly as she slipped them off and padded toward the kitchen.

A note waited on the counter, Gideon's handwriting unmistakable.

Be back by seven. Chinese or Italian tonight? Text me.

She smiled, fingers brushing the ink as if it might still be warm.

The fridge hissed open. She grabbed a bottle of water and leaned back against the counter, the ache in her shoulders a living thing, but welcome. Proof she was still here. Still moving. Still fighting.

Still Arden.

She curled into the oversized chair by the window, legs tucked beneath her, one of Gideon's throw blankets draped over her lap. Her hair, still damp from the gym shower, left dark streaks along the collar of her worn tee. She lit one of his favorite candles—cedar and smoke—and let the scent settle around her like a ward.

The journal in her lap was old. Weathered. One of the few things that had survived every move, every upheaval. Its pages were crowded with chaotic scrawls: half-thoughts, fragments, names she wasn't ready to release.

But they were hers.

She didn't know what she meant to write, only that she had to.

After the training. After the fear. After the ache, and the small, stubborn miracle of surviving another day, this was the ritual that made it real. She uncapped the pen and let her hand move before her mind caught up.

again & again
i forget who i am
sometimes.
not in the mirror—
but in the moments
i go quiet
when i should roar.
i come back slowly.
through fists
and footsteps,
through the sound of my own breath
catching fire in my chest.
i come back
not prettier
not softer—
but truer.
a little scraped up,
a little less polite,
but whole.
again.
and again.
and again.

Arden exhaled, the words humming low in her chest. Not peace, exactly, but release. Her gaze drifted toward the window as dusk deepened, the sky bleeding from gold to charcoal.

A soft sound caught her ear—keys in the front door.

Her heart kicked. This time, it was anticipation.

The door creaked open with the easy familiarity of someone who didn't need to announce himself. Gideon's footsteps were hushed but sure as he crossed the room, shrugging off his coat. He paused when he saw her curled into the corner chair, legs tucked beneath her, pen still in hand. Candlelight flickered across her features, catching the damp ends of her hair and the faint bruise on her knuckle like proof of battle.

"Hey," she said softly, without lifting her head. There was something solid in her voice now, bedrock beneath the current.

He crossed the room in a few strides, gaze dipping to the open journal in her lap. The ink was still wet, but it wasn't the handwriting that held him. It was the fight in the words.

Arden looked up then, catching him mid-stare. "Judging my emo poetry?"

His mouth curved. "Not even a little."

She tilted her head.

He reached out, brushing a thumb along her jaw as if he were memorizing this version of her. "You came back."

"I didn't go far," she murmured, though her eyes said otherwise. They held flickers of pain and progress, loss and reclamation.

"No," he said gently. "But I saw what it took—to walk into that gym. To hit back. To write this."

He nodded toward the journal.

Her shoulders dropped, the last of her tension loosening. "It wasn't pretty."

"Didn't need to be." His voice stayed low. "It was honest. That's braver than pretty."

For a moment, they simply existed together.

Then he nodded toward the kitchen. "I picked up dinner. Figured you'd be sore."

She grinned. "I'm sore in places I forgot I had."

"Good," he said, offering a hand. "Means you're still in there."

She took it.

With a firm grip and a soft smile, he pulled her back into the room again.

The journal lay closed on the table, the pen resting across it like a ribbon over something sacred. In the kitchen, the lights stayed low, plates clinked softly, and the music played on—ordinary sounds, achingly safe.

Arden walked barefoot toward the counter, drawn by the scent of roasted garlic and butter. "Mmm. Smells good."

"I reheated," Gideon said, glancing over his shoulder. "Don't give me too much credit. The place on Tenth owed me a favor."

She smiled, stepping closer. "Still counts."

He reached for two plates and handed her one. "Sit. You've done enough damage today."

"Damage?" she echoed, brow lifting.

"You punched a man twice your size, sparred with Kasha, and journaled." His mouth curved. "That's at least three emotional breakthroughs in one afternoon. I'm impressed. And slightly alarmed."

Arden laughed, full-bodied and unguarded. She brushed past him as she took the plate, the contact deliberate.

"Guess I was due."

They sat across from each other at the small round table, knees brushing beneath. Between bites, silence settled, but the easy kind. Comfortable. Alive.

"You feel different," Gideon said after a while, watching her over the rim of his glass.

"I feel like myself again," she said, gaze dipping to her plate. "At least more than I have in weeks."

He nodded, something like relief threading through his expression.

"You look like it."

"Thank you," she murmured, rolling one shoulder. "My muscles ache in all the right ways."

His head tilted, eyes darkening. "That so?"

"Mmhmm." She rose, collected her plate, and carried it to the sink. When she turned back, her grin was unmistakable. "But I'm still hungry."

Gideon's gaze tracked her slowly. He stood, closing the distance until there was barely air between them. He stopped short of touching her. "I thought you said you were full."

Her eyes flicked down to his mouth, then back up again. "Maybe I want something else."

His hands slid to her hips, firm and knowing, thumbs pressing into the fabric at her waist. "Then what are you craving now?"

Her fingers slipped beneath the hem of his shirt, light and teasing—a promise, not a claim.

"Something sweet."

He kissed her. Hot. Open-mouthed. The kind of kiss that tasted like surrender and claimed her in the same breath.

She moaned softly, pulling him closer. He lifted her onto the counter in one practiced motion, and she wrapped her legs around his waist without hesitation. His mouth traced along her jaw, down the side of her neck, finding her pulse racing.

"I can give you sweet," he murmured against her skin. "But you should know...I do better with decadent."

Arden's nails dragged lightly across his chest, her voice a rasp against his ear. "Good. I want you messy."

Gideon pulled back to meet her eyes—stormy, molten.

"Don't tempt me."

She smirked, breath already ragged.

"Too late."

HIS HANDS GRIPPED HER THIGHS, anchoring her to the counter as his mouth claimed hers again, slower this time. Less urgent. More present. Every kiss carried the echo of the storm they had weathered. Every touch became a promise that neither of them had broken beneath it.

Arden's fingers slid into his hair, drawing him closer, guiding the rhythm until it built by degrees into something deeper than desire.

Elemental.

His hands moved beneath her shirt, palms splaying across her ribs as if he needed to feel her heartbeat from the inside. She gasped when his thumbs grazed her breasts, and he swallowed the sound, his own breath stuttering against her mouth.

"You're shaking," he whispered, voice wrecked and reverent.

She nodded once, eyes locked on his.

He brushed a kiss across her cheek.

Then he kissed her again—cheek, jaw, collarbone. Lower. He pulled the shirt from her body as if it were spun silk, as if taking it off were its own kind of sacred act. His mouth followed every inch of exposed skin, worshiping the stretch marks on her side, the softness of her belly, the tattoo across her ribs.

No praise. No teasing. Only devotion, complete and wordless, as if each inch of her body were its own liturgy.

When he knelt, spreading her thighs open and pulling her underwear aside, he did not look up for permission because she had already given him something deeper than invitation.

Trust.

She gasped as his mouth met her, not with the practiced rhythm of a man proving a point, but with the lazy, devastating indulgence of a man who knew exactly how to ruin her and had all night to do it.

He took his time. Tongue slow, savoring. Hands gripping her hips as if they might drift without him. And when she started to come undone, he didn't stop. He held her through it, held all of her—even the part of her that still wanted to vanish.

When she came—shuddering, breathless—he kissed her thigh as if he were starving for it, mouth open, tongue dragging slow before his teeth grazed her skin.

Arden stared down at him, chest rising fast, lips parted in awe.

"You always do that," she said, voice rough around the edges.

He rose, mouth still wet from her. "Do what?"

"Make me feel like I belong in my body."

Gideon didn't flinch. Didn't smirk. He only wrapped his hands around her waist and pulled her close.

"That's because you do."

They didn't make it to the bedroom.

He turned her slowly, certainly, bracing her hands against the counter before he sank into her with a groan torn straight from his chest. No finesse. No choreography. Only heat and gravity and the kind of need that trusted itself enough to be honest.

The stretch. The heat. The way she whimpered his name as if it were the only solid thing she had.

He bent over her, mouth at her shoulder, moving with slow, brutal tenderness—the kind that could shatter and heal in the same breath.

No one else would ever see her like this.

No one else could.

He came with a broken gasp against her neck, clutching her so tightly she could feel the tremor in his hands. When he finally stilled, their breaths were ragged, tangled.

Neither spoke.

He kissed her shoulder. Her spine. Her lower back. Then he turned her to face him again, arms still wrapped around her as if she might slip away.

Arden brushed the hair from his forehead, and for a moment, the world was steam and heartbeat.

"You're home," she whispered.

He blinked.

Because it didn't sound like she meant the brownstone.

He kissed her again, softer now. Less fire, more flesh and vow. And this time, it didn't lead to more.

Only a bath. A soft towel. An arm tucked around her in bed while she drifted.

Safe. Claimed. Here.

CHAPTER 26
Cold Flame

The silence in the house was complete.

Arden slept with her cheek against his chest, her breath soft against his skin, one leg draped over his hip as if she had no intention of letting go.

Gideon hadn't moved in over an hour.

Wouldn't.

Couldn't.

As if shifting might wake her—or worse, fracture the peace they had fought like hell to earn.

Outside, the city exhaled.

Inside, nothing stirred.

Across town, beneath the polished gleam of glass and shadow, Sebastian Hawthorne was very much awake.

From his penthouse, he watched the storm roll in, rain streaking the windows and smearing the skyline into a fractured mosaic of light. The chaos outside mirrored the symphony he was conducting: every note deliberate, every movement precise.

His reflection hovered faintly in the glass.

Cold eyes.

A ghost looking back.

The speaker on his desk crackled. Dylan's voice cut through the static.

"The gifts have been delivered. Chad made contact...but Arden's suspicious."

Sebastian's lips curved, the barest suggestion of amusement never reaching his eyes.

"Good," he murmured. "Suspicion is a seed. Let it grow."

A pause.

"And Gideon?" Dylan asked. "He's watching. Tighter security. Fewer openings."

Sebastian's smile sharpened. "Exactly where I want him."

He crossed to the bar cart, poured bourbon into a crystal glass, and turned back to the storm.

"Predictable. Reactionary. He'll keep chasing ghosts, trying to shield her."

A sip.

A beat.

"But the real threat is already beneath his feet."

Thunder rolled, low and distant, as if the city agreed.

"She doesn't know yet," Sebastian continued, his voice softening to something almost fond. "But she's already dancing on my strings."

Dylan hesitated. "She's strong. She won't fall easily."

The faint smile vanished.

"She's strong because she's been broken. Burned. Rebuilt." Sebastian set the glass down. "That kind of strength remembers pain. It responds to it."

He turned and faced his reflection.

"She's fire, Dylan."

His gaze never wavered.

"But even the fiercest flames need something to burn for."

A silence.

"And she will burn for me."

Dylan's voice dropped. "And if she figures it out?"

Sebastian didn't blink. His attention slid to the monitor on his desk, a muted feed from Arden's old apartment building, the hallway grainy and still.

"She won't," he said flatly. "Not until it's too late."

Silence stretched. He let it. Each drop of rain against the glass felt like a countdown without end.

Arden believed resistance could save her. That clarity could outmaneuver devotion.

It wouldn't.

Her fire wasn't enough, not against the fortress Sebastian had built to contain it.

The city shimmered below, all illusion and light. Sebastian's mouth curved again, slow and predatory, as he imagined the moment she would finally see him clearly.

"Gideon thinks he's her shield," he murmured, forgetting Dylan. "But shields are made to shatter."

His voice cooled.

"And when his does, she'll understand there's only one constant in all of this."

He straightened, gaze fixed on the distorted skyline.

"Me."

His thoughts were crystalline. Arden Rivers would burn, and her fire would consume everything: Gideon, the Blackwell name, the fragile myth of safety she clung to. When the storm cleared, nothing would remain but him.

A buzz.

Sebastian reached for his phone, the screen lighting his hand.

Harlan.

Status confirmed. All preparations complete.

His smirk deepened as he set the phone aside. The plan was flawless.

It was time to move the final piece.

A disruptor—magnetic, unpredictable. Someone who could step into the gala and tilt Arden's axis enough to make the world spin.

And Sebastian knew exactly who.

CHAPTER 27

Double Meaning

The low murmur of conversation mingled with the delicate chime of champagne glasses, giving the gallery an air of curated sophistication. Penny drifted through a maze of abstract canvases, her hair a flare of red against the muted walls. She stopped in front of a painting—an eruption of reds and golds, streaks so violent they looked like the world caught mid-explosion.

"What do you think it means?"

The voice behind her was smooth, sharp as a scalpel.

Penny turned. Sebastian Hawthorne stood there, charcoal suit immaculate, posture composed, wearing the kind of control that passed for charm in rooms like this. He offered his hand.

She ignored it.

"Do I know you?" she asked, folding her arms.

"Not officially." His smile didn't falter. "Sebastian Hawthorne."

"I'm sure that works on people," she said lightly. "Just not on me."

A flicker of amusement crossed his face. "I've seen you at The Blackwell Room. You're friends with Arden Rivers, if I'm not mistaken."

At Arden's name, Penny's posture tightened.

"And you just happened to notice me?" she said. "That's dedication."

"Dedication," he echoed, unbothered. "Arden's name comes up in... interesting conversations. A person as memorable as you is hard to miss."

Penny's smirk cut sharp.

"Right. And the Tom Ford is purely coincidental. You strike me as a man who dresses for effect."

"Presentation matters."

"So does substance." She tilted her head. "What's your angle, Mr. Hawthorne? Flattery's a starting point, but I don't buy innocent passerby."

His amusement cooled, refined into something more intentional.

"Fair. I won't waste time. The gala tomorrow could use unpredictability."

She blinked.

Once.

"And you think that's me."

"I know it is." He stepped closer, his voice dropping to a conspiratorial murmur. "A presence. Someone who can command a room and upend it with a single glance. The kind of attention that shifts the temperature."

Penny studied him. The offer hummed at the edges of her instincts—dangerous, ridiculous, and intriguing in precisely the way good sense hated.

"Let me guess," she said. "You want me as your plus-one."

"Exactly."

She laughed, short and incredulous.

"You don't even know me, so...why me?"

"Because unpredictability is captivating," he said smoothly. "And from what I've seen, you excel at captivating."

For a beat, she considered him. The surprise of the invitation set her nerves on edge, then tempted them. Walking into that gala on her terms, as disruption incarnate, felt almost irresistible.

"Alright," she said at last, her smile sharpening. "But one thing."

His brow lifted.

"If this is a game to mess with Arden," Penny said evenly, "I'll burn your evening to the ground. Slowly."

A flicker of challenge warmed his dark eyes.

"Noted. I wouldn't dare underestimate you."

"Good." She turned, already moving, a wardrobe plan snapping into place—sequins that reflected light, heels sharp enough to draw blood, red lipstick loud and unapologetic. Full glam. Full Penny. Full chaos.

"See you tomorrow," she tossed over her shoulder. "Try to keep up."

Sebastian lingered by the painting, watching her disappear into the crowd. Penny Haverford—matchstick poised at the edge of a forest.

His smile returned, faint and wicked.

"Perfect."

Satisfaction thrummed beneath his skin like a live wire.

Every move had been calibrated, every thread drawn tighter around Arden Rivers. She would try to dismiss it; compartmentalize the unease, tell herself she was imagining patterns where none existed. But the cracks were already there. The seeds of doubt had taken root.

Now, he would strike the match.

The thought of Penny brought a slow, sharp smile to his lips.

Bright.

Unpredictable.

Magnetic.

She wasn't merely a guest. She was a statement. The perfect variable. A disruptor elegant enough to pass as coincidence.

Penny's boldness, her effortless charm, her ability to command attention with a single glance—it was a counterpoint Arden couldn't ignore. Sebastian had studied Penny as closely as he had studied Arden, cataloguing every sharp quip, every flash of mischief in her eyes. More importantly, he understood the bond between them: roommates once, confidantes always, the one person Arden had ever truly let past her defenses.

That was the point.

Penny wasn't about jealousy. She was about breach. Intrusion. The first crack through the sanctuary Arden clung to.

Arden would hide it, of course, behind humor and heat, behind that bright, defiant composure she wore like armor. But he would see it. The flicker in her gaze. The tightening of her jaw. The subtle tremor beneath her fire.

The ripple would spread, patient and corrosive, seeping into the spaces Arden believed were safe.

This wasn't about Penny.

It was about Arden.

About dismantling her sense of self, one heartbeat at a time.

The gala was only the stage. The performance had already begun.

Sebastian's reflection blurred in the glass as his smile deepened.

Arden.

Little Fire.

She would burn brighter in resistance, and he would watch as the flames consumed her composure.

Let her fight.

It would only make the fall more exquisite.

Her fire was already his.

And soon, she would realize it.

CHAPTER 28
Shadowed Truths

The low murmur of conversation threaded through the club, a soft symphony of glass and laughter that barely reached the quietest corners of the bar.

Arden sat with her back to the room, the glow from a nearby sconce gilding the items laid out before her: a Polaroid photograph, a gold necklace with a delicate lotus charm, and a small folded note.

Four words, written in familiar strokes.

See you at the gala.

Her gaze slid to the Polaroid. A moment frozen too close. Too precise. She was reaching for a glass, unaware of the camera inches away. Whoever had taken it had stood beside her, close enough to share her air.

The realization crept over her skin like frost.

The parcel had arrived earlier that evening. No name. No return address. The familiar handwriting had turned her stomach before she even opened it.

"Do you recognize it?" Gideon's voice was controlled, but the restraint in it carried a pulse of fury.

She nodded once. "It's his. He's reminding me he's everywhere."

Gideon's jaw flexed, a muscle ticking as he studied the items like they might confess.

"This isn't just a message," he said. "It's a challenge. He's escalating."

Arden's breath wavered. Her gaze fell to the necklace, the lotus catching the light like mockery. "He's taunting me. Taking what's mine and twisting it."

Gideon's hand covered hers. "He wants you to feel exposed. Don't give him that power."

"The lotus again..." Her voice thinned. "It used to remind me I could grow. That I could come back from anything."

His expression softened with understanding.

Arden turned the charm between her fingers, the metal cold against her skin.

"My parents' house was chaos," she said quietly. "Fear wrapped in silence. You learn to survive by disappearing." A pause. "Nursing school was supposed to be my way out. But even then—"

She swallowed.

"Someone slipped into my life. Followed me. I didn't recognize it until it was too late."

The words stayed suspended between them, raw and unfinished.

Gideon didn't rush her.

"And still you fought," he said. "You rebuilt. You grew from what tried to bury you."

She met his eyes—gray as storm clouds, darkening—and felt something inside her lock into place.

"And now he's using it," she said. "My symbol. My story."

"They can't take what's yours," Gideon said, voice firm, almost a vow. "Not your strength. Not your truth. They think this will break you." His gaze held hers. "They have no idea who you are."

Her chest loosened. The ache didn't vanish; it shifted and sharpened.

"It's not about what they can take," she said slowly. "It's how far they're willing to go."

Gideon's expression didn't waver.

"Far enough to make it personal."

She drew a grounding breath.

"And it's not just about me anymore, is it?"

"No," he said, voice low with lethal calm. "It never was. He's using you to get to me."

A beat.

"And that," Gideon finished, "is his mistake."

The necklace had been chosen with intention.

Every detail calibrated.

Every curve a study in Arden Rivers.

Elegant.

Unyielding.

Impossible to break without leaving evidence.

The lotus wasn't a flower.

It was a mirror.

The will to rise, no matter how many times the water tried to swallow her whole.

To Sebastian, it was also a declaration.

A promise.

A claim.

Gideon would never understand that. To him, meaning was surface-level, something to admire, then set aside. He collected symbols without ever needing them. But Sebastian needed them. Symbols were how truth announced itself.

Sebastian leaned back in his chair, penthouse light carving his face into shadow and bone. A single red rose rested on the arm of the leather seat, its stem bending beneath his fingers as his thoughts tightened into a singular, exquisite focus.

The photograph.

The note.

The necklace.

None of it was meant to frighten her.

Fear was crude. Fear closed doors.

This was revelation.

He wanted her to feel seen, to remember that someone noticed the details she pretended didn't matter. The way her shoulders squared when she was cornered. The way she flared hottest when she was afraid. The scars she carried beneath the fire, pretending heat alone could cauterize them.

The charm was no longer a symbol.

It was a tether.

Each time her fingers brushed the metal, she would think of him. Each time she wore it, she would remember that knowing was a form of intimacy, and that someone had claimed it first.

His smile deepened as the rose yielded beneath his grip.

Arden's resistance only sharpened her brilliance. Fire was always most beautiful when it pushed back against the wind. He could already see it—the tightening of her jaw, the measured control of her breath as she insisted she was unaffected. She would tell herself she was fine. That it meant nothing.

She always did.

But even the fiercest flames shifted when pressure was applied with intent.

Her fire was not Gideon's to shield. Not his to claim. He mistook proximity for understanding. Protection for devotion.

Sebastian knew better.

This was never about the lotus. Or the note. Or Gideon Blackwell.

It was about what Arden refused to acknowledge.

She was already his.

In every sharpened glance. Every retort that came a beat too fast. Every tremor of frustration when control slipped and she felt seen.

All of it pointed back to him.

He would wait. Let her resist. Let her burn brighter. Every spark she threw only fed what was coming.

And when the fire finally turned, when it mistook recognition for destiny, it would consume everything in its path: doubt, fear, the fragile myth of safety she had wrapped around herself.

Gideon Blackwell would think he could stand in those flames.

Think he could shield her.

But fire doesn't shield.

Fire consumes.

Sebastian's lips curved in satisfaction—not joy, not triumph, but conviction. Obsession mistaken for devotion.

When Arden's fire burned its brightest, it wouldn't be for Gideon.

It would be for him.

Hours later, the air inside Gideon's brownstone felt charged, too still, too aware.

Arden sat curled on the edge of the couch, the necklace clutched in both hands. Across the room, Christian stood before the monitors, eyes reflecting the cascade of code scrolling too fast to read.

"They're using burners," he muttered, more to himself than anyone else. "Not invisible enough."

Gideon's voice cut through. "Can you trace them?"

Christian nodded, sharp and certain. "I can intercept messages between them. It'll take time, but I'll get it."

"Do it."

Minutes bled away. Then Christian straightened, pulling up a decrypted message, the pale glow of the monitor bleaching his face of warmth.

"Harlan's burner," he said. "Sent right before the package was delivered."

He read it aloud, voice cool and collected.

The package has been delivered.

The name twisted inside Arden like a blade. Her pulse jumped, fast and unrestrained.

Gideon met her gaze, burning. "They're making this personal."

Outside, the rain softened to a whisper, tapping faintly against the glass. Christian closed his laptop, the click of it echoing too loudly.

"I'll keep digging," he said. "And I'll flag the connection to her case."

Gideon nodded once, brief and grateful. His hand landed on Christian's shoulder. A thank you. A promise. Then Christian was gone, the door clicking shut behind him.

Silence settled like fog.

Arden didn't move. The necklace glinted in her hands. She turned it once. Twice. The metal caught the low light like a snare.

Gideon crossed the room and crouched beside the couch, his presence pulling gravity back into the space.

"Christian will find something," he said quietly. "He always does."

Arden nodded, eyes still fixed on the gold. "It's not what we'll find that scares me." Her voice thinned. "It's how far they're willing to go. The way they twist things that were mine."

Gideon reached for her hand, warm against the chill of the metal. "That's what he wants. To make you feel exposed."

Her breath shuddered out. "It's working."

His voice softened, but it didn't waver. "He can't take what's yours, Arden. Not your strength. Not your story. They think this will break you."

She lifted her eyes to his, something raw breaking the surface. "I hate that I need this—that I need you. It makes me feel like I've lost something."

The admission landed hard.

Gideon's mouth curved faintly, but his eyes stayed serious. "You haven't lost anything," he said, voice gruff. "You're not exposed. You're not alone."

The words struck deeper than she wanted them to. Her spine bent toward something softer. Safer.

"This isn't intimidation anymore," he murmured. "It's personal."

"It always was," she said, steadier now. "But I'm not hiding while he plays these games."

"I know." His thumb traced her wrist. "You're not the one who needs protection."

A beat.

"But that doesn't mean you have to stand alone."

Something in her finally gave.

When he kissed her, it wasn't desperate. It wasn't frantic. It was a vow wrapped in warmth.

His hand cupped her jaw; the other pressed at her back, drawing her in until the storm inside her went quiet.

For the first time in hours, she let herself breathe.

WHEN HE FINALLY PULLED BACK, their foreheads rested together, breath mingling in the charged air. His voice was low, rough around the edges.

"I meant what I said."

Arden's fingers curled into his shirt, her answer whispered but unyielding. "I'm not backing down."

His lips curved, but the fire in his eyes didn't soften. "Good. Neither am I."

Between their hands, the necklace lay cool and delicate, a fragile promise wrapped in solid strength. Whatever Sebastian intended, whatever waited ahead, they wouldn't face it apart.

"Come on," he murmured after a moment, the edge easing from his voice. "You need rest."

She let him guide her down the dim hall, muted light giving way to the warmth of his bedroom. Outside, the world was rain-soaked and relentless; in here, it felt distant. Suspended.

Gideon's hands settled at her waist from behind, his touch light but certain. "You're soaked," he said, gentle authority threading his tone. "You'll catch a cold if you sleep like this."

She turned slightly, defiance sparking in her eyes. "I can handle it, Gideon. I've been taking care of myself for a long time."

He leaned closer, his breath warm at her temple. "I know."

A beat.

"Humor me."

Before she could argue, his fingers brushed her skin carefully as he lifted the damp fabric over her head. The intimacy of it was unhurried. Not control. Care. Presence.

"I could've done that myself," she murmured, her protest softened by a thread of reluctant amusement.

"I know." A half smile formed. "But where's the fun in that?"

The teasing wasn't seduction. It was trust. A gentle nudge toward ease.

She huffed a laugh, half sigh. "You're impossible."

"Impossible is part of my charm."

He stepped back, giving her space as she slipped into his shirt. It hung loose on her frame, the hem brushing her thighs, the faint scent of cedar and spice wrapping around her like warmth itself.

Gideon watched her with quiet awe.

Before she could respond, he swept her up, strong arms gathering her with effortless ease.

She let out a startled laugh, hands clutching his shoulders. "Gideon!"

He chuckled, low and teasing. "What? You're tired. I'm helping."

He set her gently on the bed and followed, his movements unhurried. When he braced himself over her, the teasing slipped away. What replaced it was quieter. Deeper.

He kissed her slowly. Feather-light touches brushed her skin: her temple, her cheekbone, the corner of her mouth. His lips traced the line of her jaw and lingered at the hollow of her throat. Each kiss was a silent promise.

Her hands slid into his hair, fingertips grazing his scalp as a soft sigh left her. For a breath, the air thickened with something that could have burned if he had let it.

He didn't.

Instead, he eased back, brushed his mouth once more to her temple, then rolled onto his side and drew her into him. His arm wrapped around her waist, firm and sure, holding her against his chest like she was something worth keeping.

Arden settled over his heartbeat, the rhythm quieting what remained of the storm inside her. His warmth surrounded her; his presence filled the hollow spaces the day had carved out.

"Tease," she murmured, sleepy and faintly accusatory.

"Am I?" His breath moved through her hair, his voice edged with humor... and promise. "Maybe I'm just pacing myself."

Her laugh was soft but real, breaking the last of the tension. She let herself sink into him, into the quiet, the warmth, the simple truth of it.

The world outside could wait.

For now, there was only the rain tapping the glass, the weight of his arm around her, and the slow beat of his heart against her ear.

CHAPTER 29

Quiet Nights

They hadn't planned on a movie. It sort of...happened—that peaceful stretch after dinner where neither of them moved, hovering in the space between we could and why not.

Gideon had the remote. Arden curled up on the couch, legs tucked beneath her, the silence between them easy.

Familiar.

Then she saw it.

"Wait. Go back. No—the other way." She leaned forward, pointing. "There. That one. The Lake House."

He squinted at the screen. "The one with the magic mailbox?"

"Time-traveling mailbox," she corrected, already reaching for the remote. "Don't knock it. It's a classic."

He chuckled, handing it over. "I'm not judging."

"Ah. A skeptic."

"I'm trying to grow."

The opening music drifted in, soft piano, wistful and a little too sentimental for either of them to admit they liked it.

"I was thirteen the first time I saw this," she said, eyes fixed on the screen. "Didn't think I'd care. But it got me."

Gideon didn't interrupt.

"It was the first time I'd ever seen that kind of love," she went on. "Not small. Not transactional. Not the kind that explodes and burns out." She smiled faintly. "Just...big. Completely unrealistic, obviously—but it made me want to believe in love like that anyway."

She shook her head, half laughing. "Still makes me cry."

He shifted so she could lean back into him. It was instinct now, her body fitting against his like a sentence finding its ending. His arms wrapped around her, anchoring without caging.

Halfway through, she felt it coming, the familiar ache building low in her throat. That stupid ache for something beautiful and impossible.

She blinked hard. Wiped beneath her eye too late. Sniffled once.

"Hey," Gideon murmured. Not loud. Not pushy. "You okay?"

She nodded, smiling through it. "This part ruins me. Every time. I swear I could quote it backward and it would still wreck me."

His hold tightened, comfort without demand.

Arden's gaze drifted from the screen to the faint reflection of them in the darkened window. "I think it mattered to me because..." Her voice caught, quiet but sure. "I didn't grow up around love like that. Not the kind that waits. Or believes in you without needing proof."

She let the words hang. No apology. No disguise.

Gideon pressed a soft kiss into her hair. "Maybe that's why you recognize it when you see it."

She smiled faintly, eyes on the screen but not really watching anymore. The glow painted both their faces, the movie still playing, but the story had shifted.

He was watching her now.

Not the movie.

She didn't know when she had leaned closer, or why. Maybe it was the ache the film had unearthed, or the space between them, or the fact that she didn't have to shield herself from him.

Of course she knew.

That was the reason.

She turned and rested her head against his chest.

After a few breaths, his hand found her cheek, gentle and unhurried, as if he were soothing something he couldn't name. His fingers tucked a loose strand of hair behind her ear, and she nearly broke right then.

Maybe because it was romantic.

Mostly because it felt safe.

No words. His fingertips lingered near her jaw, tracing away the last salt of her tears.

"I know it's a movie," she murmured. "I do. But back then, it made me think..." Her voice softened. "Maybe someone would wait for me. Or really see me. Enough to stay."

Gideon leaned in, not to kiss her, but to rest his forehead against hers.

"I would've waited," he said quietly. "I'd wait a thousand days for you. Longer."

Her chest tightened, not with pain, but with something fuller. She closed her eyes, breathed him in, and let the words settle where they needed to land.

When she opened them, his gaze was already there, unguarded. That look that never flinched. That made her believe she was worth staying for.

"I do believe you," she whispered.

And somewhere deep inside, the thirteen-year-old version of her—the girl who cried alone in the dark, who ached for something gentle to believe in—finally let go.

They stayed like that long after the credits faded.

He didn't move.

She didn't want him to.

Arden shifted in his arms, her cheek brushing his shirt. "Can I tell you something kind of stupid?"

"You can tell me anything."

"I used to think love was only like that in movies." A pause. Then a soft, breathless laugh. "But this—" she gestured vaguely between them, "—with you? It feels better."

He didn't answer. He drew her closer and kissed the top of her head.

When she looked up again, her eyes were still rimmed in red, but the tears had passed. What remained was warmth.

Arden studied him, really looked. The way his arm stayed wrapped around her. The way he held her like one wrong move might undo her.

"I want you," she said. Clear. Sure.

She leaned in and kissed him once. Then again, slower this time. The kind of kiss that rewrote memory.

"I'm sure," she whispered against his mouth. "I need this."

Something shifted in his gaze. Not surprise. Not hunger.

Recognition.

As if he hadn't been waiting for permission, only for her.

He rose first, offering his hand. She took it without hesitation.

Letting him lead wasn't surrender.

It was trust.

At the bedroom door, she stepped ahead, fingers still laced with his, and tugged him forward.

Gideon followed at an unhurried pace, the dim light catching the careful way he watched her—not only her body, but the spaces between her breaths, the pauses that meant something. He kissed her with the patience of a man unafraid of time.

There was no urgency when he began to undress her. No rush to rip or fumble. He moved like he knew exactly how long the moment could last, and intended to stretch it until she couldn't bear another second.

His hands touched her face first, thumbs sweeping her jaw, then lower. Her throat. The edge of her collarbone. Familiar paths, taken with fresh intent. Every pass of his fingers was deliberate, slow enough to tease, slow enough to burn.

She breathed him in, held by the weight of his attention. Then she reached up and dragged her shirt over her head, bare before him in one smooth motion. She didn't hesitate when she reached for his, pulling it up over toned muscle and heat.

The silence deepened.

"I want to feel everything," she said.

"You will," he murmured, mouth brushing the hollow at the base of her throat. "Promise."

Their bodies found their familiar rhythm. It wasn't frantic. It didn't need to be. His hands moved over her as if he had waited years to map her properly. Her breath stuttered every time his lips found bare skin—lower each time. Her sighs turned to gasps as he kissed the swell of her breasts, the line of her stomach, the inside of her thigh.

Her name slipped from his lips like it belonged there.

When she climbed on top of him, confident as ever, his hands slid to her waist, but he didn't guide her.

He let her take it.

She sank down onto him inch by inch, hips rocking once she was fully seated, the stretch sharp and hot and perfect. Her breath caught as she adjusted, then started to move—slowly at first, a testing grind of her hips that made his jaw go tight.

The look in his eyes was all hunger and restraint. His hands flexed on her thighs.

"Jesus, Arden..."

Her head dropped back, a moan catching halfway between breath and need.

Her pace deepened. She rolled her hips harder, dragging friction in every slow circle until the tension in him started to shake loose.

His chest rose in sharp bursts beneath her hands. She braced there, palms spread, fingers pressing into the heat of him. His eyes never left hers. Being watched like that made her ache in places she didn't have names for.

She rode him with slow control, shifting her angle until his breath punched out in a curse. Her body clenched tight around him, slick and open, and he answered her with his hips, jerking up to meet every grind with more pressure, more depth.

She didn't want to let go.

But she wanted him to take it from her.

His hands slid up her torso, thumbs grazing beneath her breasts before he took them in both hands—rougher now, more certain. He pinched her nipples, slow and tight, drawing a sharp gasp from her throat. She arched into it, grinding down harder.

"Whatever you want," he murmured, voice frayed. "However you want it."

She kissed him—messy, greedy, chasing the edge of his unraveling.

Then he moved.

In one fluid motion, he flipped her, her back meeting the sheets in a rush of heat. She gasped, not from shock, but relief.

He hovered over her, eyes locked on hers. One hand slid down her thigh as he pressed back inside, slow and deep.

She groaned, legs locking around his waist, pulling him deeper.

He started to thrust.

Not fast. Not hard.

Deep.

Every stroke was purposeful, dragging against every sensitive nerve until she was gasping for breath. He caught her hands and laced their fingers tight above her head, holding her open while he moved.

She felt the heat building sharp behind her ribs. Every thrust landed deep, unrelenting. His breath hit her skin in ragged bursts. She moaned, loud and unfiltered, hips tilting to take every inch.

He fucked her with nothing held back. Not domination. Not control.

Heat. Intention. Need.

Her body tightened, shaking beneath him.

He pressed his forehead to hers.

"Let go," he whispered, voice breaking.

She came—sharp and sudden, a full-body lock as her muscles clenched around him, wet and pulsing. His name broke from her throat, raw and jagged.

He followed with a groan torn straight from his chest. He buried himself to the hilt and came hard, body shaking, arms braced, breath lost. His weight dropped to hers, sweat and skin and everything they didn't have words for.

They stayed like that.

Tethered.

Spent.

And slowly, when their breath evened out, his hand found her face again, thumb brushing the corner of her mouth as if he wasn't ready to stop touching her. She leaned into it, eyes closed, body humming.

She didn't speak.

Neither did he.

ATER, she lay tangled beside him, one leg thrown over his, her cheek pressed into the hollow between his collarbone and shoulder. His chest rose and fell beneath her with a rhythm so steady it made the world feel briefly capable of staying in sync.

His fingers traced lazy circles along her spine, feather-light. Not from habit. Not from obligation. Simply because he wanted her there.

She wasn't thinking about the movie anymore.

Or the past.

Or the ache that had lived in her body so long she had almost learned to ignore it.

She was here.

Warm. Spent. Kissed raw and real.

And maybe it hadn't healed everything. Maybe it hadn't erased what came before.

But it had done enough.

CHAPTER 30
Threads of Deception

The boutique fitting room buzzed with laughter and the clatter of hangers as Arden stepped out, the emerald Elie Saab gown cascading around her like liquid light. The fabric shimmered with each movement; beadwork caught the overhead glow and scattered it like constellations. The plunging neckline and open back walked the line between daring and divine—commanding, elegant, impossible to ignore.

Penny's reaction was immediate and predictably dramatic. She clutched her chest, eyes wide in mock outrage.

"Arden, that dress doesn't say I belong. It screams bow down, peasants. Men will weep. Women will reconsider every life choice."

Rachel gave a low whistle. "You're not walking into that gala—you're storming it."

Leaning against the wall, Jade smirked. "It's not just a dress," she said. "It's power."

Arden turned toward the mirror, fingertips trailing over silk and beadwork as the gown settled against her curves. The green deepened the blue of her eyes. What stared back at her wasn't vanity, but intent. Still, beneath the glow, doubt crept in, familiar and unwelcome.

Her phone buzzed on the counter.

> Gideon: You'll look stunning in anything. But if you want my vote...neither. I prefer nothing at all.

She stifled a laugh, thumbs already moving.

Careful, Blackwell. You'll make me blush in public.

The reply came almost instantly.

That's the goal.

Her grin softened.

In the mirror, her reflection caught her eye again, and for a moment, the noise around her blurred. She could almost hear his voice, composure threaded through the teasing.

He had offered to handle the dress. She had refused, stubborn as ever. Standing here now, surrounded by friends, sequins, and the faint hum of champagne laughter, she felt him anyway. That pulse of reassurance lingered as if he were still in the room, reminding her she could own every spotlight that ever tried to burn her.

"It's...a lot," Arden murmured, teeth catching her lower lip.

"A lot?" Penny repeated, scandalized. "Arden, this dress is a damn coronation."

Jade crossed her arms, her voice softer but no less certain. "It's armor. Wear it like the queen you are."

Their confidence washed over her like a wave. Slowly, Arden straightened, her chin lifting. This wasn't only a gown; it was a declaration. Of everything she had fought for. Everything she refused to lose.

"You're right," she said quietly, her voice settling into itself. "This is the dress."

Penny squealed, grabbing Arden's hands. "I could cry. Now that we've crowned you Queen of the Gala, let's talk about me."

Arden arched a brow. "What about you?"

Penny's grin turned sly. "I'm going to the gala."

"What?" Arden and Jade said in unison.

"Sebastian Hawthorne needed a date," Penny said lightly, smirk dazzling. "Naturally, I volunteered."

Arden's stomach twisted. "Penny, you're not serious. He's dangerous."

"Dangerous is my middle name." Penny winked. "Relax. I'm not stupid. I'll keep my eyes open, and maybe have a little fun while I'm at it."

Arden's pulse spiked. "You don't understand. He's not just dangerous—he's calculated. Manipulative. This isn't about fun, Penny. He's using you to get to me. To get to Gideon."

Penny's gaze sharpened. "Then he doesn't know who he's dealing with." Breezy on the surface, steel beneath. "I can handle myself. And if he thinks he can shake you through me, he's in for a surprise."

Jade smirked. "Oh, he's in for a rude awakening. Penny's chaos is a full-contact sport."

"Exactly," Penny said, lifting a red satin gown that shimmered like spilled wine. "I've got my own plan for the night."

Rachel snorted from across the room. "This is either going to be epic or a disaster."

Arden met Penny's reflection in the mirror, unease tightening like a knot beneath her ribs. "Just...be careful, okay?"

Penny winked, too confident by half. "Careful is boring."

As Penny vanished into the fitting room, Arden's gaze drifted back to her own reflection. The emerald gown gleamed beneath the boutique lights—regal, commanding, and suddenly heavy.

The flutter in her chest wasn't vanity.

It was instinct.

Something was coming.

She reached for her phone, Gideon's last message still glowing on the screen. His confidence in her steadied her pulse, but the worry over Penny lingered, static in her bones.

This gala wasn't an event.

It was a battlefield.

Gideon's office buzzed with urgency. The desk, usually a study in meticulous order, had become a battlefield. Floor plans, scrawled notes, and red-marked documents sprawled across the polished wood in controlled chaos. Late-afternoon light cut through the tall windows, carving long shadows that mirrored the tension simmering beneath the surface.

Christian leaned over the plans, eyes sharp, movements precise. "If Sebastian makes his move, it'll be through the VIP wing," he said, tapping the corner of a blueprint. "Limited access points. Easy to control. If he wants her isolated, that's where it'll happen."

Gideon nodded once, tracking the lines on the paper. He didn't see a layout; he saw vectors. Risk. Places a man could disappear into shadow.

"He won't get the chance," he said quietly. "She'll have eyes on her all night."

Christian's mouth twitched—half smirk, half warning. "She's not going to like that. Arden doesn't exactly thrive on being boxed in."

"She doesn't have to like it." Gideon's voice softened, frustration flickering as his hand dragged through his hair. "She's too important to risk."

The humor drained from Christian's face. "You're playing a dangerous game. If this blows back—if Sebastian gets the upper hand—"

"It won't." Gideon's interruption was clean, final. He stepped back from the desk, posture settling into something immovable. "This ends tomorrow. No more games. No more shadows. He thinks he can manipulate her—use her to dismantle me." His jaw flexed, eyes darkening. "He doesn't understand her strength. Or ours."

Christian studied him for a beat.

Measuring.

"And if he takes it too far?"

Gideon didn't hesitate. The softness vanished, replaced by steel.

"Then he'll regret ever thinking about touching her."

His phone buzzed on the desk, a clean break in the tension. Arden's name lit the screen.

Do you think emerald or midnight blue? Penny's vote doesn't count. She's biased.

A rare smile eased the set of his jaw. He could see her clearly—standing in the boutique, chin tipped just so, stubborn and glowing.

You'll look stunning in anything. But if you want my vote...neither. I prefer nothing at all.

Three dots appeared. Then—

Arden: Careful, Blackwell. You'll make me blush in public.

That's the goal.

He set the phone down, her presence lingering like warmth beneath the chaos. The floor plans blurred. The noise receded. His pulse steadied around one detail.

Tomorrow wasn't about protecting a name.

It was about choosing Arden again.

❦

Across the city, daylight streamed through the rain-splattered windows of Sebastian Hawthorne's penthouse, scattering fractured light across polished marble floors. Storm clouds blurred the skyline into a dull, glimmering haze, the world reduced to reflection and distortion. The jagged rhythm of rain against the glass echoed the pressure building in his mind.

His desk—sleek, minimalist, immaculate—held a single object: a black envelope centered on the polished surface, elegant and unassuming.

Dangerous nonetheless.

The buzz of his phone broke through.

Harlan: The package is ready. Instructions?

Sebastian didn't hesitate.

Deliver it tomorrow. Make sure it's anonymous. She'll know who it's from.

He slid the phone back into his pocket and rose, every movement precise. At the window, he paused, studying his reflection in the glass.

Sharp eyes. Immaculate posture. Satisfaction flickering beneath the surface.

Control wasn't something he pursued.

It was something he embodied.

Outside, rain slicked the city in silver and gray. Glass towers cast uneven light. Umbrellas dotted the sidewalks below like restless shadows. The world continued, oblivious to the reckoning he was engineering.

Tomorrow night, the gala would loosen the final thread of Gideon Blackwell's carefully curated empire. The documents were flawless. The whispers had already taken root. Doubt was ready to bloom into spectacle.

And Arden—

Sebastian's expression darkened as his fingers traced the envelope's sharp edge.

She would finally see the truth.

Gideon couldn't protect her. He never could.

The thought sent a low thrill through him. She wasn't meant to be shielded or contained, her brilliance dimmed by another man's delusion of protection. She was fire—meant to burn, to unmake, to create something new in the ashes.

She deserved more than safety.

She deserved chaos.

Power.

Him.

The smile returned, cold and assured. He imagined Arden's faith in Gideon fracturing, realization blooming across her face, beautiful and devastating. When she finally saw Gideon as small, reactive, unworthy, she would burn brighter than ever.

And she would burn for him.

Little Fire.

His gaze dropped to the envelope. The gala wasn't an event.

It was an ignition.

Arden might rise on her own terms, crowned by fire and will. But when the ashes settled, Sebastian had no doubt who would be standing beside her.

He slipped the envelope into his coat pocket.

"She'll see the truth," he said quietly.

Outside, the rain intensified, silver light shivering against the glass. The city pulsed beneath it—alive, oblivious, waiting for the storm to break.

CHAPTER 31

Fractured Allegiances

The Blackwell estate's private sitting room exuded dominance, its opulence as deliberate as the family it housed. Gilded mirrors caught the chandelier's glow; velvet curtains framed rain-streaked windows; the faint scent of old bourbon lingered like memory. But the true weight of the room wasn't in its grandeur. It lived in generations of control. Even decadence, here, had sharp edges.

Evelyn Blackwell sat at the head of the mahogany table, poised and immaculate. Each movement of her hand scattered light from her diamonds across the polished wood, brilliance as precise as her gaze. Across from her, Alex leaned back, irritation masked by the easy swirl of amber in his glass.

"Gideon's not just making noise anymore," he said, clipped. "He's holding meetings with tenants. Digging through contracts we buried years ago. Bringing in outside counsel. He's not posturing—he's building something."

Evelyn's icy blue eyes narrowed. "Let him build," she said softly. The frost beneath the words was unmistakable. "Gideon mistakes idealism for strength. Power doesn't live in ideals. It lives in control. The Blackwell name has survived far greater rebellions than his."

The words landed clean and final.

Alex drained his glass in one swallow, setting it down with a faint clink. "And Sebastian?" he pressed. "You've seen how he looks at Arden. He's obsessed. That kind of fixation isn't useful forever. It's dangerous."

Evelyn's fingers paused mid-gesture before curling slowly around the table's edge. "Sebastian's preoccupation is...inconvenient," she said at last, voice smooth as cut glass. "But obsession, properly directed, can be useful. As long as his attention remains fixed on Arden, he serves a purpose."

"And if it doesn't?" Alex asked.

Her gaze sharpened, then slid away. "Then he becomes expendable. A scapegoat can be as valuable as an ally."

Alex exhaled sharply, frustration coiling tight. "He's already a liability. He invited one of Arden's friends to the gala."

Evelyn's head snapped toward him. "Her friend?"

"Penny Haverford," Alex said with a sneer. "The loud one. He invited her out of nowhere. Clearly trying to rattle Arden."

"Reckless," Evelyn murmured, disdain threading the word. The diamonds at her wrist caught the light again, a shimmer like warning. "Inviting one of her allies is idiocy."

"It's worse than idiocy," Alex snapped. "It's a risk we can't afford. Penny's loyal. If she senses something's off, she'll make noise, and the night could unravel."

Evelyn's expression remained unchanged, but her voice turned to steel. "If Sebastian's behavior threatens this family, he'll be dealt with. No one acts without accountability."

Alex leaned back, defeat threading his breath. "And Gideon? What if he actually pulls it off? What if he exposes everything?"

Evelyn allowed herself the faintest smile, sharp and bloodless. "Gideon doesn't have what it takes to win. He's tethered to principles that don't survive the real world. Conviction isn't power. Control is." Her voice dropped, cold and certain. "And we don't win by playing fair."

Outside, the rain intensified, striking the windows in a strong, percussive rhythm. Alex stared into the shadowed depths of his empty glass.

Evelyn remained unmoved. Serene. Certain. A woman sculpted by power, perfectly willing to weaponize love, blood, or both.

When Alex finally rose and left the room, Evelyn remained seated, her silhouette framed by the chandelier's glow. Light scattered across the polished mahogany table, fracturing into sharp reflections over the papers meticulously arrayed before her.

Contracts.

Surveillance photos.

Financial ledgers.

Each one a thread in the web she had spent decades weaving, every signature proof of her precision, her reach, her dominion.

Her fingers drifted to a photograph.

Penny Haverford.

A sharp nail tapped once against the glossy surface. The woman's wild grin and unapologetic posture radiated rebellion, a jarring contrast to the order Evelyn required. Inviting her to the gala wasn't merely reckless.

It was insubordination.

Sebastian's obsession with Arden had been a tolerable indulgence, something Evelyn could redirect or contain when necessary. But introducing a wildcard like Penny Haverford into her orbit?

That was chaos, not strategy.

"You think you're clever, Sebastian," she murmured, voice low and almost indulgent. "But cleverness without discipline is just noise."

She set the photograph aside and reached for another document. Gideon Blackwell's name stared back at her in black ink: tenant meetings, legal filings, alliances forming beyond the family's control. For the briefest moment, her composure tightened, fingers curling against the page.

Gideon was no longer the prodigal son testing his limits.

He was becoming a fracture.

And fractures, in Evelyn's world, were never tolerated. They were sealed.

Or excised.

Her attention returned to the centerpiece of the table: the gala plans. Detailed. Immaculate. Unforgiving. She leaned forward, steepling her fingers beneath her chin as her thoughts aligned, variables clicking neatly into place.

The gala would not merely display power.

It would reclaim it.

A reminder that the Blackwell name was not a legacy to be inherited, but a fortress to be enforced.

Chandelier light caught in her eyes, diamonds of reflection glinting in their depths. Her lips curved into the faintest, sharpest smile.

The stage was set.

The players assembled.

And in her house, only one outcome was acceptable.

Control.

THE HEAVY OAK door to Evelyn's private sitting room creaked open. Colton stepped inside, rain still glistening on his coat. His movements were precise, but the damp sheen betrayed the haste with which he had answered her summons. The thick carpet swallowed his footsteps as he crossed the room.

Evelyn stood by the window, her silhouette cut sharp against the storm.

Outside, rain carved jagged paths down the glass, pelting relentlessly. The diamonds at her wrist caught the light in the reflection—hard brilliance, perfectly matched to her composure.

"You called for me," Colton said. His voice was even, curiosity threaded carefully through restraint.

Evelyn didn't turn. She let the silence stretch, a reminder of who controlled the air between them. When she finally spoke, her voice was soft.

Too soft.

"Do you remember the man you tapped to frighten Arden Rivers?" she asked, each syllable measured. "The one outside the karaoke bar."

Colton stiffened. His jaw flexed. "I remember."

Evelyn turned then, icy blue eyes locking onto him.

"And do you remember how that little stunt not only failed," she said, tone unhurried, "but emboldened her?"

She stepped closer.

"She's grown bold, Colton. Too bold. And now Gideon and his investigator are digging deeper. Closer to things we've spent decades burying."

Colton's composure flickered. Just once. "I underestimated her," he said. "It won't happen again."

"No," Evelyn replied, heels clicking softly as she closed the distance. Each step landed like a metronome. "It won't. Because from this point forward, every move will be flawless."

She stopped directly in front of him.

"Mistakes are luxuries," she continued calmly. "And liabilities..."

Her gaze hardened, the rest left unspoken.

"...are removed."

Colton's jaw tightened. "I'll handle it. What do you need?"

Her smile was small. Precise. Dangerous. "Good. Because the gala will be the turning point. Sebastian will make his move. Gideon will counter. And Arden—"

She paused, letting the name linger.

"Arden will find herself in the crossfire."

Colton swallowed. "What's the priority?"

Before Evelyn could answer, a faint creak broke through the room. The unmistakable complaint of old floorboards beneath cautious weight.

Her head snapped toward the doorway. "Who's there?"

Cate stepped from the shadows, every inch of her composed. Blonde hair framed her face in soft, deceptive waves, the kind that suggested innocence without ever promising it. Her tone was smooth, casual.

"Relax, Evelyn. I was just looking for Alex."

Evelyn's gaze cut to her like a scalpel. "Alex isn't here," she said, each word clipped. "And eavesdropping is a habit that tends to invite...consequences."

Cate smiled. Too sweet. Too measured. "Eavesdropping? Of course not. But you should know—these walls are thin. It's remarkably easy to overhear things. Even when you're not trying."

Evelyn's diamonds flashed as her hand tightened on the table's edge. "Be careful what you overhear," she murmured, silk drawn over steel. "Curiosity has a way of backfiring."

Cate tilted her head, eyes gleaming with something sharper than amusement. "I'll keep that in mind." A beat. "You've always been the expert on handling...backfires."

The silence snapped tight.

Power and sheer stubbornness held the room in fragile equilibrium, neither woman willing to blink, neither willing to yield. Then Cate turned, the click of her heels a deliberate punctuation as she left.

The door closed.

Evelyn's expression didn't change.

She turned to Colton. "Keep an eye on her. If Cate becomes a liability, deal with her."

Colton didn't hesitate. "Understood."

Evelyn faced the window again, her reflection fractured by trickles of rain. The storm outside beat harder against the glass, but the fury beneath her composure burned hotter still.

Cate's insolence was a reminder: even within a fortress, cracks could form.

She lifted her glass, dark red wine catching the chandelier's glow.

The Blackwell name wasn't a legacy.

It was a shield.

A fortress.

And Evelyn Blackwell would defend it—not because it was unbreakable, but because she was.

CHAPTER 32

Lines in the Sand

The bedroom oozed opulence, its muted tones and rich textures the essence of the Blackwell legacy: luxury wrapped in shadow. Dim light from the bedside lamps spilled across polished wood and crisp linens, softening the room's edges without touching its chill.

Cate Blackwell stood by the window, her silhouette etched against the rain-slicked cityscape. One hand clutched the curtain, knuckles pale. The tension in her frame had become impossible to hide.

Behind her, Alex lounged in a leather armchair, a tumbler of bourbon balanced between his fingers. The loosened tie and unbuttoned collar gave the illusion of ease, but his shoulders betrayed him. Irritation rolled off him, unchecked.

"Are you going to keep glaring at the rain," he said finally, "or tell me what's on your mind?"

Cate turned. For the first time, her composure cracked. Anger flared in her sharp blue eyes.

"I've overlooked a lot, Alex," she began, voice even but edged with fire. "Your ambition. Your indiscretions. The way your family plays god with people's lives."

He raised his glass in mock salute, the clink of ice an insult. "And I appreciate your unwavering devotion, darling."

Her jaw tightened. "But this?" she said, stepping closer. "This is beyond shady deals and backroom politics. People are losing their homes, their livelihoods. And you're standing by."

Alex straightened, irritation sharpening his tone. "What are you talking about?"

"I overheard Evelyn and Colton tonight," Cate said, each word landing like a blade. "This isn't just about Gideon or Arden. Sebastian's involved. Evelyn's orchestrating something far beyond business. It's vile. And if you sit back and do nothing, you're complicit."

He set his glass down hard enough to rattle the crystal. "Complicit?" His voice rose. "Do you even hear yourself? This is how power works. You don't get to the top by playing the hero."

Her anger snapped, sharp and bright.

"Don't you dare condescend to me. I knew what I was marrying into, but even I have limits. I've turned a blind eye to your affairs, your deals, your moral decay. But this?" Her voice cracked, raw with conviction. "This is where it stops. This isn't business, Alex. It's monstrous."

He took a step toward her, his expression hardening. "And what do you expect me to do? Take a stand against my own family? That's not bravery, Cate. That's suicide."

She didn't flinch. "If you can't live with the consequences of doing the right thing," she said coldly, "then I'll find someone who can."

His eyes narrowed, voice low and dangerous. "Careful, Cate. You're playing with fire."

"No," she replied softly, her tone a blade wrapped in velvet. "You are."

She turned and strode toward the door, heels clicking across the marble. The door shut behind her with a clean, decisive sound.

In the hallway, Cate pressed her back against the wall. Her breath came shallow, composure cracking in slow tremors. She wasn't naïve; she knew what defying Evelyn Blackwell meant.

But silence was no longer an option.

She pulled her phone from her pocket, fingers trembling as she typed.

I need to talk to you. Alone.

The name on the screen glowed like a lifeline.

Gideon.

Cate hesitated—one heartbeat, then two. Then she pressed send.

The message vanished into the ether, small and irreversible.

For better or worse, she had drawn her line in the sand.

And this time, she wasn't the one who would burn.

Arden hadn't expected to see Gideon tonight, not with the gala looming like a storm cloud ready to break, but the knock on her door had been unmistakable.

Measured.

Familiar.

And now he was here, standing in the sanctuary of her room, his presence grounding and electric all at once.

"Careful, Blackwell," she teased, though her voice came softer than intended. "You're starting to sound sentimental."

"Maybe I am." His usual expression was gone, replaced by something raw and unguarded. His gaze held hers with a warmth that stole her breath.

The weight of the day pressed down on her shoulders, and she stepped closer, drawn by instinct more than thought. "Tomorrow feels like a storm waiting to hit."

"It is," Gideon admitted. "But we'll face it together."

The certainty in his voice wrapped around her. When his hand lifted to brush her cheek, the touch sent a shiver through her—not fear, but the promise carried in his fingertips.

"Stay," she whispered, before she could second-guess herself.

He studied her for a heartbeat. Dark gray eyes. Tender resolve. Then he nodded.

"I'll stay."

He shrugged out of his jacket, draped it over the chair, and rolled his sleeves to his forearms. An unconscious habit. Intimate. When he sat on the edge of the bed, the space between them dissolved.

Arden joined him, close enough to feel his heat, the tension humming low between them. She leaned back into his chest, his arm curving around her shoulders, anchoring her there. His heartbeat was the reassurance she hadn't known she needed.

Her fingers traced idle patterns over his hand. "Do you think she'll try something tomorrow?"

"Evelyn?" His tone stayed level, but steel threaded through it. "Always. But we'll be ready."

She smiled faintly. "You make it sound simple."

"It is," he said, pressing a kiss to the crown of her head. "Because I won't let anything happen to you."

Silence settled, rich and fragile. Rain tapped softly at the windows, keeping time with their breathing. The world felt suspended, reduced to pulse and warmth and the rise and fall of his chest beneath her.

Tomorrow would change everything.

But tonight belonged to the calm at the center of the storm.

Neither of them wanted to let it go.

The fragile peace fractured with a soft buzz.

Gideon shifted, his arm tightening briefly before he reached for the phone on the nightstand. The glow of the screen cast faint light across the room. He angled it so they both could see.

Cate: I need to talk to you. Alone.

Arden turned, brow knitting. "Cate?"

"If she's reaching out," Gideon said, focus sharpening, "it's not casual. It's Evelyn."

The implications settled between them.

"You'll meet her," Arden said.

"Yes." Immediate. Certain. He set the phone down, the sound final. Then his gaze returned to her, softer. "But not tonight."

"Gideon—"

He kissed her. The kind that stopped worry before it could take shape.

"Not tonight," he murmured. "Tonight, we hold on to this."

But when he pulled back, the silence didn't settle.

It simmered.

Arden's breath stuttered, her hands still curled in the sheet where she had anchored herself. Gideon had moved just far enough to look at her, eyes dark and too full of everything he hadn't said.

She reached for him.

He met her halfway.

Their mouths crashed together—not soft this time, not measured. This kiss didn't ask. It took. It tasted like goodbye, though neither of them was leaving yet. She felt his fingers fist in her hair, tipping her head back, forcing her to meet the full force of him. His other hand gripped her hip, dragging her beneath him in one rough pull.

Their bodies aligned without preamble. No slow undressing. No lead-up. She was already bare beneath the thin sheet, and he was already moving—shirt gone, jeans shoved low, breath hot against her neck as he shifted and settled between her thighs.

She gasped when he thrust into her in one deep stroke. No hesitation. Only heat.

Only him.

"Gideon—"

"I know," he bit out, voice cracking under everything behind it. "I know."

He didn't start slow. Didn't tease. He moved inside her with force, completely consumed, each thrust landing deep and solid. Her hands scrabbled against his back, nails dragging down muscle and sweat-slick skin. He growled low against her throat and bit down just hard enough to make her gasp again.

She wrapped her legs around his waist, anchoring herself to him as if the rest of the world were already falling away.

"You always kiss me like it's the last time," she whispered against his jaw, voice splintering.

He stilled, hips buried deep, breath shaking hard against her ear.

His grip tightened in her hair.

"Because I don't know how to kiss you any other way."

Then he moved again. Harder. Rougher. As if the rhythm could prove him wrong.

Her body arched beneath him, meeting every thrust, every frantic pull of skin on skin. The bed creaked beneath them. The air thickened around them. Every gasp, every moan, every desperate sound filled the room.

He grabbed both her wrists and pinned them above her head with one hand. His other found her thigh, hauled it higher, opening her wider, driving into her deeper.

She broke first, writhing beneath him, crying out as her body locked down around him, pleasure crashing through her in sharp, staggering waves. He didn't slow. Didn't soften.

He fucked her through it, jaw tight, eyes locked on her face.

Then he came, deep and guttural, a raw curse torn from his throat as he emptied into her, shaking with the force of it.

He collapsed over her, still inside, still breathing hard, face buried against her neck.

They didn't speak.

Didn't move.

Their bodies stayed tangled—slick, warm, joined at every point that mattered. Her wrists were still caught in his grip. Her pulse still kicked beneath his mouth.

Eventually, he loosened his hold.

She didn't pull away.

Outside, the rain kept falling.

Inside, there was only this: the quiet, the wreckage, the last calm before it all burned.

CHAPTER 33
Edge of Madness

The city sprawled beneath Sebastian's penthouse like a restless beast, its pulse visible in the shimmer of lights bleeding through glass. Thunder rolled in the distance, low and guttural, matching the storm tightening inside him.

Once a monument to control and opulence, the penthouse now bore the marks of obsession. Papers littered every surface, their edges curling in the damp air sneaking through a cracked window. Maps and photographs clung to the walls, tethered by strands of crimson twine that seemed to pulse like veins in the low light. At the center stood a board—shrine and crime scene all at once—its web converging on a single name.

Arden Rivers.

Her face dominated the space.

Arden laughing behind the bar, smile open and unguarded. Arden walking through the rain, hair catching the streetlight like flame. Arden standing her ground, blue eyes blazing.

Each image was a fragment. Stolen, rearranged, twisted into the story he needed her to inhabit.

Sebastian reached out and traced one photograph with unsteady fingers, as though touch alone could collapse the distance between them. His sleeves were unevenly rolled, his once-pristine shirt rumpled, collar undone. The man who had once built empires with precision now stood tethered to chaos by fixation alone.

"She doesn't see it yet," he murmured, voice thinning at the edges. "But she will. Tomorrow, everything becomes clear."

Behind him, Harlan Atwood leaned against the bar, a glass of whiskey catching the amber light. His composure remained immaculate, jarringly out of place amid the wreckage.

"You're walking a narrow line," Harlan said evenly, warning smoothed beneath restraint. "Fixation blinds even the sharpest minds. You're playing with fire."

Sebastian turned, conviction burning hot and unfocused in his eyes. "Do I look blind to you, Harlan? I see everything. Gideon's every move. Every lie. Every time he touches her like she's something fragile he needs to shield."

His voice fractured, then hardened.

"She isn't his to protect."

Harlan didn't blink. "And if she doesn't agree?"

Sebastian laughed. The sound was brittle. "She will. Gideon has poisoned her perspective. But when his world collapses, when the truth comes out, she'll finally see who's been there all along. Who understands her."

"And if she still doesn't?"

For the briefest moment, something flickered across Sebastian's face.

Doubt.

A hairline crack.

Then it vanished.

"Then she's trapped," he said softly, almost kindly. "But I'll save her anyway. Even if I have to save her from herself."

The storm outside pressed against the windows, thunder swelling like distant applause.

Harlan set down his glass with a soft clink, opposition contained in the small gesture. "You're risking everything. Your alliances. Your leverage. Evelyn's patience. If this collapses, there's no coming back."

Sebastian turned away, fingers brushing the chaos on the table: falsified records, forged transfers, lies engineered into evidence. His hand settled on a file with calculated care.

"Bridges are for men who retreat," he said coldly. "I don't retreat. I conquer."

At the center of the mess lay a single envelope, the name Dr. Lila Whitaker scrawled across it in bold ink.

"She'll testify," Sebastian muttered. "She understands the cost of disobedience."

Harlan's voice dropped. "Lila's looking for an exit. Push her too hard and she'll take it."

"She won't," Sebastian snapped. "She knows what happens to people who cross me."

"And Arden?" Harlan asked quietly.

Sebastian's expression softened. Not warmth—conviction.

"She'll come to me. I've made sure of it."

On the table lay a note in his elegant, deliberate hand.

You deserve the truth.

Meet me by the east wing terrace.

Alone.

Harlan frowned. "And if Gideon reaches her first?"

Sebastian's jaw tightened. "He won't. By the time he understands what's happening, she'll already see him for what he is. A coward. A fraud."

Midnight bled into the storm as rain lashed the glass. Sebastian returned to the board, his shadow stretching over Arden's photographs. A single red rose rested beneath her image. He picked it up, the thorns biting deep into his palm until blood welled against the petals.

"She doesn't understand yet," he whispered, voice trembling. "But she will. When this is over, she'll know I'm the only one who truly sees her."

Harlan paused at the doorway, his silhouette cut by storm light. "Like I said before, this kind of interest blinds men, Sebastian. Remember that."

Sebastian didn't turn. Blood slipped from his hand onto the white envelope.

"Blindness is for those who fear the outcome," he said softly. "Tomorrow, fear won't matter. Only victory."

The door shut behind Harlan, leaving Sebastian alone with the storm. He set the rose beside the letter, its petals darkened with blood.

Lightning fractured his reflection in the glass: one man, split by obsession.

"Tomorrow," he murmured, almost tenderly. "Gideon will fall. The Blackwells will burn. And Arden—"

He smiled.

"Arden will finally be mine."

Harlan's departure had sounded like a gavel. Silence, then rain—small percussion on glass, the city murmuring far below, oblivious to the weather inside this room.

Sebastian stood amid his ruin; the penthouse no longer a monument to control but a map of a mind unstitched. Papers lay like fallen leaves, inked trails like arteries. The air tasted of damp paper and intent.

His fingers found the board—the collage of Arden. Her life sliced into frames: laughing behind a bar, hair haloed by rain, the flame in her ocean-blue eyes. He touched one photograph as if blessing it or breaking it; the gesture was both.

"She's not yours," he whispered, the words trembling on the edge of agony. "Not yet."

Rain carved the city into shards of light; his reflection fractured in the glass, wild, taut, raw. They didn't see her, Gideon, Evelyn, the whole tidy world of inherited privilege. He did. He saw the fire she carried; he saw what they mistook for weakness.

He moved like a predator circling its prey, then crossed to the table where a single red rose rested atop a black envelope. He turned the bloom in his hands; a thorn bit his thumb. He let the sting stand, blood as ledger, as proof.

"She'll bleed," he said softly. "Not because I want it. Because it's the only way she sheds what binds her, loyalty, blind trust, safety dressed as a cage."

He inhaled the rose. His thoughts unfurled: ash and light, her hand in his as the world burned away.

"They'll call it madness," he mused, a bitter smile curving his mouth. "History celebrates the bold."

His fingers closed around a photograph of Gideon and crushed it; paper surrendered beneath his fist. "Gideon Blackwell," he snarled. "The shield. The liar. The fraud."

The image fell among the papers, the rose, the black envelope.

He returned to Arden's face, tracing the curve of her mouth with his eyes. She was incandescent. Untamed. The storm ratcheted louder; lightning stitched the sky. He stood long and still, mania threaded through a chosen calm.

"This isn't madness," he whispered into the rain. "This is destiny."

Outside, the city drowned in the storm. Inside, his resolve was absolute.

Tomorrow: fire.

Tomorrow: ruin.

Tomorrow: Arden, his at last.

CHAPTER 34
Fragile Threads

The ballroom hummed with elegant disorder, gleaming beneath the soft glow of crystal chandeliers. Caterers moved in precise rhythm, florists adjusted the last blooms of their arrangements, and the faint strain of strings tuning drifted through the air like anticipation made audible. Every detail bore Evelyn Blackwell's mark: measured, immaculate, merciless. Everyone present knew better than to fall short; even the florists moved as if they were being watched.

Gideon had arrived hours earlier, his timing as purposeful as the event's choreography. He moved through the room with practiced ease in a crisp tuxedo and undone bow tie—his single act of rebellion against the empire he had inherited. The Blackwell name pressed heavy on his shoulders, but his mind refused to stay there.

Evelyn's gaze cut through the bustle as she swept across the marble, her diamond bracelet scattering light with every sharp gesture.

"Make sure the centerpieces are symmetrical," she snapped to an assistant. "And the mayor's aide must be seated where he'll be seen. Appearances matter."

Then her eyes found him.

"Gideon." Her tone held that familiar demand, cold as crystal. "Everything must be flawless. We cannot afford even the appearance of a misstep."

"It will be," he said, steel threading his voice.

The conviction in it made her hesitate a fraction. Then her lips tightened, and she turned away to issue another string of corrections.

Gideon exhaled, the mask slipping as he stepped into the shadow of the grand staircase. The clamor faded behind him. He drew out his phone, Arden's name glowing softly, her last message an anchor in the noise, holding him where marble never could.

Be careful tonight. I'll see you soon.

He brushed a hand across his jaw, a rare smile ghosting there. The memory of her still clung to him: the warmth of her body against his last night, the promise pressed to her temple before he left. Now, surrounded by marble and mirrors, the thought of her was the only thing that steadied him.

Footsteps interrupted the moment. Alex appeared at the base of the stairs, glass in hand, his smirk already loaded.

"Still hiding, brother?" he drawled, the amber liquid catching the light. "The perfect Blackwell heir—avoiding the spotlight."

Gideon slid the phone into his pocket and straightened, composure restored. "I'm ensuring everything runs smoothly," he said, voice cool as stone.

"Always so dependable." Alex leaned against the banister, savoring the taunt.

"Better dependable than irrelevant."

The smirk faltered, but before the next blow could land, Evelyn's voice carried across the room, summoning Alex by name. He tossed back the last of his drink and stalked off, the echo of crystal and resentment trailing behind him.

Left alone again, Gideon glanced at the clock. The hour was drawing close, anticipation tightening in his chest like a pulled wire. Arden's presence was the only light cutting through the storm that loomed ahead.

When she arrived, he would be ready for whatever tonight demanded.

Arden stood at the kitchen counter, watching as Penny transformed their cramped living room into a makeshift salon. The table had become a scatter of curling irons, brushes, open palettes, and glittering tools laid out with alarming purpose.

"Step one," Penny announced, brandishing a curling wand like a scepter, "ensure you look so devastatingly gorgeous that Evelyn Blackwell has no choice but to hate you on sight."

Arden smirked, arms crossed. "That's the official strategy? Intimidation by beauty?"

"Damn right." Penny's green eyes sparked. "Step two: slay the room. Preferably with a single glance."

"Ambitious."

"Efficient," Penny corrected. "Now sit. You're my masterpiece tonight."

Arden obeyed, lowering into the chair. "You know I'm fine doing this myself. I keep telling you—"

Penny interrupted in a singsong voice, "And I keep telling you to just let me have this."

Outside, the city murmured its low, constant hymn while Penny's movements sharpened into focus. The curling iron clicked off. Then came the brush, lightly twisting strands of Arden's dark hair into a braid that felt less like ornament than intention.

Her phone buzzed on the counter. Gideon's name lit the screen, and something in her chest eased.

See you soon. And for the record I'm already in awe.

A smile ghosted across her lips, loosening tension she hadn't realized she was carrying.

Penny caught it immediately. "Was that lover boy?" She arched a brow. "Did he send one of those texts that knocks the air out of you?"

"Something like that." Arden typed a quick reply, the weight of the night briefly held at bay.

"You're grinning like an idiot," Penny said, pinning jeweled clips into place. "Good. Keep it. You're going to need it."

The smile faded a touch. "You'll be careful tonight, right? With Sebastian?"

Penny's hands stilled. Their eyes met in the mirror, humor gone, resolve burning clean beneath it.

"Relax," she said softly. "Sebastian thinks he's running the game. He isn't."

Arden nodded, unease threading beneath her silence. Penny's bravado had always been her shield. Tonight, it looked thinner than usual.

When Penny stepped back and lifted the mirror, Arden barely recognized herself. The emerald gown flowed like liquid light, beadwork catching every stray gleam. Her hair framed her face with meticulous grace; her features had sharpened into something regal, dangerous, and impossible to dismiss.

"Holy hell," Penny breathed, hands settling on Arden's shoulders. "You're not walking into that gala. You're commanding it."

Arden laughed quietly, gratitude rising sharp and bright. She squeezed Penny's hand. "Thank you."

Penny pressed diamond earrings into her palm, the grin returning. "Don't thank me yet. Chin up—"

She met Arden's gaze in the mirror.

"You've got a dynasty to shake."

❦

Evelyn surveyed the preparations like someone fluent in command, unimpressed by the pageantry surrounding her. Every detail was purposeful, a reflection of her taste: florals restrained yet exquisite, champagne chosen as much for implication as flavor. Her diamond bracelet caught the chandelier's glow as she adjusted the angle of a crystal centerpiece, the gesture small but final.

The assistant who had placed it hesitated, then withdrew without a word.

The ballroom shimmered, an immaculate illusion of the Blackwell dynasty at full bloom. Beneath the polished surface, however, Evelyn was conducting something far more intricate.

Alex approached, irritation threaded through the ease he affected. Her gaze flicked to him, quick and assessing.

"The board?" she asked.

"Seated exactly as you wanted," he said, jaw tight.

A faint smile curved her lips, devoid of warmth. "Good. Tonight is about the Blackwell name. Not Gideon's rebellion. Not Sebastian's theatrics. And certainly not anyone's lapses in judgment."

"Speaking of theatrics," Alex drawled, "have you seen Sebastian? He's practically vibrating with whatever scheme he's nursing."

Her expression didn't shift. Her voice cooled. "Let him entertain himself. Sebastian's usefulness ends where his obsession begins."

She let the silence finish the thought.

Alex's smirk flickered, then steadied. Evelyn noticed.

She always did.

"And Cate?" she asked lightly. "Where is she?"

His fingers curled against the table's edge. "Getting ready. You know how she is about appearances."

Something sharp passed through Evelyn's eyes, a memory quickly sealed.

"Make sure she understands her role tonight," she said. "We don't need surprises."

"I'll handle it."

"See that you do."

Alex disappeared into the hum of the room. Evelyn moved toward the edge of the ballroom, her reflection gliding across the polished floor. She pressed one manicured finger to the discreet earpiece at her collar.

"Colton," she said, voice balanced between silk and steel. "Arden Rivers is your priority. No one else."

A pause.

"Understood."

Evelyn smiled and lifted her gaze to the grand staircase, already anticipating the moment the first fracture would appear in her flawless design.

THE PENTHOUSE, once a monument to precision, now mirrored its owner's disarray. Papers littered every surface: documents, photographs, fragments of plans spilling into one another in chaotic unity. A web of red thread stretched across the walls, taut and frayed, every line converging on a single name.

Arden Rivers.

Sebastian stood before the windows, the city below glittering like a living organism. Its pulse should have thrilled him. Tonight, it only amplified the static in his mind. His reflection stared back, hollow-eyed, unraveled, barely recognizable. The knot of his tie hung loose; cufflinks lay abandoned beside a crumpled velvet box.

Inside it, an amethyst ring caught the lamplight, cool and immaculate.

Waiting.

"She doesn't see it yet," he murmured, as if speaking a truth that required patience. "But she will."

He lifted the ring, metal biting into his palm. In his mind, the moment unfolded, crystalline: Arden standing before him, eyes wide not with fear, but recognition, as he slid it onto her finger. Then she would understand. Then Gideon's careful distortions would collapse beneath the weight of what was real.

Sebastian began to pace, uneven and uncontrolled. His gaze snagged on a photograph of her—head tilted, defiant, luminous. The image both enraged and grounded him. His thumb brushed the edge of the frame.

"He doesn't see you," he said, voice tightening. "Not your fire. Not what it costs you to carry it."

The air felt dense, pressing in. He leaned closer to the glass until his breath fogged the surface, his reflection warping, splitting, reforming. He searched the eyes staring back at him for control. For something solid.

All he found was motion.

The photograph seemed to watch him. With a sharp movement, he seized it, fingers curling until the paper bent and buckled.

"After tonight," he whispered, the promise edged with steel, "there won't be any confusion."

The ring slipped from his grasp and struck the floor with a soft, forgotten clatter. His attention had already shifted to the table.

To the note.

You deserve the truth.
Meet me by the east wing terrace.
Alone.

A slow smile curved his mouth, satisfaction settling into something calmer, more resolved. The chaos around him aligned, every thread tightening into place. The jewelry could wait.

The terrace would be the moment.

He dragged a hand through his hair, forcing order where he could.

"Tonight," he said quietly. "Gideon will fall. The Blackwells will fracture. And Arden—"

His voice softened, almost tender.

"—will finally understand."

Outside, the city hummed, indifferent and unaware. Light pressed against the glass, but Sebastian saw only her.

By morning, his world and hers would be irrevocably bound.

And there would be no undoing it.

CHAPTER 35

Whispers in Gilded Shadows

The Blackwell Annual Charity Gala unfolded like a symphony of wealth and deception, every note composed to dazzle and distract. Crystal chandeliers spilled light across the marble floors, breaking into fractured halos. Every gilded flourish dared scrutiny, its perfection almost taunting. Beneath the shimmer and laughter of New York's elite, a quiet rot pulsed—corruption wrapped in gold, sanctified by applause.

Gideon had been here for hours, a still point amid the storm of preparation. His presence wasn't merely expected; it was mandatory. The heir apparent. The symbol of control. He wore the role flawlessly, greeting donors with a firm hand and a measured smile, the practiced ease of a man born into performance, muscle memory honed long before he learned how to resist it.

Evelyn's sharp directives cut through the air. Alex's barbs landed where they could. Gideon absorbed them all, composure unbroken, restraint immaculate. Yet beneath the veneer, pressure gathered, coiling tight behind his ribs. The weight of the night pressed harder with every passing minute.

His thoughts were already elsewhere, drawn toward the moment Arden would step through those doors.

The night air carried the promise of a storm, a fitting prelude to the tension simmering beneath the gala's sheen. Arden stepped from the sleek black town car, the hem of her emerald gown brushing the damp pavement. The fabric clung to her curves with unapologetic elegance; beadwork caught the stray light and scattered it like something alive. The slit along her leg wasn't vanity. It was declaration—bold, defiant, entirely her own.

Behind her, Penny emerged with effortless grace, her silver gown rippling like liquid mercury beneath the estate's glow. Alexandre Vauthier; all sharp lines and unrepentant glamour. She looped her arm through Arden's, a playful smirk already in place.

"Ready to set this place on fire?" Penny asked, her voice equal parts challenge and charm.

Arden's lips curved faintly, though her pulse thudded. "I'm aiming to survive the night, not scorch it."

"Survival's overrated," Penny said, her grin bright enough to blind. "Let's walk in there and outshine every chandelier."

A soft laugh slipped from Arden as Penny tugged her forward, their heels clicking in unison against the marble. But as the estate rose before them, its grand façade washed in gold light, her smile dimmed. The air itself seemed to tighten—charged with expectation, with memory, with everything waiting on the other side of those doors.

She lifted her chin.

Whatever waited beyond them, she would face it on her own terms.

The Blackwell estate's ballroom unfolded like a monument to excess. Gold accents shimmered across every surface, the soft strains of a string quartet threading through the low hum of conversation. Waiters moved with choreographed ease, trays of champagne catching light as they passed between guests draped in couture and diamonds. The air carried a charge, the faint metallic tang of power—intoxicating to those who chased it, suffocating to those who knew its cost.

Arden entered with the poise of a woman who understood the room expected spectacle and intended to give it something sharper. The train of her gown whispered across the marble as her gaze swept the crowd, sharp and assessing, every movement measured. The predators here didn't bare their teeth. They smiled. Their weapons were laughter and civility.

"Miss Rivers."

The voice cut cleanly through the music.

Smooth.

Familiar.

Unwelcome.

Her stomach tightened as she turned. Sebastian Hawthorne stood only a few feet away, his midnight tuxedo cut to precision, cufflinks catching the chandelier's glow. His smile was effortless; his eyes were not. Something jagged lived beneath the polish. Something that watched too closely.

"Sebastian," she said, tone even and edged just enough. "What brings you out of the shadows?"

His smile deepened, predatory in its restraint. "I'm not one to linger in them," he murmured. His gaze swept over her, slow enough to feel deliberate, before shifting to Penny. "Though I must admit, the light is captivating tonight."

Penny arched a brow, her grin immediate and irreverent. "Flattery and tuxedos? What's next, a dance-off?"

Sebastian laughed, low and practiced. "Miss Haverford. Always the spark in the room." He extended an arm, courtly to the point of mockery. "The evening awaits. May I?"

Penny's eyes flashed with mischief as she slipped her arm through his. "Don't wait up," she called over her shoulder, tossing Arden a wink before vanishing into the crowd beside him.

Sebastian glanced back once. The look was brief, barbed.

A promise.

Or a warning.

Then he was gone, swallowed by glitz and glamour.

Arden remained still, her pulse a taut rhythm beneath the music. Penny's laughter drifted back, light and careless, doing little to loosen the knot tightening in her chest. Straightening, she drew a measured breath and turned toward the sea of guests.

Whatever game Sebastian was playing, she had already decided.

He wouldn't win.

Dan stood near the entrance, scanning the crowd with the vigilance of someone who missed nothing. Gideon caught his eye, a brief, silent exchange confirming everything was in motion, before his attention shifted—pulled inexorably toward the one person who made the rest of the room fall away.

Arden's heart quickened as her gaze swept the ballroom. She didn't have to search long. Gideon stood out even among power players, as if the air itself adjusted around him. His tuxedo—Tom Ford, of course—was luxury made real, silk lapels catching chandelier light, amplifying a magnetism that felt both effortless and deliberate.

He moved like a man who didn't attend rooms.

He claimed them.

When his eyes found hers across the polished floor, the tension coiled in her chest loosened, replaced by a steadiness she hadn't realized she needed. Something settled.

Something familiar.

In a few measured strides, he reached her. His attention locked onto her as if nothing else existed. His gaze traced the emerald gown, lingered on the way it held her, then lifted to her eyes. His mouth curved, small and private. He leaned in, his voice dropping low, belonging only to her.

"You're stunning," he murmured, warmth threaded through the words, unmaking the last of her nerves.

Heat crept into her cheeks, but she held his gaze, a real smile breaking free—soft, unguarded. "You look pretty damn good yourself."

His smile tilted, but his eyes stayed serious. Without hesitation, he offered his arm.

She took it.

The simple contact anchored her amid the social noise, the message between them clear as they stood together: whatever this night intended to take, it would have to go through both of them first.

As they moved through the crowd, a shadow crossed Gideon's features, concern tightening into something sharper. His voice dropped, edged and controlled.

"What the hell is she doing with him?"

Arden followed his gaze, and the knot in her stomach cinched. Penny and Sebastian cut through the room like a staged distraction, Penny all silver light and easy confidence, Sebastian polished, predatory, too smooth by half.

"I didn't know until the last minute," Arden said, her breath thinning. "He asked her. I couldn't believe she actually said yes."

Gideon's jaw set. His grip closed around her hand, firm and stable. "Sebastian doesn't make moves without intent. Penny with him isn't accidental."

"She's sharp," Arden replied, steadier now, conviction taking hold. "She won't let him play her."

"That doesn't mean she's safe," Gideon said, his tone hardening. "Sebastian uses people. He doesn't care who bleeds."

Arden stopped. Her fingers pressed to his chest, instinctive and calming. "I'll watch her," she said quietly. "But tonight is bigger than him. We can't lose focus."

The contact eased something in him. His shoulders loosened a fraction as he exhaled.

"Stay close tonight," he said. "Sebastian isn't the only threat in this room."

Her chin lifted. She met his gaze without flinching. "I'm not running, Gideon. This is your shot to expose them. I won't be scared off."

His hand slid to her waist, thumb brushing the delicate fabric of her gown—protective, intimate, saying more than he could afford aloud.

"Your safety comes first," he said, voice firm and weighted. "Promise me you'll be careful."

"I can handle myself." Her voice held, unyielding.

His eyes darkened, not with doubt, but recognition. He knew what this night could become. His grip tightened once, then softened as his other hand lifted, brushing a loose strand of hair from her cheek.

"I know you can," he murmured, voice rasping with restraint. "But I'm not losing you. Not tonight. Not ever."

The words settled between them, heavy and alive.

She covered his hand at her waist, pressing it there. "You won't."

For a beat, the gala fell away: the music, the laughter, the shimmer reduced to static. Then a shift in the room broke the spell.

Gideon's focus snapped toward the far end of the ballroom. Evelyn and Alex stood beneath the chandeliers, their composure brittle beneath the light.

Resolve replaced the softness in his eyes. His hand lingered one final heartbeat before he stepped back.

"I need to handle something," he said quietly. Steel, unmistakable.

Arden straightened, composure sliding back into place. "Go," she said. "I'm fine."

He hesitated, committing her to memory, then turned and disappeared into the glittering current.

Arden watched him go, her chest tightening as the weight of the night settled once more across her shoulders.

The gala shimmered with opulence, every detail radiating the Blackwell family's particular brand of curated power. Penny moved through the crowd with practiced ease, her silver gown catching the light, sequins flashing like liquid courage. Her smile stayed playful, effortless, a mask she had perfected long ago. Beneath it, her attention was razor-sharp.

Across the room, Sebastian held court, charisma coiled and deliberate as guests leaned in, hungry for proximity. Penny drifted closer, feigning interest in a nearby art installation, her body angled away while her focus locked onto the cadence of his voice.

A reporter leaned in, conspiratorial.

"These documents are ironclad," she murmured, fingertips brushing the edge of a manila folder. "Once they're leaked, the media will have a field day. It'll be impossible for Gideon to deny involvement."

Sebastian's smile didn't waver. "Make sure it's tonight," he said quietly. "Timing is everything."

Penny's pulse kicked. She lifted her champagne flute, letting the motion disguise the tightening of her grip.

"Gideon's fall will be spectacular," Sebastian continued, the words smooth, venom threaded beneath them. "And when he's gone...we'll see who Arden turns to."

Cold settled in Penny's gut, then burned off, replaced by something sharper. Anger, yes, but clearer than fear.

She slipped back into the current of glittering guests, posture loose, expression untouched. Inside, every instinct snapped into focus.

Arden needed to know.

And she needed to know now, before the night shattered completely.

CHAPTER 36
Fractured Foundations

The weight of the Blackwell legacy clung to Arden like a silken shroud. As she moved through the ballroom, marble gleamed beneath her heels and chandeliers scattered gold across every polished surface, turning opulence into something colder than beauty. A crown, perhaps, but one built with bars. Every reflection seemed to watch her back. Every laugh carried a subtle edge. Conversation braided itself into a careful symphony of veiled intent, while smiles sharpened to glass and glances passed like blades beneath the music.

Gideon's hand rested at the small of her back, light enough not to restrain her, deliberate enough to be read. A claim, yes, but also a warning to the predators orbiting them: she was not alone.

"Stay sharp," he murmured, voice low and contained. "If Sebastian or my family make a move, we need to be ready."

Arden nodded, her gaze sweeping the room. The emerald of her gown shimmered beneath the chandeliers, beadwork catching the light in flashes that looked fragile only from a distance.

"I can feel it," she whispered. "They're circling. Waiting."

"They always are." Frustration threaded his voice, tempered by the grim familiarity of a man who had been raised inside the cage and taught to call it legacy.

His attention shifted toward the far end of the room, where Evelyn and Alex stood in practiced command, their composure immaculate beneath the chandelier light. Cate lingered nearby, her smile polite enough for public viewing, the strain beneath it impossible to miss once Arden knew to look.

Near the terrace doors, Sebastian stood at the edge of the crowd, posture deceptively casual, his attention fixed on her with unnerving patience. The faint curve of his mouth sent a chill skittering down her spine. Not hunger. Promise.

Christian appeared at her side without announcement, so quiet he seemed less like a man crossing a ballroom than a shadow changing position.

"He's been watching you all night," he said. "Stay close to Gideon. Don't give him an opening."

"I won't let him rattle me."

"Good." His gaze swept the room once more, clinical and exact, before he melted back into the throng.

Arden found Penny near Sebastian, too close for comfort and far too composed for accident. Her silver gown shimmered like moonlight over a blade, her laughter bright enough to pass as ease, but the tightness in her shoulders told the truth her smile refused to confess.

"She's too close," Arden murmured. "She's smart, but she doesn't know how far he'll go."

Gideon's jaw set. "Christian's watching them. For now, we stay focused on my family."

Across the room, Penny's green eyes met hers. For one heartbeat, the sparkle slipped, and worry flashed beneath the charm. Arden tilted her head, a silent question.

Penny answered with a grin and formed a tiny heart with her fingers.

The familiar gesture cracked the tension just enough to let air through. Arden smiled despite herself and echoed the motion, small and quick and fiercely loyal across a room full of enemies.

Her friend was chaos wrapped in rainbow and sparkles, impossible and reckless and bright; somehow, in the middle of all that gold-veined rot, she was still the closest thing Arden had to safe harbor.

Evelyn Blackwell stepped into the light with the poise of a monarch addressing her court.

Her black gown caught the chandelier shimmer, every razor-cut line echoing the precision of her gaze. Conversation thinned around her as if the room itself knew better than to interrupt. The gala's glittering hum receded into something quieter, watchful and expectant.

"Miss Rivers." Her tone was honeyed steel. "I see you've managed to survive another evening in our company."

Arden straightened, meeting her gaze without flinching. "Survival," she said evenly, "is mostly a matter of adaptability."

Evelyn's smile curved—measured, bloodless. "A useful skill. One that will serve you well, if you remember your place."

Gideon stepped forward before Arden could answer, his presence shifting into an unmistakable barrier. He didn't raise his voice. He didn't need to.

"Evelyn. This isn't the time."

"On the contrary." Her attention never left Arden. "It is precisely the time. Your choices have consequences, Gideon. It's past time you acknowledged them."

The air tightened, but Arden refused to give Evelyn the satisfaction of retreat. Fear moved through her, cold and bright, then settled into something she could use.

"Your threats don't scare me," she said softly. "I've faced worse than you."

Evelyn tilted her head, studying her with something almost like curiosity. The smile that followed was nearly kind, which made it all the more obscene.

"Oh, my dear," she murmured. "You should be."

Penny found Arden near the edge of the ballroom, still as a blade beneath the chandelier light, her composure drawing attention in the quiet, dangerous way motion never could. She caught Arden's arm, fingers firm, and leaned close enough that the urgency in her voice belonged to Arden alone.

"Arden, we've got a problem."

Arden's focus snapped into place. "What is it?"

"Sebastian," Penny said, low and fast. "He's feeding the press forged documents—trying to pin the research site reopenings on Gideon."

Arden's pulse kicked hard. "You're sure?"

"I heard it myself." Penny's grip tightened. Beneath the glitter of her silver gown, every reckless, bright edge of her had gone sharp. "He's using an opportunistic journalist to leak it tonight. I came straight to you—after looping in Dan. He's lingering near the terrace in case Sebastian makes a move."

Arden's gaze cut across the ballroom, already searching for Gideon. The noise around them blurred into static: laughter, music, crystal, the soft predatory rustle of expensive fabric. "Then I need to warn him."

"You should," Penny said, urgency softening into something more serious. "But be careful. Sebastian's watching you."

Arden's hand settled briefly on Penny's shoulder, gratitude pressing through the fear. "Thank you. You just changed the game."

Penny's grin flickered back into place, bright and reckless as a match struck in a dark room. "Please. Causing chaos *is* the game. Now go save your man."

CHAPTER 37
Shattered Illusions

The ballroom glittered with ruthless perfection, every gilded surface and crystal chandelier reflecting the illusion the Blackwell name had spent generations demanding from anyone reckless enough to enter its orbit. Beneath the dazzle, whispers moved like pressure beneath ice, hairline fractures spreading through glass.

Arden stood at the room's edge, emerald silk catching the light in quiet flashes. To the casual observer, she was composure itself: chin lifted, shoulders relaxed, gaze steady enough to be mistaken for calm. Beneath it, her thoughts moved fast and exacting. Penny's warning burned hot in her bloodstream, every detail sharpening into strategy. She had to reach Gideon without drawing a single curious eye.

She threaded through the crowd with unhurried grace, her breath even, her expression untouched. Roses and champagne thickened the air, all sweetness and ceremony, clashing with the pressure building beneath her ribs. When she reached him, she brushed her fingers against his arm, a signal so small only he would feel it.

He turned immediately. The tension in his jaw sharpened, then smoothed into control.

"What is it?" he asked, voice low.

Arden leaned in, close enough that her words vanished beneath the music. "Sebastian planted forged documents," she said evenly. "They link you to the research sites. A reporter has them. He plans to confront you tonight—publicly."

Fury flickered through Gideon's eyes, bright and lethal, then disappeared behind discipline. His hand closed around hers for one brief, grounding second before he let go.

"Thank you," he murmured. "I'll handle it."

Arden nodded once, resolve locking into place. She stepped beside him, shoulder to shoulder, letting the room see what it wanted to see and misunderstand the rest.

Together, they looked untouchable.

Beneath the chandeliers, the fractures were already spreading.

ACROSS THE ROOM, Sebastian lounged against the bar, casual and calculated, every movement too precise to be mistaken for ease. He lifted his glass in a mock toast, dark eyes gleaming with satisfaction. The smirk at his mouth should have unsettled her.

Instead, it lit her.

He thought the night was unfolding exactly as he'd planned.

He was wrong.

Arden met his gaze, serene and unflinching, as if she were looking straight through him to the hollow architecture beneath. Marble-cool on the surface; fire underneath. She was no longer moving inside the shape of his expectations, no longer bending beneath the invisible hand of his design. Whatever game he thought he'd built around her, she had found the seams.

Sebastian's smile stretched, confidence thinning at the edges, brittle where it mattered. When Arden's attention shifted to Penny—poised near the art displays with practiced ease, silver gown catching the light like a blade slipped beneath moonlight—her mouth curved into the faintest, knowing smile.

He had underestimated them both.

Then came the sound that cut the room clean open.

Evelyn Blackwell's heels struck marble, each sharp click slicing through the murmurs. Conversation stilled. Glasses lowered. Breath held. She ascended the stage with the composure of a queen taking her throne, her black gown gleaming like cut obsidian beneath the chandeliers.

When she reached the microphone, her gaze swept the ballroom: icy, regal, unyielding.

And the room obeyed.

"Good evening."

Her voice carried effortlessly, smooth and measured, filling the hush she had commanded. "On behalf of the Blackwell Foundation, thank you for joining us tonight in support of a cause that has always been close to our hearts—renewal."

Polite applause followed. Evelyn smiled, perfect and practiced, every inch of her calibrated for admiration.

"For generations, the Blackwell name has stood for progress. We've rebuilt. We've invested. We've given our time and resources to help this city rise from its own ashes." Her tone softened, sincerity arranged with surgical care. "But true progress demands sacrifice. It demands vision. And it demands that those in power bear the weight of expectation with grace."

Her gaze moved again, lingering on Gideon just long enough to register as coincidence to anyone who needed the lie.

"Tonight, we celebrate not wealth, but responsibility. We stand beside our partners in government, our colleagues in finance, and those committed to urban revitalization. Together, we are not merely funding projects." A pause, immaculate in its timing. "We are shaping legacies."

Approval rippled through the crowd.

"Our city is changing. Brick by brick. Dream by dream." Her smile warmed, then thinned. "And while some may question the pace—or the methods—of that progress, I assure you our intentions remain pure. Our goals transparent."

Another pause. Another blade turned slowly toward the light.

"We invest not for profit," she said lightly, "but for promise."

Crystal glasses chimed softly as hands shifted.

"Every partnership. Every contribution." Her eyes gleamed. "Every headline we generate serves one purpose—to ensure this city continues to shine as a beacon of endurance and opportunity."

She lifted her glass, the gesture both benediction and command.

"To progress," she said. "To loyalty. And to the legacy we all share."

Applause thundered, chandeliers trembling with sound.

Beneath the brilliance, Arden felt the undertow: a decree delivered in silk, corruption polished to a mirror shine, a queen reminding the room exactly who ruled the board.

When Gideon stepped onto the platform, the room stilled as if the air itself had been held in check.

Every gaze turned toward the Blackwell heir. He moved with command: tailored suit, measured stride, composure honed to a blade. Control, embodied. The very thing Sebastian had hoped to shatter.

His jaw tightened as he met his mother's gaze. One beat passed between them, old and loaded, an unspoken challenge sharpened by blood and history, before he reached for the microphone.

The air crackled. The empire leaned toward its breaking point.

"I've been made aware of some troubling allegations circulating tonight," Gideon began, his voice resonant, controlled, impossible to dismiss. "Allegations designed to tarnish my name—and distract from the truth."

A murmur rippled through the ballroom. Crystal glasses froze mid-lift.

"These documents," he continued, gesturing toward the unseen evidence, "are forgeries. Careless ones. Easily disproven. A desperate attempt to derail a vision founded on accountability and transparency."

Flashbulbs erupted. Reporters leaned forward, instincts sharpening at the scent of blood in all that perfume and candlelight. Across the room, Sebastian's smirk faltered, confidence draining into disbelief.

Gideon's gaze moved again until it settled on Evelyn. Her composure held, but only just; the faintest fracture appeared in the marble.

"To those who believed lies could be weaponized without consequence," he said, voice low and precise, "understand this: the truth has a way of surfacing. No matter how deeply it's buried."

He let the silence stretch, and for once, it did not belong to Evelyn.

It obeyed him.

"For decades," Gideon continued, the weight of his words pressing into every gilded corner of the room, "the Blackwell name has been synonymous with power. But beneath that power lies a history of exploitation, corruption, and devastation."

A collective breath moved through the ballroom.

"My family's empire was built on the suffering of others," he said, unflinching. "And tonight—" his gaze swept over the chandeliers, the donors, the reporters, the carefully curated faces pretending not to hunger for ruin "—that truth steps into the light."

Gasps scattered like glass breaking.

Evelyn's expression froze, still regal, still composed, but stripped of even the pretense of warmth. Sebastian pushed away from the bar, fury flashing raw and uncontained, no longer polished enough to hide what lived beneath the charm.

And in that suspended heartbeat, the Blackwell legacy began to tremble—not from scandal, but from exposure.

Gasps rippled through the ballroom, the air charged with disbelief. Cameras flashed in sharp bursts; reporters leaned forward, instincts honed by the scent of blood beneath all that perfume and gold. Evelyn's composure finally fractured, her lips pressing into a bloodless line.

Arden's stomach knotted as Evelyn's gaze found her across the room. It wasn't outrage alone. It was promise. Whatever came next, one truth was unmistakable: Evelyn Blackwell would not fall quietly.

"This is slander," Evelyn snapped, her voice cutting through the hush. "A desperate spectacle staged by a foolish son determined to dismantle his own family."

Gideon turned toward her without haste. He looked almost calm, which made the fury beneath it feel more dangerous.

"The damage doesn't belong to me, Mother," he said, each syllable measured and precise. "It belongs to those who believed the truth could stay buried."

Her eyes flashed. "You think this changes anything?" she hissed. "You're as naïve as your grandfather. He believed principles would protect him. They didn't. They destroyed him."

Gideon didn't flinch. When he spoke, his conviction carried without force, steady enough to make the room listen.

"My grandfather believed in justice—values you suffocated beneath ambition. If standing where he stood makes me naïve, then I'll accept it. Proudly."

A curious murmur stirred, then spread, a subtle shift in gravity as the room recalibrated around him.

Evelyn's fury burned cold and controlled, lethal in its restraint, but Gideon had already turned back to the crowd. His voice reclaimed the space.

"For decades, the Blackwell name has functioned as a shield for power and greed," he said. "It was built on the backs of those without the means to fight it. My grandfather envisioned integrity. That vision was stolen—replaced with profit, silence, and harm."

The chandeliers trembled in the quiet that followed.

"To those who suffered under that legacy," Gideon continued, his voice carrying clean and clear, "know this: it ends tonight. The Blackwell name will no longer be associated with fear. It will answer for what it has done—and it will rebuild what it destroyed."

The words hung there, bright and dangerous.

One clap sounded. Then another. Then more, until applause rolled through the ballroom—not celebratory, but resolute. A verdict delivered in sound.

Evelyn stood motionless, fury carved into every line of her face, her stillness the only thing holding her together.

And beneath the chandeliers, under the glare of cameras and consequence, the Blackwell dynasty did not shatter.

It fractured.

From the bar, Sebastian's smirk curdled into something darker.

This was not how the night was supposed to unfold. Gideon was meant to buckle beneath the weight of accusation, not stand taller beneath it, and certainly not with Arden at his side as if she had chosen him in front of everyone.

His gaze found her across the room. The emerald of her gown caught the chandelier light, radiant enough to make something cruel twist behind his ribs. She should have been his. She was supposed to be his. Instead, she stood unyielding and loyal, her fire burning beyond anything he had ever managed to shape, contain, or command.

Bitterness surged, hot and venomous. The crystal glass trembled in his hand, the delicate stem creaking beneath the pressure of his grip. The night was slipping away from him, every careful calculation warping into mockery before his eyes; every glance toward Gideon felt like betrayal, every breath Arden took outside Sebastian's design felt like theft.

If Gideon wanted to play the hero, Sebastian would make sure the victory tasted like ash.

The night wasn't finished yet.

Arden moved through the throng with purpose, her emerald gown catching the light like bottled flame. The daring slit and intricate beadwork set her apart from the sea of muted elegance around her, defiant by design, every shimmer a refusal to shrink. She was a woman their world had tried to measure and dismiss, and she had answered by becoming impossible to overlook.

Her focus wasn't on the glances that followed.

It was on the folded note tucked inside her clutch.

You deserve the truth.

Meet me by the east wing terrace. Alone.

Sebastian's handwriting. The words coiled in her chest like a fuse, waiting for flame.

Across the ballroom, her gaze found Gideon. Even amid the bright lights and the polished violence of all that wealth, his eyes were already on her. The exchange lasted only seconds, but it carried everything: the warning he hadn't spoken, the resolve she hadn't yielded, the tension stretched tight between them.

You're not going, he'd said earlier, voice clipped, his grip on her wrist firm enough to betray what restraint cost him.

We need to know what he's planning, she'd answered, calm but immovable. *This might be our only chance.*

It's too dangerous.

She had rested her hand against his chest, soft but sure, feeling the thunder of his heart beneath the immaculate cut of his tuxedo. *I can handle him. Trust me.*

Now those words echoed with heavier weight.

As she slipped free of the crowd and approached the terrace doors, the air changed. Cooler, sharper, carrying the faint metallic promise of rain. Behind her, the ballroom's warmth fell away by degrees, music and voices dulling beneath the hush of the corridor ahead.

Gideon's last instruction pulsed through her thoughts.

Christian will follow at a distance. Don't take any risks.

Her fingers brushed the clutch, the note still hidden inside. Paper-thin. Dangerous. Every instinct she had screamed the same truth.

This was a trap.

And still—

She went.

Back near the terrace doors, Penny sidled up beside Arden, her silver gown shimmering like liquid moonlight. Her eyes flicked between Arden and Sebastian, sharp despite the teasing lift of her mouth.

"Your boyfriend's making big moves tonight," she murmured.

"My boyfriend?" Arden's smirk barely surfaced, her gaze still fixed across the room.

Penny snorted. "Please. So he's just the man you'd storm a ballroom for."

Arden didn't answer.

The humor slipped from Penny's face, replaced by something quieter and far more dangerous: instinct, concern, the look she got when she sensed a line being crossed and had already decided she would not ignore it.

"What's going on?" she asked softly.

Arden hesitated, then exhaled. "Sebastian left me a note. He wants to meet outside."

Penny's expression hardened instantly. "Absolutely not."

"We need to know what he's planning," Arden said, calmer than she felt. "Gideon agrees—mostly."

"Mostly?" Penny's grip tightened around Arden's arm. "Arden, that man has been orbiting you all night like he owns the air around you."

"I'm not going alone." Arden lifted her wrist just enough for the terrace light to catch the slim band there. "Christian's covering me."

Penny studied her, frustration flaring beneath the glitter. "This feels like a trap."

"It is," Arden said simply.

The honesty stopped Penny cold.

"Then why—"

"Because traps tell you who set them," Arden said, her voice steady. "And how far they're willing to go."

Penny's jaw set, protective fury sharpening her features. "If he so much as breathes wrong—"

"You signal Gideon," Arden said gently. "Promise me."

A beat passed between them, tight with all the things Penny wanted to argue and all the things Arden would not yield. Then Penny nodded once, hard. "Fine. But I'm not waiting quietly."

Arden's lips curved, gratitude threading through the tension. "I know."

Penny lingered one heartbeat longer before she turned back toward the crowd, already scanning. Her eyes found Dan, her posture squaring beneath silk and sequins as if chaos itself had just been given orders.

Arden drew a steadying breath and pushed through the terrace doors.

The ballroom's noise fell away as she stepped outside. Cool air brushed over her skin, carrying the rustle of leaves, the distant pulse of the city, and the faint metallic promise of rain. Beyond the terrace, the skyline shattered into stars, beautiful and indifferent; behind her, the gala dulled to a wash of gold and muffled voices.

Shadow and light stretched in uneasy symmetry across the stone.

She straightened her shoulders, heels clicking softly as she moved farther from the doors.

Then she saw him.

Sebastian emerged from the dark with practiced composure, every line of him immaculate. But his eyes gave him away, too bright and fixed, the charm worn thin over something fevered underneath.

This was intent, not courtship.

Movement flickered beyond him, a shape slipping between shadows near the edge of the terrace.

Colton.

Her stomach tightened.

Of course.

"Arden," Sebastian said, his voice smooth, almost fond, as if this were some private indulgence she had finally granted him. He stepped into the light. "Thank you for coming. I wasn't sure you would."

She didn't move closer. "You said you had the truth. So talk."

His smile deepened, admiring and wrong. "Always direct. I like that about you."

"I don't have time for nostalgia," she said. "Say what you came to say, or I'm done."

He took a step closer. Too close, but not close enough to make her retreat. His voice softened, threaded with something unsteady. "You don't belong in there. With them. They'll never see you as anything but leverage. A pawn." His gaze burned. "Not like I do."

Her pulse kicked, but her spine stayed straight. "What is this?"

"It's me offering you a way out," he said quietly. "Gideon's world is poison. He's part of the machine that grinds people down and calls it progress. He doesn't even recognize it—but I do. I can protect you. I can free you."

Her fingers hovered near the slim band at her wrist, close enough to signal if the night tilted. When she spoke, her voice cut clean.

"Protect me?" A breath moved through her, controlled and furious. "You're confused, Sebastian. I don't need saving."

Something fractured in him. The polish split, obsession bleeding through the cracks.

"You don't understand," he said, his voice tightening. "No one else sees you. Not Gideon. Not anyone. You're wasted in his shadow. With me—" His breath shuddered. "You'd be unstoppable."

Arden stepped back, power settling into her stance. "You don't love me," she said evenly. "You love possession. You love control. And you hate that I won't give you either."

His face twisted, pleading curdling into menace. "That's not true," he whispered. "I see you. I've always seen you." His eyes burned. "I'm the only one who ever has."

He reached for her arm.

His fingers closed too tight.

Her heart slammed, but her voice didn't rise. It dropped, cold and lethal, as her thumb brushed the hidden signal.

"Let. Me. Go."

The words cracked through the night like glass.

THE TERRACE DOORS BURST OPEN.

Gideon strode through without hesitation, every step purposeful, the storm in him finally breaking its leash. His gaze swept the scene—Arden, Sebastian's hand locked too tightly around her arm, the shadows beyond them—and fury flared white-hot before settling into something far more dangerous.

"Get your hands off her," he said, voice low and lethal.

Sebastian froze. The wildness in his expression cooled into something sharper, calculation sliding over the fracture.

"She doesn't belong with you," he hissed. "She never did."

Gideon didn't raise his voice. He didn't need volume when restraint carried this much violence.

"You don't get to decide where she belongs. Step away."

For one suspended heartbeat, the night held its breath. The terrace seemed to crackle around them, cold air and chandelier spill and the distant pulse of music gathering between two men who had mistaken very different things for power.

Then Sebastian released her.

He stepped back, laughter spilling out of him, bitter and edged with threat. "You think this is over?" he sneered. "This night isn't finished, Gideon. You'll see."

Then he vanished into shadow, his footsteps swallowed by stone and distance.

Gideon's hands found Arden's shoulders with exquisite care, as if his rage had been forced to kneel before the more immediate need to know she was whole. When he spoke again, all that fury narrowed into focus.

"Are you hurt?"

She shook her head, breath still uneven. "He's unraveling. This isn't about you anymore." A beat passed, cold and clear. "He thinks it's about me."

Gideon went still—not in surprise, but in recognition.

For weeks, they had treated Arden as collateral. Leverage. The pressure point his enemies would press because she mattered to him. Evelyn had seen her that way. Alex had. Even Gideon, for all his careful strategy, had built the night around the fear that someone would use Arden to reach him.

But Sebastian had not been aiming past her.

He had been aiming at her all along.

Gideon's jaw tightened. "Then it ends tonight."

They turned toward the doors, but Arden stilled, her gaze cutting back toward the darkness.

"Wait." Her voice sharpened. "Colton was out here. Watching. He disappeared when Sebastian started talking."

Gideon's expression hardened, calculation flickering behind his eyes. "Then whatever move comes next won't be accidental."

Together, they stepped back into the ballroom, into crystal light, murmured conversations, and secrets dressed as civility.

The night wasn't over.

It was only changing shape.

CHAPTER 38
Breaking the Chains

Sebastian cut through the ballroom like a blade drawn too fast.

Conversation faltered around him. Laughter thinned, then died. The glittering ease of the evening fractured as guests shifted away, instinct recognizing what manners could not name. His composure, once immaculate, had splintered; every step carried urgency, fury barely leashed beneath the ruined elegance of his tuxedo.

At the edge of the room, Arden stood beside Penny, emerald silk catching the chandelier light. She laughed at something Penny said, but the sound rang hollow even to her own ears. The air tightened. She felt him before she saw him, the pressure of his attention moving over her like a hand at her spine.

Then he was there.

His grip closed around her wrist, sudden and crushing. Her bracelet bit into her skin as he pulled her half a step closer.

"Sebastian." Arden's voice cut sharp and clear through the gathering hush. "Let me go."

"Not here," he hissed, leaning in, his breath hot with desperation. "They don't deserve this. You don't belong with him. You need to hear me."

Her jaw locked, but she didn't lower her voice. "This isn't a conversation," she said, cold and precise. "It's assault."

Penny reacted instantly.

"Sebastian," she said, stepping in, her voice steady despite the flash of fear in her eyes. "Let her go."

His head snapped toward her, eyes wild. "Stay out of this."

The warning carried enough weight to freeze the guests nearest them. A champagne flute paused halfway to someone's mouth. A woman's hand tightened around her husband's sleeve. Then Sebastian yanked Arden toward the terrace doors, dragging her off balance.

Pain flashed up her arm. "You're hurting me," Arden said, outrage burning clean through the fear. She shoved at his chest, but his grip only tightened.

"You're not listening," he barked, control finally unraveling. "I'm trying to save you—from him, from all of this."

She twisted against him. "You don't get to decide my life," she shot back. "You never did."

Penny lunged.

Her hand locked around Sebastian's arm, nails digging in. "Let. Her. Go. Now."

Her voice shook, not with fear, but with rage—the kind that ignited rooms.

In that charged instant, the ballroom stood witness: every chandelier, every polished surface, every carefully curated face reflecting the truth Sebastian could no longer outrun.

His head snapped toward Penny, irritation curdling into something darker. He didn't hesitate.

His elbow drove into her shoulder, sharp and brutal, sending her stumbling into a nearby guest. A startled cry broke loose. Glass clinked, tipped, and shattered against the marble.

"Stay out of this," he barked, his voice stripped raw.

Then his attention snapped back to Arden.

For a fraction of a second, his grip faltered. Desperation flickered through his eyes, naked and pleading, all the uglier for being sincere.

"I'm the only one who can protect you," he said, lowering his voice as if intimacy could make the lie holy. "I see you, Arden. Not like him."

"Sebastian."

Her voice dropped, lethal and unwavering. "You don't see me. You never have. Let me go. Now."

The words landed hard.

Pain flashed across his face, real and unguarded, before it twisted into something more dangerous. His fingers tightened again, a fractured smile pulling at his mouth as control slipped for good.

Across the room, Gideon's gaze locked onto them.

The champagne flute shattered in his hand.

He didn't look at it. He was already moving, fast and precise, the crowd parting before him as instinct recognized threat before reason could catch up.

"Sebastian."

His name cracked through the room.

Sebastian froze. His grip tightened around Arden's wrist as if she were the last thing anchoring him to reality. Slowly, he turned, that brittle smile reassembling across his face, cornered and feral.

"Of course," he sneered. "The hero." His eyes flicked to Arden. "Always ready to claim what doesn't belong to him."

"Let. Her. Go."

Gideon's voice stayed low, controlled, dangerously so.

Sebastian laughed, jagged and wrong, dragging Arden closer until his fingers bit deeper into her skin. "You think she's yours," he snarled. "Like everything else you've stolen—my place, my legacy, my life. You don't deserve her. She deserves someone who sees her."

Arden's voice cut through him, clean and final. "You don't know me," she said coldly. "And you never will."

The words staggered him.

For one breath, the room held.

Then the smile returned, broken and hollow. "I know you better than anyone," he murmured. "Every gift. Every plan. It was all for you. You're fire, Arden, and he cages you. I can set you free. I can make you unstoppable."

Her eyes hardened. She didn't raise her voice. She didn't need to.

"Those gifts terrified me," she said. "Your plans were fantasies. What you call devotion is obsession."

Sebastian's face darkened. The last shards of control splintered as his free hand slipped into his jacket.

Metal flashed beneath the chandeliers.

The gun came up.

The room froze.

Gasps broke the silence like glass shattering. Conversation died mid-breath. Even the air seemed to still, thick and waiting.

"You've taken everything from me," Sebastian said, his voice cracking under the weight of years he could no longer contain. His gaze jerked between Gideon and Arden, wild and unfocused, but his grip on the weapon was firm. "You don't deserve her. You don't deserve anything."

The ballroom became a study in terror: no music, no movement, only the faint electrical hum of light and the harsh sound of Sebastian's breathing.

Gideon didn't move.

Slowly, he raised his hands.

"Sebastian," he said, voice low and even. "Put the gun down. Let her go. We can stop this. It's not too late."

Sebastian barked a laugh, broken and jagged. "Stop it?" he spat. "You don't stop betrayal. You don't stop someone stealing your life."

His eyes snapped to Arden.

"Everything I did—everything—was for you."

The barrel pressed against her temple.

Cold. Real.

Her pulse thundered, but her voice didn't betray it. When she spoke, it cut clean through the chaos.

"Sebastian," she said quietly. "This isn't love."

For a fraction of a second, his grip loosened. Doubt flickered, thin and fragile.

"You can stop," she continued. "Right now."

The doubt shattered.

"You don't understand!" he shouted, the sound raw and unhinged. "I'm the only one who can save you. Gideon doesn't see you. He never has."

Arden held his gaze.

When she spoke again, her voice was lower, unafraid and absolute. "This isn't about saving me. It's about control. About needing to own what you can't have."

A beat passed, taut enough to break.

"And it ends here."

The words landed.

The gun wavered.

The tremor spread from his hand to his shoulders, into the breath he could no longer steady. The room inhaled as one silent, terrified body.

Gideon took a single step closer, measured and careful, his eyes never leaving the weapon. One wrong movement could end everything.

"Sebastian," Gideon said, his voice cutting through the taut air like a drawn blade. The calm had thinned, leaving authority beneath it, cold and absolute. "You think this is about her," he said, each word deliberate. "It isn't. This is about you being too weak to accept that you've already lost. Let her go, or I will make sure you lose everything."

No one moved. Dan edged closer through the sea of frozen faces, his attention locked on Sebastian's hand. Somewhere in the crowd, Christian's team waited, still and unseen, ready for the breath where violence tipped into action. The air itself seemed to vibrate, the weight of the gun pressing down on the room like gravity.

Each second stretched.

Sebastian's hand trembled, the barrel wavering as the storm inside him cracked. Arden felt the shift—the small, dangerous instant when control slipped and instinct took over.

"You never wanted me, Sebastian," she said quietly, almost mournful. "You wanted someone to mold. Someone to fill the emptiness you refuse to face. That isn't love. That's fear."

The words struck with surgical precision. Doubt flickered across his face again, brief and fragile.

His hand faltered.

Arden moved.

Her stiletto came down hard, heel driving into the soft joint at the top of his foot with brutal precision. A sickening crunch tore a howl from him. The gun dipped as his body lurched forward in shock.

"Now, Gideon!" she shouted.

The world snapped back into motion. Arden tore free of Sebastian's grasp, stumbling backward, her emerald gown a slash of color against the polished marble. The crowd erupted in screams. Glasses crashed. The once-perfect ballroom unraveled into pandemonium.

Gideon moved like the storm finally breaking loose. He lunged forward, shoulder slamming into Sebastian's chest with enough force to drive the air from his lungs. Their bodies hit the marble hard. The gun skidded loose, spinning in a blur of chandelier light before clattering to a stop near the edge of the crowd.

A single ringing note of metal lingered in the stunned air.

Sebastian swung wildly, fists fueled by rage and desperation, every movement reckless and uncontrolled. Gideon met him with precision, discipline and wrath braided together. His strikes were sharp, contained, brutal only where they needed to be, every motion carrying years of betrayal finally given form.

"You stole her from me!" Sebastian roared, voice cracking.

"You never had her." Gideon drove him back against the marble, the impact echoing like a gavel. His voice dropped, deadly calm. "You don't even know what love is."

Sebastian's gaze darted wildly. Then, in an instant of pure madness, his fingers closed around a shard of broken glass, its jagged edge catching the light. With a savage cry, he lunged.

Gideon twisted aside. The shard sliced empty air. In one fluid motion, he caught Sebastian by the collar and drove him back to the floor. The glass skittered across the marble, and the fight left Sebastian all at once. He crumpled beneath Gideon's weight, chest heaving, eyes fixed on the chandelier above as if seeing nothing at all.

Arden was already moving.

Her gown trailed behind her like green fire as she crossed the marble and dropped to the floor, fingers closing around the fallen gun. The cold metal bit into her palm, its weight startlingly real.

She rose slowly, breath steadying. The ballroom seemed to still around her, every sound swallowed by the pulse of adrenaline. She leveled the weapon with both hands, shoulders squared, gaze unflinching.

"It's over, Sebastian."

Her voice rang through the silence, low and resolute, a clean cut through the chaos.

Sebastian's wild eyes darted to her. For a fleeting moment, the fire in them guttered as her words sank in. Then his lips curled into a sneer, bitterness twisting what little humanity remained.

"You'll never be free of me," he spat. "I'll always be watching."

Christian and his team swept in like a tide, surrounding him in one seamless motion. Sebastian struggled, fury reigniting as they wrenched him upright.

"You'll regret this, Gideon!" he roared, his voice echoing through the shattered ballroom. "You can't save her. You can't save yourself."

Christian's reply was cool. "You're done, Hawthorne."

Gideon exhaled hard, the fury draining from his face as he turned to Arden. In two strides, he was there, his hands finding her cheeks, his touch trembling with everything he had refused to let himself feel while the gun was still in play.

"Are you hurt?" he asked, breath uneven.

She shook her head, the words barely forming. "No... I'm okay."

Her voice broke on the last word, adrenaline leaving her hollow but whole.

He pulled her close, his arms wrapping around her like an anchor in the storm's wake. His mouth brushed her hair, his voice low enough for only her.

"You were incredible," he murmured. "You're safe now."

The ballroom lay in ruin. The music had gone silent; the façade of perfection had cracked beyond repair. Guests stood scattered among broken glass and overturned champagne, their jewels flashing under the chandeliers as if beauty had survived by accident.

Amid the wreckage, a bruised red rose lay on the marble floor. Its petals were crushed, its beauty marred.

But it wasn't destroyed.

Neither was she.

The fight had not only been against Sebastian. It had been for herself—for the life no one else would define, the fear she refused to obey, the future she had chosen with blood in her mouth and her hands steady around the truth.

And she had won.

CHAPTER 39

The Tilted Crown

The ballroom was no longer a monument to opulence.

Polished marble lay littered with shattered glass, crushed roses, and the glittering debris of a night unmasked. Jagged shards caught the fractured chandelier light, each flicker reflecting the chaos below in broken pieces: overturned champagne, trampled petals, diamonds flashing at the throats of guests who no longer knew where to look.

The air was thick with contradiction. The sickly sweetness of roses clashed with the metallic tang of blood and spilled champagne; decadence had turned sour.

Arden stood beside the wreckage of an overturned floral arrangement, her emerald gown clinging to her like a second skin. The beadwork shimmered faintly beneath the chandeliers, defiant amid the ruin. Beside her, Gideon remained a pillar of resolve, jaw tight, eyes still burning with the fury he had not entirely put down. Blood marked his palm where the champagne flute had shattered; more stained his knuckles, a silent testament to battles fought, truths exposed, and the cost of surviving both.

Together, they were the still point in a spinning world.

At the center of the chaos stood Special Agent Lauren Bishop. Her navy blazer was crisp, her presence cutting through the noise with the clean authority of a blade. The folder in her hand carried a weight far heavier than paper and ink: legacies collapsing, names losing their power, a dynasty finally meeting the record.

"Evelyn Blackwell. Alex Blackwell. Colton Blake," she announced, voice steady, the steel in it unmistakable. "You are under investigation for conspiracy, fraud, racketeering, assault, and numerous other federal crimes. The evidence against you is comprehensive and irrefutable."

Evelyn's composure sagged by the smallest degree, a fracture so slight most people would have missed it. Arden did not. She watched the older woman raise her chin, diamonds scattering broken light across her wrist as if wealth could still perform immunity.

"You have no case," Evelyn said coolly, each word honed to wound. "This is nothing but a desperate attempt to tarnish the Blackwell name."

Lauren arched a brow, unflinching. "Your testimony may carry weight in certain circles, Mrs. Blackwell, but it means little against sworn affidavits, digital transfers, and recorded directives. Your actions speak louder than your denials."

Evelyn's gaze flicked across the room, precise and searching, until it landed on Cate. She stood near the edge of the chaos, posture composed, eyes clear. For one lethal beat, the faintest tension at the corner of her mouth gave everything away.

Not regret.

Resolve.

Lauren didn't miss it.

"Cate Blackwell has provided a full account of your orders," she continued, voice honed to surgical calm. "From the intimidation of Arden Rivers to falsified land deeds and unethical medical trials. Her testimony, corroborated by financial records and internal communications, establishes a clear and sustained pattern of criminal conduct."

She closed the folder with a soft, final snap.

"There is no ambiguity here."

Evelyn's glare found Gideon across the room, fury coiling tight and venomous beneath the last tatters of composure.

"Do you think this spectacle absolves you of your betrayal?" she hissed. "You've humiliated this family."

Gideon stepped forward, his voice steady and unyielding. "The Blackwell name was tarnished long before tonight, Evelyn. I'm only shining a light on what was always there."

Her laugh came sharp and brittle. "You think you're free of us?" she snapped, rage threading every word. "You'll never escape this family. It's in your blood."

"I'm not trying to escape it," Gideon said evenly. "I'm reclaiming it."

The smile that crossed her face was thin as glass. "You sound like your grandfather," she said softly, cruelly. "Do you think you'll succeed where he failed? He died believing morality mattered."

Gideon's gaze didn't waver. Something old and unbreakable steadied behind his eyes, a legacy deeper than the one she had spent her life corrupting. "If standing for what's right makes me like him," he said, "I'll take that as a compliment. And for the first time, this family will be remembered for something other than destruction."

Evelyn's reply never came.

Two agents stepped forward. The metallic click of handcuffs rang through the ballroom, final and unforgiving. For one heartbeat, Evelyn held Gideon's gaze, her power burning down to a single, feral stare.

Then she was led away.

Not a queen.

A consequence.

Alex erupted next, his composure disintegrating. "This is insane!" he shouted. "You can't do this—we built this empire!" His words collapsed into rage as agents restrained him, his voice scattering uselessly across the wreckage.

Behind him, Colton watched with a poisonous smile.

His voice carried far enough to be heard. "This isn't over."

The room shifted. The chaos had stilled, but the energy remained heavy, charged like the aftermath of lightning. Reporters surged forward, cameras flashing, the pop of bulbs strobing against the ruined grandeur while agents moved through the wreckage with grim efficiency.

From the periphery, Leo leaned against a marble column, his expression unreadable. He caught Gideon's eye and gave a single nod, the smallest acknowledgment of truth finally wrested from power.

Lauren's lips curved into a faint smile. "Justice takes time, Mr. Blackwell," she said, "but tonight, you've given it a fighting chance."

The tension eased by degrees, replaced by the low hum of reporters, agents, and survivors cataloging what remained.

Then Penny broke the solemnity.

"I'd like to point out," she said, brushing a silver-streaked curl from her shoulder, "that Evelyn didn't even spare me a glare. I mean—am I losing my touch? My hair is a masterpiece tonight."

Arden laughed softly, the sound threading through the ruins like light through smoke. "Maybe she was intimidated," she said, her smile faint but real. "You did kind of steal the show."

Penny struck a mock pose, the familiar glint returning to her eyes. "Obviously."

"Obviously," Dan echoed as he joined them, his tie loosened, tone bone-dry. "Figured I'd check in before the feds start charging for emotional damages."

Penny arched a brow. "We're billing Evelyn for that, Daniel."

"Good luck collecting, Penelope," he said, lips twitching.

Arden's laughter softened what remained of the night's edge. Gideon shook his head, the ghost of a grin tugging at his mouth, and for the first time in longer than he could remember, it didn't feel heavy.

He turned to Arden, his hand brushing hers, the contact brief and necessary. A silent thread tying them together amid broken glass, federal evidence, and the ruin of everything his family had tried to keep polished.

"It's not over," he said softly, steady amid the fading chaos.

Arden met his gaze, resolve clear. "Then we'll finish it together."

The ballroom emptied slowly, grandeur giving way to aftermath. Shattered glass caught the last tremors of chandelier light, gleaming like a thousand tiny victories.

For the first time, the weight of Gideon's inheritance didn't feel like a curse.

It felt like a promise.

CHAPTER 40

The Mask Unveiled

The fluorescent lights buzzed faintly, casting a sterile, unforgiving glare across the room. Sebastian Hawthorne sat slouched in a metal chair, the cuffs at his wrists clinking softly each time he moved. The immaculate image he had spent years cultivating was gone: tailored suit wrinkled and stained, tie crooked, hair damp against his forehead. Stripped of polish, he looked less like the puppet master he fancied himself and more like a man perched at the edge of collapse.

Detective Ronan Hawkes sat across from him, all hard lines and quiet patience. His stare was unyielding, the kind that left nowhere to hide. Against the wall, Leo Marcus leaned with his arms crossed, his stance deceptively relaxed. The faint smirk tugging at his mouth wasn't amusement.

It was certainty.

After months of pursuit, the hunter had finally cornered his prey.

Sebastian drummed a restless rhythm against the table. "You can sit there smirking all you want, Marcus," he rasped, the edge in his voice barely covering the tremor beneath it. "But you don't know what you're dealing with."

Leo pushed off the wall, unhurried, and dropped a thick folder onto the table. "Oh, I think we know exactly what we're dealing with." He flipped it open and slid a glossy photograph toward him. "Recognize him?"

Sebastian's eyes flicked down.

Dylan Tate, caught mid-exchange with red roses in hand.

The faintest tic betrayed recognition before his sneer returned. "A delivery boy," he said. "That's what you've got?"

Hawkes leaned in, voice sharp as glass. "It's not the roses we care about, Hawthorne. It's the notes. The threats. The way you made her look over her shoulder every damn day."

Sebastian scoffed, reaching for disdain and landing somewhere closer to desperation. "So what? A few flowers and poetic words? You'll have to try harder."

Leo's hand came down hard on the table. The metallic thud ricocheted off the walls. "And Richie?" His voice cut through the sterile air. "The guy Arden chased down? He's talking. Turns out loyalty dries up fast when the paychecks stop."

A flicker crossed Sebastian's face, uncertainty giving way to rage. "They're all cowards," he hissed. "None of them would've been anything without me."

Leo studied him for a long moment. "You keep telling yourself that."

His voice sharpened as he leaned closer and slid another photograph across the table. "And then there's Chad Dawson. You remember him, don't you?"

Sebastian's sneer snagged. His jaw tightened as his gaze touched the image: Chad in a dim parking lot, mid-conversation with one of Sebastian's proxies.

"Arden's ex," Leo continued, each word deliberate. "He wasn't hard to find. Bitter, broke, clinging to a grudge against the woman who left him behind. And you?" Leo tilted his head slightly, his eyes cold with disdain. "You turned that grudge into leverage."

Sebastian's lips twitched into a brittle smile. "Chad's a fool. His own failures ruined him, not me."

"I'm sure that's how you sold it," Ronan said evenly. "You gave him validation, whispered just enough poison to keep him hooked. Fed his insecurities. Made him feel like you were the only one who understood." He leaned forward by a fraction. "All while you were using him to map out Arden's life. Her routines. Her past."

Sebastian leaned back, metal scraping beneath him, his composure slipping like a badly tied knot. "If Chad was dumb enough to believe anything I said, that's on him," he snapped. "I didn't make him do anything."

"No," Leo said smoothly. "You didn't have to. You dangled the right bait: a chance to feel in control again, to hurt her the way he thought she hurt him. And Chad took it. He practically gift-wrapped her life and handed it to you."

Sebastian's eyes flicked toward the mirrored wall, his breath quickening. "Chad didn't know anything important," he muttered, lower now, the edges fraying.

"Didn't he?" Ronan's tone sharpened. "Because according to Chad, you knew exactly where to find her. What to say to unnerve her. The book she loved as a kid. The lotus tattoo and why it mattered."

Sebastian's fingers twitched against the table, his pulse visible in his throat. "She's not as closed off as you think," he said defensively. "People notice things."

"Not like that," Leo shot back, voice cold and calculated. "Chad's bitterness gave you access no one else had. He opened the door, and you walked through it armed with every intimate detail you could weaponize."

Sebastian let out a jagged laugh, hollow and humorless. "You think that makes me some kind of monster? Everyone uses people. Even you, Marcus. Don't pretend you're any different."

Leo's expression didn't shift, but something in his tone turned lethal. "You're right. I'm not above using people," he said. "But I don't destroy them to feed my own delusions." He leaned forward, his shadow cutting across the table. "You didn't just use Chad. You turned him into a weapon and pointed him at her."

The silence grew taut, the weight of Leo's words pressing down like a vise. Sebastian's jaw flexed, misplaced arrogance draining as he stared at the photograph still resting on the table.

Ronan leaned in, voice low and ominous. "It wasn't just Chad. You manipulated everyone in Arden's orbit—every friend, every ghost from her past. But here's the thing about manipulation: it leaves fingerprints. And thanks to Chad, Dylan, and Richie, we've mapped every single one."

Sebastian's head snapped up, fury flaring in his eyes. "Chad doesn't know anything that matters," he hissed. "And Dylan's a liar. Richie's a scared little punk. None of them can touch me."

Leo leaned closer, his tone dropping further. "They already have, Hawthorne. You just haven't realized it yet."

The silence that followed was sharp enough to cut.

Leo slid another photograph across the table: Dylan, seated in a mirrored interrogation room, eyes red-rimmed.

"Dylan's been talkative," Leo said. "The roses, the notes, the deliveries—he's filled in every blank. He knows who paid him, and why."

Sebastian's sneer faltered, his eyes flicking to the photo before snapping back up. "Dylan doesn't know shit," he snapped, denial coming too quick, too thin.

"And the forged documents?" Ronan's tone sliced clean through the air. "The ones you used to try to bury Gideon Blackwell? Dylan mentioned those too."

Sebastian's laugh came jagged. "Dylan's an errand boy," he spat. "He doesn't know how those documents were made. If you want the truth, ask Harlan Atwood."

The name landed like a blow.

Leo's gaze sharpened. "Atwood," he repeated slowly. "You're saying he forged them?"

Sebastian's smirk returned, faint but cruel. "I'm saying Harlan's always been the better chess player. He knew how to vanish when the board turned against him."

Ronan's eyes narrowed, reading every twitch of the man across from him. "So you're admitting the documents were fake."

Sebastian leaned back, his chair groaning beneath him, a gleam of satisfaction reigniting in his eyes. "I'm admitting it doesn't matter," he said softly, a smile curling like smoke. "You can catch Dylan. You can even catch me. But you'll never stop Evelyn—or what comes next."

Ronan leaned forward, his voice cutting through the room. "You mean Evelyn's involvement in Arden's assault outside the bar? The man who roughed her up while Colton watched?"

Sebastian's head snapped up. Realization burned hot in his wild eyes, then faltered. The mocking grin that should have followed never came; his lips pressed into a tight, colorless line.

"That wasn't me," he hissed, the words brittle with indignation. "I would never hurt Arden. Never."

Ronan didn't blink. "So you're saying you had nothing to do with it?"

"I don't need to repeat myself," Sebastian shot back, composure fraying. "If you're fishing for a confession, you won't get it. I wasn't involved. That was Evelyn's work."

Leo pushed off the wall and leaned on the edge of the table. "Then why didn't you stop it, Sebastian? If Arden meant so much to you, why did you let Evelyn and Colton use her as bait?"

Sebastian's expression twisted, rage and desperation colliding. "You think I knew?" His voice cracked. "Do you think for a second I would've let them touch her if I'd known? Evelyn does what she wants. Colton obeys. They kept me out of it because they knew I wouldn't stand for it."

"Convenient," Ronan said coldly, skepticism sharpening his gaze. "But it doesn't change the fact that they carried it out while you were too busy orchestrating your own chaos."

Sebastian slammed his cuffed hands against the metal, the clang echoing through the room. "Don't you get it?" he shouted. "I wanted to protect her. Not hurt her. Everything I did—everything—was to show her she didn't belong in their world."

Leo's voice dropped. "And look where it got you. Caught in your own web while the monsters you served did exactly what you claim to despise."

Sebastian sagged back, breath ragged, the fire in his eyes dimming but not extinguished. His fingers curled against the cuffs, a small, desperate motion, grasping for power he no longer held.

"Evelyn set it up," he muttered bitterly. "Colton carried it out. They thought it would scare her off. Make her back down."

He exhaled a tremor of something perilously close to awe. "Evelyn always knew how to make fear look like mercy."

Ronan's jaw tightened. "That's what abusers tell themselves."

Sebastian's gaze lifted, fever-bright now. "But Arden... she's not like the others. She's not a pawn to be moved or silenced. She's fire. Untamed. Unforgiving. She fights back. She doesn't fold. Doesn't run. Not like they expected."

He leaned forward, voice dropping to a near-whisper, fervor trembling beneath it. "They didn't count on her strength. They didn't see how perfect she is—how alive she makes everything around her. Evelyn, Colton, all of them, they see her as an obstacle to crush. But they don't understand. She's not meant to be controlled. She's meant to burn."

Leo's eyes flicked to Hawkes; a silent exchange passed between them.

Hawkes's tone cut through the haze. "And that's why you put her through hell? Because you couldn't stand to see her slip out of your grasp?"

Sebastian's smile fractured, jagged and bitter. "You don't get it," he rasped. "She needed to see. To see me. To see what I could do for her—how I could free her from them. From him."

"Free her?" Leo's scoff was low and cutting. He stepped closer, his shadow spilling across the table. "You call manipulation and stalking freedom? You didn't want to save her, Sebastian. You wanted to own her. To twist her into your fantasy."

The last of Sebastian's composure broke. His fists slammed against the metal, the sound a thunderclap in the sterile room. "You're wrong!" he shouted, voice raw with desperation. "You don't know her like I do. She's not supposed to end up like the rest of them—like Evelyn and her hollow, soulless world."

His chest heaved. The mania drained from his face, leaving something darker behind. "I was supposed to show her. To save her. They'll destroy her like they destroy everything."

Hawkes leaned in, ominous and steady. "And what do you think you were doing? From where we're standing, you're no better than Evelyn or Colton. You're not her savior. You're the monster she had to fight."

Sebastian's cuffed hands tightened on the table, knuckles white.

"She wasn't supposed to fight me," he muttered, trembling. "She was supposed to understand. But damn it, she did fight me. She's stronger than any of you realize." His mouth twisted, ugly with need. "And that's why she'll never forget me."

Silence fell, heavy and suffocating.

Leo straightened, his expression hardening to iron. "No, Sebastian," he said quietly. "She'll remember you for exactly what you are: a cautionary tale of what happens when obsession devours reason."

Sebastian's head tilted back. His eyes narrowed as the words settled like a stone. "So what now?" he muttered, hollow.

"Evelyn's fingerprints are all over this," Ronan said, constant as a metronome. "Thanks to you, we've got testimony. A witness connected the dots."

A beat.

"Cate," he added. "She corroborated Colton's involvement and Evelyn's orders."

Sebastian's grin thinned into a hard line. "You don't get it," he hissed. "You'll never pin Evelyn down. She's untouchable. She'll go down dragging the whole ship."

Leo exchanged a look with Ronan, calm and sure.

"That's exactly what we're counting on."

Sebastian laughed, short and brittle. "You think that will make a difference? Evelyn will bury you all before this goes public."

"Not when Cate testifies," Ronan said, unblinking. "We know Colton had a man grab Arden on Evelyn's order. Colton carried it out. Evelyn made the call. She didn't count on Arden fighting back."

"You think you've won?" Sebastian snarled, desperation rising. "You think this ends with me? Evelyn, Alex, Lila—they'll walk away like they always do."

"Not this time," Leo said, folding his arms. "Thanks to you, we can drag them into the light. Evelyn. Colton. Lila Whitaker. Harlan will resurface once he realizes there's nowhere left to hide."

Ronan leaned back, unwavering. "They won't walk away. You handed us the map."

For all his plotting, Sebastian had become the pawn he loathed; the board had flipped against him.

Ronan closed the folder with a decisive snap.

"This interview is concluded," he said.

Sebastian looked up sharply. "You think this is over?"

Leo didn't answer. He simply turned toward the exit.

The lock clicked as they left.

Sebastian sat alone beneath the fluorescent lights, the hum pressing in from all sides. No audience. No leverage. No Arden.

For the first time, there was no one left to convince.

Leo Marcus leaned against the cool brick wall of the precinct hallway, phone in hand, thumbs moving rapidly across the screen. He fired off a message to Gideon.

Sebastian cracked. Evelyn gave the order for Arden's attack. Harlan and Lila are implicated. This web is breaking apart.

The message sent just as footsteps echoed down the corridor. Lauren Bishop's presence arrived before she did, sharp and no-nonsense, her crisp blazer and badge giving her the kind of authority no one with sense bothered to test. She stopped a few feet from him, dark eyes studying him with a blend of curiosity and concern.

"Well?" she asked, her tone sharp but not unkind.

Leo straightened and slipped the phone into his pocket. "He sang like a canary," he said. "Confirmed Evelyn orchestrated the assault. Colton carried it out. And he gave us plenty of breadcrumbs to follow Harlan and Lila straight to the heart of this mess."

Lauren crossed her arms, brow furrowing. "And you're sure this holds up? Testimony helps, but the moment Evelyn realizes she's cornered, she'll turn this into a circus."

Leo's smirk was faint, edged with determination. "It's more than testimony, Bishop. Between Cate's corroboration, the forged documents Dylan outlined, and the financial trails Harlan left behind, you've got enough to tie Evelyn's empire into knots."

Lauren's gaze sharpened. "That assumes Harlan doesn't vanish completely. He's slippery, Leo."

"Slippery, sure," Leo admitted, easing back against the wall. "Not invincible. The guy's a ghost, but ghosts leave traces. Someone like Harlan always resurfaces when the money trail runs dry or when he thinks the heat's cooled."

Lauren gave a small nod, conceding the point, though her expression hardened. "And what about you? How far did you push him? Because if you overstepped—"

Leo raised a hand, cutting her off with a dry laugh. "Relax. I know exactly where the line is."

Her brow arched. "And you love dancing right on it. Look, Leo, you might not wear a badge anymore, but if this blows back, it's not only you on the hook. We've been building a federal case here, and the last thing we need is to hand Evelyn's lawyers ammunition."

Leo's smirk softened into something more serious. "I get it, Bishop. I'm not looking to screw this up. But let's be honest—you need someone who can move faster than the Bureau's playbook when the situation calls for it. I'm the guy who can get where you can't."

"That doesn't make you untouchable," Lauren countered. "It means you've been lucky, and smart enough to keep your hands clean where it counts. Don't forget the difference."

He nodded, expression briefly sober. "Noted."

Lauren studied him for another second before her shoulders relaxed by the slightest degree. "You've done good work here, Leo. Better than I expected."

"I'm flattered," he said, though the warmth threading his voice made it clear he took the compliment seriously. "And to ease your mind, Sebastian sealed the deal himself. His obsession with Arden unraveled him faster than we could've planned."

Her lips tightened, a shadow crossing her face. "Evelyn isn't like him. She won't crack. She'll weaponize everything she can to stay out of reach."

Leo's expression hardened. "She can try. We're ready for her."

Lauren's gaze lingered on him, assessing, before she gave a curt nod. "I hope so. Because if this falls apart, the fallout won't stop with her."

With one final glance toward the interrogation room, Lauren turned and walked away, her heels clicking sharply against the floor. As the sound faded, Leo leaned back against the wall and exhaled slowly. For all the battles fought in that room, the war was far from over.

Justice was within reach, but the path forward would be anything but clean.

Leo stared at the reflection in the glass across the hall, at the faint, distorted image of a man who had learned the hard way that truth did not absolve anyone. It only exposed what they were willing to live with.

CHAPTER 41

After the Storm

The morning papers hit like a tidal wave, their headlines screaming across front pages and screens alike:

"Blackwell Dynasty Topples: Evelyn Blackwell in Custody" – The New York Times

"Gideon Blackwell Breaks Silence: Exposes Family's Corruption" – The Washington Post

"Fall of an Empire: The Secrets Behind the Blackwell Name" – The Guardian

"Multiple Allegations Surface Against Hawthorne in Ongoing Investigation"– The Daily News

Television loops replayed the same footage again and again: Evelyn Blackwell being led out in handcuffs, her diamond bracelet glinting like irony beneath the morning sun. Her expression remained a study in provocation, every line of her posture daring the world to pity her, doubt her, underestimate the damage she could still do.

Beneath the flashes and shouted questions, the cracks showed.

The twitch of her hands. The rigid set of her jaw. The small, furious adjustments of a woman discovering that composure was not the same thing as control.

For the first time in her life, Evelyn Blackwell was not controlling the story.

The world was watching.

A banner scrolled across the bottom of the broadcast:

"Former Associates Allege Blackwell Family Bribery, Blackmail Of Politicians And Public Figures."

The revelations painted a grotesque tapestry of power and decay: bribes paid to bury investigations, blackmail used to silence opposition, entire communities exploited to feed the Blackwell empire and keep its machinery gleaming. Whistleblowers emerged from the shadows—former employees, ruined partners, victims whose stories bled together into a collective reckoning. One by one, they spoke of intimidation, financial ruin, careers dismantled with a phone call, and the quiet, efficient ways dissent was punished until fear became compliance.

Then came the Daily News exposé.

Sebastian Hawthorne's sins, laid bare in black ink and raw testimony.

Women came forward, their stories hauntingly similar: the stalking, the manipulation, the gifts that looked romantic only from a distance, the way he inserted himself into their lives like a shadow that refused to leave. One described how her career vanished after she tried to press charges, silenced by the same machine that had protected him for years.

The story went viral. The internet caught fire with outrage and disbelief.

The empire had not merely fallen.

It was rotting in public.

Inside a waiting SUV, Evelyn watched the chaos through tinted glass. Cameras flashed like gunfire outside, each burst of light a reminder of the control slipping from her grasp. Her diamond-hard composure held by force alone, but her hands betrayed her, fingers curling once against the leather seat before she stilled them.

The door slammed, sealing her away from the noise.

For the first time, Evelyn Blackwell looked less than untouchable.

She looked haunted.

Gideon's televised statement swept across the globe, the image of him standing before the press a sharp contrast to the chaos now bearing his family's name. Cameras flashed. Microphones pressed forward. Voices rose and tangled at the edge of the frame, but his composure never wavered.

"My family's wealth and influence were built on exploitation and deceit," he began, his voice even, weighted with remorse. "For generations, the Blackwell name was used as a shield for corruption, silencing anyone who dared to stand against it. I can't undo the damage that's been done. But I can, and will, fight to make it right. This isn't only about dismantling power. It's about rebuilding trust. The Blackwell name will no longer stand for privilege built on pain. It will stand for accountability, justice, and healing."

The response was immediate, but restrained: measured applause, bowed heads, silence where outrage had once lived.

The speech marked a turning point not only for the Blackwells, but for those who had lived in their shadow. Survivors of the empire's reach—workers, tenants, whistleblowers, families who had learned to lower their voices when Blackwell lawyers entered the room—watched with cautious hope as the heir to their suffering finally broke the silence from inside the house that had profited from it. Gideon's acknowledgment of the family's crimes—bribery, blackmail, intimidation—rippled through every screen, every feed, every conversation.

For the first time, the Blackwell name was no longer only a symbol of control.

It was a promise.

And a debt.

The next morning, the city woke beneath a cautious kind of hope.

Beyond the brownstone's balcony, the skyline stretched in soft gold and pale blue, a canvas of resilience against everything the night had tried to ruin. Below, traffic murmured awake. Distant voices rose with the light. Life kept moving, imperfect and insistent, even as the weight of what had happened lingered in the air like smoke.

Arden stood at the wrought-iron railing, a steaming cup of coffee cupped between both hands. The crisp morning air kissed her skin, grounding her while her mind returned, again and again, to the ballroom: the arrests, the headlines, the flash of cameras, the sound of glass breaking, the reckoning they had finally dragged into the light.

"Do you think it's really over?" she asked, her voice barely above a whisper, threaded with wary disbelief.

Gideon joined her at the railing, his steps measured, his presence the kind of calm she was still learning to accept without bracing for its cost. He looked out over the city before answering.

"For Evelyn, Alex, and the others? No. Their reckoning is only beginning." His hand found hers, his thumb brushing slow circles over her skin. "But for us..." He exhaled, quiet and deliberate. "Maybe it's time we stop running. Just breathe."

She looked up at him, the faintest smile softening her mouth. "It feels strange, doesn't it? To finally exhale?"

"It does," he admitted. "But it isn't only about exhaling. It's about what comes next. Taking what's left, all the broken pieces, and rebuilding. Slower. Wiser. With less to prove."

Her gaze met his, blue to steel. Something unspoken passed between them, not a promise made lightly, but a vow shaped by everything they had survived. She leaned into him, resting her temple against his shoulder, his heartbeat steady beneath her ear.

"Together," she murmured, the word carrying the weight of all they had fought for.

His arm slipped around her waist, drawing her closer. "Together," he echoed, low and certain.

They stood that way as the morning sun climbed higher, gilding the city in warmth that did not erase the damage, but touched it anyway. For the first time in what felt like forever, the future did not arrive as a threat.

For Arden, the fight was not finished, but it had changed shape. She was no longer standing alone against the storm.

For Gideon, the weight of his family's sins no longer chained him to the past. It anchored him to something worth saving.

Below them, the city stirred, alive again.

Above, the light kept growing.

The storm had broken.

What came next was not peace.

But it was possible.

CHAPTER 42
Where Light Lingers

The club had never felt so empty.

Its usual rhythm—the clink of glasses, the low hum of conversation, the distant melody of the piano—had vanished, leaving behind an almost sacred stillness. The chandeliers cast a muted glow across the polished floor, their light glinting over a room still trembling with truth's aftershock.

Arden sat at the bar in jeans and a soft sweater, the quiet defiance of ordinary clothes after the emerald gown that had made her look untouchable less than two days before. A glass of wine sat untouched in front of her, its surface unbroken as her fingers traced slow, absent circles around the rim. Her posture was relaxed enough to fool someone who didn't know where to look, but her eyes betrayed the storm beneath, still cataloging every revelation, every fracture, every horror now dragged into the light.

Gideon stood beside her, steady and close. His hand rested lightly on the bar, his gaze moving between Arden and Leo Marcus, who leaned against the counter opposite them with a manila folder in hand. Leo, composed as ever, opened it with a decisive snap and spread its contents across the polished wood.

The air thickened. The silence was no longer empty.

It was charged, truth waiting to detonate.

Leo tapped a photograph with his index finger and slid it toward her.

A grainy mugshot.

Hollow eyes.

A cruel smirk frozen in time.

"Jason Tillman," Leo said evenly. "Your original stalker. Still in maximum security. No visitors. Hasn't left his cell since sentencing."

Arden went still. "So...it wasn't him." Her voice thinned around the realization. "It was never him."

Leo nodded. "No. But someone used his shadow to get to you."

He pushed forward another photo: a younger man, scruffy, confident, reckless.

"Dylan Tate," he continued. "One of Colton Blake's errand boys. He ran Sebastian's off-the-record jobs. Clean. Quiet. Deniable."

Gideon's jaw flexed. "And how does he tie back to Tillman?"

Leo's gaze cut to him, sharp as a blade. "Sebastian's obsession wasn't only revenge. It was fixation. Dylan was his instrument. Every message, every rose, every carefully timed delivery was engineered to make Arden look over her shoulder, then look for the man who claimed he could make the fear stop."

The realization hit with cold, ugly force. Arden's hand tightened against the bar. "He wanted to own me," she said, voice low, fury shaking beneath the control. "Not just hurt you. Possess me."

Leo's nod was grim. "Sebastian saw you as the center of it. His hatred for Gideon fed the obsession, but you weren't only a pawn in his game." He let the words settle. "You were the game."

Gideon reached for her hand, his grip sure and warm, fury coiled beneath every careful breath. "He failed," he said softly. "He never understood that you can't possess fire."

Arden met his gaze, the edges of a fierce smile curving her mouth. "No," she said, her voice steadying into something bright and dangerous. "I'm not a possession. I'm a goddamn wildfire."

Leo slid another stack across the bar: emails, transcripts, timestamps. The paper whispered like confession.

"This is everything," he said. "Dylan's correspondence with Sebastian. Every instruction. Every manipulation. Enough to dismantle what's left of his illusion."

Arden's eyes skimmed the pages, each line another cut, each revelation another scar turning to steel. "What happens to Dylan?" she asked, cool and controlled.

Leo's smirk went knife-thin. "He's singing like a canary. Every detail. Every thread. Between his testimony and what we pulled from Sebastian's penthouse, Hawthorne isn't seeing daylight again."

Arden's spine straightened. "Good," she said simply. "Let him rot in the dark he created."

Something softened in Leo's expression, rare and fleeting, gone almost before it arrived. "You're made of something rare, Arden Rivers. They underestimated it."

Gideon's hand stayed over hers like a promise. "You faced every trap they built and walked through fire," he said. "You didn't just survive. You won."

Her gaze met his, bright as morning light filtering through crystal glass. "No," she said quietly. "I'm not surviving. I'm reclaiming."

The words hung suspended, a vow and an exorcism all at once.

Above them, the chandeliers caught the faint pulse of dawn, their glow no longer harsh but softened by the hour. The Blackwell Room, once a sanctuary for corruption, felt altered in the quiet after violence—not cleansed, not absolved, but changed by the truth it could no longer keep hidden.

The light did not erase the darkness.

It proved what the darkness could not kill.

After Leo left, the club fell into a profound, expansive quiet.

The muted chandeliers cast soft reflections across the polished bar, their light gentler now, less opulent than human. Arden traced the rim of her empty glass, her fingers moving in slow, absent circles as her thoughts finally began to settle. The fractured chaos of the past weeks had not vanished, but it had loosened its grip, leaving behind a tentative weightlessness she did not yet trust.

Peace, unfamiliar but welcome all the same.

Across from her, Gideon stood watchful and still. His presence held without trapping, steadied without demanding. He leaned against the bar, sharp gray eyes fixed on her, not assessing, not protecting from a distance, but seeing. That kind of attention used to unsettle her. Now it felt like gravity: inescapable, necessary, and chosen.

He moved closer, his voice low and inviting. "Come with me."

Arden tilted her head, curiosity sparking through the last of her exhaustion. "Where are you taking me this time, Blackwell?" she asked, teasing, though her hand was already reaching for his.

He smiled, a rare, boyish curve that cracked something tender through the last of her guardedness. "You'll see."

His hand found hers, warm and certain, and he led her through the lounge, past gleaming wood and mirrored glass shimmering in the low light. The farther they went, the softer everything became: the room, the air, even the space between their steps. As if the club itself had finally stopped holding its breath.

A melody began, soft at first, then blooming into something soulful and low. It filled the quiet like memory, curling through the stillness with a gentleness that made Arden slow. She let the music wash through her until the edges of her thoughts went smooth.

"Gideon," she murmured, a half-smile tugging at her lips. "What is this?"

He turned to her, his eyes shadowed with warmth. "We're dancing," he said simply. "After everything, I think we've earned it."

Her breath caught. For once, she didn't argue. She stepped into his arms, her hands settling on his shoulders as his slid to her waist. His touch was careful, certain, reverent in a way that did not ask her to become fragile beneath it. The world narrowed until only their rhythm remained.

"Everything you've faced," he whispered. "And you're still standing. You're incredible, Arden Rivers."

Her throat tightened at the tenderness in his voice. "I didn't do it alone," she said softly, fingers brushing the nape of his neck. "You believed in me when I didn't."

"And I always will," he murmured. "No matter what."

They swayed to the music, unhurried. The past did not disappear; the fear, the fire, the ghosts did not become harmless simply because the room had softened around them. But for this moment, they loosened. For this moment, what remained was a quiet haven, a shared heartbeat, the fragile mercy of standing still and finding no threat in it.

As the last notes faded, neither moved to break the spell. Gideon brushed a thumb across her cheek, his touch feather-light.

"You amaze me," he said, voice barely audible. "Every single day."

Arden's lips curved into a smirk, wit glinting through the tenderness. "Careful, Blackwell. Keep this up, and I might start believing you."

His chuckle was low and unguarded. He rested his forehead against hers. "Good," he said softly. "Because you should."

The chandeliers flickered once before their glow steadied, warm across the empty club. The shadows had not vanished entirely; shadows never did. But they had lost their claim. What remained was light, quiet and stubborn, and the promise of everything still to come.

CHAPTER 43

Reflections in the Rain

The café was a haven of warmth and chatter, its rustic charm bathed in late-afternoon light. Outside, sunlight rippled across the waterfront; inside, the scent of coffee and buttered pastry wrapped around them like comfort itself.

"To Arden and Gideon," Penny declared, lifting her rosé with theatrical grandeur, eyes glittering with mischief. "The power couple who burned down the Blackwell empire and walked away without singeing a single hair."

Arden groaned, tracing a slow circle along her cup's rim. "At least let the ink dry on the arrest warrants before we start myth-making."

Dan chuckled, leaning back with easy amusement. "Come on, Arden. You two have the kind of story people binge-read in a weekend."

Arden's smirk tilted toward Penny. "I'll leave the dramatization to her. She's the one collecting New York bartenders like trading cards."

"Please." Penny took a sip from Dan's mug, unbothered. "My memoir would outsell any novel. Shakers, Makers, and Trouble Takers." She lifted her chin. "Tell me that's not a bestseller."

Gideon leaned back in his chair, his hand slipping beneath the table to find Arden's. Their fingers laced, the gesture easy and grounding, more intimate for not needing display. "We're still figuring out what normal looks like," he said, amusement woven through the fatigue.

Penny snorted loud enough to draw a glance from the next table. "Normal? After all that? Forget it. You're rewriting the definition—and you're welcome, by the way, for the assist."

Dan gestured toward her with mock outrage. "You mean you're rewriting it. Let's not forget the pep talks, the late-night phone calls—"

"Rallying the troops," Penny cut in, grinning. "Someone had to keep the spark alive."

Laughter rolled between them, unrestrained and genuine. For the first time in months, Arden's chest loosened.

Then something beyond the glass caught her eye.

Across the street, beneath the wide arms of an oak tree, a figure stood perfectly still. Hood up. Face hidden. The café noise dulled to a hum as her pulse spiked, instinct sparking hot and immediate through her body. Her shoulders tensed before her mind could catch up.

She blinked.

The figure was gone.

Arden forced her breath to slow. Not today. They had fought too hard for this peace, and she would not surrender it to a shadow.

"Hey." Dan's voice softened, all teasing gone. "You good?"

Arden met his gaze and managed a quick nod. "Yeah," she said. "A momentary ghost."

Penny leaned in, the steel beneath her charm glinting through. "Ghosts don't stand a chance with us," she said lightly. "And for the record, I've got Daniel on speed dial. He can weaponize a dad joke at fifty paces."

Dan pressed a hand to his chest, feigning insult. "Dad joke? I prefer precision-engineered pun."

"Refined as a gas-station latte," Penny shot back, nudging his shoulder.

Then her voice softened. "Seriously. You're not alone, Arden. Not now, not ever."

The sincerity reached deeper than the joke, settling warm and heavy in Arden's chest. She glanced between them, throat tightening with gratitude she did not have to dress up to make understood.

"I know," she said softly. "And I'm grateful."

Across the table, Gideon's thumb brushed her knuckles, a silent vow. "Ghosts don't stand a chance," he murmured, for her ears only.

The tension unraveled. Arden smiled and turned back to their friends as sunlight poured through the glass, gilding the table, the cups, Penny's glittering earrings, the ordinary miracle of all of them sitting there together. The shadows of her past still existed somewhere beyond that light, but they no longer owned her.

They were fading, outshone by laughter, warmth, and the people who refused to let her stand alone.

Outside, the water caught the sunlight and threw it back tenfold, bright and unbroken.

Some storms end in silence.

Others end in light.

Later, rain whispered against the glass, a soft melody filling the room around them. The only other sound was the rhythm of their breathing, steady and entwined.

Arden lay sprawled across Gideon's chest, her fingers tracing lazy patterns along his skin, grounding herself in the slow rise and fall beneath her hand. The storm had left its marks on them both, but here, in the hush of rain and warmth and tangled sheets, the world felt small enough to hold.

"You're everything to me," he murmured, his voice gentle, stripped of pretense. His hands rested at her waist, holding her with a care that no longer felt like fear.

She lifted her head, finding his gaze. What she saw there—love unhidden, unguarded—stole her breath. She brushed a damp strand of hair from his forehead, her touch certain.

"And you're everything to me," she whispered back, the words trembling but true. "Completely."

A rare smile softened him. His arms tightened around her as he pressed a kiss to her forehead, her cheek, then her lips, each one unhurried, each one a promise made in silence before it reached the mouth.

"Whatever you want," he breathed. "However you want it."

Her fingertips skimmed his jaw, slow and gentle, though nothing in her felt fragile now. "Then don't hold back," she said, her voice a vow of its own. "Because I won't."

He drew her closer, their foreheads touching as another kiss sealed the words between them. Outside, the rain kept falling, a rhythm of renewal after the ruin, soft against the glass while the night opened around them.

Wrapped in each other's arms, they let the hours stretch on, unbroken. The world beyond the window no longer felt like a threat.

Together, they were enough.

Together, they had everything that mattered.

CHAPTER 44
Promises in the Rain

Morning sunlight poured through the wide windows, bathing the room in a gold so serene it almost felt unreal after everything they had endured. Outside, the city hummed softly, its muted rhythm threading through the walls like a distant symphony.

Arden sat curled on the couch, wrapped in a soft knit throw, her legs tucked beneath her. The mug of coffee in her hands radiated warmth, grounding her as sunlight spilled across the floorboards in slow, gentle bands. Everything about the moment felt fragile, as if peace itself might splinter if she moved too quickly.

Across from her, Gideon leaned back in the armchair, sleeves rolled to his elbows, stubble shadowing his jaw. His eyes—those sharp gray eyes that had once measured every threat—had softened in the morning light. He watched her quietly, without urgency, without calculation, as if silence had finally become something they could share.

Her phone buzzed on the coffee table, cutting briefly through the quiet. She glanced at it, sighed, and left it untouched.

"Another admirer?" Gideon teased, his voice low, a smirk tugging at his lips.

She rolled her eyes and set her mug down. "Let's hope not. I think I've reached my lifetime quota."

A laugh escaped him, deep and rich, filling the space. He leaned forward, brushing a loose strand of hair from her face, his fingers lingering with familiar care. "You're sure? I'm rather fond of exclusivity."

Her smile curved, slow and certain. "You've got nothing to worry about, Blackwell."

For a moment, time held its breath. The sunlight stretched. The quiet deepened. Finally, it did not feel like absence.

Then his voice came again, gentle but sure. "We've made it, haven't we?"

Her chest tightened. She met his gaze, relief and devotion stealing the air from her lungs in equal measure. "I think we have."

He straightened, his eyes glinting with familiar purpose. "Come with me," he said, mischief threading through the warmth.

She arched a brow. "Where?"

His grin was disarming. "You'll see."

Without hesitation, she took his hand. His touch was a welcome tether in a world that had finally stopped spinning. He led her to the window, then through the hall, down the stairs, and out into the city.

Rain had begun to fall, soft enough to cling to the air rather than cut through it. The city shimmered in reflection, gold and red and silver rippling across the wet pavement.

Arden tilted her face toward the sky, letting the cool drops kiss her skin.

"I love how you love storms," Gideon said quietly, his voice as steady as the rain.

"They remind me that even chaos can be its own kind of beautiful," she replied. Her eyes lifted to meet his, shining with a peace that had not come easily, the kind born only from surviving what once tried to destroy you.

He took a step closer, and the world narrowed to the space between them. Slowly, he reached into his pocket and pulled out a small velvet box. Its edges were worn, the mark of something carried, waited on, meant.

Her breath caught.

He opened it.

Inside, the ring glimmered like captured starlight: a round diamond framed by two emerald-cut stones, the platinum band timeless and sure.

"Arden Rose Rivers," he said, his voice roughened by everything he was trying to hold steady. "You turned my world upside down. You challenge me. You make me better. And I can't imagine a life that doesn't have you in it." His thumb brushed once over the edge of the box, the smallest betrayal of nerves. "Will you marry me?"

Tears welled in her eyes, catching the light like rain. She nodded before she could speak, then whispered, "Yes, Gideon. A thousand times yes."

Relief broke across his face like sunrise after a storm. With steady hands, he slipped the ring onto her finger; it fit perfectly, as though it had been waiting for her all along.

He cupped her face and kissed her softly, then deeper, the rain gathering in their hair and on their lashes. The city blurred around them, sound falling away until there was nothing but heartbeat and rain, his hands warm against her skin, her yes still trembling between them.

When they finally broke apart, their foreheads rested together, breaths mingling in the cool, rain-washed air.

"I love you," he murmured, his thumbs brushing rain from her cheeks. "More than anything. Always."

Tears spilled freely now, her smile breaking through them like light. "I love you too," she whispered. "Completely. Always."

They stood there as the rain fell harder, the storm no longer something to survive, but something to stand inside together.

This was renewal.

Gideon smiled, his voice low and sure. "Whatever you want. However you want it."

Her laugh came light and certain, mingling with the rain. "Good," she said, eyes shining. "Because I want it all."

Beneath the storm's gentle fury, the city glowed around them, new and alive.

The dawn was theirs.

Epilogue I: Vows

Morning light poured through the tall windows, wrapping the room in gold. Arden stood before the mirror, her gown cascading around her in a sweep of ivory silk and silver-threaded starlight. The embroidery caught the sun and scattered tiny constellations across the floor, as if the morning itself had decided to bless her in pieces.

Her hands trembled slightly as she adjusted the bracelet on her wrist, her grandmother's heirloom cool against her skin. Strength. Resilience. Survival. The words moved through her like a familiar prayer, but softer now, less armor than inheritance.

She studied her reflection. The woman staring back was both familiar and new.

A soft knock broke the quiet.

Penny burst in, green eyes already brimming. "Okay," she warned, holding up both hands, "don't freak out, but I'm about to cry."

Arden smirked. "We agreed—no crying. You're the one keeping me composed."

"Impossible." Penny sniffed, fanning her face. "You look like a goddess. This is entirely your fault."

Arden laughed and pulled her into a hug. "If you smear that eyeliner, I swear—"

"Too late." Penny dabbed at her cheek with her sleeve, grinning. "But don't think marriage gets you off the hook, Mrs. Blackwell. You're still bound by our friendship vows: late-night ice cream, trashy reality TV, and existential crises at two a.m."

"Always," Arden said softly. "You're family. Non-negotiable."

"Speaking of family—" Penny rummaged in her bag and pulled out a small velvet box, eyes gleaming. "Something blue."

Arden lifted the lid, and her breath caught. A delicate sapphire pendant rested inside, set in a platinum starburst that echoed the embroidery on her gown.

Penny clasped it around her neck. "He said it reminded him of you."

Arden's fingers brushed the cool stone, emotion rising in her throat. "He's impossible."

Penny grinned. "He's impossible, but he's yours. Now let's go knock his perfectly tailored socks off."

Arden turned back to the mirror. The necklace caught the light at her throat, blue and silver and bright as a promise. She smiled, radiant and ready.

"More than ready."

The soft hum of strings swelled as she stepped into the aisle. Arden walked alone, head high, each step a reclamation. Every scar, every trial, every breath that had carried her here wove itself into the rhythm of her stride. The aisle was more than a path to Gideon; it was a testament.

Then she fixed her eyes on him.

Gideon stood at the end of the aisle, his gaze steady and unguarded. In that single heartbeat, the world fell away. All she saw was the man who had met her fire with reverence and never once tried to extinguish it.

When their hands met, the world narrowed to what mattered.

The officiant began, but the only words that mattered were theirs.

Gideon's voice carried through the hush. "Arden, you are my light in the darkest moments, my courage when I falter, my home when the world feels unsteady. You've taught me what it means to love, to hope, to believe in something beyond redemption. From this day forward, I am yours—fully, freely."

Tears pricked at her eyes. Her own voice trembled, but held steady.

"Gideon, you saw me when I could barely see myself. You loved the broken, the scarred, the imperfect, and gave me the courage to do the same. You are my beginning—and the place I stand. From this day forward, I am yours. Always."

When the officiant pronounced them husband and wife, Gideon didn't wait. His kiss was fierce and tender, sealing a promise made in front of everyone they loved. Applause rose like thunder, but they barely heard it.

Under a canopy of lights, the reception glowed like a dream. Lanterns swayed in the ocean breeze, carrying the scent of salt and jasmine. Laughter mingled with music until the night felt alive around them, warm and bright and impossibly gentle after everything it had taken to get there.

When their first dance began, the melody wrapped around them, soft and timeless. Arden's gown moved in ripples of silk and lace, catching the lantern light as Gideon drew her close. She felt the weight of his hand at her waist, the gentleness in his eyes undoing her in a way no danger ever had.

"You're stunning," Gideon murmured, his voice low against her ear.

She smiled, ocean-blue eyes gleaming. "That's only because you see me in a way no one else ever has."

His smirk deepened. "Then they've never truly seen you."

Around them, the world blurred into gold and laughter. For Arden and Gideon, there was only this: the rhythm of their hearts, the whisper of silk, the echo of storms long past.

A love built in the storm.

A promise to keep the light.

The ocean stretched before him in silver and blue, the horizon blurred by morning haze. The air smelled of salt and rain, the tide whispering against the shore like a secret. Gideon stood at the edge of the balcony, coffee cooling in his hand, watching sunlight drift across the water.

It had been a year since everything broke—and rebuilt.

He had thought peace would feel foreign, like wearing a life that didn't quite fit. But it didn't. It felt earned. Fragile, yes, but real. The chaos was gone, replaced by unhurried mornings like this one: the water breathing below, the city waking in the distance, possibility returning without demanding proof.

Inside, he could hear Arden moving—soft footsteps, the faint rustle of fabric, the low melody of her laugh as Penny said something ridiculous over the phone. Even now, that sound rooted him more deeply than any vow ever could.

He had spent so much of his life fighting ghosts: his family's legacy, his own reflection, the weight of everything that came before. He used to believe redemption meant erasing the past, cleansing it until nothing ugly remained. Arden had taught him otherwise. Healing was not erasure; it was reclamation.

He set the mug down and leaned on the railing, letting the sunlight warm his hands. From here, he could see the faint outline of their initials etched into the wood—A + G. Penny's idea, scrawled during a late-night celebration and too imperfect to erase.

He smiled. Arden had rolled her eyes at it, of course. Then she had added a rose beside the letters.

A storm and a rose, he had thought. Always that balance: wildness and grace, strength and tenderness. Hers, his, theirs.

A soft breeze shifted the curtains behind him. Moments later, her arms slipped around his waist, her cheek resting against his back.

"Morning," she murmured.

He turned in her arms and brushed a kiss across her hairline. "Morning, Mrs. Blackwell."

She tilted her face up to him, that familiar spark of mischief in her blue eyes. "You're still not tired of calling me that?"

"Not even close."

Her smile deepened as she looked past him toward the water. "Do you ever think about it?" she asked softly. "Everything that happened? How close we came to losing it all?"

"Every day," he said. "But not with regret."

She frowned slightly, curious. "Then what?"

"Gratitude," he replied. "For what survived. For who survived."

Her hand found his, fingers fitting perfectly, effortlessly, like they always had. They stood in silence, the waves below catching the morning light, the world stretching out before them—vast, unknowable, beautiful.

Gideon looked at her, at the woman who had turned the wreckage of his life into something extraordinary.

"You once told me you loved storms because they were proof that chaos could be beautiful," he said quietly.

Her gaze lifted to meet his. "I did."

He brushed his thumb across her ring. "You were right. And this—" He gestured to the sun, the sea, the space between them. "This is the calm that made the storm worth surviving."

Arden smiled, the kind of smile that always undid him.

He kissed her, slow and certain. For once, there was no battle waiting beyond the horizon, no inheritance pressing like a blade against his throat, no ghost demanding blood for the privilege of peace.

Only this.

The morning.

The sea.

And her.

Epilogue II: A New Day

The ribbon fluttered in the breeze, deep plum silk chosen not for formality, but for meaning.

Arden pressed her thumb against the shears. The crowd gathered before her was small and intimate: no podium, no politicians, no polished speeches disguised as charity. Just women from the city, a few local families, the Haverfords clustered near the fence line, and one little girl in rhinestone-covered sneakers craning to see the garden.

Behind her, The Willow House stood warm and bright. Whitewashed wood. A wraparound porch. A kitchen that always smelled like bread rising. The swing out front was not decoration; it was for tired hearts and second chances. And the garden—the garden was its own kind of scripture.

She had spent her whole life stitching herself together. Now she had built a place where no one had to do that alone.

Gideon stood beside her, close enough to feel. He didn't speak. He never filled silence for the sake of comfort; he only stood inside it with her until she was ready.

Arden lifted the shears and cut the ribbon.

Applause followed, gentle and brief, but it was the hush afterward that stayed with her. A stillness that said: We see you. We've been waiting.

A woman approached, somewhere in her forties, shoulders drawn in like someone accustomed to shrinking. A toddler rested on her hip, one small hand tangled in the collar of her shirt.

"Thank you," the woman said softly. "For not just building this, but for believing we'd come."

Arden blinked hard. "I was hoping you would."

The woman nodded and stepped inside, crossing the threshold into a softer world.

Arden lingered, letting the moment land. Letting it matter. She thought of her mother, of all the women who had been too scared, too shamed, too broken by fear to speak. She understood now what terror could do when it had nowhere to go, how heavy it became when someone had to carry a child inside it.

The Willow House wasn't built in her mother's name.

But it was built because of her.

For the girls left standing in rooms no one saved them from. For the women who never got to unlearn survival.

"This place won't fix everything," she had told an interviewer the week before. "Healing isn't tidy. But choosing it still matters. And sometimes, having a place to make that choice changes everything."

She stepped down from the porch just as the little girl from earlier ran up and caught her hand.

"Are you the garden lady?" the child asked, wide-eyed.

Arden smiled and crouched beside her. "I am today."

The girl nodded as though this made perfect sense, then skipped down the lavender path.

Gideon met Arden's gaze from a few steps away, the corners of his mouth lifting into a proud grin—not the kind meant to be seen by anyone else, but the kind that said, I know what this means to you.

Arden turned toward the house again, the wind tugging at her hair. The breeze smelled of rosemary and clean earth, and for once, the future did not feel like something waiting to take from her.

She had lived through the storm.

She had named the shadows.

And now—

Now, she had built something that would outlast both.

For the Discerning Reader: A Deeper Dive

Stories live twice: once on the page, and again in the hearts of those who carry them. ♡

When I wrote *The Storm and Shadow Duology*, I didn't only want to give you a dark, romantic escape. I wanted to write into the tradition of the gothic—a genre where passion and peril, inheritance and obsession, survival and defiance all bleed together.

Every rose in these books has thorns for a reason. Every storm carries both ruin and rebirth. Arden's fists, Gideon's restraint, Penny's laughter, Evelyn's diamonds—none of it is accidental. This is a modern gothic tale, shaped with intention.

This guide exists if you want to dive deeper. Whether you're reading with a book club, unpacking the story in class, or simply reflecting on your own, you'll find your paths here:

Book Club Questions → for conversation, debate, and imagining yourself in Arden's storm.

Literary Critique Notes & The Symbolic Index→ where I've shared my own thoughts beside critical insights; I've also included the symbols and choices that built this duology.

Take what you like. Skip what you don't. Argue with me in the margins—I'd love that.

But above all, know this: the shadows, the storms, the roses... they were all planted with purpose.

With fierce gratitude,
T.L. Johnson

P.S. You can vibe with my moody writing playlist here: https://bit.ly/storm playlist

Book Club Guide

Discussion Questions

1. Arden refuses to be "saved." How did that shape your reading of her relationship with Gideon?

2. Roses are both beautiful and dangerous throughout the duology. Which rose moment stayed with you most, and why?

3. Penny's humor and lightness often cut through darker moments. How does she function as an emotional counterbalance in the story?

4. The Blackwell family dinners feel like battlegrounds. Did they remind you more of *Succession* or a classic gothic manor—and why?

5. Trust is a quiet but central theme. Was it harder for Arden to trust Gideon, or for Gideon to trust himself?

6. The stalker's obsession is deeply invasive. Did it feel more terrifying because of his actions—or because of his intimacy with Arden's private life?

7. Which scenes best captured the "modern gothic" atmosphere for you: the storms, the velvet rooms, or the stalker's gifts?

8. Arden's independence often borders on self-protection. Where do you think her strength becomes her shield?

9. Gideon wrestles with love and legacy throughout the duology. Which ultimately wins out—and at what cost?

10. The storm functions as both weather and metaphor. When did it feel most symbolic to you?

11. Mirrors, glass, and reflections recur repeatedly. What truths do they force the characters to confront?

12. Setting plays a powerful role—from urban isolation to rural intimacy. How did place shape the emotional tension for you?

13. This story explores survival after trauma. Did it change how you think about what healing can look like?

14. Love in this world is messy, fierce, and imperfect. What does the story suggest about loving someone who's still learning how to love themselves?

15. If Penny were to star in her own book, what genre would you want for her—and why: rom-com chaos or dark romance with teeth?

16. If you had to choose one word to describe the emotional tone of the duology, what would it be—and why?

Literary Critique Guide

Prompts for Deeper Analysis

This appendix is designed for readers, reviewers, and educators who want to look beneath the story's surface—to examine its literary bones and emotional architecture more closely. These prompts and annotations reveal the duology's Gothic lineage and modern reinvention, blending author insight with critical context.

Each entry contains two perspectives:

Author's Note: the creative intention behind the scene or motif.

Critical Note : a scholarly or analytical observation that situates that choice within literary and psychological frameworks.

1. The Byronic Hero: How does Gideon echo classic Byronic figures (like Heathcliff or Rochester)? In what ways does he resist those archetypes?

Author's Note: Gideon isn't just brooding for aesthetic—he's battling legacy versus integrity. His restraint is intentional; he's passion on a leash.

Critical Note: This creates tension where love becomes rebellion rather than rescue—a modern twist on the Gothic hero.

2. The Haunted Heroine: How does Arden's trauma parallel gothic heroines of the past (*Jane Eyre*, Rebecca's unnamed narrator)?

Author's Note: Arden's not designed to faint or freeze. She trains, fights, bleeds. Her agency is my deliberate break from old gothic scripts.

Critical Note: By giving her fists instead of just fears, the text modernizes the gothic—trauma is acknowledged but not romanticized.

3. Legacy as the Gothic Estate: In classic gothic novels, the "haunted manor" is often a symbol of oppression. How does the Blackwell empire serve that role here?

Author's Note: Marble boardrooms and velvet-curtained clubs are my gothic castles. Wealth becomes just as claustrophobic as stone walls.

Critical Note: This resituates gothic tropes in corporate America, where inheritance is as binding as any ancestral curse.

4. Obsession vs. Devotion: How does the stalker's twisted logic mirror gothic villain archetypes?

Author's Note: He reframes intrusion as love. That's intentional—because real-world predators often do.

Critical Note: This blurs gothic "haunting" with psychological realism, making his menace more chilling than a monster.

5. Symbolism of Roses & Storms: What do roses and storms symbolize across both books?

Author's Note: Roses = beauty with thorns; storms = transformation and inevitability. Both are forces Arden must pass through to claim herself.

Critical Note: These motifs elevate the duology from plot-driven suspense to allegorical gothic fiction.

6. Love as Resistance: How does romance function beyond the love story?

Author's Note: For Arden and Gideon, love is not escapism—it's survival, rebellion, resistance.

Critical Note: This positions the duology in literary gothic tradition: passion not as cure, but as defiance against ruin.

7. Trauma as Narrative Structure: The story's rhythm mirrors trauma—looping, fragmented, repetitive. How does that affect pacing and reader experience?

Author's Note: The form mirrors the mind. Recovery isn't linear, so neither is the story.

Critical Note: Drawing from trauma theory, the duology's nonlinear rhythm echoes the cycles of memory, repression, and release—transforming structure into emotional truth.

8. The Modern Gothic Intention: What makes *The Storm and Shadow Duology* distinctly modern in its Gothic approach?

Author's Note: This isn't about ghosts in the hall—it's about the ones that live inside us.

Critical Note: By reframing the Gothic through psychological, relational, and cultural lenses, the duology shifts from fear of the dark to empathy within it. It's not imitation—it's reclamation.

The Symbolic Index

Storm

Chaos. Cleansing. The breaking point that becomes the beginning.

The storm doesn't destroy—it reveals what can withstand the wind.

Rose

Beauty entwined with pain. Proof that something fragile can still bleed and bloom.

To love like a rose is to accept the thorn and the perfume alike.

Mirror

Truth in reflection, distortion in denial.

The mirror is memory—it shows what's left when illusion cracks.

Shadow

The part of the self that hides but never disappears.

To face the shadow is to become whole.

Legacy

The chains we inherit and the choice to remake them.

Inheritance isn't destiny—it's material for transformation.

Candlelight

Hope burning small but steady.

The Gothic heart beats between light and smoke—what endures and what fades.

Silence

A language of its own.

Sometimes it's survival. Sometimes it's surrender. Sometimes it's the loudest truth.

The House

A living body of secrets. Every door a decision. Every hall a history.

What we build around ourselves is always a translation of what's within.

Glass

Transparency and fragility—both illusion and clarity.

It divides and reflects, but it also lets the light in.

Night

Stillness and revelation.

Everything true becomes visible in the dark if you're brave enough to look.

Blood

Inheritance, sacrifice, survival.

It binds and betrays; it keeps the story alive.

Smoke

Memory fading, trauma rising.

What burns never fully disappears—it lingers in the air between us.

Touch

Connection as confession.

Every touch in the duology means *I see you and I stayed.*

Mercy

Power, softened.

The Gothic heart isn't cruel—it's just honest about what it costs to be kind.

Acknowledgments

This book—this ending—was not built alone.

To my husband, who has seen me at my most unguarded and loved me anyway: you know what it means to live beside a survivor. To witness the sleepless nights, the trembling hands, the 3 a.m. typing, and the endless rewriting of both story and self.

You remind me to eat when I forget. To breathe when I spiral. To step away when the words blur into ghosts. You have watched me chase this book from midnight to morning, whispering goodnight while I promised just a few more paragraphs. And when the sun rose again—and I was still writing—you were there. Steady. Patient. Believing.

You are the quiet grace behind every storm; the reason I kept building even when the walls shook.

Thank you.

To my daughter, my sunshine, my fiercest muse, my greatest gift: watching you grow has been the purest joy of my life. You are the light that reminds me why stories matter. You cheer me on through every edit and remind me to eat, too. You have listened to me say I'm done writing more times than I can count, and every time, you ask, "But why?"

You see the fire in me even when I'm content to let the embers cool. You love that I'm a pharmacist and a mom who happened to write a book. You're my reminder that ambition and gentleness can live in the same heart. You are already fierce in your own right, and watching you rise is my favorite story of all.

To my dearest friends and readers:

Linda and Kristen, thank you for reading every version of this duology, from its messy 38K-word beginnings to its 210K-word finish. Your honesty, insight, and faith in these characters carried me through every rewrite.

Holly, thank you for believing in me and my writing—and for loving Dan and Penny so much that I may need to publish their romantic comedy. Your notes, feedback, and encouragement were instrumental in the final days, especially when I very nearly stopped.

Wanda and Leeann, thank you for championing The Storm and the Rose and for stepping early into The Rose and the Shadows. Your excitement and encouragement mean more than you know.

To the readers who simply couldn't wait: thank you for trusting me enough to dive into an early read of book two after loving book one.

And to the readers who get me and this genre, I am endlessly grateful for your messages. Flattery will get you everywhere.

To my coworkers, especially my night shift crew: you have seen the feral, slightly delusional version of me muttering plot ideas at 3 a.m., and you still show up the next night. Thank you for the humor, the grace, and for keeping my secrets.

Please—to the grave and beyond.

To Sarah H., my free-spirited friend and one of the sparks that started it all: a casual BookTok conversation—book boyfriends and thirst traps—that somehow turned into, Hear me out... a guy walks into a bar.

And just like that, everything changed.

I owe you this entire storm, and I am forever grateful for your presence in my life.

To every person who stood in my corner, who asked, *What happens next?* or *When's the next book coming out?*: thank you from the bottom of my heart. You believed before I did. You believed in the story, but more than that, you believed in me.

To the ones who called me author before I could say it out loud: your belief built this dream's foundation. Every kind word, every whisper that said you are allowed to have this, lives between these pages.

And finally, to anyone still finding their way out of the dark—toward healing, toward hope, toward a love you never thought you deserved:

This story is for you.

Your survival matters.

Your dreams matter.

Your heart matters.

This book is a hand reaching back through the shadows, whispering...

You made it.

You are worthy.

If You Need It

Stories like this touch real wounds and real strength.
If you or someone you love needs support,
I've created a Resource Library with information
on healing, advocacy, and hope.

Visit: midnighthaven.co/resources

*If you or someone you love is in need of support,
please don't hesitate to reach out.*

The National Domestic Violence Hotline is available 24/7
at 800-799-7233 or by text at 88788.

If you are struggling with thoughts of suicide or need
immediate emotional support, the Suicide and Crisis Lifeline
is available 24/7 by calling or texting 988.

Author's Note

For those who walked through the storm and stayed: you made it.

The Rose and the Shadows is not a story about endings, but about what lives in their wake. It is about the slow, sacred work of becoming; about rebuilding on the bones of what was lost; about love that does not ask for perfection, only presence.

If *The Storm and the Rose* was survival, this is resurrection.

The ache does not vanish. It transforms. The shadows soften. What remains is what was always yours: your strength, your softness, your self.

If you carried pain into these pages, I hope you also found power. If you came seeking closure, I hope you found a beginning.

Thank you for walking beside Arden and Gideon through the aftermath—the wreckage, the rebuilding, and the grace of what is real. You are proof that healing is both an act of defiance and an act of devotion.

You are the rose and the shadow.

You are what remains.

And what rises.

With gratitude and awe,

T.L. Johnson

P.S. If these pages lingered with you—if you found a piece of yourself in their light or their dark—your review would mean the world. It does not have to be long; even a handful of words can help another reader decide whether to step into this story.

Thank you for reading, for feeling, and for supporting indie voices.
Goodreads: https://www.goodreads.com/tl-johnson
Amazon: https://www.amazon.com/author/tl-johnson

About the Author

T.L. Johnson is a lifelong lover of stories that explore resilience, strength, and the beauty found in life's storms. A Mississippi native now calling West Virginia home for more than a decade, she draws inspiration from both her Southern roots and the mountainous landscapes she's come to love. A homebody with a love for travel, she enjoys spending time with family and friends, savoring gray days, getting lost in a good book, and writing stories and poems during midnight meanderings.

facebook.com/thetljohnsonauthor

instagram.com/tljohnsonauthor

threads.com/tljohnsonauthor

goodreads.com/tl-johnson

amazon.com/author/tl-johnson

www.ingramcontent.com/pod-product-compliance
Lightning Source LLC
Chambersburg PA
CBHW030346120726
47901CB00007B/1929

* 9 7 9 8 9 9 2 3 6 6 6 5 5 *